SINS
HAVOC OF SINS

To all those who wait out their enemy. You got this.

CHARACTER GUIDE

<u>Gates Family</u>

Jim Gates: Grim's father and owner of Indulge Hotel

Laurel Gates: Grim's mother

Grim Gates: Owner of Secrets and oldest of the brothers

Leo Gates: Middle of the three brothers

Knox Gates: Youngest of the three brothers

Leal and Zhar: Grim's Doberman Pinschers

Darcy: Dog walker

<u>Extras to the Gates Family</u>

Jesse: Grim's right-hand man

Cartwright: Grim's main driver

Louis: Grim trusts him to ride his bike

Janelle: In love with Grim

Deborah: Real estate advisor

Tayla Canos: Cartel daughter (Dark Water Series)

Jerry and Elva Canos: Tayla's parents (Grim lived with them for 10 years when in Mexico)

Tame Family

Cameron Tame: Kenna's father, Lawyer to Jim Gates

Claudine Tame: Kenna's mother, travels the world for work

Kenna Tame: Goes by Lodge to keep her job separate from her family

Calli Tame: Kenna's younger sister, doesn't get along with Kenna

Extras to the Tame Family

Simon Gable: Private Investigator, works for Cameron

Zara: Cameron's secretary

Extras

Jayden Wallace: Manager to super hosts

Mr. Salazar: Client of Kenna's

Yen Hong: Client of Kenna's

Elio Capri: Head of the Capri mafia family in Italy (Quiet Wealth Series) and friend of Grim

Vinni and Niccola Capri: Elio's cousins

Martin Castillo: Head of Cartel (Dark Water Series)

Hannah: Kenna's old friend

Gavin: Elevator operator at Indulge Hotel

Shore: Kenna's favorite driver at Indulge Hotel

Devil's Reach Motorcycle Club

Location of official clubhouse: Santa Monica, California

Trigger: President, married to Tess

Brick: Vice President, Minnie's longtime boyfriend

Tess: Married to Trigger, best friend to Brick and Minnie and owner of Dirty Deeds Club

Minnie: Kenna's best friend and owner of a sex house and Dirty Demons strip club.

Rail: Good friend of Kenna's and dates whoever he can

Morgan: Good friend of Kenna's. Holds the rank of Sergeant of Arms

Stripe Backs Motorcycle Club

Rival club to Devil's Reach

Location of official clubhouse: Venice, California.

Club weak and scattered as many members were killed over the years. Power struggle within the membership as they try to rebuild.

ONE

GRIM

Blood sprayed as my fist met his face. Everything blurred while I pounded out my anger. I grabbed him by the collar and sent one into his chest and quickly repeated it with one to the gut. Darkness filled me as I grabbed his hand and broke all the small bones. His screams seemed to come from a distance and were like a salve to my insides, but it wasn't enough. Nothing could soothe the pain or heal the scars left from Leo's death. I was no longer human; I was a machine designed to kill anyone who had a hand in my brother's murder.

"That all you got?" his pulp of a face asked as he spat. His blood-lined teeth morphed into a grin. "You better finish me off, Gates, because I'll be coming for ya."

I switched hands and drilled my knee into his stomach, and when he buckled, I drove a knee into his face. A little voice told me to keep going with the promise of peace at the end. That was a lie. There would never be peace for me; that would mean Leo came back from the dead.

"Grim! No!" my mother yelled from the doorway, and someone yanked at my arm throwing me off balance. I whirled around to take a swing when Knox's face appeared. He wore a crazed expression. He grabbed my arm and held on.

"Not him," Knox shouted. "No, Grim, not like this!"

I glared at the asshole who had managed to slither over to the wall. He propped his battered body upright.

"Yeah, not like this." Sonny laughed, and I lunged at him, only to be pulled away from him again. I was yanked backward, and my father's voice boomed through the chaos in my head.

"No!" Dad wouldn't let go, even when I ripped my arm away from Knox. "Son, no."

"Snap out of it," Knox yelled. "You're gonna hurt Dad!"

"Yeah, listen to your brother, Grim." Sonny coughed. "You only have one left."

Dad tightened his grip on me as I went in for a third time.

"Enough! All of you, enough!" Mom's voice got through, and I tried to force myself to focus on her.

"Sonny Conti," if she could breathe fire she would have in that moment, "one more word out of your mouth and I'll put a bullet through your heartless chest myself."

"Yes, ma'am." He snickered, and Dad reached for his gun.

"Jim," Mom warned, and like me, he knew to step back. Mom rarely used that voice, and we all knew to listen. "Knox," she kept her eyes on me, "get your brother out of here."

I slapped Knox's hand away and spun toward the door. I grabbed the handle and slammed the door into the wall as I stomped out. I could hear the glass smash as I left.

"Conference room," Dad ordered from behind me. "Jesse, look after this, will you?" Dad waved at the mess against the wall.

"Of course, sir. Sorry I wasn't here sooner." He glanced at me. We both knew what he'd done had given me a head start.

Once inside, Dad shut the door behind us, and the only sound I could hear was my own gasping breath. I forced myself to take a moment to breathe. I was too amped to sit, so I grabbed one of the high-back chairs and clenched the top of it with my fists. I desperately needed something to anchor me.

Knox was the first to speak. "What do you know?"

I shook my head. I wasn't ready to tell them yet; I wanted to end his fucking life first.

"Laurel?" Dad turned to Mom. "How did this all happen?" I appreciated him giving me a moment to gather myself.

"I was up talking to Gavin up in the security room when I saw Grim race through the lobby, then he went to the restaurant where the Tames normally have their family dinner. When he headed up to this floor, it didn't take much to see he was looking for Cameron." She smoothed out her hair as she settled in a chair.

"So, why Sonny?" Knox pushed.

"Because..." I felt everything rush to the surface, and I could tell I was going to blow.

Knox took a step toward me, and I raised my hand to stop him. "Because?"

"Because they're all fucking in on it!" I screamed, and Mom jumped. "It wasn't supposed to be Leo. I was the mark. Me!" I jabbed a finger at my chest. "Cameron ordered a hit to take me out, but Leo had my jacket on, and the stupid hired fuckers thought he was me."

Silence.

Fuck!

"How?" Knox shook his head, confused. "You're

like a fucking Picasso painting." He waved a finger at all my tats. "Leo was a blank slate, for shit's sake."

"I don't understand, Grim." Mom leaned forward in her chair.

"Me either." Knox pursed his lips. "Even if he had your jacket on, he looks nothing like you."

"Hired men don't get photos, they get marks." I tried to calm my nerves and remember Knox wouldn't know this shit. "They get a text, a bit of information, that's it."

"Why? That's stupid."

I pinched the bridge of my nose. "It's all about tracing shit back." I slammed my fists into the chair. "You'd know this shit if you actually paid attention."

"Grim!" Mom warned as she pressed her hands flat on the table. "What do you mean, Cameron ordered the hit? What evidence do you have?"

"Kenna." As her name slipped past my lips, I had a sudden vision of her still handcuffed in my room. "She found an envelope in her father's office. It had Leo's cufflinks and some of that straw that was found in Leo's room."

"Proof of a kill," Dad spelled out for Knox, who had suddenly paled. "Any chance it could be a fluke?"

"No." I rubbed my head. "Jesse found out Cameron sent Sonny to New Orleans. To see where we were, maybe? I'm guessing, but to me, it's enough, with the cufflinks—"

"That's not why he sent Sonny there." We all turned to stare at Knox. "He wanted confirmation that you and Kenna were together."

I swallowed hard as Knox slowly shook his head like something was coming back to him. "What do *you* know, little brother?"

"More than I realized, I think." His face morphed into visible pain, and for a moment, I took pity on him. "I'm not as stupid as you might assume." His eyes went glossy. "I know I party too much, but it's because I'm not ready to deal with the shit you all do. You all walk around like you carry this big secret on your shoulders, and Grim is always angry or just plain covered in blood."

I shrugged. "We have a lot of enemies."

"Don't we have people to keep them out?" His youth showed in his face, and I saw the little boy I'd helped shield from our world for so long peek through. Yet another mistake I'd made. I shook the thought away and slipped back to business. "Knox, what do you—"

"It's a lot," Dad cut me off, and I moved to sit next to him, "and we're carrying a big secret, son. One I think you might be in the middle of without knowing it." He gave Knox a sad smile and pointed at the chair across from us. "Grim may be right, Knox. If we can figure out what Cameron's up to and what else you might know, maybe we can end this nightmare and move on." Dad reached across and patted his arm tenderly. "What else do you know, son?"

"Well, I know Calli likes to feed me drinks." He squeezed his eyes shut as he thought. "At first, I thought she just wanted us to have fun, but over time, I noticed she never really touches much alcohol at all. One time when I wasn't feeling the best, you know, from the night before," he made a face and looked down, "I pretended to drink whatever she gave me, but I poured them into a planter next to me. Later, when I was zapped from the sun, I drifted off in the cabana. I wasn't totally asleep and overheard Cameron telling Calli he'd sent Sonny to New Orleans to get proof that you," he looked at me, "were fooling around with Kenna."

"That's probably what made him snap." I slammed my fist into the table. "After I beat his face in, I'm going to slice his throat and break every—"

"Calm down, Grim," Mom said firmly. "Knox, I know you care for Calli, but you see what's happening here, right?"

"I do. But, Mom, I really love Calli. She's different than them." He didn't get it, blinded by easy pussy and a cute smile. "She's just as blind to her father as Kenna is."

"Don't," I snapped. "Don't clump the two of them together." I suddenly felt wildly protective of the woman I'd ripped apart emotionally and still held captive in my bedroom.

"She feels stuck in her job because she works for him. You guys don't know the Calli that I do. She's loyal to her father. Surely that counts for something?" Knox looked at Dad, and I saw red. Dad must have sensed my change in mood because his tone changed.

"It does," he said soothingly. "I love that you see the good in everyone." He stood and walked around the table and kissed Knox on the head like he was twelve and not in his mid-twenties. "And you're right. We don't know Calli, and maybe given what's going on, we need to. Why don't you invite her to dinner tonight? Kenna too." Dad gave me a look, and I wanted to laugh at what I was hearing.

"Sure, I'll ask." Knox cautiously looked at me then at Dad. "Just make sure Kenna will be there so Grim doesn't take a swipe at Calli."

I found it humorous that he thought Kenna could stop me.

"I will." Dad smiled warmly. "Why don't you head out, and we'll deal with this Sonny situation?"

"Okay." He looked relieved to go. "Sounds good." He headed for the door.

I blocked his path and pushed a finger into his chest. "Just remember what blood you carry and where your loyalty lies."

"And *you* don't forget he was my brother, too." He

swallowed hard. "You grieve with violence and I with emotion. You might want to try it sometime before you push everyone who loves you away." He shoved my arm aside and left.

As the door slammed shut, Mom let out a light cry.

"He's not wrong, Grim." Dad poured himself a drink. "If you don't deal with this right, it'll consume you."

"Who says it hasn't?" I grunted and pulled my head back on track. "So, we can't trust Knox or Calli right now."

"No, we can't," he agreed, "so we'll pull her in and keep her close." His phone rang, and he cursed. "I have to go."

Mom and I sat in silence. I knew this was hard on her, and I wasn't making it any easier, but shit, I could have eliminated one of our enemies tonight if she hadn't come in. Sonny was trouble and clearly knew more than any of us realized.

"Please," she rubbed her face, "don't do anything else unless we know about it first. We've been waiting this out far too long to have Cameron think we know anything."

"Yeah."

She dropped her hands heavily on the table. "Seriously, Grim."

"I understand, and you're right." I nodded. She was right; I'd let myself slip, and I needed to be careful.

"One last thing." I tapped a finger on the table. "It might be wise if you were the one to ask Kenna to join us tonight."

"Why? Are you two fighting again?" She leaned back with an exasperated sigh.

"Because she knows I was headed to kill her father, and she's, ahh, handcuffed to my bed right now."

"Grimson Gates," her mouth dropped open as I quickly slipped out the door, "you better be joking!" Her voice followed me.

My head was in pure chaos when I left the office. When I stepped onto my suite, Zhar immediately sat up, then got to his feet as he sensed my mood and followed me toward the bedroom. I listened outside the door, but it was quiet. I pushed it open and saw Kenna curled into a ball, her head against the head-board with Leal curled up next to her. He lifted his head to look at me and gave a low growl as I moved farther into the room. Apparently, he had an opinion on the situation. He looked at Kenna then stared at me.

I eased onto the bed next to her then slowly reached over her head to unlock the cuff. I could spot a hit a mile away, but she caught me totally off guard when she swiped out her hand and something sliced across my collarbone. I snagged her hand and squeezed her wrist to make her release the knife.

"You missed," I growled and snatched the knife up and shoved it back in her hand. I yanked her arm up and held her hand with the knife tightly in mine and pointed the tip of the blade to my throat. "Go big or be killed," I tempted her. I waited for her to apply the necessary pressure, but instead, she stiffened.

"Let go of me!" She pulled her arm away, sending the knife to the bed. I tried to grab her wrist again, but she was extra feisty. Instead, I grabbed her legs and tried to hold her down. "Why are you such a bastard?" She was like a wild animal, and I found myself turned on by her temper.

"I never claimed to be anything else." I flipped her onto her stomach, careful not to hurt her arm too much, but the little devil was ready and bucked upward. I snagged her ankle and slid her back across the mattress to a better position. I pushed her down with my arm, and her wild breathing made her sexy chest strain against her lacy bra. "Are you quite finished?" I kind of hoped she wasn't because I really was a sick bastard.

I saw the anger fade from her puffy eyes as she took in my battered and bloody knuckles. She dropped defeated against the mattress, and I watched her fall apart.

"Did you?" Her voice was barely a whisper.

I grabbed the knife and tossed it on the bedside table, making Leal jump. "I couldn't find him," I admitted, and her chest fell as she let out the air she held with a relieved sob. I wasn't sure why she was relieved; after all, it was only a matter of time.

I leaned over her to unlock the cuff, and her gaze followed mine. She leaned back as I leaned in. Her bra strained against my dress shirt, and I took in her beauty. She was a gorgeous woman, and it crossed my mind I should just keep her locked up here.

"Grim, please don't do this. Please. "Don't forget, he's my father."

Rage rushed to the surface, and I felt my walls shoot back up.

"So, it's okay that he killed my brother? It's okay that it was meant for me?" I seethed as I let her arm drop.

"No, but—"

"Would you be so forgiving if he'd killed me?" I interrupted.

She pushed me back and sat upright. "No! I'm just saying there was a different way to handle the situation." She rubbed her raw wrist then jumped up and grabbed her dress off the floor. "And it's a lot to process, but you don't have to kill him. There are ways to deal with these things," she shouted.

"Listen, sweetheart," I grabbed her arm and made her look at me, "when you live in my world, it's my way. You come at me, I come at you. He knows that."

"Who are you to live above the law!"

"There is no law in my world. It's live or die. Your

father killed my brother and tried to kill me. He failed. He knows retaliation is coming."

"You're infuriating." She tried to pull away, but I wouldn't let her go. When she moved to slap me, I blocked her hit. I towered over her, and she cowed as she saw she'd fucked up.

"Listen to me, Kenna." My voice was eerily calm. "I know where our fights lead us, and as much as I might want to be inside you right now, be careful." I jerked her toward me. "Because I will destroy you."

Her face fell into an expression I couldn't read, and she pulled her hand out of my grip. "You already have." She grabbed one of my dress shirts from the back of a chair, covered herself up, and left.

TWO

My prison life had become a game of dodgeball. I constantly had to dodge the monsters who wanted their way with me, and I grew exhausted with all the hiding. I had little protection, and they knew it. I soon found solace in the library. Who would have thought they had one? The library was huge, and they had an entire wing designated just to books on the law. I had to laugh at that one. Given that I was a model inmate, I soon earned the respect of Sprinkles, the manager, who just so happened to be best friends with CM, my cellmate.

I remembered the day I asked the manager why he was called Sprinkles. He just smiled and said he added that extra little touch to those who stood in his gang's way. The image *that passed through me sent goosebumps. I quit asking about nicknames after that.*

I eyed CM as he thumbed through a law book and scribbled something down in his notebook. He always had that book tucked in his breast pocket.

"Curiosity will get you killed in here." He didn't look up, so he must have felt me watching him. "Go ahead and ask."

The load of books in my arms was heavy, so I started to stack them as I spoke. "How much time do you have left?" I pushed my glasses farther up my nose. "Here, I mean."

"I can leave at any time." He shrugged, and I chuckled, but when he looked up, I saw something flash across his face.

"I guess I could, too, but I don't want to be shot or thrown into the hole like you were just in last month."

He closed his notebook, tucked it away, and moved closer. "See this?" He pulled up his sleeve and pointed to a part of his tattoo. "That symbol right there?" I nodded. "That means I'm a recruiter. I pop in and out of prison to check on my men here and the new guys coming in."

"For your club?" I tried to follow.

"Yes, my club." He smiled like he thought it was cute I called it a club. "I wasn't in the hole. I was in west Los Angeles checking on a," he tilted his head as he thought, "client who got himself into a real bad situation."

A smile broke out across my face when I realized he was playing me. "You had me there." I chuckled.

"You don't believe me?"

"I don't." I lowered my voice when a guard came in with his lunch. "It's impossible."

He jumped up on the table, and I held my breath, waiting for the guard to snap at him. "Nothing is impossible when you have money. We," he tapped his tattoo, "have money. Lots of it, in fact."

"How?" I shook my head and thought how crazy this all sounded. "Who are you, really?"

He pursed his lips and studied my face. "So, are you ready to share who you really are?"

I pulled my glasses off and used a rag to clean them. I needed a moment to think. "Why do I get the impression you knew who I was before I stepped into our cell?"

"He said you were smart." He grinned.

"Who?"

"Come." He chin-pointed to the door. "We should talk, but not here."

I jumped back to the present as Cameron tossed open the door to his office, then I slammed into his back as he stopped short. I bounced off his heavy body, but he didn't turn around.

"What the fuck happened to you?" he barked at someone I couldn't see. Out of the corner of my eye, I saw Jesse, Grim's right-hand man, turn swiftly on his heel and head in the opposite direction. That was odd.

The sound of a bullet being pushed into the chamber pulled my attention immediately back to the office.

"Whoa!" Cameron dropped his bag and raised his hands. "What the hell?"

I shimmied around Cameron and saw a badly beaten Sonny sitting in one of the chairs. He had a gun pointed in our direction.

"This, you fat, fucking ass, was meant for you!" he shouted as I slowly closed the door. I didn't want to give Jesse a reason to head back this way.

I inched between the two of them. I figured Sonny had reached his limit. "Who did this to you?" I tried to be the rational one.

Sonny winced as he stood and pressed his other hand to what I could only imagine were several cracked or broken ribs. "I'm tired of this." He moved closer to Cameron. "I've had enough of your constant bullshit. I'm—"

"Calm down, Sonny." Cameron stepped back with his hands out in front of him. He stopped as he hit the wall. "Who did this?" Sonny raised the gun, so it pointed at Cameron's face. I knew I should stop him, but there was a part of me that liked seeing Cameron nearly soil himself.

"He was looking for you," Sonny's voice made my mouth go dry, "but found me instead."

I moved into Sonny's line of vision, in fear he'd go too far and really shoot Cameron. "Who are you talking about?"

"Grim Gates." I watched as that news sank in for Cameron. "I took a beating for you, motherfucker."

Cameron's face turned three shades of red as he took a deep breath. "Impossible. He can't know. There's no proof."

"The missing cliff links," I reminded him.

He swung his gaze over to me. "But those were sent to me. I didn't take them."

I shrugged. "Does it matter? Possession is nine-tenths of the law."

"Hang on, hang on." Cameron held up a hand as he thought. "Let's back this up a moment. Why would you think Grim was after me and wasn't looking for *you*?"

"You want to try that sentence again?" Sonny hissed.

"*You* went to New Orleans to discover if that inked-up mongrel was involved with my daughter. *You* were supposed to keep a low profile and report back to me. Instead, *you* made a mockery of yourself, swinging your hurt ego around when you saw they *were* together. Then you go and make a big show of your power. Maybe, just maybe," Cameron's face twisted into a grin, "he believes it was *you* behind his brother's hit." He paused as Sonny's face grew red. "No, I don't think that beating was for me. I think he was looking for me to find you, and you just so happened to be in my office when he came in."

"Cameron," I warned. I knew shit was about to hit the fan.

"If Grim Gates believed it was me behind Leo's death, I can assure you I'd have a sniper laser between my eyes right now."

If he would only be so lucky.

"If you want to blame me for that," Cameron pointed at Sonny's swollen face, "bring me more proof."

The sound of spit being pulled from halfway down someone's throat filled the silence, then Sonny spat a bloody ball of mucus at Cameron's chest.

I closed my eyes in disgust. I totally understood why Sonny was so upset. Cameron was an idiot and incredibly hardheaded. He refused to see anyone's side of things if he didn't want to. He was impossible.

Sonny dropped his arm and groaned in pain. As the gun lowered, I let out the breath I held. "We need to get you looked at, Sonny." I hoped he would let it go for now.

Sonny looked at me, then his face twisted in an ugly scowl as he looked over at Cameron. "Let's not forget your role in all of this."

THREE

KENNA

"Whoa." Minnie caught me as I stepped out of the Wet and Wild cage in a fishnet dress. "Are you crazy? What do you think you're doing?"

"Dancing." I snagged a towel from the peg and wrung out my hair.

"Kenna, no," she held out an arm to stop me, "we're not ready. What if that sicko shows up? What if he's already here?" Minnie's concern was understandable, and I knew it, but I was way past being sensible.

"Then he saw me dance." I shrugged.

"But, Kenna, he beat, threatened, and blackmailed you, then he hired some tweaker to send you a message that he's still around. That isn't the average shithead we have to deal with every day here. This is on a way higher messed up level."

"I know." I wanted the bastard to show up. If anyone should be beaten to a pulp, it should be him. "But if he shows up, then we'll know who it is."

Minnie looked at me like I had two heads. "What happened to you tonight? You look different." She scanned my body then homed in on my wrist. "Tell me this was from doing something kinky."

"No, this was Grim making sure I didn't get to my father before he killed him." I dropped my damp fishnet dress on the floor, stepped out of it, and wrapped my towel around me.

Minnie's mouth dropped open. "Okay, wait. Start again."

"Turns out my father did get Leo killed, and now Grim is on the warpath."

Minnie gasped, pulled out her phone, and made a call to Brick. As she filled him in, I gathered my things.

"Wait, Kenna, where are you going?"

I stopped at the door and drew in a deep breath. "Now that I've had a chance to get my head on straight," I pointed back to the cage, "I need to speak to that murdering son-of-a-bitch father of mine."

I didn't wait for her to protest. I shot outside and rushed back to Indulge. Benny called out as I entered the lobby and hurried toward me. I hadn't realized he was still in town.

"Hey," he reached out as I rushed by and spun me right around as he snagged my arm, "where's the fire?"

Flashbacks of Grim's hotel Secrets being on fire came screaming back to me, but I quickly pushed them away.

"I'm late for—"

"Your dinner?" he asked in a tone that made me look at him strangely, and he pointed a finger in the air. "Your father's upstairs with Calli and some guy in that restaurant with the glass box. They seem to be looking for somebody. I just assumed it was you."

"Yeah, they are." I nodded through my lie.

He smiled like something ran through his head and let go of my arm.

"What?"

He shrugged. "I understand why your boyfriend is so protective." I dropped my gaze with how much his words bothered me. "Well, don't let me keep you."

"Thanks." I rushed away and slid into the elevator just as the doors were closing. I smiled at the old couple who were already inside out of habit then focused on what I needed to do.

I watched my father from a few yards away, He might as well have had a spotlight directed on him. He was making such a show of himself from his favorite "everyone can see me" table in the restaurant. He let go a loud belly laugh, head tipped back, and mouth wide open. Food spat from his mouth as my sister said something else and laughed along with him.

My temper shot to the surface as I clenched my fists. How could he have fun at a time like this? What an insensitive asshole.

He banged on the table and made a few guests look over as he laughed harder. Simon sat with them, but he seemed to be the only one who was conscious of the spectacle they made. He looked around a few times almost as if embarrassed.

My feet started to move on their own as a million different thoughts raced through my head. Every scenario I came up with ended with me making a scene. My blood pressure spiked. I felt my cheeks burn, and my heart pounded against my chest to the point of pain as I headed toward their table. The memory of Leo's smile popped up in front of me, and pain mixed with the anger. Tears prickled my eyes as I grew closer. He was my father, but how could he do such a thing?

Suddenly, an arm wrapped around me, and I was steered in a different direction.

"What are you doing?" I snarled at Grim.

He waited until we were far enough away not to be heard by my father or the others. "Mom needs a word."

"I was in the middle of something."

He wouldn't look at me. "I know." He led me

toward a table and pulled out a chair. Laurel Gates greeted me.

"Please," she pointed to the chair, "have a seat."

Grim took a chair then entwined his fingers and rested his hands calmly on the table. I found that odd, considering the man he wanted to kill was across the room from us. "You weren't in the pool, and you haven't been to your suite yet, and why is your hair wet?"

"What? Are you watching me?" I shook my head, confused about why he'd bring that up right now.

"Grim, please," his mother said quietly. I turned my attention to her and took in her rigid posture and the heavy bags under her eyes. "I'm going to address the elephant in the room." She nodded over my shoulder, and I didn't need to turn to know she referred to my father and the others who sat across the room. "It's true, dear, all of it." She placed a hand on mine. I immediately felt the weight of my father's actions slam down on my shoulders. I tried to fight the tears that pooled in my eyes, but it was impossible. It was true; my father was a monster. "Your father killed my son." She paused to swallow while I sat stiffly in my seat. "We have all the proof we need."

"I'm so sorry, Mrs. Gates," I said softly, not knowing what else to say. "I truly had no idea."

"I know you are, and I know that too." She tugged at her yellow cardigan and shivered. "Because if you did, this conversation would be going very differently."

Now I was the one who shivered.

The sound of my father's laughter made me cringe, and I noticed Grim's finger had started to tap on the table.

"My son isn't even laid to rest, and that miserable man is stuffing his face with Chef Dan's finest food." She rubbed her tired eyes. "And tomorrow I have to stand there and watch him pretend to mourn for my baby." Grim reached over and squeezed her hand. "To think we let him in all those years ago." She held back a sob and closed her eyes to regain control. "We thought he was our friend."

"People with money like we have don't have friends, mother," Grim growled.

I wanted to run away like a child. I didn't know how to handle this situation. Nothing could prepare you for when your father murders your boss's son.

I shifted in my seat, unsure what to say next, so I opened my stupid mouth and spoke without a filter. "What's going to happen to my father?"

"I have a few ideas," Grim hissed, but Laurel said something to him in Spanish I didn't catch. Whatever it was, he gave a tight nod and shut up. I wished I had that power over him sometimes.

"As much as I want to tear his eyes out for what

he's done, Kenna, we all have to take a step back. We have to wait."

"Wait?" I didn't follow.

She nodded and let her gaze move over my shoulder, and a darkness I'd only ever seen in her son's eyes flickered across hers. "He suspects Grim knows, and he probably wonders if we know, but a part of me thinks he might not suspect that *you* know." Her fingers tapped the table. "I'm sure it's why he's making such a scene in the middle of the restaurant. If people are watching, he knows we won't make a move."

"For someone who's fucking stupid, he has his moments," Grim added.

"And when he's alone?"

"Then we return the kindness he so lovingly cast on my brother." Grim's voice sent another shiver through me. "But until then," his lips spread into a chilling smile, "we play."

"Play?" I repeated and leaned forward in my seat as I looked up at him. "As in handcuff him to your bed for several hours?"

His mother's gaze dropped to my wrist as I rubbed the angry red mark from where I'd tried to free myself. "Grim!"

"Don't worry, Mother," he huffed. "She held her own just fine." He pulled his shirt down at the neck and revealed the cut where I'd slashed him with the knife.

She closed her eyes and took a deep breath. "Please, don't make me worry about you two."

"I can assure you anything we might have had is over." I licked around my dry mouth, and Grim smirked and shook his head. "Mrs. Gates, what can I do to help?" I wanted to be kept close to this.

"Act like you don't know anything," she shifted gears, "and keep an eye on Knox for me?"

"Knox?" That confused me.

"Your sister has her claws in him," Grim grunted, but I wouldn't look at him. "They keep him with a belly full of liquor and pump him for information whenever they feel like it."

"Grim," his mother shook her head, "Knox is still young. Kenna, I think he really loves your sister, but I don't think it's returned. I've lost one child to your family. I'm not about to lose another."

Although she had every right to be devastated, her words slashed. It was as if she'd said it had been my doing.

"Of course. I'll keep a close eye on him." I didn't want to hear anything else. My heart hurt for everyone, and there was no making it right. I got up and left the way I came.

I stood in the back while everyone piled into the church, the Gateses stood in a row and greeted people as they came in. I hadn't slept at all the previous night, and the more I tried to make sense of things, the more twisted up I became. How did you process something like this? How did you not feel the judgement from others, and how could you not blame them?

Minnie caught my eye from where she sat next to Brick and Tess. She waved me over, but I shook my head, just wanting to be alone. The only thing that almost brought a smile to my lips was the row of reapers that lined the pew from the guy's motorcycle cuts. A few older ladies clutched their pearls as they walked by. If only they knew.

"Are you not going to join the others?" Elio Capri, the mafia boss of Italy, inquired kindly. I loved that he'd taken the time to be here for the Gates family. It showed how strong his friendship with Grim was. I shook my head. "Why is that?" His accent was thick, but his English was perfect.

"I don't feel overly welcome, given the…" I paused as someone walked by, "situation."

"Mm." He stroked his chin. The huge black ring he wore caught the light, and I saw what looked like a family crest engraved on it. "Do you know my wife's story?"

"I've heard a bit about it." I'd heard a lot more than

a bit, but I didn't want to admit it. Her past could be a book in itself.

"Sienna had no control over who she was; I would never hold that over her."

"Perhaps, but let me ask you this." I couldn't believe I was speaking so freely with this man. He could snap his fingers and end my existence. "When you first found out, weren't you shocked? Didn't a sliver of doubt ever run through your mind that maybe, just maybe she wasn't who you thought she was? What if she was just playing a game with you for years?" I stopped myself at his raised eyebrow. I'd already said too much.

He smiled and shrugged. "So, you have heard the story." He put a hand on my arm. "I would be lying if I said there wasn't a moment of doubt in the beginning, but that's to be expected. I'm only human. Not to mention my responsibility to protect my people."

"And no one should ever think to judge you for that, Mr. Capri. I mean Elio," I corrected myself when he gave me a look. "So, you see why I'm standing back here on this day of all days. They only just got confirmation it was my father who did it. There'd be some doubt there, wouldn't there? In the forefront of their minds?" I looked down as my chest squeezed tight. "The way Laurel looked at me yesterday," I cleared my throat, "it broke a tiny piece of me."

"And what about Grim? How does he look at you?"

"With regret," I answered honestly.

I caught movement and nearly passed out as my father, mother, and Calli came through the doors dressed in their finest. Dad looked in the direction of the family pew and seemed to think twice about sitting there. He steered them all into seats farther back.

I noticed Elio caught Trigger's look and something passed through them, but as fast as I felt it, it was gone.

"Can I ask you something, Elio?"

He looked straight ahead. "Of course."

"I just hope my mother didn't know anything." Elio peered down at me and gave me a puzzled look. "I feel like a loose balloon stuck on a tree branch about to pop. I'm close with my mom, and I need to know I can trust her." He shifted uncomfortably. I felt weak in the knees.

"It's difficult to say if she could have known about the hit on Grim. I certainly can't comment on their relationship. Perhaps you should talk to your mother."

"Great." I felt myself invert even further.

"Perhaps a good friend, then? Minnie and Tess are there if you need someone. Both of them are good people." I nodded with an attempt at a smile.

Elio looked over as the priest entered and asked everyone to take their seats. The service was about to begin. Elio pointed for us to sit in a half pew off to the side.

"No, please, be with your friends." I pointed to Trigger and the others.

He ignored me and moved to the pew and waited for me to sit down then he slid in beside me. "I am, *mia amica.*"

"Thank you, Elio."

The service was beautiful and filled with stories of Leo and how he brought laughter to everyone's life. I was pleased that Elio took my arm and walked with me to the reception after.

"Hey, sweetie," Minnie wrapped a loving arm around me, "I've never been one to beat around the bush, mainly because I've never had one, but how are you dealing with all this?" She nodded toward my father, whose dress shirt did nothing for his weight problem.

I grimaced. "Just trying to digest it all."

Elio excused himself to go to speak to someone.

"God, that man is sex on a stick," Minnie sighed. "We're going back to my club after this to toast Leo. You're coming." She rested her head on my shoulder. "You'd have known if you answered my calls."

I felt like a shitty friend, but I also suddenly felt like an outsider looking in at my life. "I'm sorry."

My father caught my attention. It seemed he'd finally gotten up the nerve to speak to Jim and Laurel. I held my breath, curious what might happen, but the

Gateses stayed true to their word and played it off well.

"Breathe, Kenna," Minnie reminded me. "You have friends all around you."

"It's not that. I'm worried about—"

She cut me off. "You know your father."

"No, it's not that." I waved my hand at her. "What if my mother's involved?"

"What? Oh, good God." She patted my arm. "I can't imagine." She chewed her cheek for a beat. "I guess only time will tell. I'm so sorry sweetie. I hadn't even gone there." Minnie spotted Brick, who beckoned for her to join him. "Look, hang in there, okay? See you tonight?"

I shook my head. "I think I just need a night alone."

"I disagree."

I set my glass down and slid my purse under my arm. "I know." I squeezed her arm and left, ignoring her protests.

I pushed open the doors to the chapel and slipped back inside. Everyone had gone, and it felt so peaceful. Candles were lit on a little table; they flickered in a sudden draft.

My heels clicked loudly on the wooden floor as I made my way up the aisle. The cross above me grew larger as I approached the altar. The evening sun shone through the pieces of stained glass and created shapes against the wall. It was lovely, and I felt a calmness come over me as I slowly lowered myself onto the polished wooden pew.

A sudden tap on my shoulder sent my nerves firing. To my horror, Sonny Conti asked me to move over. His appearance was shocking. It looked like he'd been through a bar fight. Then it hit me like a bag of rocks. Grim's battered knuckles.

"Yeah, your boyfriend's handiwork." He read my mind.

My back went up. "He's not my boyfriend," I corrected.

"Right. Well, all this," he waved a finger around his face, "was his doing. For no reason."

"Pfft, if he did it, I'm sure he had a good reason," I shot back without thinking, and his expression went hard. I swallowed. I needed to be careful.

He smelled like cigarettes and alcohol, and I turned my face away. I wanted to run, to scream, to God knew what, anything but sit there like a stone and let him fill me with fear. I realized my effort to be alone had left me vulnerable.

"Funny how people turn to the church for solace whenever anything bad happens. And what is this place but a building filled with things that bring some people comfort? Just a house, really. The only difference between this and a house is that someone stands up there," he pointed to the pulpit, "in front of two crossed sticks and tells us how we should be good people." My hands shook in my lap, and I wondered if I should try to call Minnie for help. "Are you good people, Kenna?" He put a hand heavily across my shoulders. I refused to flinch. I wouldn't give him the pleasure of knowing the depth of my fear.

"Are you?" I countered.

"No." He shrugged. "But the difference between you and me is that I'm honest with myself."

"Just because you admit you're bad doesn't justify the behavior." I shirked out from under his arm and leaned forward against the other pew.

"Maybe not, but at least I sleep at night." He turned to look at me, and I knew he saw my exhaustion. "You worried about dear old dad?" I locked my face in place. This was a test. I knew it was. He wanted to know if I knew the truth.

"Why?" I shook my head and acted like I didn't follow. "What happened to Dad?" I went for my purse like I was going to call him. Sonny's cold hand slammed down on mine, and he leaned close, so his swollen-ugly face was only inches from mine.

"We all have sins, Kenna, and it's only a matter of time before we have to deal with the consequences." He squeezed my thigh hard, then, as fast as he'd appeared, he got up and left.

FOUR

Dad beamed at me. "You did an amazing job, son." It was the first time since we'd left for New Orleans that I'd seen him smile. "We've been through so much this last while, but your mother and I are very proud of you, and Leo would be, too."

"Thanks, Dad." I looked around the beautiful lobby of Secrets that was now filled with potential guests, new guests, and press. As much as the fire had set me back, it also had brought the hotel twice the amount of attention. I was very pleased with the grand opening so far.

I glanced around and spotted some staff from Indulge and noted Jayden and his father Walter Wallace were in conversation. To my surprise, Victor

Conti had made an appearance. Thankfully, his son hadn't dared show his battered face.

Salazar lifted a glass to me with a nod as he caught my eye from across the room, I tilted mine back at him as a thank you for coming. It had been an excellent turnout, and I felt confident that Secrets would be a success. I went back to scanning the lobby. Several other guests either waved or smiled, and a sense of accomplishment filled me. Perhaps we'd get through this thing without any trouble, after all. I scanned the lobby again.

"She'll be here." My father patted my shoulder.

"I was just checking out the guests." It was partially true.

"Uh huh." He smiled.

It had been ten days since we laid my brother to rest, and ten days since I'd seen Kenna. She had disappeared right after the funeral and apparently only let Dad know where she'd gone.

"If you'd only told me where she went, I could settle." I held my glass up to my mouth as I spoke.

Dad tucked a hand in his pocket and made an effort to look relaxed, as many were watching us. "Like I explained, I'm honoring her wishes. I understand why she left," he gave me a look, "but I need you to make things right." He pressed his lips together when Minnie appeared at my side.

"Is she here yet?"

"Not yet." My father smiled down at her. "I should go sit for a while." He chuckled quietly and headed toward a chair off to the side. I saw Mom make a beeline for him. She made a show like a "mother hen" for a few moments then sat down beside him.

"I still can't believe she left and didn't tell me where she went. Just texted that she left." Minnie blew out a breath as she pulled at her tight dress. "Holy mother of air conditioning, I'm like a helpless sausage wrangled into a casing." She waved at herself, trying to cool down. "Jesus, even my vag is suffocating in this thing."

"I'll take things I didn't need to know for five hundred." Tess chuckled as she came up behind us.

"It's like a water park down there. I'm slipping and sliding."

"Minnie," Tess shook her head, "these people don't need to hear how your vag is a summer amusement park."

I laughed. "Agreed. Please stop." I spotted Knox with Calli and fought the urge to roll my eyes. Just what I needed, a fucking spy at my hotel opening.

"Meh." She shrugged and snagged a champagne flute off a waiter's tray as he walked by. "No sighting of Kenna yet," she said in response to Tess's question as she looked around.

"Fucking Sonny," Tess huffed. That drew my attention, and Minnie's eyes went wide at Tess.

"Why do you say that?" I looked at the two of them, and Tess closed her eyes with a curse. "Speak, ladies," I ordered.

"We had it covered," she started, and I cocked a brow. I didn't like how this story started. "Basically, Kenna left Leo's reception early and went back to the church because, well, you know, struggling with the family murder-ness." She waved her hand. "Anyway, Sonny must have been watching her because the moment she was out of sight, he followed her in."

"And?"

"And I don't know, but whatever it was, she wouldn't share. Then later that night, I get a text from her saying she's leaving town but would be back for the opening."

What the hell?

"And why was I not told this?"

"She brought it straight to Trigger," Tess added quickly, "and he said he'd handle it because you had enough to deal with."

"I see." I didn't like it, but I would have done the same for Trig, so I understood it. As for Sonny, I would deal with him again soon. I smirked to myself as I remembered Jesse had told me I'd broken his nose and fractured his cheek.

My mind drifted back over the past week. I thought of Talya's warning that her parents, Jerry and Elva

Cano, had been behind some of our problems. Retaliation had been sweet. We'd tipped off some of the rival Cartel families and shared that the Canos planned to take over Martin Castillo's empire. Now they had a whole new set of problems. *Karma.* Of course, I made sure whoever took over Rosarito knew they'd have my support as long as they left my run alone. My contract for drug distribution to Vegas was carved in stone.

Suddenly, Minnie's hand slapped on my arm, and I followed her line of sight. Kenna entered the lobby on the arm of Yen Hong. She was in a dress that nearly took my breath away. A long, form-fitted, red number. It flowed over her willowy frame and hugged her curves. Her shoulders were bare, as the top of the dress was attached to a matching red scarf that was wrapped around her slender neck.

When she turned to smile at someone, I caught her bare back. The dress was open all the way down to just above her sexy bottom, where it cut into a V shape and gathered across her hips. The red scarf hung from her neck at the back and swooped down to trail along the floor. I froze when she laughed at something Yen said and he smiled down at her. It didn't help that the rich Asian bastard looked like he'd stepped from a fashion magazine himself.

"Oh, shit," Minnie squeaked. She looked at Tess like she knew something I didn't. Then she squeezed my arm with something like panic on her face. "So that's where she was!"

"Where?" I wasn't following.

"A while ago, Yen Hong made her an amazing offer to come work for his hotel in Hong Kong. She didn't say yes but didn't shoot the idea down either."

"What the hell, Minnie? I need to know these things!"

"No," she corrected me, "only a boyfriend needs to know these things, and you've stated a few times now that Kenna isn't your girlfriend."

"I'm her boss. If she's being poached, I need to know."

"Then go be a boss and win her back, because so help me Jesus, if you don't and something breaks up our trio, I will strip you bare and beat your fine ass for all to see."

"Oh, I want in on that, too." Tess glared at me.

Where are the fucking guys when I need them? I caught sight of Brick, who just smirked at me from the far corner of the room, like he knew what a handful they could be. The Devil's Reach wanted nothing to do with fancy parties but everything to do with watching my back.

"Good evening, ladies." Yen was in front of me. "Mr. Gates, your hotel looks exquisite. Congratulations on your opening."

"Thank you." I tried my best to curb my frustration that he had Kenna on his arm. "I'm glad you could join us. I thought you were out of town."

"I was," he smiled lovingly at Kenna then back at me, "but Kenna made me an offer I couldn't refuse, and, well, here we are." *What the hell does that mean?* Someone called out his name and he inclined his head at me. "Forgive me, but I must go attend to something." He turned to Kenna and bowed and kissed her hand. A beautiful gold Chow Tai Fook bracelet sparkled from her wrist. "What a pleasure it's been." He winked, and her cheeks pinked.

My blood boiled to the point of pain, but when Kenna brushed back the piece of her hair that hung from her low bun, I caught a whiff of her perfume, and my fingers twitched to grab her. The only reason I didn't was I felt my father's eyes on me. I'd promised to behave, but I never promised for how long.

"Kenna," Minnie moved closer to us, "please tell me you didn't sign with Yen?"

Kenna slapped a smile on as someone she knew said hello. "Now is not the time to discuss this."

"Is that a Fook bracelet?" Minnie grabbed her arm. "Tess, look at this, it's positively fuck-worthy!" She studied the bracelet, and my skin grew hot.

Tess snagged her arm and took her time studying it while I studied Kenna's face. "Yen bought you a gift?"

"It's not that big of a deal." She brushed them off

and glanced at me like I was just any other man in the room. "The place looks lovely. You should be pleased."

"I am with the hotel, just not with certain people who leave on vacation without so much as a warning when I have an opening planned." I hadn't liked it when she was away. I'd grown quite accustomed to her being around. Even when I was an asshole to her.

"Well, I see you managed."

"It wasn't easy."

"Did I miss a single one of your *business* requests?" She raised a brow. "No, I handled everything I needed to, and then some. Clearly, you don't need me here in person."

"I disagree."

She stiffened, and it took me two seconds to understand why.

Jenelle threaded her arm through mine. "There you are," she purred, clearly pleased to have me speaking to her again.

"Yeah, he's in the same space he was when you watched him five minutes ago from across the room." Minnie rolled her eyes at Jenelle. "And he hasn't moved since you arrived."

"How nice of you to notice me." Jenelle chuckled in the bitchy way she always did when women were around me. "Dad thinks tomorrow would be a good time for that dinner."

Excellent.

"Great, I'll have my assistant make the reservations for six people at seven." I smiled down at her and watched as her face morphed into a frown.

"Six?"

"That's the number that comes after five," Minnie's voice dripped sarcasm, and it made Tess smile.

"Yes, six. Kenna is the lead hostess for Secrets. She needs to be at all business meetings with prospective clients." Kenna's face hardened as Jenelle shot her a nasty look.

"Shit just got real," Tess muttered as she turned away.

"I didn't see that on my calendar," Kenna shot back. "I believe I have a night with Salazar tomorrow."

"See," Jenelle beamed up at me, "she's entertaining another man tomorrow night." She clapped her hands. "Five, it is."

Minnie raised her glass in the air. "Well, tie my tits in a bow, she *can* do math."

"I took the liberty of clearing your schedule," I countered and watched Kenna's face grow angry. "Perks of being the boss."

"Boss isn't the word I would use," she muttered, but her eyes lit up when Chef Dale came out of nowhere.

"Mr. Gates," he pumped my hand, "this place is something else." I nodded politely as he turned to greet Kenna.

"You're back!" He wrapped her in a hug. "Damn, girl, you look hot enough to start a fire in that dress. Remind me why we broke up."

"'Cause you're a man-whore," Minnie teased. I knew there was a lot of truth behind her words.

Kenna bypassed his question. "Did you meet Chef Trahan yet?"

"No." Dale took her arm. "Introduce us?"

"Sure." She slipped away, and I wanted to stop her, but Jenelle moved in front of me.

"Dance with me?"

I shook my head. "I have to make some rounds." With that, I left her with Minnie and Tess and went to fulfill my role as the owner of the newest hotel on the strip. I felt a sense of pride that it had finally come together and that it was everything I'd hoped for.

I searched the faces in the crowd for Cameron, in spite of the fact that if he even showed his face for a moment, I'd know. Elio and his cousins, Niccola and Vinni, were back at Indulge watching things from there, while the Devil's Reach had this place surrounded. I refused to have anything else go wrong.

I kept an eye on Kenna as she worked the guests after she'd linked up the chefs, Dale and Trahan. As I whisked by the two of them at one point, I caught their conversation about various dishes they had in common. Kenna worked expertly around the room. Her charisma and charm as she talked with people was interesting to watch. Even the most high-powered men and women met their match with her. She fielded all their comments and raised them one.

I saw her face fall when Calli and Knox pulled her away from someone she was talking to. I moved through the crowd to intercept but got tangled up with an art dealer and missed what was said.

My phone buzzed. I pulled it free and excused myself from the art dealer.

> Morgan: Your ten o'clock, green shirt.

I scanned the crowd in that direction and spotted Simon, who had his eyes on Kenna. Maybe it was Calli he watched, but I'd take bets it wasn't.

> Morgan: He arrived alone five
> minutes ago. Figured we'd let him
> through and watch what he did.

"I think I'll turn in," I heard Kenna say. "Thanks for everything. I'll see you tomorrow."

"No thanks needed." I recognized Yen's voice. "I've always got you."

She strolled by and greeted people along the way.

> Grim: Don't lose him.

I moved quickly through the crowd to my private

elevator. Because it was opening night, the main staff had been given rooms so they could properly celebrate; I was pleased to see Kenna was going to use hers.

I heard her door open, and as she came into the room, I turned on the light and she jumped.

"Why do you insist on doing that?" She dropped her hand from her chest as she tossed her keycard on the side table. "Shouldn't you be downstairs at your opening?"

"The last person I'd thought you'd show up with tonight was Yen Hong." I rubbed my finger over my lips. "Did you sign his contract?" If she was surprised by my knowledge, she didn't show it.

"I'm confused." She twisted the top off a water bottle. "Why are you here? Because you made it very clear that you had no desire to see me. I'm a Tame, remember?"

I leaned forward and rested my elbows on my thighs as I studied her. "Answer my question."

She ignored me and reached down to undo her heels. She tossed them to the side then reached up and undid her hair. It tumbled down her bare back.

"You know, it's funny that you think you can control all aspects of my life." She headed to the bar and poured herself a glass of red wine. She took her time, and I watched her throat constrict as she took a good swig then set the glass on the bar. When she turned back around, I was standing right behind her.

"Where were you?"

"Your father knew."

"Were you with Yen?"

She held my gaze. "Yes."

"Why?" I felt all tangled up inside.

"It's none of your business." She went to turn, but I grabbed the tie around her neck and used my free hand on her hip to draw her back to me. I saw her nipples harden through the thin fabric when my lips brushed by her ear.

"Whatever you do is my business." I breathed her in. "I make it my business."

"Well," she leaned her head back to look at me, "that's a you problem, isn't it?" She tried to slide out of my hold, but I tightened my grip. "Grim," she rolled her eyes, "yes, I was with Yen Hong in Hong Kong, and yes, he offered me a contract. I haven't turned him down but haven't accepted his offer either. I like having options."

A cold prickle shot down my back. "Why? Don't I give you enough here?"

Her face fell and her shoulders straightened. I could see a change come over her. "You've offered me more than enough here."

"So?"

"Grim," she wiggled away and put a hand on her hip, "it's complicated."

"I'm listening."

"All right. One minute I'm a just a hostess for your father's hotel, and the next I'm trapped under someone I just killed, then you show up and…" She shook her head. "Next I'm being attacked, then I'm being stalked." Her hands whirled about as she tried to find the words. "Then you and I suddenly become like animals and it's like we can't keep our hands off each other." She stopped and her eyes pierced mine. "Then there's you and Jenelle." She sucked in a deep breath. "One moment I think we just might have something, then…" She stopped herself and closed her eyes. "I don't know. Sometimes I wonder if it's a good idea for me to stay at Indulge."

"It's not."

"Really," she scoffed. "That's what you've decided to say."

"I have plenty more to say." She waved for me to keep going. "For starters, what did Sonny Conti talk to you about after Leo's funeral? Why did you sit in the back with Elio, and why did you leave the reception alone, anyway? You're a smart woman, Kenna. You know people are watching you. You know who you killed. Why would you leave alone, knowing all that?"

"Seriously?" she yelled.

"I'd like *you* to take this seriously."

She raised her chin in the way I hated yet loved because I knew we were in for a fight. I felt my pants tighten. "Grim! You flung insult after insult at me, trying to take me down so I'd hurt just as much as you did! You'd let me in then tossed me out just as fast." She was pissed and hot. "You chose vengeance over me," she spat.

"I also chose you over my brother, and look where that got me!" I boomed when she hit that nerve.

"I know that!" She pushed my chest with both hands, but I didn't budge, and that pissed her off further. "You've reminded me many times. Like it was my fault or your fault." Tears suddenly filled her wild eyes. "It wasn't either of our faults. It was a horrible thing that happened, but blaming me or you isn't going to help."

"Why the hell do you think I went after your father?" I shouted in her face, but she didn't back down.

"No, you don't!" She stepped closer, and I couldn't help but glance down at her heaving chest. "What you need to take ownership for is to see that I was only trying to help protect you. I had to stop you from leaving. I was on your side, Grim. I knew we were being watched and that your family had to play it the right way." She swiped away a tear that had slipped down her cheek, and her mouth opened and closed as though she was about to say something, then changed her mind. "And you knew by walking out that door that if you killed him, we were over, yet you still left."

"He put a hit on me and got my brother instead," I

hissed and put a hand on her shoulder. "Anyone in my situation would have left."

She slapped my hand away. "And anyone in my situation," she poked my chest to drive her words home, "would have left too. So, I did." She turned away, and I grabbed her hand.

"But I didn't kill your father."

Her mouth twisted as she thought. "Would you have if he was in his office that night?"

Fuck yes.

Well, maybe, yeah.

I thought for a moment as I took in her hurt expression, and something nagged at me. *Would I have?*

"Look," her shoulders sagged, and she looked exhausted, "Sonny came to let me know the truth is coming. Whatever the hell that means. I can't tell if he knows, but he made sure to scare the hell out of me."

I hated that he got to her. "If he knew you killed Matt Mayers, you'd be dead, church or not."

She nodded. "Then I guess I have my head for another day."

Her phone rang, and I grabbed it off the bar and fought an internal battle not to look at the screen. I handed it to her and watched her send it to voicemail. She cursed under her breath as I moved closer to breathe in her scent. She was like a mantrap.

"Well, I can tell you, I'm over all of this." She moved to sit on the couch, and I shut my mouth about how she was in too deep to hide her head in the sand now. "And I'm not going to dinner tomorrow night."

I smiled and thought it was cute that she thought she had a choice. "You will go to dinner tomorrow night because I am your boss and it's part of your job." I poured myself a glass of wine from the open bottle and carried both glasses over to the couch.

"How is part of my job dealing with your bitch girl-friend?" She took the glass. "Do you enjoy the insults she flings at me?"

"I enjoy that you hold your own." I took a sip of the cab sav. "What I don't enjoy is another man poaching what's mine."

"And when did I become yours?" She set her glass down. "Because the last I remember, you had me tied up in your room, about to go kill my father without so much as listening to a word I said."

A flash of her chained to my bed made my head go light. It was a beautiful sight. I loved the idea of having her all to myself and at my mercy. "Don't think it won't happen again," I grinned, "having you there all to myself. You're lucky you got away as easily as you did."

Her eyes narrowed. "Next time, I'll be more prepared."

I grabbed her by the waist and hauled her onto my lap and snagged her wrists to hold her in place.

"Don't threaten me with a good time, sweetheart." I

thrust my interest between her legs, but something flashed over her face I couldn't pinpoint.

She pulled her hair over one shoulder and licked her lips as she looked down at me. She raised on her knees and shimmed her long dress up her thighs. I felt hungry for her as I skimmed my fingertips up her bare skin and over her smooth bottom. I loved that she wasn't wearing anything under her dress; all that stuff just got in the way.

She reached back and slid the tie free from around her neck and allowed her breasts to break free. I leaned forward and kissed her across her collarbone and up her neck, and her breasts were warm as I palmed one.

"I need this." I drew in her skin as I confessed without a care.

"And I needed you to hear me the other day," she pulled back, "but you wouldn't. So why should I give you my body?" Before I realized what was happening, she pushed off me and took a few steps back. Instantly, I felt a flash of anger.

"Kenna," I warned, my head warm with wicked thoughts.

"If you care about me even in the slightest, leave." She fixed her dress back in place. "Prove to me that you hear me when it counts."

Fuck me!

I pushed to my feet. If she was anyone else, I would

have lost my shit, but for some fucking reason, this woman had a hold on me.

I moved to tower over her as I weighed my decision. Everything screamed at me to take her, everything but one little spot in my fucking chest that gnawed at my core.

"You better be at that fucking dinner," I growled. As the door shut, I swore I heard her exhale.

FIVE

KENNA

Dinner was at one of the brand-new restaurants at Secrets. Grim had changed its name at the last minute to "The Leo." I loved that he honored his brother in that way. Of course, the Italian food was divine, and it was Leo's favorite food. I knew we were meeting up with the bitch and the bitch's father, so I had dressed to impress in a white cocktail dress that put the girls on show. I'd caught her father checking them out countless times, so I figured I'd play into that a little too. Anything to piss off Grim's future wife. I chuckled at the thought, but then a strange ping hit the center of my stomach. Christ, maybe Minnie was right. Maybe I was falling for him harder than I realized.

A videocall pushed through, and Zara's face

popped up on the large screen on my dresser. I pursed my lips and blew out a little air at the sudden thought that my father's secretary, who I considered a friend, might know something. I shook it off.

"How can you look slutty and gorgeous all at one time?" She sighed, then jumped into business. "All right, so, I did a little digging, and the Duggan Brothers are two self-made millionaires from Saskatchewan, Canada. They invented—ready for this—a solar-powered battery designed for fancy sailboats. Odd thing to invent for a province that doesn't even have ocean access." She shrugged. "Anyway, I did my thing and sent you over all the extra details."

"Thank you so much for doing this, Zara. I know it's extra work, but I'll make it up to you."

She waved me off. "Your dad's been extra quiet lately, so the work's been light. It made the day go faster. Go give that bitch and her highfalutin' daddy a taste of how smart you can be. It'll make my day."

"Well, I appreciate it." I laughed and blew her a kiss. Once I ended the call, I grabbed my purse and iPad and left my room. As I walked toward Secrets, my phone pinged.

> Minnie: Girls' Night at Dirty Demons, eight thirty!

I chuckled. I knew the girls were concerned I was

going to take Yen's offer at his hotel, so I really needed to show up.

Kenna: You had me at Dirty.

Something hit me in that moment, and a newfound sense of strength and determination came over me. I turned around to look back at Indulge.

Fuck it.

I slowed my walk to make sure I'd show up after the others, more just to make Jenelle think for a moment that I wasn't going to show. Her face as Grim pulled out my chair said it all.

"Yesterday was a one-time thing," Grim growled in my ear. "I'm pent-up, hard, and won't be responsible for my actions."

"I'm feeling quite relaxed," I whispered back and settled in my chair. I pulled my napkin onto my lap when I caught sight of the others watching me. Grim made quick introductions and scowled when he saw Jenelle's father stare shamelessly at the girls.

We jumped right into business, as Grim took the lead. He was impressive to watch. These dealings came easily to him, and in no time, they'd worked out a contract so they'd stay at Secrets whenever they were in Vegas. It also helped that Grim had contacts at a high-end marina in Malibu. It just so happened to be a place the clients had been looking at as a possible site to build one of their vacation homes. I showed off my knowledge, thanks to Zara, and everyone seemed to be impressed except Jenelle, who only seemed annoyed that Grim wasn't paying attention to her.

"Kenna, do you sail?" one of the brothers asked me after our meal arrived.

"Grim just took me out on his sailboat last week," Jenelle cooed loudly. "That man just loves a fast boat."

I had to refrain from rolling my eyes. She sounded like a twat.

The brother closest to me perked up. "What kind of boat do you have, Mr. Gates?"

"It was one of those boats with the two sails," Jenelle interrupted again as she beamed at him. I swallowed a chuckle. "He calls it the Escape." *Yup a total twat.*

"She's a ninety-foot Oyster," Grim corrected and went on to describe the boat in more detail.

As the guys dug deeper into their world of boating, I noticed Jenelle's father's eyes had glazed over. I decided to chat him up a little.

"So, Lloyd," I smiled warmly, but it quickly faded when his gazed dropped to my chest again, "what do you think of Secrets? Pretty impressive."

"I think it fits my clientele better than Indulge. Not to downplay Jim's hotel, of course," he quickly added. Then he leaned over and draped an arm over the back of my chair. "Indulge is a little subdued, shall we say, for the younger taste."

"I see. Well, I'm glad Grim will be able to provide that for you at Secrets. I think you'll find DJ Clay an excellent choice. He's been a huge hit on the nightclub scene. Plus, Cajun Cat will be here, and they offer a unique taste of the south."

"Oh, yes," Jenelle blurted again, "Grim and I already planned coordinating outfits for their debut this week." When her father didn't look over, she cleared her throat. "Daddy, when are you going to show Grim your new Corvette?"

That caught his attention. "Maybe after dinner." He nodded at her then turned back to me. "Have you ever ridden in a Corvette before?"

"Yes," Grim said over my shoulder, "she had the pleasure of riding in mine the other night when we attended the midnight party at the Encore." He gave me a look, and I caught his drift. Lloyd had creep vibes, and I didn't need another person giving me trouble.

Lloyd squinted then looked at Jenelle. "I thought you two were supposed to go to that party." She glared at me and shrugged. "You know," her father moved in too close, and I dug my knee into his as if to say back off, "these two have been dating on and off for years. It's only a matter of time before Grim gives in and asks my little Nelly to marry him."

"I'm sure *Nelly* will make an excellent wife." I nearly gagged. "I know how Mr. Gates loves a woman who submits." I eyed Grim, and he moved a hand to my bare thigh and gave it a tight squeeze.

Jenelle sucked on her straw. "A man like Grim has many challenges in his business. He doesn't need that at home as well."

"Like I said," I smiled wide and pushed Grim's hand away, "you'd make an excellent wife for him."

Grim chatted with the others as I followed and texted Minnie that I was about to head over.

"Want to see Daddy's car, Grim? We're heading over to the Bellagio for a game. Join us." Jenelle's voice was like someone "bagpiping" a cat.

Grim pulled out his phone and tapped the screen. "I have to meet Dad, but I'll touch base later." She pouted as the valet rolled up with Lloyd's car. He opened her door for her, and she leaned up to kiss his cheek. He didn't move away, just gave her a pat.

I hoped she'd trip and dent Daddy's car with her pointy chin.

She didn't.

Once they drove out of sight, Grim turned his hungry eyes on me, but I strolled over to where Shore, my driver, waited for me.

"Where are you going?" His mood dipped, and mine lightened.

I tossed my hair over my shoulder and looked back.

"Girls' night!" I slipped inside and watched him hit the screen on his phone.

"Jesse," I heard him say, "we're heading out."

Have fun with that.

Two things that don't go well together are nerves and two best friends who are scared you're going to leave them. They were keying off my anxiety, and in turn we were popping champagne bottles like we were living the high life. I was scared to tell them the truth, and they were scared to guess the truth. All in all, it made for a night of drinking, not talking.

My head spun.

"I don't think I can feel my lips." Tess pressed them together as Minnie poured her some more bubbly. We all lounged on the furniture out by Tess's burlesque themed pool. "Yeah, I definitely can't feel my lips."

"Good to know." Trigger slapped her ass as he walked by with a platter of meat for the barbecue.

"You know," Minnie moved the fan mister toward her and kicked up her legs, "if I angle this just right, it creates this mini tornado down by my own mister."

"That's quite the pun, ha-ha." Brick laughed and reached over and turned the mister toward himself.

I loved that girls' night was really the guys and us. They gave us space, but they couldn't help but watch over us. I felt safe when I was with them.

"Dogs are done!" Morgan yelled, holding up a

plastic bottle of mustard. He tossed it to Denton, Trigger's nephew.

"So, how's it going with you and Grim?" Minnie wiggled her eyebrows, and I downed my glass and went in for another. "That good, huh?"

I didn't bother to hide my smirk, thanks to the booze. My filter about giving a fuck had already gone out the door. "Actually, he wanted some last night after he broke into my hotel suite at Secrets, and I said if I meant something to him, he'd respect me enough not to have sex."

"He listened?" Rail took a seat next to me. He hated to miss any kind of drama being spilled. "I'm shocked. I mean, when I'm horny enough, nothing can stop the beast, and let me tell you, Grim's always horny for you."

Tess laughed so hard her face turned red. "The fact that you know that."

"Keep your eyes a little north of the Boy Scout camp," Minnie joined in giving Rail shit, "though I guess Grim isn't pitchin' a Boy Scout tent."

"No." I laughed, thinking how true that was. "Oh," I pointed over Minnie's shoulder, "I see our entertainment has shown up."

Minnie sat straighter, and I knew we were in for a good time. "Tess, what the hell is that broad doing in here?" She pointed at Glory and Keller, who were looking around the pool.

"She tried out for the pole last week and couldn't even do a fireman spin. I felt bad and gave her a free day pass. Maybe I can still make some money off her in one of the rooms." She pointed to one of the blackened-out windows for the client's privacy.

"Well," Keller eyed me up and down as they drew closer, "I didn't know you were on the menu tonight."

"Like you could afford me." I waved him off. "I see nothing's changed since Dirt's, and you're still slummin' it with diseases of the world." My stomach rolled at Glory, who had one of Trigger's hot dogs between her shit-stained fake nails.

"Aw, you jealous, Kenna?" Keller grabbed his crotch. "I know it's been a while, but just say the word and I'll fill your hole."

"You couldn't fill my piss hole," I blurted, and the girls burst out laughing.

His face scrunched when the guys started tossing him insults, too. "You wanna find out how big I am?"

"After that thing?" I tried to catch my breath as I pointed at Glory munching on the end of the hot dog. Her teeth were going at it like a hack saw. Bits of mystery meat dropped down onto her shirt, and I couldn't hold back anymore. "How you got the nickname Glory Hole is beyond me."

"Nothing's glorious about those choppers." Minnie mimicked Glory. "It's the first time I've actually felt bad for you, Keller." We laughed harder, and Glory swallowed when she realized how she looked.

"But do we?" I dried my tears. "I mean, a hot dog is a step up from Keller, here." He flipped me the finger.

"Are you offering your finger?" Tess chimed in. "Because that might be the next best thing."

Glory used a napkin to dig the mustard out of her nail. "Kenna, shouldn't you be entertaining somewhere?"

"You know what I find funny?" I ignored her lame dig. "That you had Big Cat as a pimp and yet you're Glory Hole."

"That's true," Morgan smirked as he sat down on the arm of my chair, "and who the hell calls himself Big Cat anyway? You're basically calling yourself a big pussy, which is ironic because it's you who has the big, gaping pussy. Oh, man, this is fun." He snorted, and we all laughed hysterically in a liquor haze.

"Kenna, you're such a whore," Glory shouted, only making us double over further. Minnie lost her footing when she tried to stand and fell on her ass. Three of the empty champagne bottles tumbled off the table and rolled toward them.

Keller grabbed her arm. "They're wasted. Let's go have some fun."

"Glory you're going the wrong way," Brick called. "The alley's over there!"

"Fuck you, Brick!" she snarled as Keller pulled her arm to get her away from us. "Fuck all of you."

I stood. I felt especially wound up on my asshole high. Any worries about my plan for the rest of the night had completely dissolved. I giggled, full of liquid courage, and stepped back to grab a bite from Tess's burger. When I popped back up, I hit my arm into someone.

"Oh, shit, sorry." I turned to find Salazar with a group of guys. "Hey!" I couldn't help but notice his face went six shades of red and his eyes widened then narrowed.

"How drunk are you?"

"Enough to know I shouldn't be around a client right now." I hiccupped and put a hand to my mouth. "But probably not enough to forget this when I join you on the green tomorrow."

"Whoa." He held up his hands and broke out in a grin, and his friends laughed.

"Oh, please," I waved him off, "this is my girls' night. Besides, who do you think expedited your membership in this place?" I pointed dramatically to myself.

"Well, in that case, I owe you a round." He grinned and ordered us another three bottles then slipped away with his buddies.

"I love my job." I popped the cork and swung around to look at Morgan.

"Oh, shit," he groaned, "I know that look."

I took a swig. "Hear me out, but I did something."

Five minutes later, we were all walking down the back hallway of Minnie's club.

"I'm not even sure how we made it." Minnie stumbled, lost her balance, and almost took someone out as we passed them. Tess grabbed her waist with a laugh, and they both almost fell into a wall.

"Good Lord, it's only a block away." Tess laughed as Rail grabbed Minnie and steadied Tess.

The bouncer, Nate, had eyed us up when we arrived, but after a word from Minnie, he walked with us to unlock the door to the Wet and Wild room. "I don't know what you all have been into tonight, but you certainly are having fun."

"Bubbly!" Minnie pulled a bottle from her bag. How it hadn't smashed with the number of times she'd fallen trying to get here was astonishing. "Tess named me Mary Poppins way back, and here I am still livin' up to my name." She grinned happily.

Tess laughed. "God only knows what else she has in there."

Minnie did a Vanna White move next to the outfits. "Pick your poison." I studied the costumes and chose a cute little white and blue sailor outfit.

"No, no." Rail snatched the hanger from me and studied the other clothes. Smoke poured out of his mouth as he grinned and held up a very thin, almost see-through little black dress. "It'll make your nips pop."

"I'll be right back." Morgan laughed. "I love that one, Rail."

"And what song?" Minnie asked, and I opened one eye and tried to study the screen.

"*Earn It*, by The Weeknd." Tess moved to stand next to Minnie.

Rail grabbed the phone. "If this goes sideways, you will not ruin *Fifty Shades* for me." He glanced over. "Don't worry, it won't go sideways," he assured me as I shifted the dress in place. "I just can't risk it." The girls tried so hard not to laugh as Rail ignored them and then turned the phone around for me to see *Closer* by Nine Inch Nails. "This fucked-up situation needs a fucked- up song."

"I couldn't agree more." I took a deep breath and another swig of alcohol and went to stand in front of the cage door. I looked back at Minnie and Tess, who now held weapons and waved them around like a bunch of drunks, then I stepped into the cage behind the viewing room.

"You got this baby girl." Rail checked his gun clip while he popped another beer. "It's pitch black for you, so let us do the rest." He was right. We couldn't see into the viewing room unless the person was really tall. Sometimes, we'd only see their shoes. That was a draw for those clients who only wanted to watch. They remained anonymous, unless they pressed a button to ask the dancer if they could enter. It was nice for the dancer, too, as they didn't have to watch someone gawk at them and could relax and just dance without inhibitions.

"Yeah, I got this." I squinted at the time on the wall. It was a little after one a.m., the time I'd told Tracy to tell my stalker I'd be dancing. I'd paid her well. This shit needed to end.

When the music started, I stepped into the water, turned my head off, and started to dance. The beat vibrated the cage walls, and the water drops that flew off me pulsated in the light. I was safe inside the cage. He couldn't get to me. The only way he could was if I opened the special door myself.

The liquor did its job and helped push all my fears away. It was reckless, but after a few moments, I fell into my normal rhythm and tuned in to the lyrics of the song as I forgot all else and danced.

That was until I caught sight of a pair of shoes. Holy shit, he was here.

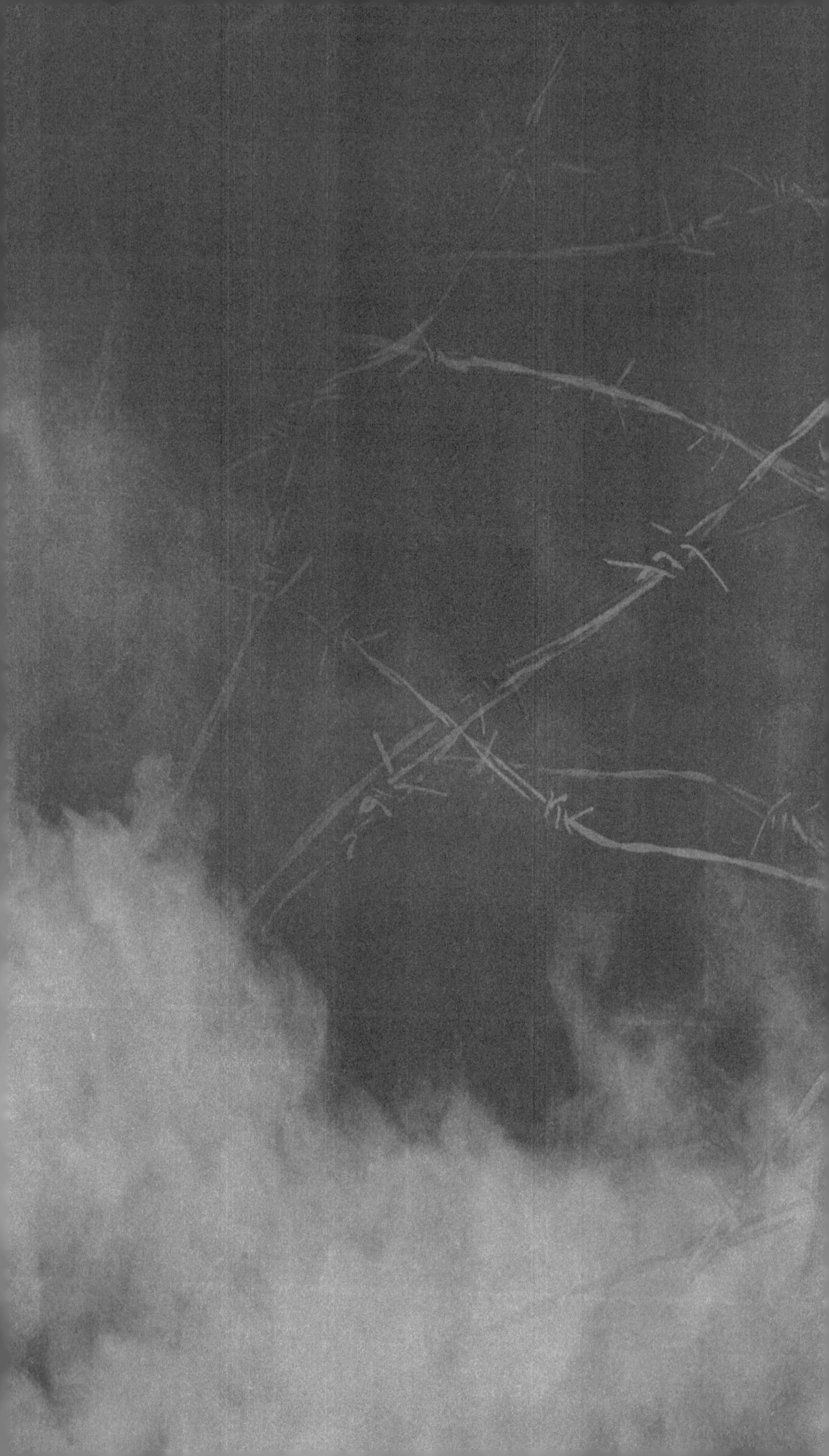

SIX

SIMON

The sun beat down on my face as I ate my lunch outside the library. I enjoyed my alone time away from the other inmates. Though I didn't belong here, it gave me time to think. Think of a way I was going to get my revenge on Allen. I had to play it carefully. He knew a lot of people, but there was a rumor I wasn't the only one who wanted him dead. It turned out his own son, Trigger, leader of the Devil's Reach motorcycle club, was after him, too. I hadn't realized he had pulled away from his gang and now rode with only a few guys.

CM pulled me from my thoughts and handed me a cold bottle of beer. My mouth watered as I snagged it from his hand.

"Where on Earth did you get this?"

He opened his, not at all hiding it from anyone who could look our way. "I told you I have pull here." He looked at me. "Go on. They," he nodded at the guards, "won't do anything."

I took a sip and let the bubbles dance along my tongue and the taste soothe my senses. My eyes closed, and I leaned my head back with a happy grin. I never drank much on the outside, but this was pure bliss.

"Good, right?"

"Great. Thank you, CM, truly." I tipped back the bottle and had a little more in case someone took it from me. "How did you get your hands on a Kona Longboard? I would have been happy with a Coors Light at this point."

"Nah," he chuckled, "I know you like the finer tastes in life."

I blinked away the memory and focused on the man in front of me.

"You asked me where he's workin'," he handed me a piece of paper, "and that's where."

I slid the paper out of his calloused fingers. Perfect. It was a true sign he was a blue-collar worker. "And you're a hundred percent sure that this is where he is now?" I eyed the address and was relieved I had a solid lead I could give Brick. The big guy squinted at me and folded his arms. His whole persona showed he had no time for me, or maybe it was just that I looked nervous. Meeting someone in the wee hours of the morning at some dive bar off the Strip was nerve-wracking.

"Buy me another beer." He pointed to his nearly full Bud Light.

I pushed up my glasses and nodded. "Another, please," I called to the bartender.

"Yeah." He snorted then swallowed. *Charming.* "That's him."

Thank God.

I couldn't risk another day going by without something. Trigger was one scary look away from shoving me in a burlap sack and beating me to a bloody pulp for not being able to track down Brick's brother. I'd never forgive Cameron for opening his mouth to him.

"I'm not questioning you," I assured him. "I just hadn't realized he was back in construction work." I tried to ease the tension. "When I knew him, we both lived that life for a while."

"I saw him two days ago when I was at the site." The man leaned back and wiped his mouth with his sleeve. "There's not a whole lot going on up in there, if you know what I mean." He pointed to his head. "Had a few knocks to the head."

I twisted my nose at the thought of what made him seem off. "What kind of knocks?"

"I got one rule on my work sites. No fighting. But this guy loves to go at it. He got his head rapped a few times too many before he even came to me. Didn't help he got run into by a forklift a while back." He chewed on a chipped nail. "Doesn't matter, though. He's a hard worker and he doesn't talk back."

"Good." I let out a breath. "That's a good thing."

"He gets off at seven most days. I don't care when you speak to him. Just don't come before then."

"Understood." I dropped some cash on the table and held up the paper. "Thank you for this."

"He's a good guy," he gave a tight nod, "so don't fuck with him, or you'll have me to deal with."

"Understood." I repeated and headed for the door. I needed to change and shower off the smell of beer and roasted peanuts. It didn't help that I knew I had to have a face to face with Trigger very soon.

SEVEN

GRIM

I sipped my scotch as the girls moved around Jesse, and I and tried to put on a show with their best moves. But, damn, I just couldn't get into it. It didn't help that Kelly spotted me the moment we arrived at Minnie's club. I hadn't seen her since Trigger's desert party.

"I've had a little PTSD from what happened in the desert." She tried to pull my attention from what Brick had been talking about. "My therapist thinks I need to revisit the trauma and have something good come from it." Her hand slid over my thigh, and Jesse eyed me around the lap dancer. "Maybe that good thing could be you and me."

"I have no idea where the girls ended up." Brick

laughed at something Trigger said. "Last I heard, they were on a mission somewhere. But, shit, Morgan's with them, so we'll hear soon enough."

"Morgan's right there." Jesse pointed to Morgan as he made a beeline toward us when he spotted me. Jesse gave the dancer a bill and she moved on; she knew something was up.

Kelly squeezed my leg again. "What do you think?"

Morgan pulled out a card and leaned down so Kelly couldn't hear. "Though I have it somewhat covered, I'd suggest you head here." I took the card and studied it. "And just so it's said, I never told you anything." I signaled Jesse to come over.

"Stay put. I'll let you know if I need you."

"Grim?" Kelly stood, and I turned to face her.

"Look, nothing's ever going to happen between us."

Her face pinked. "Because of that skank?"

I gave her a half smirk. "Because you try too hard." She opened her mouth, but I shook my head.

"You're an asshole, Grim."

"So I've been told." I headed to the private viewing rooms knowing that the card Morgan gave me was for one of them. I glanced at the number on it. The hall was dark, only a red outline glowed for each room and number. A man came out of the room next to the one I was about to enter, but I couldn't see his face in the shadows. He gave me a grunt and moved on. I tapped the card to the door and pushed it open. A woman danced in a cage to a Nine Inch Nails song. When she leaned back to grab the pole, water flung from her hair, and I saw her face. It was Kenna.

Well, fuck me.

I sat on the couch, rested both arms along the back, and kicked out my feet. I knew from being in these rooms before that she couldn't see my face, only my legs and feet, and I smiled to myself at Morgan's play to get me there. *He's a good guy, I'm going to enjoy this.*

My pants grew tight as I watched her wet body move to the music. She was so fucking sexy. I knew Tess had been a dancer back in the day, but now, married to Trigger, she only hired them. I chuckled at my good friend and his over-the-top protection for his wife.

I reached for the button to call the waiter for a drink when it hit me. What if Kenna worked here on the side when she wasn't working at Indulge? She had, after all, been in Tess's playroom with another man, but that was different. That was then; this was now. My mind ran with frustrated thoughts, like who else had sat in this very seat and seen her this way? I wasn't sure why that bothered me so much, but shit, it did. I shook my head, but the intrusive thoughts wouldn't stop. My fists tightened at the thought of some man working himself up for release with Kenna a mere few feet away. Somehow, it was even worse than someone else having sex with her. Well, not really. Damn it, I wasn't making sense even to myself.

I bolted to my feet when the door flew open across the room, and Tess, Minnie, and Rail all held guns. They screamed liked banshees as Rail, hard on their heels, tripped and slid across to land at my feet with his weapon pointed at my face.

"Freeze it, bitch!" Minnie squinted at me. "Wait, you're Grim." She waved her gun around, and I was scared it would go off. She looked at Tess, who looked to be way more drunk than I'd ever seen her. "Tess, that's Grim."

"You," Tess blinked, "you're Grim. Wait. You're supposed to be Kenna's attacker."

"You're Grim." Rail laughed. "That's not the attacker, Tess. It's Grim." He grinned, and I pushed the gun away from my face. "Sorry, man. You're not her attacker. Right?" His gun wavered in his hand.

"What the fuck, Rail? Put that thing away." I wasn't laughing.

Then the lights flickered on, the cage opened, and Kenna had a gun pointed in my direction. "Grim?"

Bang! She shot it at the ceiling and Minnie burst out laughing.

"Oh, shit, Minnie," Kenna covered her mouth, "I think the gun just went off."

"What the fuck!" I lunged forward and pulled the gun out of her hand and removed the clip. I hauled her out of the cage and stood her on her feet. She grabbed my arm as her wet feet slipped on the floor. "How drunk are you? Put those fucking weapons away. And what the hell is happening?" I demanded as Trigger and Brick came running in.

"The fuck?" Trigger boomed and made the girls jump, then it turned into laughter again. *Gone are the days that Trigger was scary to these chicks.*

Kenna held up a hand. "That's a lot of questions to ask in a short amount of time Grimmy." I glared down at her, and she beamed up at me with glazed-over eyes.

"Gr-immy," I growled.

"I lost count after the fourth bottle of champagne." Tess tried to count on her fingers, and Minnie added her own to the count. Christ, they were shitfaced.

"Morgan?" I turned to look at him. "What the hell's going on?"

"Kenna paid off Tracy," Morgan sighed, "to tell her stalker to be here tonight so they could trap him."

My temper spiked to the point of pain.

"It was a really good idea," Kenna added. "Well, until you showed up instead." She looked at the girls with a giggle. "Hell, I should have had better aim." She giggled again.

"What you have is a death wish," I muttered. She scrunched up her nose at me. "You heard me."

Trigger rubbed his face and huffed out a breath like he was trying to control his temper. "This place is crawling with bikers," he growled. "Fucker wouldn't show his face here tonight."

"But he did the other night." Kenna shrugged like she wasn't realizing what she was sharing with us. "Tracy said he followed me here when I danced the last time. 'Member, Min, when you got mad at me. Turned out you were right." She fluttered her hands. "He didn't come in, but he knew I danced. He told her that."

"Wait. What?" Minnie said from behind me. "You never mentioned that earlier."

"Well, no," she looked around, "no one would have gone along if I shared that." She looked at Morgan. "You certainly wouldn't have." She seemed to suddenly sober up a little.

He folded his arms, clearly not impressed. "No."

"You're so naughty," Tess scowled at her playfully.

Trigger shook his head. "Tessa!" he barked, and she pressed her lips together and made a naughty face. "Let's go."

"Ohhh, girl," Tess rubbed her hands together as she moved past Kenna, "he used my full name. I better get the good sex goin' tonight, baby."

"You'll get somethin'," Trigger muttered, and she hauled ass toward him while Brick whispered something to Minnie. She wasted no time following him out the door.

We were alone, and I wasn't sure what my actions were going to be.

"It's McKenna," she smirked, "if you want to use my full name. I'll gladly take a beating if you want to punish me." She winked as she stepped toward me. "That's assuming you're pissed at me."

"There are no words for how pissed I am." My gaze went down over her see-through dress. I couldn't help myself. I licked my lips and tried not to show how turned on I was.

"I can imagine." She didn't miss a beat. "But, you know, I had my girls, my boys, and my liquid courage." She brushed past me, and I scratched my head as I thought how sideways the night could have gone. Thank hell Morgan was smart enough to tell me.

I whipped out my gun at the sound of someone trying to open the door.

"Relax, Grim." Kenna chuckled. I turned to find her hopping up on the cage floor. "You need the key to get in. Oh, and apparently, you have it." That was true. I did.

"How long have you been dancing for others?" I demanded. I had to know.

She hit a button and put me in the dark and her in a sexy red light. She reached up high on the pole and started to walk around it. "Not long."

"You don't move your body like that if you've only

been dancing a short time." I shrugged off my jacket and draped it over the arm of the sofa.

"I've been dancing for years," she dragged her feet through the water, "but you asked how long I've been dancing for others." She hit something with her hand, and the song she was just dancing to started over again, *Closer* by Nine Inch Nails. She jumped up kicked her feet out and swung around the pole in a sexy turn. I started to unbutton my dress shirt as I watched her body move effortlessly despite how much alcohol flowed through her veins. I ditched my shirt then stripped down to nothing. I'd respected her wishes twice now, but a man only had so much restraint when a woman was moving her body the way she was.

The bottom of the cage rested just at the top of my thighs. I stood there and watched her body as it moved around the pole. She reached above her head, spread her thighs, and slid down in front of me.

"So, how many men have you danced for?" I repeated, my voice hoarse.

"Two, apparently," she flicked her wet hair back over her shoulder, "but the only man I want to dance for is you."

I lost it.

I grabbed her hips, and in one motion I swung her from the pole and held her above me. She wrapped her legs around my waist, and as water dripped from her hair, there was fire in her eyes. "And I'll be the last." I fisted the thin fabric of her dress and tore it away. Then something clicked. All those times I'd seen her with wet hair, she must have been here dancing. A spark of anger pinged through me at the thought that her fucking stalker had seen her like that. I forced myself to push it aside. At least he'd never have her like I could.

Her wet body was glued to me, and her head went back to expose her neck as an invitation. I could barely contain myself, but I stopped. "Are you sure?" She was drunk, and I didn't want to take her the way I wanted to without her consent.

"Well, if it's not you, it's gonna be me tonight." Her hand slid down between us as her eyes held mine and she dipped between her legs. *Oh, hell no.*

I laid her on the floor of the cage, grabbed her hips, then fed myself into her, inch by inch. I savored every inch and fed off the look on her face. I leaned down as my stomach coiled into a delicious knot and dragged my tongue along the water drops on her shoulder. Her fingers guided my hand up to her neck. I lapped at her skin and flicked my hips. When I heard her breathing catch, I increased the pace. I moved her legs to hook over my shoulders. She was in a frenzy and her feet pounded against my back as she lost control.

I caught the point in the song and growled the first line of the chorus into her ear.

"I wanna…" I felt her grin against my cheek, and I dragged my erection over her sensitive spot. My mind shifted again, and I couldn't get enough of her. I swung her legs down to roll her hips to one side and increased the pace again. The ripples in the water around us caught the lighting from underneath. The song switched to something else, but I didn't care. All I cared about was being inside this woman. My muscles locked in place when I felt her spasm, her mouth opened, but the music was too loud to hear her screams. Her eyes found mine as she let go, and something intimate passed between us, and for once, I didn't feel uneasy. Instead, I felt more alive than ever before.

I needed more.

When she came down from her orgasm and relaxed, I used the opportunity to flip her onto her stomach. I jumped up, sank onto my knees, and pulled her slick body back onto my lap and eased back into her. She pressed her hands onto my thighs to steady herself, then she ran her hands through her hair, arching her back. We moved well together; my hands were everywhere as I chased my own release. She turned her head, and I caught her lips without thinking. Her taste made me growl from deep down. I ripped away, pushed her down so she had to turn her head to the side to breathe, and yanked her hips as I balanced on my knees. I leaned down and held the base of her spine so she wouldn't slip.

Sounds and colors morphed together in my head as

I ravaged her. I held nothing back, and the cries from her lips pushed me to the point where I was without a care of going too far. This was what I needed; it was what we both lived for.

Finally, my body gave in, and I came, nearly drowning her in the process. I lost my sight for a moment as my skin heated. My fingers bit into her flesh as I rode the last of it out. I flipped her back over as my chest heaved, and I stared down at the woman who let me be me without judgement. Her satisfied expression met mine, and I suddenly realized what I was feeling. Happiness.

As the morning went on, I found myself growing angrier at Kenna. I was reckless, but I could handle myself. What in the hell was she thinking, drawing her stalker out of the shadows like that? Let alone shit-faced. I pinched the bridge of my nose as Zhar rested his head on my thigh. I scratched behind his ear the way he loved.

"When did the room start spinning?" Kenna groaned from my bed.

Leal, who had also decided to sleep in, lifted his head to look at her. *Nice of you to decide to wake up, pup.*

I leaned forward and felt my anger surge. I studied her from where I sat in my chair. "I would think it started to spin about the time you polished off your first bottle of champagne." I gave her a glare—not that she noticed. "And picked up speed around the fourth bottle."

She pushed up to lean against the headboard and let the blanket fall off her gorgeous tits. Her hair was messy, and she looked positively ill, but my pants strained against my zipper.

"What time is it?"

I glanced at my watch. "Eight."

Her eyes widened, but I held up a hand. "Salazar pushed his game back until eleven. Seems he too had a fun night." I lifted a brow.

"I bet he did. Wait," she squinted, "did he call you?"

"No, he called you."

"You answered my phone?"

"I did." I shrugged. "When a client calls three times in a row and you fail to wake, I step in. You're welcome."

"Thanks," she couldn't hide her irritation, "but you could have woken me, and how did I end up at your place and in your bed, anyway?" Leal wiggled out of his own bed and stood at the change in our voices. He was making excellent progress and could walk without much of a limp.

I scoffed at her comment. "You needed sleep. Do you remember last night?"

"Some of it's foggy," the corners of her mouth went up, "and some was pretty memorable." She reached over and patted Leal, who rested his head on the side of the mattress. Zhar looked at me for permission to do the same, and I reluctantly gave a nod. He carefully made his way over, and Kenna smiled and patted him, too. She whispered something, but I couldn't make it out. I'd never seen them take to anyone before, so I chalked it up to the fact that Kenna found Leal that night at Secrets and he'd had to let his guard down. Kenna did have a way of working her way into people's lives.

"Well," I stood and used my leg to move the boys back and handed her two pain killers and a water glass, "now that you tried and failed to take matters into your own hands, things are going to change around here."

She swallowed the pills. "Change?"

"You'll be sleeping here from now on." I held her gaze but hadn't expected her reaction. She burst out laughing.

"Yeah, okay, sure." She swung the blankets back then groaned and put a hand to her head when she stood. "I mean, your girlfriend Jenelle will love that one."

I cleared my throat at her jab. "I'm not kidding."

"Who knew you were this funny?" She laughed again and disappeared into my closet and reappeared with one of my dress shirts on. It looked like a dress on her. I hid the satisfaction that she seemed comfortable enough to wear my stuff. When I didn't say anything, she turned to look at me. "No, Grim, that's not going to happen."

"But it will."

She grabbed her purse and phone from the nightstand, but I stood in her way.

"You swung at a hornet's nest last night." I felt angry again but pushed it down. I took another approach. I slid my hand under the shirt and over her smooth, naked hip. "Kenna," I kept my voice even, "he got to you before. What makes you think he won't now?"

"I know I messed up." She pushed a finger against her temple. No doubt her head pounded. "But how is sleeping here going to fix that?"

I pulled her into my chest. "Because you'll be with me."

"Mm," she nodded and chewed her cheek as she looked at me, "and the last few times we were together, I believe I was the one who got pushed away and lashed out at when I was only trying to help." She clamped down hard on my hand that had moved to her bottom. "I'm not taking your shit anymore, Grim."

She stepped back with a sexy smile, and I scowled. "If you really want me to stay with you at night, make an effort." She reached up and cupped my cheek. "And then, and only then, I might consider it."

"The fuck you say?" She moved around me, and I turned on my heel to see her reach down and pat the boys as she opened the door.

"Thanks for the shirt, *sweetheart*." Her tone dripped with sarcasm then she disappeared.

What the hell just happened? Frustration flashed through my chest as Leal looked over his shoulder at me.

"Don't look at me like that," I growled. "You two are just as bad as she is."

"Am I interrupting?" Jesse stepped into the room. The shit-eating grin he wore told me he'd caught wind of things.

"No."

"Good," his tone deepened, and I knew something was up, "because you need to see this."

EIGHT

KENNA

The hangover drink Dale made for me shook like Jell-O as it sat in the cupholder of the golfcart. He claimed the drink worked miracles, but now I wondered if I'd been the butt of a nasty joke. It looked like green cement and snail sludge blended to taste like what I assumed a cat's asshole would be like. Every sip was a constant battle with my stomach to keep the shit down. Thankfully, Salazar suffered just as badly as I did, and a few times he looked like he might be sick as well.

"Where were you two?" his friend asked as we rolled up late, and Salazar slowly shook his head as he didn't want to answer. "You think you can do the next one?" The guy chuckled and swung like a pro.

We rode in silence to the next hole. To say we were both hungover was an understatement, but at least we were in this hell together.

Salazar pulled a big plastic cup from between the seats and gagged as he took a sip.

"He got you too?" I held up mine and showed him the name the shit had written on the side of it. *Hate me now, thank me later.*

"Did you see what he put in this thing?" He dropped the cup back in the holder and took the iron the caddy held out. "Green tea, coconut milk, and tomato juice. The man should be punished. What a combination." He made a face.

"I'm willing to conspire on something violent if you're up for it." I pulled my ball hat down, hoping to block more of the sun, but it didn't work.

"This is why we're friends, Kenna." He chuckled lightly.

"I've yet to see you swing." His buddy came up. "And you're trying to sell me." Salazar shot him a look, and he shut up but winked at me. Clearly, they had a good relationship. "Have you seen him play before?"

"I have." I felt my phone vibrate, but the idea of even moving to answer made my head swim.

"He any good?"

Salazar got out and walked to the tee then immediately took a swing and launched the ball straight toward the flag on the next green. My eyes hurt as I watched, but I saw it had landed only about a foot away from the cup.

"Damn," his buddy muttered, "here I was thinking I had a leg up because I got him so drunk last night."

I grinned, knowing Salazar's play. "Did he tell you he was a righty too?"

His face fell. "He did."

"Yeah," I chuckled as Salazar returned and handed his club to the caddy, "he's ambidextrous."

"Shit!" He rubbed his mouth and I realized he must have bet a lot on each hole. "Since you look like shit, my friend, maybe we should do this another day?"

"No." Salazar climbed back onto his seat in the cart, and we tore off toward the next green. When we were far enough away, he turned to look at me. "The next hole, he bet his beach house in Bali for a month."

I grinned. "Let's take him down."

It wasn't until three that I felt human again, and maybe it was because of the burger I swallowed down with no shame at the Iron Bar with Salazar.

"Can I ask you something?" I downed some lemon water.

He leaned back in his chair and seemed more relaxed now that we'd found some shade and food. "Is it about last night and where it was we met?"

"No, we don't ever need to discuss that night."

He smiled. "Then ask away."

I dabbed my mouth with the napkin. "How are you and Yen Hong?"

"Better, actually." He thanked the waiter who took his plate away. "We even had lunch the other day."

"I'm impressed." I dove into my fries.

"To be honest, so am I. Yen isn't the most forgiving man. But I think he knows what happened wasn't intentional, and that I don't conduct business that way. I didn't mean to take his business deal from him, but business is shady in our world, and we can't always predict what a seller is capable of." He ran a hand through his hair. "I also appreciate that you said something to him."

I held up my hands, but he tilted his head to show he knew. "I hope I didn't overstep, but I was in Hong Kong, and we got to talking."

"It means a lot that you had my back. You're good people, Kenna."

"Kenna!" Grim's sharp voice made me jump in my seat. I looked up and saw he wore quite the usual scowl. "Excuse the interruption, but I need to steal Kenna away."

"Of course." Salazar sat straighter. "Is everything all right, Mr. Gates?"

"No." Grim held out a hand and helped me stand. "Enjoy the rest of your day."

I threw an apologetic smile to Salazar as Grim pulled me toward the car where his driver, Cartwright, waited with the door open. I slipped inside and held myself back from blasting him until I had a better handle on what was going on.

I didn't react as Grim sat and snatched my purse from where it lay on my lap. Cartwright took off so quickly I lurched in my seat, and Grim's free hand landed on my lap as if to anchor me. Once the car hit the main road, he removed my phone and hit the screen. "Ah, so, it is working." I noticed several missed calls from him.

"I was with a client." I plucked it from his hand. "What the hell is going on?"

"Repercussions, that's what."

I wasn't following. "What the hell does that mean?" I felt my temper simmer as he refused to answer.

We turned down a familiar side street and came to a stop. Grim gave me a strange look as if trying to decide about something then opened the door and waited for me to follow. I hesitated as a cold feeling crept over me and replaced my anger. I stepped out and headed toward him but stayed a foot or so back. I followed his gaze, and that was when I saw Tracy. Her body had been thrown among the trash. Her freckled face was stark white above the terrible red slash at her throat. I saw her mouth had been taped shut.

"Oh, my God," I whispered, "we're only a block from Minnie's club." I covered my mouth as I felt my stomach roll. "I did this. I paid her to say where I was."

"No," Grim growled, "Potens did it." He pointed to the figure drawn roughly on her forearm with black marker. Just like Leo's. "I did warn you there'd be consequences, Kenna." At my reaction, he seemed to relent a little and put a hand on my shoulder. "Let's go. Jesse'll be here with the police any minute."

I let him direct me back to the car, and once inside, he draped his arm along the back of the seat. "I showed you that because it could have been you."

"I know," I looked out the window as a shiver went through me, "but she deserved it." I wanted to justify it. "She took that video of me killing Matt and sold it to him."

"That she did." His fingers fiddled with the strap of my dress. "That being said, you see why I want you to sleep at my place?"

"No, I really don't." I wasn't in the right frame of mind to argue, however, and let it go. Thankfully, Cartwright pulled up to Indulge, and I hopped out before Grim could hold me hostage.

"Ding-dong, the bitch is gone." Minnie grabbed my arm as I entered the lobby. "You good? Because, really, who are we to stand in the way of destiny?"

"I moved out of the way." I chuckled darkly. "We might be able to find a lead on someone's camera when he dumped the speckled bitch."

"Kenna," Grim growled from behind me, but I kept

walking, and he turned and headed toward the elevator.

Minnie looked over at me, and I shot her a smirk. "What's he done now?"

"It's about what I'm doing." I felt a new sense of control over myself.

She squeezed my arm. "Tell me."

"He wants me to spend my nights with him due to all that's going on." Minnie rolled her eyes, and I nodded and rolled my eyes in agreement. "I told him if he wants that, he's going to have to earn it. He's hurt me too damn many times for me to just cave. Why should I do as he says?"

"Well, that just tickled my twat, Kenna!"

"Mine too." I waved at Yen Hong as he rushed by with an entourage. "I'll never be a doormat for anyone."

"No, the hell you won't, but um, Jayden is coming this way, so say the word and I'll nut punch him so hard it'll swell up and knock the other one right off the twig they hang on."

"I'd pay to see that." I laughed as Jayden came up to us.

He stopped and glared at Minnie until she left with a wink at me. "There's been a complaint filed against you. The client says you haven't fulfilled your duties as a hostess."

That made my face fall; I'd never had a mark on my record. "Who was it?" I thought of my three top clients, Salazar, Yen, and Harris. I took excellent care of them.

"Sonny Conti."

I burst out laughing, and when Jayden looked at me, unamused, I calmed myself. "Trust me, Jayden, you can go ahead and delete that complaint. It's a bunch of bull."

"You know I can't do that, Kenna, and to be honest, I'm a little concerned you don't see how bad this is."

"First, that claim is ridiculous. I've never been assigned as Sonny's hostess in the first place, and second, Sonny isn't even a client anymore, and third, if you must know, the man tried to roofie me. So, we can take this to Mr. Gates on the twentieth and he'll set you straight on this horseshit."

"What?" Jayden stepped forward and placed a hand on my upper arm. "I had no idea. Are you okay?" I looked at his hand and thought *how dare he touch me* as he spoke again. "Would you like to go somewhere and talk about it?" He moved his hand, and when he did, he very obviously brushed my breast.

"If you don't remove your fucking hand, I'll kick you in those tiny balls of yours." I raised my chin and glared at him. So, we were back to the creep stage. His hand dropped instantly, and his fake smile twisted into a scowl.

"Lucky for you Mr. Gates always seems to be around." He rubbed his nose, clearly annoyed, and probably shocked at my reaction. "Are you two dating now?"

I had to contain my distaste for this man, at least in public, so I refrained from kicking him. "I hardly think it's professional that we talk about a member of the Gates family like this."

"Nor is it professional for you to be sleeping with your boss," he muttered, "but I'll keep that to myself because I wouldn't want to get fired." He stepped back quickly as I pivoted. "I'll pass this complaint along and let upper management cover it up—I mean, deal with it." His smarmy smile made my blood boil as the meaning behind his words sank in. I was about to let loose as Minnie returned, and I got hold of myself.

"You know, Jayden," I closed the gap between us, "people have underestimated me before, but they're no longer here to tell about it."

He stood still and studied me. "What's that supposed to mean?" His eyes narrowed.

"Think about it."

"Whoa!" Minnie pushed between us. "That's enough, folks. We're in the lobby of the place you both work, and people are staring. As much as I love a fight, walk away." Jayden stared at me a beat longer then left.

"Kenna," Minnie got in my face, "Jesus, girl, I know Jayden pushes your buttons, but watch what you say."

"I know," I let out a long breath, "but he went too far, and I just lost it."

"And that's why we let the guys handle assholes like that, because they know what to say and how to say it."

"You're right." I closed my eyes and wished I could take back the last three minutes. It had been reckless to say what I had. "Thanks."

I hauled ass to the meeting on the twentieth. I was now a few minutes late and knew I'd have to hustle. When I arrived, everyone was sitting around the conference table. I quickly took my seat and mouthed a sorry to Jim, and he gave me a kind smile in response.

We discussed breaking ground on the new property they had purchased and how Knox was interested in having more of a hands-on position. I noticed Jim glance at Grim a few times as Knox spoke. Again, I felt that twinge of discomfort about my family. I knew they were concerned with how much control Calli had over Knox. They weren't wrong; she played him like a fiddle.

Jim went on to talk about Secrets and how some of his clients had indicated an interest in moving there for a change from Indulge. Jim was pleased about that, as it would free up the hostesses for fresh clients. Jim reminded everyone that he wanted Indulge to cater more to the older clients who were into a more traditional style, while Grim's Secrets would offer a fresh upbeat vibe to the younger clientele.

"Is there anything you'd like to add, Kenna?" Jim asked as we finished up.

"Actually, yes," I cleared my throat and felt Grim's eyes penetrate my brain, "but I'd like to discuss it privately, if you don't mind."

"Why?" Grim cut in, and I glared at him.

I looked at Jim for help then turned to Grim. "Because what I have to say to Jim is between him and me. Besides, you aren't exactly known for your even temperament, Grim." His face turned to stone.

"She's not wrong, Dad," Knox chimed in. "Grim's at a ten all the time, especially when Kenna's involved." I fought a blush.

Grim ignored his brother and glared at me. "What happened?"

Jim raised a hand when he saw what I did, that his son was about to go from zero to a hundred. "Of course, Kenna. The meeting's over, everyone. Let's all get on with our day."

Grim waited a beat then moved to stand next to me and leaned over to whisper in my ear. "Don't make me tie you up again."

I raised a brow. "Is that a promise?"

He chuckled darkly then gave me a warning that he wasn't kidding before he left.

Once we were alone, Jim placed a cup of coffee in front of me. He was always such a kind man, no matter what was going on in his life.

"I won't beat around the bush with you, Kenna. I'd like to think we've grown close, especially since you started working here. How are you holding up, given all that's happened?"

I tapped a finger on my coffee cup as I thought about his question. I loved Jim like family, so I wanted to be honest when given the chance. "I'd be lying if I said I wasn't struggling, but I know where my loyalty and heart lie, and it isn't with my father or my sister." I pushed aside how terrible that sounded, but it was the truth. "At the risk—" I stopped myself.

He waved a hand at me. "Please, go on."

I took a deep breath. "At the risk of bringing up something that's upsetting, I want you to know that Leo's death has been difficult for me to process. Mostly due to," I shifted in my seat, "how and why he was killed." Jim nodded. "I'm so sorry for what happened, and I'm sorry for running off to Hong Kong. It's just that I felt uncomfortable by association. I mean, Cameron's my father, and I think I needed to reassure myself that I had other options if things became too difficult for me here."

"I can totally understand that, Kenna. It would be a perfectly natural way to feel." He leaned back in his chair. "But just so it's said, we never once blamed you or thought you were in any way a part of our son's death."

"I think I know that now. Thank you for that. I can't imagine how you all are managing, what with Cam—"

"We're managing, dear." He held his hand up. "I'll admit it's difficult living every day with your son's murderer so close and trying to pretend all the time. I wish I could just handle things the way I want to, but there's too much at stake. There's a lot more going on, and we can't afford to lose sight of our goal. He'll pay for what he did." He looked at me, and I held his gaze and nodded.

"Yes, he will." It had finally sunk in over the past weeks that my own flesh and blood was a murderer.

"So, have you made a decision, then, about the offer from Yen Hong?"

I pressed my lips together, and Grim suddenly popped up in my thoughts. I shook him away, but he wouldn't leave. "Ah," I stumbled over my words, which must have looked bad, "if I didn't love my job here, I would consider it, but my friends are my family, and I wouldn't want to leave them behind."

A smile broke free. "That's good to hear. I'm sure Grim is pleased to hear that, too?"

"Mm," I shrugged with a playful smirk, "sometimes it's good to keep Grim on his toes."

He tossed his head back and laughed. "Spoken like

a woman who understands how my son works." His face was so full of life at that moment that I found myself joining in. God, it felt wonderful to laugh with him again. "Well," he swiped a finger under his eye, "now that I don't have to look for a lead hostess anytime soon, I can relax."

"I don't have any intention of leaving," I reiterated. "I do have a concern I want to bring to you, though."

"Of course." He sipped his coffee.

"I'm concerned about Jayden Wallace." His face fell just the way his son's did. "Honestly, I wouldn't bring this up, given everything that's going on, but he's becoming quite inappropriate. He's overstepped before, but now it's gone too far." I raised my chin. "I can handle myself, but if he's like that with me, I'm very concerned about the other girls."

"I see." He took a moment to think. "I'm going to be honest here and let you in. His father is another one I'm watching. Walter Wallace came on the same time as Cameron, and they're quite close." I noticed he didn't say *your father*. "For now, leave him to me. Let's have you spend most of your time at Secrets. Mr. Salazar is leaving tonight, and Mr. Hong is busy with his clothing line. Mr. Harris is in town with some businessmen I think you should engage with. They'd be excellent potential clients for Secrets."

"Of course," I agreed.

He pulled out his phone and texted someone. "I

appreciate that you came to me with this and know it will be dealt with at the right time. I'll have one of my men watch him. Make sure he stays clear of you and isn't bothering the others."

"I like that idea." I hooked my purse over my wrist. "That's it, I just wanted to bring it to your attention."

"Thank you." He stopped me as I stood. "I know it's a lot to ask that you join in and keep up this facade that we don't know Cameron killed Leo." He pressed his hands on the table. "It's been the hardest thing I've ever faced, but knowing this situation is a lot larger than we even thought, we need to keep it up a bit longer. We can't risk it blowing up before we're ready."

"I've had to swallow a lot of things from Cameron my entire life." My heart stung at my own admission. "A few more days or weeks won't kill me."

"You're a strong woman, Kenna. Please come to me if you need to talk again."

I gave him a nod and left.

I stepped into the empty elevator and sagged against the wall. I was pleased with my conversation with Jim but also exhausted. I could only imagine how hard this must be for him and Laurel, not to mention Grim and Knox. On a sudden urge, I pulled out my phone and texted Mom.

> Kenna: When you have a free
> moment, I'd love to chat. Things are
> heavy here.

The elevator stopped on my way to the lobby, and I found myself face to face with my father. His face was in a panic as he stepped inside. He, of course, was with several men; he wouldn't dare be alone at this point. He must be in a constant panic, as he had no idea who knew what and when someone might strike. I had no sympathy. *The curse of being the Devil, I suppose.*

"Humph. I hardly know you still work here anymore." He stepped forward, and the men moved in behind him. "I might add, you've missed two family dinners as well."

"Hello, Dad. How are you?" I rolled my eyes and thought about how nice he'd been only a short time ago. Even bringing up my childhood. I now realized it was mostly because he'd thought Grim had been killed on his order then found out it was Leo. He couldn't even get that right.

"Don't be smart, young lady," he grunted, keeping his voice low as he glanced at the other men who spoke quietly behind us. "This has been a difficult time for all of us."

How dare he!

Breathe, Kenna.

I closed my eyes and channeled all my control not

to throat-punch him. It probably was another attempt to see what I knew. My fingers rolled into fists as I gave myself a pep talk inside.

"It's been heartbreaking." I barely managed to get the words out. "Have you spoken to Jim yet? Does he have any leads? I've been away in Hong Kong, and I'm not caught up."

"You're needed here, not galivanting around in Asia. Jim needs space right now." He was such a coward. "You should remember that and pick up the slack at work." How was I related to such a monster? "Grim, too. He doesn't seem to realize his father isn't well. He should be more supportive."

I blinked at his words and looked up at him. "What does that mean?"

"I know you two are dating." His large neck contracted against his tightly buttoned collar. "Do you really think it's smart sleeping with the boss's son?" I opened my mouth to tell him off, but his words seemed awfully close to, if not the same as, Jayden's. Maybe Jim was on to something. Maybe Jayden had been talking to my father. Christ, was no one safe anymore? Were we all living in a den of vipers? "Grim is not the man your mother or I would choose for you, McKenna."

Instantly I felt my back go up. "Thankfully, you don't have a say in who I date, or in any part of my life, for that matter." He sucked in a sharp breath at my disrespectful tone.

"Hey," he grabbed my arm as the doors opened. Grim stood in the lobby speaking to someone, and he took in what was happening. "I mean it, McKenna." My father squeezed my arm a little tighter. "I want you to stay away from him, if you know what's good for you."

Grim was already heading toward us. I looked down at my arm and then back up at my father. "First, I am your daughter, yes, and I'm asking you to please let go." He didn't. He was an ass like that. "Second, I'm not Calli, and I won't let you dictate my life." As he still hadn't let go, I pried his fingers from my arm. "It's sad that this is where we are now."

"That's not my fault." He stepped back when Grim appeared. I stepped out as he pressed the button to close the doors.

"Don't ask," I warned. "I'm playing my part." When he didn't say anything, I glanced up and saw an odd look on his face. "What?"

"I want to invite you to dinner." He sent my head in a spin. Then it hit me; he was trying. *Okay, this is nice.*

"All right, where?"

"My place." I caught a smirk on his face.

"Try again."

"Fine. Seven-thirty at Desert Breeze." One of the

new restaurants on Secret's rooftop? That was a good choice for a nice date.

"So public?" I teased him.

"We can always pivot back to my original idea." He chuckled.

"Desert Breeze it is."

Good as Hell by Lizzo pounded through my speakers as I sang at the top of my lungs. I checked myself in the mirror and added a little more lipstick. I'd chosen a tight white dress, as I knew he'd wear his classic black suit. I kind of liked that we played the heaven-and-hell look off each other. Though I was anything but heaven these days.

I kept my hair straight and loose. I decided on a sparkly gold bracelet on each wrist and matched it with one around my ankle, then added gold hoops earrings. Sometimes simple was more.

I spotted him at the bar as I arrived. He leaned an elbow against the counter as he nursed a glass of whiskey. As I predicted, he was in one of his wonderfully classic black suits. I loved that he and Elio had similar tastes when it came to clothing. They were both a perfect balance of raw and wild, yet refined and sophisticated at the same time. Trigger blended well with the two of them, perhaps never in a classic suit kind of way, but all three carried that wonderful dose of darkness I loved. It was something that pulled at every part of me, and I felt a surge of desire as I looked at Grim.

He must have felt me watching because he turned and looked directly right at me. His eyes went slowly down my front without an ounce of shame before he pushed off the counter and walked toward me. One hand was tucked in his pocket, and the other held his glass.

My skin heated as I held his gaze. I put my chin up and took a step toward him. His hand slipped from his pocket and slid around my waist as he leaned in for a kiss on my jaw.

"This dress," his fingers flexed as he breathed me in, "is going to get you into a whole lot of trouble later."

That's the hope.

I played along. "And you look like trouble." I loved Grim's playful side. "This place looks amazing." I looked around at his new bar. Lights twinkled in the distance and created a lovely atmosphere. Rooftop bars were always my favorite places, and I loved taking clients there. I knew this one would be a hit.

He turned and steered me to a table where we sat in a booth with a view of the desert. In fact, all the tables were half-moon shaped to provide privacy and a spectacular view. In the center was a dance floor, a pool, and a DJ who already played music.

Then I heard *her* voice, and my mind went from turned on and relaxed to white hot anger.

"Did you know Jenelle was going to be here?" I leaned forward and slit my eyes as I spotted her with her father two tables down. She was like a damn cockroach.

"I did," he sipped his drink like it was nothing, "but I don't care. Do you?"

I thought for a moment, and the anger that had come so quickly fizzled out as I mulled over what he said. He knew she was here, yet he sat across from me and didn't hide that he couldn't wait to get me alone.

"I don't care, not in the least. But they better not come over here."

"Good." He nodded. "You're feisty tonight." He seemed amused.

I pulled his glass from his hand and took a large sip. "You have no idea."

"Does this have anything to do with Jayden? Dad told me."

I cursed under my breath. "I see."

"You know you could have come to me."

I twisted the napkin on my lap. "Truth, I wasn't sure how you'd react, and I didn't want a scene."

"You act like I have temper." He chuckled at his own joke as though entertained. "I need to know these things." He paused as the waiter set my favorite dirty martini down and took our orders. "They're my staff, and if someone is touching something that's not," he paused, "theirs, I need to be aware."

"All right, I suppose that's fair."

"Good." He let it go. "Now, I have something for you." He pointed to my phone. "Check your email." I quickly opened my phone and saw an email had arrived from him just moments ago.

"What's this?" I tapped on the attachment. "Blueprints?"

"Yes. You know my tastes, so I was thinking you could design my penthouse."

My jaw dropped, but I caught myself. "This is unexpected." I studied the layout.

"The second attachment is for the Silk and Lace Room. I'm not pleased with how it turned out, and I thought about that drawing you did on the last page in your notebook. It would be perfect, sexy."

I lowered my phone. "You remember that?"

"I do." He sipped his drink. "I bow to your skill as a hostess. You go the extra mile, but I've seen your drawings, and I like what I saw. I want to use you as a designer. You pick up on what I see in my head but find hard to get across."

"Is it really that, or because you don't want me working with male clients and fulfilling their requests?" I smiled playfully, while I secretly felt a sense of pride that he liked what he'd seen.

"I would be lying if I said it wasn't partially that." He leaned back as the waiter placed our meal in front of us. Everything smelled amazing.

I set my phone down and decided to speak candidly. "Grim, I haven't accepted the offer from Yen Hong, and to be truthful, I don't see myself there. However, if this is your way of trying to keep me here—"

"Don't insult me, Kenna," he interrupted. "You've got talent, and I want you to design those rooms for me. I want to see what you can do because, as you know, we have another hotel going up soon, and I could use your ideas." He took a bite of his roasted potato and chewed slowly.

"Wow." I pushed at a piece of asparagus and thought how exciting that would be. "All right, yes, I'll do it. Thank you."

He smiled with pleasure. "You're talented." He gave me a quick glance. "Don't hide it."

I sighed and looked out at the view of the twinkling lights that could be seen far out in the distance. The summer was coming to an end, and there was a tiny bit of a nip in the air. I loved the relief our clients felt when the temperature dropped, but winter was just around the corner, and Vegas just wasn't the same without the heat.

Grim stood and draped his jacket over my shoulders. He really could be a gentleman.

"Thank you." The material was like butter on my skin, and I found myself breathing in his fresh, clean smell. I licked my lips and tamped down the sudden urge to rub myself.

He sliced into his perfectly done rare tri-tip and savored the taste for a moment. I tried to hide my amusement. "What?" He tilted his head.

"You've eaten the finest of meals all over the world, yet you still get so much enjoyment from every meal you eat."

He thought for a moment and took another taste. "I want to make sure it's up to par."

"See, I don't think it's that." I wasn't going to let him get away with that. I loved that he had shown me a moment. I liked this side of him. "I think this might be one of the times in your day that you stop and actually enjoy something."

"Perhaps." He shrugged. "I never really thought about it. I guess I've tried to focus on things that bring me enjoyment lately." He made a point of side-eyeing me.

I focused back on my plate, and we both enjoyed the small talk that came with it.

A while later, I slid out of the booth, and he wrapped an arm around my waist as we headed toward his private elevator. I swore everyone watched us, and I suddenly felt unsure if I wanted that kind of attention. There was nothing between us at this point, and I wasn't totally sure what I even wanted from him.

"Join me for a nightcap at my place." He pulled out a keycard and tapped his button.

"Well." I took a moment to think about it. I didn't want to sound too eager. "I guess I really should check on Leal. But," I raised my chin, and he gave me a serious look, "tomorrow is a new day, I'm not asking for dinners or for you to spend money on me. I'm just asking for a little effort. I deserve it."

He smiled. "Understood."

NINE

SIMON

"You got anything to drink?" Kurt slammed into the living room table with a curse. He reached for my best bottle of merlot, but I plucked it from his hand and replaced it with a bottle of J&B scotch. I kept one on hand for the times he made his late-night calls such as this one. I turned on the lights and used my foot to gently push back the vase that was in danger of being knocked over. Kurt was a damn fine investigator, but he turned to the bottle too often for my liking.

"Why don't you take a seat?" I practically shoved him into a chair so he wouldn't send my Death Star model crashing to the floor, "and tell me why am I so lucky to have you visit," I checked my watch, "just after midnight?" I tucked the bottle of wine into a cabinet, to keep it out of sight.

He spun the top off the bottle and chugged the scotch. I touched my nose to hold back my rection. "I'm worried about Cameron."

"I'm worried about you," I countered, but when he took another sip, I sighed and eased into the chair across from him. "When have you ever worried about Cameron?"

"Since he fucked up the Gates hit."

"How can you be so sure it was him?" I felt a jolt to the chest. That had been one of the biggest blindsides I'd experienced yet with Cameron, and I'd had a few. I had no idea he'd been responsible for the hit, but I knew now by the way he'd been acting; he'd done it.

He's acting guilty as fuck. I've known him longer than you have."

"I knew he was growing more and more frustrated with Grim, but I never dreamed he'd go to such extremes." I looked away and rubbed my hands on my thighs. "And then to find out it was Leo." I shook my head. "Fuck."

He hiccupped. "Even I could see Grim was moving in on Kenna, but it was stupid reckless of him to do something like that."

"Yeah, it was." I saw him scowl as I inched my glasses up my face but didn't say anything. He always let me know he hated my glasses.

"If the Gateses know Cameron's behind their son's death, why aren't they making a move?" He pulled at the collar of his shirt. "I feel like I'm looking over my shoulder waiting for the repercussions because of my association with him."

"I suspect they know." I huffed out a breath. "As far as why they're not moving on it, if they do, I've no idea. Cameron told me he ran into Kenna, and things seemed normal. Claws out and lots of snapping back and forth. She didn't seem nervous, but then again, Grim was right there when the doors opened, so…" I shrugged. "Apparently, they were spotted having dinner together at Secrets, so nothing seems to out of the ordinary."

"I see." He kicked his feet up on the table, and I cringed at my copy of Home and Hearth that was being crumpled by his shoes. "Do you think it's just a front? The two of them?"

"No," I hated the idea of that tainted man touching something as flawless as Kenna, "and I don't think Sonny would have outed himself the way he did if he didn't believe they were together either."

"He's such an asshole." Kurt took another swig. "Sonny's always been in love with her."

"Yes, he has." I didn't blame him; Kenna was a whole different level of a woman.

He looked around the room, and his eyes became

heavy. The scotch was clearly catching up to him. "The time is coming," he murmured.

I watched as his eyes closed, and I took a deep breath, happy he'd passed out already and nothing had been broken or ruined. His ball hat slipped down over his eyes as a snore fell from deep inside. The bottle wobbled in his slack hand, and I lunged to grab it before it crashed on the floor. It wouldn't be the first time I'd had to clean up after one of his visits.

I froze when I saw the black smudge on his little finger and side of his palm. I studied it further, and my blood started to boil. "What the hell?" The telltale sign of a permanent black marker smudge. It looked faded, like when someone tries to scrub the ink off, but you can never get it all. It was a dead giveaway. "Hey!" I smacked his cheek, and he jolted back to the living with a yelp. "What's this from?"

"What are you talking about, for fuck's sake? I dunno," he muttered and shut his eyes again. I covered my mouth and was immediately hit with a memory.

"Hey, Wanda." CM jumped off the table he sat on and nearly knocked over the books I was organizing. He ran up to the guard on duty. She eyed me uncomfortably, and I looked away. When I first met her, I thought she was nervous of me because I was in prison for murder, but I soon realized over the last few months it was because CM had become way too pushy with her. She'd made the mistake of crossing that line with an inmate, and I knew she regretted it. CM was charm-

ing, but she'd made a mistake when she flirted with him. She hadn't banked on how much he wanted her to always be around.

He brushed her arm, and she quickly moved it back. He didn't pick up on her hints that she was no longer interested. I knew there'd been more than a few female guards who moved quickly away from him when he was around. He would just wink at me and smile then walk off.

"God, she's a beauty." He sat down and leaned in. "We're gonna meet up tonight." He wiggled his eyebrows and made a rude gesture. I pushed the ratty spine of James and the Giant Peach into its rightful place and glanced over my shoulder at how uncomfortable Wanda seemed.

Suddenly, a letter was dropped on the table by another guard, and I caught the name on it. CM grinned at me and shrugged as he picked it up. "I guess we're buddies now. Maybe it's good you know my real name." He held out his hand. "Kurt Moore. Pleased to officially meet you." He smiled wide.

"Fuck." I spun out of my memory and pulled out my phone. I looked at Kurt as he snored away in my chair. I tapped the screen to make a call then stopped myself and studied him a moment. "My old friend, you've gone too far this time." I sighed deeply. The writing was on the wall, and I hated to see it. "Dammit! Okay, okay." I tapped my temple and thought it might be the time. "All right." I closed my eyes and centered myself as I sat back to hatch a plan.

By the time morning came, I knew what I needed to do. The place smelled of warm muffins, and I put two on a plate and set them on the table in front of Kurt along with a bottle of water and a couple of painkillers. I grabbed my keys and headed for the door. Kurt loved anything carb, and I knew from his past he wouldn't be able to resist the painkillers and the smell from the Ativan-laced pastry. I was sure he'd be out for a while.

TEN

GRIM

Imoaned as I shifted and was pleased to find I was still inside Kenna. I buried my face in her neck and breathed in deeply as I moved slowly in and out a few times.

I couldn't wait to get her to Italy. We were already packed and ready to leave the following day. Elio had sent word that it was time to celebrate and had invited our family and friends to help him party. I wouldn't miss it for the world. I'd been there many times and knew Kenna would love it. Elio never spared any expense when it came to celebrating, and I sure as hell wasn't going to leave Kenna behind.

"Morning." She bowed her back, and I palmed her breast and rolled her nipple between my fingers.

"I need you." I kissed her shoulder. The memory of last night's sex came back to me. We had kept it up until neither of us could move and had fallen asleep totally spent. I eyed my bookshelf, and more than half of them were on the floor thanks to some wild moves. I couldn't get enough of her. I craved her. I turned her on her front and rolled to my knees and took her from behind. Her arms went up to act as pillow for her head, and a lazy smile spread across her lips as I pumped into her. The early morning sun began to peek through the open shades.

My phone lit up and vibrated against the nightstand, but I knocked it aside and sent it flying across the room. Leal growled his displeasure at the noise.

Kenna peeked up at me from behind her long lashes. "You keep this up, I won't be able to walk right."

"That's the plan." I picked up the pace, and she reached between her legs and cupped my balls. "Christ, woman, you have a death wish." Her phone vibrated under my knee, and I pulled it free and saw the screen.

> Benny: I leave tomorrow. I'd love to
> see you. Dinner tonight?

Anger bubbled to the surface, and I leaned over her body and showed her the text message. "Decline this."

She pulled it closer to read the message. "No."

I ran my fingers along her neck and across her stomach, then I tugged her up onto all fours. I tilted her chin to look at me. "He wants you." I thrusted a few times to drive my point home.

"Do you want me?" she countered.

"I want you like this." I stopped myself from saying anything else.

"Seems to me, you have me the way you want." She turned to push her lips to mine then pulled back. "So, what's the problem with me having dinner with an old friend?"

I didn't like the feeling that ran through me, so I grabbed her hips and finished what I started. Perhaps I was a little rougher than I meant to be, but her screams made it worth it. She held on and took everything I gave her. I wanted her to feel me for the rest of the day.

She looked royally fucked by the time we stepped into the elevator and headed down toward the rest of the world. I smirked when she yawned and sagged into the wall with a sleepy look. I had both boys with me, even if Leal avoided eye contact with me when he stole pats from Kenna every so often.

"Hey," I grabbed her hand when she went to step out and pulled her back to me, "have dinner with me."

"Instead of Benny?" She gave me a knowing look. "Give me a reason that doesn't end with you inside me."

"Are you complaining?"

"Are you deflecting?" she challenged then waited a beat before she stepped back. "He's just a friend, Grim."

"He wants you."

She walked backward, and I followed. The boys shifted instantly into business mode. "And what if he does?"

My insides twisted and I felt my face twist into a scowl. "I'll kill him."

"Your kill list is pretty long, baby." She grinned. "Besides, Benny is the least of your problems."

"We'll see about that. Don't forget that gorgeous pink bikini when we leave for Italy tomorrow."

"Already packed. Have a good day, Mr. Gates." She chuckled and waved over her head as she swayed her hips away from me.

Zhar stiffened, and his ears told me someone was approaching from behind me. *Fuck me, now what?*

"Mr. Gates?" I found Simon with both hands in his pockets. He looked like he'd gotten less sleep than I had. "May I have a word?" He looked around. "Alone."

Intrigued, I nodded and waved him toward a quiet room. Something told me Cameron wasn't aware of this meeting. I opened the door and let him go first. I couldn't help but be amused when he sidestepped Leal, who looked back at me for permission for a taste.

I shook my head, and he huffed as he followed us. I closed the door and told the boys to sit.

"I'm worried about Kenna," he blurted, and I was instantly on alert. "I care about her, and I know you do too," he cleared his throat like he was nervous how that came across, "but in different ways, of course. This isn't about Cameron, though I don't blame you if you thought it was…" He started to babble, and I checked my watch.

"I'm a busy man, Simon," I cut in, "and you have the five remaining free minutes I have left."

"Yes, sorry." He pushed his glasses up his nose as he muttered something. "I know we are often on different sides of the fence, given my employer, and I stay working for him for my own reasons, but I need you to know I would never hurt Kenna."

"Good. Then I won't have to kill you," I said, deadpan, and his eyes widened. "Now, get to the fucking point."

"I think I know who Kenna's stalker is." He seemed to just blurt shit, but at least we were getting somewhere.

"And who might that be?" I wasn't about to get excited until I had some real proof.

"Look, you may or may not know I spent some time in prison," his face went apologetic as he added hurriedly, "for a crime I never committed."

"And this is important, why?"

I knew Leo had done a background check on Simon. There were a few things that had seemed off about what he'd been accused of, but I didn't give a shit because it wasn't anything I thought would come back on our family. Besides, he worked with Cameron, so that meant I kept him as far away from my life as I could.

"I made friends with my cellmate," he went on. "He had a bit of a problem with women and often became obsessed with them, but I kept my distance and turned the other way whenever I saw it. He had a lot of pull, and I wasn't going to mess with him. In the end, he helped get me an early release through Cameron." He rubbed his arm. "I didn't see it with Kenna until it was too late."

"See what?" I folded my arms and fought to keep my anger down. I was impatient for him to get to the damn point. "And what do you mean, too late?" The hairs on my skin prickled, knowing something dark was coming.

"I think he's her stalker. He came over last night, drunk, and when he passed out, I noticed a black Sharpie smudge on the side of his hand." Instantly, both dogs cued in to my change in heartbeat and were on high alert. My jaw locked tightly in place. "I heard that Tracy girl who was involved in all of this was killed, and I also heard there was a drawing on her body, and it was done with marker." He licked his lips and waited for me to speak.

"And how do you know this?"

"I don't know for sure, of course, but when I saw that marker, it just hit me. I'm a PI, and Kenna's my boss's daughter. Cameron pays good money for me to know things, and I like Kenna. I also know my friend, and –"

"Where is this man?" I ground my teeth as I tried to control my desire to lose my shit on the man in front of me.

"At my place."

"Take me there." As we headed out, Jesse joined my side with confusion on his face. "Where's Kenna?"

"At the pool with Harris. He arrived last night."

"Grab her and get Cartwright to meet me at my spot." He looked at me with a question. I switched to Mandarin and filled him in. He veered off as Simon and I headed for the exit with the boys. I spotted Shore, and when he caught sight of me, he rushed over to open the door of the limo. The boys hopped inside. Simon prattled off his address to Cartwright.

"Get in," I ordered Simon as he leaned down and looked inside. I saw him hesitate and had no doubt he might be rethinking his options of how he was going to get home. If the situation wasn't so serious, I might have found some humor in the fact that Zhar had squeezed to sit on one side of Simon and Leal the other.

They all swayed in one direction when the car took off. He looked like the meat in a sandwich. I was sure there was some familiarity there from his prison days.

I got to work and began to send messages. I made sure Dad knew I'd miss the morning meeting but hoped to make the afternoon one. I also texted Knox to get him to escort a client to the vault in Secrets. It was a low-risk task, given that they'd be surrounded by security, and these were the things I had to start getting him involved in more, now that...I stopped my thought and pushed away the pain that immediately filled me at the thought of losing Leo.

> Jesse: I have Kenna. We'll see you there. She's not pleased.

I was sure she wasn't. I switched chats.

> Grim: Normal spot. 40 mins.

> Trigger: Just dealt with a situation. I'm already here.

The car stopped, and I tucked my phone away and got my head in the game. "He's, ah, just inside." Simon hesitated as Shore opened the door. Leal started to growl. I ordered the dogs out then waited for him to follow. I wasn't about to take my eyes off him yet.

We approached the house, and Simon unlocked the door with the dogs on his heels. We all went inside, and I finally laid eyes on the man who had possibly hurt and stalked Kenna.

"See, right there," Simon whispered as he pointed to the marker smudge, but I was more interested in his ball hat. It was the same hat I'd seen in the photos of the man who had dumped Tracy's body in the trash.

It was him.

Pure, white-hot rage filled me and burned deep in my chest. It was much the same as the rage I had to swallow back whenever I looked at Cameron, but this time, I wasn't going to hold any of it back.

I pulled my arm back and punched him square in the face. I felt his cheekbone break, and it fueled me. It also brought him out of his drunken stupor with a cry of agony. Simon cursed and hurried to put some space between us.

"What the fuck?" the guy howled as I hauled him to his feet. He took one look at me, and his eyes bugged out. He made a pathetic attempt to swing at me, and I punched him in the gut. He caught sight of Simon, and his face turned red. "What the fuck? You brought him here? You goddamn traitor!"

"You went too far this time, Kurt." Simon shook his head. "What was next? What was your plan with Kenna?"

"He's in love with her, you know!" the guy named Kurt screamed at me as if to try to find an out.

"No," Simon sighed calmly, "I'm not in love with

Kenna." He looked at me and held out his hands. "I'm in love with her sister." I believed that one. I'd seen evidence of it myself. "But, Kurt, there's a big difference between loving someone and hurting them."

"I'd never hurt her!" he blubbered.

"You already did, you bastard," I barked, and he cowered in my hold. I shook him like a rat and tossed him to the floor. I drew back my foot and kicked him. He landed against the wall and cried out as he held a hand to his cheek.

"I loved her," he pleaded. "How could you not? You know what I mean, Mr. Gates. You…I mean—" He changed tactics. "It hurt me to see her with you. It made me angry. I didn't mean…" Kurt's gaze moved to the dogs and his eyes went wide again.

His face twisted as he squinted at Leal, who was always on my left side. "You're supposed to be dead."

I lost it.

I punched him in the temple and knocked him out cold. I wasn't going to let myself ruin my fun prematurely. I dragged his body out the door and dropped him like the trash he was into the trunk of the limo.

"I'd like to stay here," Simon said behind me. "The less Cameron knows, the better."

I whirled around and stuck a finger in his face. "If I find out you were a part of this in any way, you're next."

He nodded. "And you know where to find me. I

can promise you, Mr. Gates, I wouldn't have told you about Kurt if I'd anything to do with it." He looked at the car then back at me. "Lord knows Kenna deserves some kind of revenge."

I nodded once and headed back to the car. We certainly agreed on that.

The desert was only a short ride away, but, in that time, I let myself retreat into the darkness that begged for a chance to take over. It felt good to let the need for a kill fill me with that welcome surge of adrenaline. When we stopped, I waved to Shore to leave Kurt in the trunk. Trigger, Brick, Rail, and Morgan were sitting on their bikes, and Minnie and Kenna were in conversation. When Shore opened my door, I saw the relief on Kenna's face. I knew she must have wondered what was going on.

"I didn't share anything," Jesse told me as he joined my side. The dogs jumped out and sat down by the trunk.

"Grim?" Kenna carefully walked in her high heels over the unforgiving desert floor. I reached out and slid my hand over her bottom and drew her to me. She looked up and made a face. "I know that look." Her lips pressed together. "Tell me what's going on."

I ran my fingers through her hair then swooped down to catch her startled lips. Normally, when I let the darkness in, I pushed her away, but this time it was different. I wanted to feed on her.

She let me have my way. She pressed her tight body to mine and matched my intensity for a moment but then pulled back and studied my face. "Tell me or I'm leaving."

I smirked. Like I'd ever let that happen. She glared at my reaction. "Grim?" she demanded, and I nodded at Shore, and he opened the trunk.

"An unexpected person led me to your stalker."

"Oh, my God," she covered her mouth, "I know this guy!"

"You do?" That was news to me.

She bent down and eyed him. "Well, I mean, I've seen him around. He talked to Simon a few times." She gasped. "Shit, was Simon involved in this?"

"No, he's the one who told me about him. Apparently, his name's Kurt." I really didn't think Simon had anything to do with it, although he puzzled me at times. I couldn't quite figure the guy out.

"Thank God."

"If he did, he knows what I'd do to him," I growled. Kurt groaned, and I waved at Jesse to help me lift him out of the trunk. We dropped him down in the dirt, and I threw a look at Trigger and the others. They all moved forward to surround him.

"Nice to have a break in the fuckin' heat." Trigger scratched his chin. "Shapin' up to be a good day." He grinned.

Kurt lifted his dusty head off the ground and took

in his surroundings. Then he broke into a chuckle as he rolled onto his back. "I wondered when this day would come." He turned and spotted Kenna and sat up with a deep groan. "She's gorgeous, yeah?" I squeezed my hand into a fist as Kenna made her way over to me. She was careful to keep out of his reach. "I bet she's great in the sack." Kenna ran her hand up my chest and made me look at her.

"He'll never know." She gave me a hungry expression, and I smirked because she was right. He never would, not with any woman ever again.

She dropped her hand and turned to look at him. "Why attack me?" She screwed up her mouth. "Was it because of Matt Myers?"

He spat on the ground and felt his broken jaw. "That was just the cherry on top." He grimaced. "No, it was just to piss him off."

"Who? Grim?" She bent down and caught herself as she balanced carefully on the tiny sticks for heels on her shoes.

"No, please," he laughed and glared at me, "though he shouldn't have touched something that should have been mine. I saw you first, way back when those tits of yours were only just starting. It was long before he laid eyes on you."

"You're disgusting, and I belong to no one," Kenna spat back, and I caught Trigger's expression and held up a hand. He could read my mind, but I wanted to give Kurt a little more rope. "Then who did you want to piss off?" Kenna asked.

He slowly got to his feet and leaned toward her, and the boys instantly jumped to either side of Kenna. "Your father, of course."

"I see." She stood, and Leal whined. He anxiously awaited my command to rip this guy's face off. "Did you hurt the dogs because of my father, too?"

"No, I wanted them dead because you never hesitated to put your hands all over them. The two of them practically drool when they see you." He dove at Kenna, but in that same second, I swung her by the waist into me, Leal launched himself at Kurt's throat, and Trigger and the others had their weapons out ready to fire. Kurt screamed as Leal hung on tight, and I gave him a command to let go. He immediately did as I said. I held up a hand to Trigger and the guys, but they never lowered their guns.

"You're okay." I brushed her hair off her face and saw her wild expression. "I got you."

"Okay." She had a death grip on my forearms. I could see that had really rattled her. She wasn't prepared for him to go for her like that. I'd been ready because I'd read his body language. Kenna was feisty and could hold her own, but she was different from the other girls in that she wasn't physical. Minus that one time with Kelly, but that was just a good, old-fashioned catfight. "He's not walking away from here, right?"

"Not in one piece." I gave her a quick kiss and waved for Minnie to come over. "Go with Minnie and let me deal with him."

"Yeah, okay."

I turned and faced him as she walked toward Minnie. Slowly, I walked over as I thought about how much I was going to enjoy this.

"The fifth year I was in Mexico," I said in a conversational tone as he sat on the ground with a hand pressed against his bloody neck, "I met a man who trained dogs for the Cartel. He had these two little pups who had just been taken from their mother. Their ears were taped, and their tails clipped. I never understood why people did that, but they weren't mine, so…" I shrugged. I moved around him as I walked the perimeter of the circle created by the guys. "I would sit on the hood of his car and watch him run drills with those pups for hours. He told me you earned their trust first, then they'd earn yours."

"How much longer is this story gonna take, for fuck's sake?" He rolled his eyes, but I ignored him.

"For a year, I'd visit him off and on, and he taught me everything he knew about working with those dogs. I learned what commands he used for what, when to let them go, when to pull them in, and I gradually earned their friendship."

"Touching." He snickered, and I smiled at him.

"Then one day when I visited him, I found my

friend on the ground with a bullet in his head and the pups playing with the killer's body. They'd ripped him open and torn him limb from limb. That," I stopped in front of him, "is true loyalty." Kurt's eyes went wide. "And they're here to protect me," I looked at Kenna, "and her."

"I didn't actually hurt them." He tried to act tough, but I could see the fear was setting in.

"And I'm not actually going to hurt you." I hauled him to his feet and looked at him dead in his eyes. "Run."

He didn't waste a beat; he swiveled and ran flat-out toward the open desert. The dogs growled and whined next to me as they strained against my legs and pawed the ground, but they stayed exactly where they were. Until…

"*Comer*," I ordered. The command meant *eat* in Spanish.

They took off after that son of a bitch.

ELEVEN

SIMON

"Stop fidgeting," CM hissed at me from where he sat backward on a chair to one side of the table. Unlike me, who was cuffed and had to sit facing the window. CM, or rather Kurt as I now knew him, had assured me no one watched from behind it. He had hookups everywhere. The guard eyed me from the corner of the room, and I swallowed hard and tried to sit still. I didn't want to give him a reason to put me in the hole. "Remember," Kurt leaned forward, "don't look him in the eye, don't talk back, and most importantly, if he tells you to bend over, you do it."

"What?" My head shot back.

"Nah," he hopped to his feet, "I'm just fucking with you. Hey." He whistled to the guard and pointed to my cuffs. The guy glared at both of us but stepped over and reluctantly unlocked my handcuffs. "Just relax, and by this time tonight we'll be having beers out on the Santa Monica pier."

"Anywhere but Santa Monica," I muttered, knowing that was neutral ground for biker gangs and that was the last thing I needed. Thanks to Kurt, I'd been able to keep tabs on Allen until he disappeared down in Mexico. He must have paid good money to disappear because he hadn't been spotted by any of Kurt's connections for years. The only thing he could dig up on Allen were a couple rumors he'd been posing as a priest, but it had never been confirmed. If it was true, he'd have demons to answer to someday.

"Fine. You name the place, then, and we'll go there."

"Deal." The word faded off my tongue when the door opened and a red-faced, heavyset man dressed in an expensive suit and carrying a briefcase came in followed by another man. The big guy gave a tight nod to Kurt.

"How are ya, Sonny?" Kurt said to the second man, who stood back slightly.

"Been better." He pointed with his chin at the red-faced guy. "Babysitting our inhouse lawyer, as usual." The man dropped his briefcase loudly on the table and threw Sonny a nasty look.

"Shitty." Kurt acted like the lawyer wasn't even in the room until he looked at him. "I trust you looked over Simon's case file, Cameron."

"I did." The lawyer sat in a chair but wouldn't look at us as he pulled out a stack of papers and clicked a pen to expose the tip.

"Great. Then do your thing and get him out."

The lawyer looked up at the camera in the corner and cleared his throat as he opened a file. "Name, age, and birthdate."

"No, no," Kurt reached for the file, "and don't worry about them." He jerked a thumb at the cameras. "Simon's getting out. Just do this part since the paperwork's completed. Oh, and he'll be your PI."

"PI?" He looked confused, and my stomach sank as things seemed to go south.

"Yes, Cameron, he's a PI. He's like a Russell Crowe in **Beautiful Minds**, plus, you'll love this, you share the same distaste for bikers."

Cameron pulled at his collar and finally looked at me. "Same distaste, how?"

"Allen." I cleared my throat. "He set me up. It should be in the file."

"The file's been altered, my friend." Kurt shook his head and shrugged. "Allen has people too."

Great.

"Half the city of Los Angeles is looking to take Allen down." Cameron tilted his head at Kurt. "What's makes this guy a good fit to be my PI?"

"I've lived with this guy for nearly six years." Kurt dropped his arm to the table like he was frustrated Cameron even questioned him. "It's my job to observe, inspect, and recruit for the Potens in this hole. Besides there's an up-and-comer in the Devil's Reach, goes by the name Brick. I wonder *what he did to get that name." He chuckled. "Anyway, he's real close with Allen's son Trigger, who took over the pres seat since Allen's MIA. Your new PI did a few jobs with this guy Brick's brother. It could be an in."*

Kurt gave me a nod, and I pushed my glasses up my nose.

"His real name's Matt Montgomery." I let that sink in, but when he didn't react, I added. "He's been searching for his brother for years. When the time's right, I can tell him where he is, and maybe we can use it as leverage or something." The skin around Cameron's eyes smoothed out and I could see he was intrigued.

"You can find him, even after all this time?"

"Yes."

"All right, then," he quickly closed the file, "let's get you out of here."

The smell of sweat, sewage, and human cattle jolted me out of my memory. My knees went weak as we walked through the second door to where the solitary inmates were held.

"I still can't believe you talked me into this," Cameron muttered as he showed his ID for the third time since we arrived. "It's not safe."

"Avoiding a client who's more powerful behind bars than he is out isn't safe," I reminded him. "He's been trying to call you for nearly a month. You're lucky it's just a call and not something else."

Mr. Griple's dark eyes glared at Cameron as we

took our seats behind the glass. I was happy for the layer of protection, but I wasn't stupid. I knew what kind of pull men like Griple had, and we were anything but safe.

Griple jumped right in. "So, here I am in a fuckin' jumpsuit, and you sit there in your fancy Swiss suit looking like a fat pimp."

"I'm working on your case—"

He hit the glass and we both jumped. "Don't lie to me! You promised I wouldn't spend more than a few nights in here, that you had that fool Martin Castillo all set to take the fall. You couldn't even make that happen!"

"I had no idea Grim Gates planned on taking him out. If I had—"

"You'd what?" His eyes burned. "You'd send out a hit?" He laughed. "I heard what happened the last time you sent out a hit."

"Such an ass," Cameron muttered behind his hand, and I kicked him to warn him to be careful.

Griple's face turned to stone, and I pressed my heels into the floor, waiting for the fire to come.

"Ten years ago, you promised my uncle would walk free. He didn't even make it the first night in this shit hole." He waved around. "You sold yourself to us that you were the best, that you could get anyone out, but you didn't come through, did you?" He stabbed his finger against the glass. "Then when we came to collect, you bargained like the little weasel you are and said you had the Gateses in your pocket, that you'd earned his trust after he got sick, so the Potens sat back and waited. We provided you with what you needed to take them down along with that fucking Devil's Reach. And you know where that got us?" Spit flew from his lips. "My nephew gets killed by that rat bastard, that's what!"

"Sasha went too far," Cameron interrupted, and I put a hand on his arm. This was bad.

"No, you son of a bitch!" Griple slammed his fist into the table, and I noticed one of the guards looked over, but he didn't make a move. Again, the power of money. "*You* went too far, and now it's time for you to pay up."

Oh, shit.

"Which daughter?"

My stomach bottomed out.

"Which daughter?" He repeated his words without so much as a blink.

"Kenna." Cameron didn't miss a beat as he sealed the fate of his own daughter to this monster.

"Cameron!" I blurted then flinched at my outburst as Griple looked at me. I took a deep breath and moved back as far as I could into the chair. I felt sick as he swung his attention back to Cameron.

"Firstborn, it is." He pressed his lips together and nodded.

I couldn't form a word as we exited the prison, and it wasn't until I ripped open the car door that everything hit me.

"How could you do that?" I felt my anger burn a hole in my stomach. "She's your daughter."

"Would you rather I picked Calli?" He gave me a knowing look. "Don't play me, boy. I know you two have been screwing around."

"Don't call me boy." I gritted my teeth. I didn't give a damn if Cameron knew about my relationship with Calli, but the word *boy* brought me back to my father days, and I fought to swallow down a mouthful of bile.

"Messing with Calli is damn risky, by the way, given what Calli needs to do with Knox."

"But Kenna? You know Griple will kill her."

He tossed his suitcase in the back seat and leaned against the roof to look at me. "She chose what side she wanted to be on."

Who was this monster?

"How heartless can you be? You didn't even hesitate when you chose which daughter." I felt physically ill as a cold sweat broke out over my back.

"We all have choices, Simon. Surely you can understand that one." He grunted as he heavily got into the car and slammed the door.

TWELVE

KENNA

The flight to Italy was a fun one. Minnie and Tess were in fine form and ready to celebrate the death of my stalker, and I was just happy to be on a vacation where I didn't have to constantly look over my shoulder. To top it all off, Dad and Calli were six thousand miles away, and I was surrounded by great friends who were ready to party it up mafia style in Montepulciano.

Security was tight on the way in. Our car was third in line with two more following us. Sienna, who had joined us girls in our limo, gave us a brief history on the place as we drove. The sun was just about to set by the time we passed through the gates and started to climb a long, winding hill lined with tall, beautiful trees that came to a sharp point at their tops. I was told they were cypress trees. They reminded me of the ones from my childhood Dr. Seuss book. The Hill house, as Sienna called it, sat at the top of the property, and she said you could see anyone approach for miles in any direction. Several houses had apparently been added to the property since it was first purchased, but we would stay at the main house.

I wasn't prepared for how gorgeous it was. Fields of sunflowers blanketed one side of the hill, while rows and rows of vineyards graced the others. Mason jars of twinkling lights swung from trees and truly showed how vast their property was.

"Welcome to our home." Niccola grinned as we came to a rolling stop, and he and the guard with us got out and opened our doors. The sunset alone took your breath away. The different shades of oranges and reds looked like someone had tipped over two cans of paint and let them flow together.

"Wow," I sighed, soaking it in.

"This is my fifth time here," Tess threaded her arm through mine, "and it never gets old."

Sienna, absolutely stunning in a soft green sundress, smiled over at us. "It will always be here for you to stay whenever you want." She was so welcoming and sweet. It made me smile to know she was a mafia princess and married to one of the most ruthless men in all of Italy. "I know it's been a long flight. Your bags will be placed in your rooms, so let's get you something to drink." She waved at the guys, who chatted happily together as they stood near the cars, and they followed us inside.

We were introduced to Elio's parents, Andrea and Piero, and then to the twins, Marabella and Filippo. They were adorable and were the spitting image of their parents. Francesco, a longtime family friend, was introduced next. Sienna said she considered him like a father. The love that filled the household was tangible and could be felt in every touch and look, especially when Elio came in and scooped up his wife and kissed her like he hadn't seen her for weeks.

It filled my heart being there, and I found myself looking at Grim where he stood near the wall with a drink in his hand, deep in conversation with Vinni. It looked to be serious, so I didn't engage in case it burst the happy bubble I was enjoying. I sipped the delicious glass of wine Sienna handed me and smiled at my friends. Minnie and Tess were obviously enjoying themselves as they laughed and talked with Elio's cousin Niccola.

Sienna came and stood next to me, and we watched the others for a few moments. "Want to see one of my favorite spots? Bring your wine."

"Sure, I'd love to." I followed her through the house and out back to a cobblestone patio that looked over a gorgeous field of sunflowers.

"Elio planted those," she said over her shoulder as I followed her down a little path that hid us amongst the tall flowers. "He wanted me to have a spot that was just mine where I could be alone." She smiled at me then reached out and pushed aside some of the huge flower heads. I gasped as I took in the white hammock tied up between two trees and tucked into the garden in a way that allowed a private view of the property. "When you're here, no one can see you. It's where I come when the outside world becomes too much."

"It's beautiful." I stepped by her and sat in the hammock to get the full effect.

She joined me, and we swayed and sipped our wine in the cool night air. "I know you're only here for a few days, but I also know you've been dealing with a lot. So, if you ever need to slip away, I'd be happy to share my spot with you."

My father's face flashed in front of me, and I let out an unexpected sigh. "I appreciate this so much. Thank you, Sienna."

"I'm happy you came along." She ran her hand down her necklace and fiddled with the two pendants at the bottom. "I would never pry, but I want you to know I understand the position you're in. I've been there."

"Yeah?"

"Yes." She cleared her throat. "It's been years, but

that feeling of thinking you're adding to the problems that storm around you doesn't go away very easily."

"No, it doesn't." I knew exactly what she meant. "It's lonely at times," I confessed.

"Very." She looked down. "I know they all love me," she nodded back toward the house, "but the looks on their faces when..." She shifted in her seat. "The truth is scars don't always heal smoothly, and the memories don't always fade completely away either. I'm just saying if you ever do need to talk, I'm here for you. I don't want you to feel the way I did and think you're all alone."

I let her words sink in. "I don't think I realized how much I needed someone from the outside to say that to me." I squeezed her hand gently. "Thanks, Sienna." She smiled, but I could see her own past still hurt her at times. We both tuned in to the night as the crickets started to play their evening song and a breeze swayed through the garden.

"As much as I could spend the night here," Sienna pushed to her feet, "we should go back up before the others begin to look for you."

"I suppose." I hated to leave, but she was right. It would be impolite to leave my friends much longer.

When we stepped out of the high flowers, I found Grim waiting for me. When Elio saw me, he slapped Grim on the chest.

"See, they're never far." Elio reached for his wife,

and they walked arm and arm back to the house. Sienna gave me a wave as they left.

"It might be wise for you tell me when you're going to sneak off." Grim undid the top button of his shirt. He sounded frustrated.

I licked around my mouth, suddenly irritated with his comment. "I was with Sienna, Grim. I hardly think that was sneaking off." I brushed past him, and he followed me.

"I don't like it when I can't see you." He tapped my hip when I wasn't sure which way to go when we reached the house.

The rest of the evening went by quickly, and after our goodnights, Grim led me upstairs. I had no idea where my bedroom would be, but he seemed to know exactly where to go.

"Ah, yes, this place probably isn't crawling with cameras like back home." I chuckled. I knew it would piss him off. "I think I'm going to enjoy this vacation." He steered me left down a very long hallway. I spotted an open door and saw my suitcase inside. "Well, on that note," I stepped inside and turned to find him towering over me, "good night."

He reached back and kicked the door shut with a smirk. "We're sharing a room, sweetheart. Now, lose the dress."

Grim lay heavily against me, his arm over my back and his hand cupped around my breast in a near dead sleep. The man was a beast—not that I would ever complain—but I needed to move, and I was determined not to miss a single moment of Italy. I managed to shimmy out of the bed, shower, and dress without waking the man who looked like a sketchbook drawing against the crisp white sheets. God, he was gorgeous. I snatched my sunglasses and my bag and headed downstairs.

"Good morning," Piero, Elio's father, greeted me as I entered the kitchen. He was perched at the large island reading the paper while a man dressed in a chef's outfit was rolling out some pastry dough. I liked the fact that Piero was here in the kitchen and not secluded in an office away from the family and staff. All signs that it was a big, happy home, and everyone co-existed as one big family.

"Good morning. Is anyone else awake?"

Just as the words came out, Sienna walked in. "I love that you're up early," she said, beaming. "I'm heading to the market. Would you care to join me?" Piero gave her a glance, and she sighed softly. "Vinni's pulling the car around."

"Good." He leaned over and kissed her cheek. "Be careful."

"When have I not?" She playfully rolled her eyes. "The men in my world are so protective."

"Don't I know it." I laughed as she led the way to the car.

Vinni was something else. He was kind, funny, and gave Sienna a massive amount of shit, which she happily took and gave right back. I wished the other girls were there to witness it. I knew my friends, though, and Minnie and Tess loved to sleep in.

When the car stopped in the plaza, Vinni and three other members of their security got out. Each was attractive in their own way, but one in particular was very handsome.

"I know." Sienna seemed to read my mind as we made our way toward the fresh vegetable tables. "His ass is so tight you could bounce a dime off of it." She laughed.

"It's not just the ass, it's the arms, the hair..." I played along as Vinni glanced back with an impressed grin.

Sienna crossed her arms. "Don't act like you never stared at him."

Vinni rolled his eyes and went back to scanning the area.

My head was on a swivel with all the stonework and history Italy offered. Not to mention the gorgeous flowers and friendly faces. "Are you happy here? Do you miss Sicily?"

"At first, yes," she threaded her arm through mine, "but Montepulciano has my heart now."

"I'm glad." Suddenly, something amazing found its way to my nose and I headed for it. "Sienna, what is that smell?"

"Oh! That's soup." She tugged my arm, and we turned down a different street. The guys had to pivot to keep up.

We stopped at a vendor who was set up a little away from the others. "They have to sell down here, because at mealtime the line is so long it clogs the rest of the market." She handed the lady some money, and we watched her pour the soup into a bowl, then she held it up for me to try. As soon as the taste smothered my tongue, I let out a moan. It was as if someone poured heaven in a cup and *he* himself served it to me.

"I know. I swear after I discovered this soup I paid for their children's first year of school." She spoke to the couple, and they thanked me a few times as they bagged some for me to take with me. We thanked the couple, and as we did, two shots rang out, and in a split second the bag that held the container of soup flew in all directions and I felt myself being tackled hard to the ground. My heart dropped into my stomach as something sticky dripped down my face.

Sienna's scream found my ears, and then I was jerked up and shoved behind Mr. Hotness. The security guard bled down his arm from a wound in his shoulder. More shots came, and he pressed my head down under the table. We kept low as he directed me to move with him behind two cars where Sienna was hunkered down with Vinni.

The four men communicated in Italian, and I kept watching their body language, trying to understand. Vinni raced off as more shots came, they seemed to be closer than before. I screamed as a bullet hit the tire very close to my side. More shots rang out, and Sienna shifted close to me and wrapped an arm around me.

"Who are they?" I somehow asked.

"I don't know," she yelped when another bullet got too close for comfort, "but there are a lot of them, and they're close."

Squealing tires found their way through the chaos, and a vehicle stopped in front of us. Mr. Hotness crouched and tried to reach up to open the car door, but dropped his hand as the door was sprayed with bullets. Finally, he managed to reach the handle of the back passenger door, it flew open, and we were both lifted off the ground and pushed inside.

Bang! Bang! Bang!

I screamed and tried to make myself smaller even though the car was bulletproof. Vinni wasted no time peeling out of there and around a corner at full speed. I was flung across the car and right into the arms of the hot security guard. He clamped a bloody arm over me like a seatbelt, and I had no choice but to hold on to him.

"Everyone okay?" Vinni called over his shoulder as he fought to keep the car on the road. "Sienna?"

"Yes." She pressed a hand to her chest and tried to catch her breath. "Kenna?" I nodded in fear my voice would betray how terrified I was. "She's okay, Vinni," she answered for me.

I closed my eyes and counted my wild heartbeats. The gunshots echoed in my head, and I fought the fear that tightened around my chest. *But it's supposed to be over!*

The car stopped, and I nearly trampled everyone to get out, but when I stood, my head went light. I twisted and reached for the car, only to have Mr. Hotness swoop me up as I lost my balance. Thankfully, I didn't pass out.

"Sorry," I whispered.

He looked at me intensely. "Don't be sorry, *signora*." His low voice grounded me.

"Get your hands off her!" Grim barked and pulled me into his arms. I sagged with relief at his familiar scent.

"I want a full report." Elio threw out orders to the men, and they scattered. He pulled Sienna from the car and checked her over feverishly, then, relieved, he pressed his forehead to hers. He spoke softly to her in Italian, and she nodded and hugged him. He then looked at me, and I gave a small nod that I was fine as well. "Grim, your parents are on their way back. They turned around as soon as they heard the news."

"Okay." Grim ran a hand down my back.

I wanted a moment alone and was grateful Elio took Sienna toward the house as they saw his parents run outside.

"Hey," Grim's tone was soft, but still carried his normal edge, "what the hell just happened?" I hated that I wanted him to pick a fight because I felt all twisted and rattled inside.

I stepped back and wiped my sweaty forehead with the back of my hand. "Apparently, I have some pretty shitty karma banked, because I can't even fly halfway around the world without someone wanting me dead."

"Or maybe they were after Sienna."

"Well, there were enough bullets for all of us, so…" I raised my hands and dropped them. "God!" I covered my face and tried to push the tears back, but they insisted on coming.

"Just take a breath." He tried to soothe me, but I felt a flash of anger instead.

"Can't you just say something prickish so we can fight?" I swiped my cheeks with a hiss, knowing I was being a bitch, but I couldn't contain my emotions. "Seriously, stop being so damn nice. That's not what we—" In a flash, he wrapped a hand around my throat and pushed me back into the car door to tower over me in that delicious way he did so well. His chest heaved against mine, and his pupils dilated to let me see the dark predator inside.

"You'd be wise to remember my dark side's never far from the surface." He swiped his tongue along my jaw as he breathed me in, and all the fear from before was replaced with a deep ache between my legs. "Don't mistake my kindness for weakness." He kissed my pulsing heartbeat. "But I crave you, *sweetheart*, and if anything happens to you…" he pulled back, and so much darkness flickered from his eyes that I swallowed hard, "it'll rain blood." His promise held so much truth goosebumps burst over my skin. He dipped down and caught my lips with his. I had to clench my legs at that moment. "The girls are looking for you, so let's get inside before I lose it with you any further."

I pushed him away, but he caught my hand and pulled me back to him with an odd look. "Yeah?"

"Stay away from that guard," he warned.

I smirked and tilted my head, loving that Mr. Hotness had gotten under Grim's skin. "For someone who doesn't care, you sure seem jealous." I didn't wait for a response. I headed inside; I needed my girls.

"See, he does want you!" Minnie beamed after I finished my story. She was stretched out like a lazy cat on the lounge chair by the bedroom window.

I shook my head. "No, he craves me physically," I

corrected. I pulled my dress up over my hips, "he's addicted to our sex. I totally get it because I can't imagine giving it up either. We're addicted to each other. It's amazing, but he doesn't care for me in the way you think. I can only wish."

"It's Grim, Kenna." Minnie's face showed she cared. "He's not a hearts and flowers kind of guy. Some men write poetry, some send you flowers, and then men like Grim threaten to kill anyone who touches you." She swung her legs around and sat up. "Tess, I think it's time."

Tess flipped her hair over her shoulder and ran her fingers through her soft curls. "It's been long enough since the desert."

I looked at both of them in confusion. "Time for what?"

"This shade of lipstick," Sienna eyed Minnie as she held up a tube of lipstick, "would match your dress perfectly."

"You know what?" I took it from her and headed for the vanity, "I don't even want to know. I have enough going on inside here, anyway." I circled my head with my finger.

"Insert Rail." Rail laughed as he popped out of nowhere with a joint between his fingers. "Some people call me a gift from God, but we all know I spread the breath of the Devil." He puffed out a smoke ring, and I chuckled and reached out. I took a hit from it, and just as I sucked the warm smoke into my lungs, I caught Minnie's glance at Tess. What were these three up to?

The party was held in an enormous room on the first floor of Hill House. Grim told me they'd go all out for this party, but no one could have prepared me for when I walked down the hallway to the top of the stairs and looked down.

The color theme was black and gold, and their family crest was hung proudly above the stage where a live band played. Black and deep red roses graced the tables, gold silk wrapped the chairs, tall pillars filled with water and gold dust sparkled and created what could only be described as a dream-like environment. Elio wore black, and Sienna dressed in a lavish gold dress as they greeted arriving guests.

I took my time to enjoy the incredibly striking scene below as I stepped down onto the first stair with my hand on the rail. I felt radiant in my sheath-style silhouette black and lace gown. It hugged all the right places, and the slit was perfectly placed to reveal my thigh as I descended to the dance floor. My hair was swept up, with a few pieces free to soften the look.

"Kenna." Laurel was at my side in an instant. Her hands slid down my arms as she studied my face. "Are you hurt? We barely got back in time for the party. A truck had tipped over," she rambled. "I just want to make sure you're not hurt."

I smiled warmly at Grim's mom and loved that she cared enough to find me right away. "I'm fine. I just felt bad for Sienna. It was a close call."

"For both of you," she corrected. "Thank goodness you're okay." She dabbed at the corner of her eye. "I just needed to see you for myself." I leaned in and hugged her. I was sure the fear of losing someone else was fresh on her mind.

"I'm fine, really," I assured her, and she smiled and dabbed her eyes again.

"Good. In answer to your question earlier, I had Vinni check, and the couple who made the soup are fine. No one was hurt at the market."

"Oh, I'm so glad. They were lovely."

"Now," she patted my hand, "I insist you put all that aside and enjoy this wonderful evening. I'm going to go and check my makeup. Isn't this all so incredible?" She waved around at the room then touched my cheek before she rushed off, leaving me alone, or so I thought.

"Some requests are worth their weight in gold." Niccola grinned as he held out his arm to me.

I threaded my arm through his. "Requests?"

He patted my hand but didn't reply as he led me across the room. "Shall we get you something to drink?"

"Please." I nodded. As we walked, a few people stopped to ask who I was, and we filled them in.

"It's not often a beautiful new American face is invited and introduced at such an important gathering," Niccola explained as we moved through the crowd. "Not since Sienna has there been such excitement. Everyone is dying to know who you are and how you fit in. But most importantly, the vultures." He glared at a few older men who gawked at me. "Are you single and looking? They wonder."

"I feel like I'm on an episode of Bridgerton." I chuckled, and his brows pinched. Of course, he didn't follow, and I waved it off. "Just a popular television show back home."

"I see." He patted my hand again. Something told me Niccola didn't watch a lot of TV. "We'll I've been asked to bring you here, and…" His voice trailed off as we approached Minnie. She stood by the tables and wore one of her smiles, the one that always meant she was up to no good. Her pretty face looked positively devious. She nodded to someone, and I tried to spot who, but I only saw Sienna, who nodded again at someone else.

"Why do I feel I'm missing something?" I moved my hands to my hips when Niccola stood straight as if uneasy. "I might look little, but I've been known to be scrappy."

"I have no idea what you're talking about." He looked over my head and eyed someone.

"Pardon me," Mr. Hotness the guard from earlier

held out a gold hoop earring, "but this must have come off when you got out of the car."

I rolled my eyes in Minnie's direction. "Or did my friend over there," I pointed at Minnie, "give you that so you had a reason to come over here?"

His grin was impressive as he stepped toward me. He totally ignored Niccola's advice to keep moving. "Or maybe *I* asked her for the earring, so *I* had a reason to come over and speak to you." He took my hand and gently laid the piece of jewelry in my palm. "A woman like you deserves to be swept off her feet." He folded my fingers around the earring and turned my wrist to kiss the back of my hand.

It was all very romantic, at least it would be to some women, but as lovely as it all seemed, and I saw Minnie swoon, I was never the type to connect with that sort of thing.

His arm fell away when a hand clamped down on my hip and lips brushed my neck, drawing every nerve in my body to attention.

"There you are," Grim muttered against my skin. "Emiliano, I see you've met Kenna." *Emiliano.* So Mr. Hotness had a nice name.

He smiled and inclined his head to Grim then looked back at me. "*Mi scusi*, I didn't realize you belonged to anyone."

Me either.

"Now you do." Grim's lips brushed my ear. "Let's go, sweetheart."

I held up the earring. "Thanks for returning it." I smiled at Emiliano.

Grim pulled me away toward Minnie and Tess, who tapped their champagne glasses together with Cheshire Cat grins.

They were always causing shit.

His hand stayed firmly planted on my waist as we walked, and when we were far enough away from Emiliano, he cleared his throat. "I told you to stay away from him. I don't like to repeat myself." His face positively glowered.

I glanced around and saw an older couple gawking at Grim's expression. I smiled, not wanting to make a scene. "First, he approached *me,* and second, who are you to tell people who I belong to? We aren't even dating."

He spun me and pressed my back to his front then slid a hand around my stomach. "When I have you in my bed," he inched his fingers down and pressed them against me, "you belong to me and only me."

My jaw dropped, and I fought to curb my temper. "Says the man who has women dripping off of him whenever he wants."

"I'm not sleeping with any of them." His other hand slid up over my mouth. "Fight me all you want," he kissed my neck again, "but we both know it's where we'll end up. Where we belong."

I went from fuming anger to a sudden, deep sadness. Everything hit me at once, and my chest heaved at the realization that I wanted more from Grim. I wanted it all. His arms loosened when he sensed my change in attitude, and I whirled to look up at him.

His face fell when he saw the pure devastation written across my face. I didn't want to want Grim, but no matter how much I tried to push the feelings away, they somehow returned. He only saw me as a sex play-mate, and the worst thing was, that was all my fault.

He reached out, and I stepped back. "What the hell just happened?"

"Ladies and gentlemen, family and friends." Elio's voice carried through the mic and around the room. I looked over and found Minnie watching me with a concerned expression.

"Nothing." I swallowed back my heartache and tuned in to Elio.

"As you know from personal experience or from the articles released about our story, things have been anything but easy these past few years." The crowd chuckled. "After much hard work, we are proud to say the Capri blood will live on as the one true blood to rule all of Italy." He reached for Sienna and threaded his fingers through hers with a smile that would have melted the sun. "And the next in line for the thrones," he laughed, "are our twins Marabella and Filippo He waved to the stairs, and we all turned to see their two youngsters., Filippo dressed in a black tux with a gold tie and Marabella in a black dress with gold flakes in the tule around the skirt. They held hands as they took the stairs carefully, one by one. The crowd clapped and cheered, and their little faces glowed with excitement.

Something caught my attention, and I swung my gaze over to Trigger dressed in a handsome suit and a scowl. Tess smirked at me. I knew she loved it when he had to dress up because he positively hated every minute of it. I had to smile, and I gave her a wink before I moved my attention to the stage.

Elio handed Sienna the mic, and she waited for the crowd to quiet down. "I know many of you still wonder about the future. I've been asked many, many times which of our twins will rule one day, who will run the family business, but we've decided they can do it together, or perhaps one can take the lead, but only time will tell. That is for them to decide." She looked at Elio and mouthed "I love you," then looked back at the crowd. "I think our own story is proof that making such large decisions for someone else is not always the right choice."

"I love you, too." Elio stepped forward, dipped her backward, and kissed her. Everyone went nuts, and I got it. They were madly in love. I felt despair, then it turned to disgust. What was I thinking? This wasn't me. I didn't want to be in love.

My head swam, and it felt like the room was too small.

I vaguely heard Elio announce something before a video came on of an old woman with devilish eyes. She hissed at the camera. The screen then split in two, and another man came into view. He had heavy bags under his eyes as he begged for mercy.

"We have provided a viewing room for those that wish to see the final moments of the Coppola bloodline." Elio held up his fist. "History will be made on this day.

I decided I'd skip this one. A double murder wasn't something I wanted to view on any given day.

"I need some air," I muttered at Grim. I knew he couldn't come after me because Elio was about to call him on stage. He'd warned Grim to be ready, as he wanted to thank him for his help.

"Hey, babe, where's the fire?" Rail took a sip of his beer and soaked the cigarette that hung from his lips. He too was dressed up, minus the biker boots that peeked out from under his pants.

"Restroom." I didn't give much more as I rounded a corner and walked down a few halls then found a door that had been left open to reveal a lovely garden.

The garden was a great place to think. There were so many little pathways and turns. I was able to take a deep breath and mentally kick my own ass for being that person. Falling in love, that just wasn't me. Then why did I feel the way I did, damn it? The soft earth under my heels made it easy to walk, and the smell of the fresh flowers helped ease the storm inside.

Deep breaths, Kenna.

It was then that I tuned in to a strange sound. I started to follow where it came from but stopped short when I caught sight of Vinni in a passionate kiss with another man.

I had no idea he enjoyed men. I turned around slowly, not wanting to break their moment, to find Sienna in front of me.

"Hey." She looked over my shoulder, and I could tell by the way she smiled she was aware of what was going on around the other side of the trees. "They think they're fooling me," she whispered and motioned for me to follow her farther away from them, "but I know they've had something for years now."

"You know who Vinni's with?"

"*Sí.*" She chuckled but didn't go any further, which I honestly respected. People should be entitled to their privacy.

"Shouldn't you be on stage right now?"

She shrugged. "Grim and Elio can handle it. The two of them could win over a priest to commit a sin, so…" She laughed at her dark joke. "Frankly, I don't need to waste another breath on Rosa and Tieri's death.

Once it's truly done, that will be enough for me." There was a lightness to her voice. "Knowing those two are finally gone forever will bring renewed peace for our family." She looked concerned. "I saw you run out. Are you all right?"

"I'm fine. I just needed a little air." I turned away to look at some flowers.

"I heard you met Emiliano."

I eyed her. "You heard? Or were you roped into something by those two matchmaking friends of mine?"

"He's not hard on the eyes," she side-stepped my comment, "and he's also very single."

I crossed my arms and huffed out a breath. "Honestly, between everything going on back in Vegas, our close call, and… and, well, Grim, I think I'm about done right now. Men, especially single ones are very low on my priority list." I sagged onto the bench, feeling the weight of my life press down on me.

She studied me for a moment then touched a purple flower that hung off a bush. "I'm sorry, Kenna, that you got wrapped up in my life here. What happened at the market is just part of it all."

"Sadly, it's not overly new for me either."

She sat next to me. "No, I guess not." Her nose scrunched as she looked at me. "Have you been getting much sleep? No matter how many times I've been shot at, it takes its toll."

"Grim tires me out," I confessed, "but I'm fine in the sleep department. And yeah, this whole thing has been utterly exhausting." I rubbed my forehead and sighed.

She stood and held out a hand. "Will you do something for me?"

"Sure. What?" I pushed to my feet and took her hand.

"Just humor me, okay? Come with me."

I followed her back inside as thoughts of a soft pillow began to sound like a lovely idea.

The next morning came all too fast. The sun beat through the windows and woke me out of my deep sleep. Sienna had given me a tour of her library on the way upstairs the night before after I did as she asked. She said it was the perfect place if I needed time alone. She brought me a cozy blanket and urged me to rest there.

Tears prickled my eyes when I felt my phone vibrate in my pocket. Four missed calls from Grim and an endless number of text messages, also from Grim. Sienna had promised to explain my absence and make it okay with the others. I had been too exhausted to entertain the idea of going back to the party. I needed time to think.

I slipped out the side door and froze when I heard a voice.

"Why someone would look so guilty leaving a library makes me very curious as to what you might have read." Vinni grinned.

"It's a gift." I smiled.

He took my arm and walked with me. A fancy breakfast table was set outside the open garden doors, and Andrea and Laurel enjoyed coffee in the lovely setting. Vinni gave me a hug and retreated into the house.

I straightened my shoulders and tried not to show I had shed tears the night before. "You're all up early." I smiled at them. It was just after seven thirty. "I figured you'd be tired after such a successful celebration."

"Most everyone is still sleeping, but we're on grandkid duty." Andrea smiled proudly. "We wanted to let their parents have the morning off."

"That's kind." I squinted at the sun and thought how nice it felt on my face.

Laurel slipped her hand into mine. "Are you feeling all right? You left the party early."

"Yes." I looked down. "I think yesterday took a toll on me." A shiver ran through me. "But I'm feeling much better."

"I'm so sorry all that happened. It must have been very frightening for you." Andrea shook her head.

"It's not like it's something I haven't been through

before." I huffed a breath and patted her shoulder. "Please don't worry about it. I think I could use a walk in this beautiful sunshine, though."

"Of course, dear." Andrea smiled. "It's a lovely day." Then her face turned serious. "Just don't venture off the grounds."

"I can promise you I won't."

I waved and headed down the backside of the hill out toward a field that called my name. It was yellow for as far as I could see, the sunflowers swaying in the wind like ripples in the water.

The first row of giant sunflowers cast their shadows against the rich earth, and as I pushed through them, there was something comforting about the way they closed around me and seemed to shield me from the outside world. I snapped a photo from between the vibrant yellow petals as I looked up at the puffy clouds that stood out against the bright blue sky. I breathed in the heavenly scent of damp earth and flowers and kept walking deeper into the field.

The farther I went, the lighter I felt. My head seemed to let go of the heaviness, and my thoughts began to untangle. I knew the truth needed to be faced at some point, but I let my mind slowly find its way.

Sienna's kindness came to me, and I couldn't help but shed a tear at her expression the night before. *"We're more alike than you might realize, Kenna. Remember that whenever you feel alone."*

I loved my girls, but Sienna was different, quieter, and insightful. She was a survivor. She'd been put through hell in her life yet had come out of it all with soft edges. I could relate to that. Minnie would have torn my stalker to little bits and stomped on them and Tess may have blown his head off, but I didn't have that inner animal inside. I was feisty and could deal with horny, difficult men, but that was about the extent of any killer instinct. I hadn't forgotten that I'd killed someone, and it would stay with me forever, but in my heart, I knew it had been accidental. I had only wanted to talk to him. Matt Myers would always haunt my dreams.

I brushed my fingertips along the stems as I wove through the sunshine-colored flowers, deep in thought. My life had taken many turns in the last few months, and I wasn't sure what the next few would look like. Maybe I should take the job with Yen Hong and…I stepped out into a clearing and saw a beautiful old church across an old, beaten road.

I listened for cars then crossed the road and followed a grassy path to where little steps led up to the doors. By the look of the place, it hadn't been used in a very long time, but I wondered if Piero and Andrea had been married there. I could imagine the sound of people singing. Perhaps it had been here for hundreds of years, and my imagination saw it as it could have once been. It was so peaceful. It took a few tries, but I managed to open the door and step inside.

My phone lit up and spoiled the atmosphere. I glanced at it; it was a text message from Zara. I ignored it, but it reminded me I was holding a handy flashlight. I turned it on and shined it around the room. Dust and droppings were scattered around the floor, and the windowsills showed evidence that an animal or two lived there at some point. I moved down the aisle and spotted an old hymnal tucked in the back of one of the pews. I couldn't help but wonder how many people had cracked open its spine and sung along to a long-ago service.

As I moved toward the podium, I admired the simple cross that had been carved and placed against the wall. I was entranced by the old building, and it felt wonderful to let myself explore. Curiosity got the best of me, and I followed the winding staircase to the very top. Sunlight streamed and dust flickered in swirly patterns as I looked up. Two large copper bells with an old ship rope hung in the center of the platform. I wasn't a fan of heights, but I'd been brave enough to try the zipline in Vegas with a client a couple times. I shuffled over to the edge and looked over.

The view was spectacular. The Capri property was like a patchwork quilt. Yellows, greens, and browns swept right to the horizon. I snapped a few pictures to preserve the memory, but as I held the phone up to center the house in the middle of the screen, something moved into the frame. I lowered it to see a man looking around. He seemed to search for something…or someone. I was instantly on alert. A second man popped out of the sunflowers right where I had been earlier, and he too seemed to be searching. He stayed low as if he did not to want to let the first man see him.

Then another man appeared, and another. My heart began to thump like a drum. A call pushed through, and I quickly tapped the button to answer it and crouched so no one could spot me.

"Hey, girl, I have a sexy-ass bikini on, a morning margarita here at Elio's house, and no one's ar—"

"Tess," I whispered harshly, "Tess, there are men here." I tried to get my words out as a painful dose of fear raced through me.

"Shit," I heard glass break, "where are you?"

"I'm at a—"

"Jesse!" she screamed into the microphone. "It's Kenna. She's—where are you, Kenna?"

"A church." I heard the door open below, and I squeezed my eyes shut and took a breath to calm myself. "At the end of the flower field, there's an old church," I whispered. "They're close, but they don't know I'm up here."

"Find Grim!" I heard Jesse bark at Tess, then the phone made a sound, and he took over the call. "Kenna, stay low and keep out of sight." I nodded like he could see me, but there was no place I could hide except to stay put, and it wouldn't keep me hidden for long. "Can you work your way back to the house? Or to a road?"

"No." I pulled my knees to my chest as I heard his shoes pound the pebbles. "Do you think they think I'm Sienna?"

"I'm thinking not." He sounded like he jumped over something, and I stifled a squeak when I heard a crash at the bottom of the stairs. Suddenly, footsteps echoed up the steps, and I knew I had moments left. I pressed myself into a shadow and tried to make myself smaller.

"Jesse," I was panicked but somehow managed to keep my voice low, "they're here." I licked my lips, and my mind spun with all the things they could do to me. "Jesse, I need to tell you something."

"I'm here," he cut me off with a pant. "Where are you?"

Tears ran down my face. "I'm up in the tower," I screamed as my legs were yanked and I was dragged straight out on my back. I screamed so hard that it felt like the tissue was torn from my lungs. I kicked hard as hands grabbed my waist.

"Smile, *bella*." A phone was thrust in my face. I screamed and bucked as I felt his grip tighten. He tried to take a picture, and I knocked his knife away from my throat. It cut into my collarbone but missed my artery. He grunted something in Italian and squeezed my wrist hard enough to fracture a bone. I screamed again, knowing Jesse was nearby.

This man was skilled; he knew exactly what I was going to do before I did. In one smooth motion, he had zip-ties around my wrists, and I was pulled to my feet.

A shot rang out, and he flinched.

Jesse!

My attacker slumped and fell back down the steps, but before I could take a breath, another man's head appeared.

No!

THIRTEEN

GRIM

"**M**orning," Brick grunted from behind his steaming mug of coffee. "Just brewed it." He pointed at the counter, and I poured myself a cup. Sienna came in and reached for an apple. "Heard your old lady didn't come to bed last night." I shot him a glare, and he chuckled as Sienna turned and hurried back out. "What'd you do?"

"No clue, and she's hardly my *old lady*," I growled. I knew bikers referred to their girlfriends as old ladies, but that description hardly fit Kenna.

"My fat clam, you don't know what you did." Minnie came in and rode my ass as per normal. "You're so fucking blind, man."

"Oh," I sipped my coffee, "you're awake. Great." I lifted a brow at her.

Brick grabbed a fist full of her ass and kissed her hard. "Share what you know, woman."

"Fine." She leaned over the island, and her bracelets hit the marble top with a clank. "Truth, Gates, if you don't want her, fine, because that fine-ass man, Emiliano, has his eyes on her. And let me tell you, you American men have nothing on the Italian accent."

"It's true." Rail nodded from behind Brick. "They sound very sexy."

"Good to know," Vinni called from another room. He came out last year as being bisexual and was fully embracing it.

"I don't do dicks." Rail looked huffy, then stood straight when Piero and Trigger came in with smirks on their faces. "Morning, sir."

Trigger rubbed his face. "The shit I hear I from your mouth."

"Good morning," Piero said to us as he plucked a muffin from the basket on the counter. "If Kenna didn't go to your bed last night, it's for one of two reasons." I glanced at Brick. He loved that Elio's father had jumped right in. "You somehow made her *arrabbiato*. That means angry." He laughed at Brick's face. "You American's might say you, perhaps, 'screwed up' or—" His face went to stone like he heard something. "Niccola?"

"Yeah, I heard it, too." Niccola moved to the door; the mood instantly shifted. "Trigger."

"Grim!" Tess's voice broke as she burst through the door. "Grim! Trigger!"

Trigger was already on his feet as we all hurried toward a frantic Tess.

"It's Kenna." She swallowed hard as Trigger pulled her in close. "They're after her."

"Where?" Trigger asked the question I was trying to form.

"A church by the end of the property somewhere. Jesse went after her!" Niccola ran, and I followed hard on his heels.

I saw Piero jump in the car and peel out of the driveway as the rest of us raced down the hill. My heart pounded like a wicked drum against my ribs, and the vision of someone after Kenna all but took my sanity. I slipped on the wet dirt. Damn, I wished I'd worn sneakers. I caught my balance and kept moving.

"Head straight!" Niccola pointed ahead through the tall sunflowers. "I'll circle around." I picked up speed, and just as I broke free of the shadows, I heard her scream.

"Grim, help!" Her cry nearly brought me to my knees. I shaded my eyes and looked toward the sound and saw her bent over the ledge of the bell tower. A shadowy figure behind her held a gun that glinted in the sunlight, and it was pointed at her head.

A man hollered, and I saw Trigger take a swing at his face. I rushed through the door and found Jesse taking on two guys inside. I grabbed a wooden chair and smashed it into the back of one man's head then jammed the broken piece into his neck.

Bang! A gun went off above us. My insides twisted, and my murderous head went darker.

"Stairs." Niccola pointed, and I beat him to the narrow stone staircase. Two bullets were fired at us. We ducked as stone chips flew but continued up the steps. I held up my weapon with two hands.

A man flew down toward us. I flatted to the wall, and he collided with Niccola, and they tumbled down together.

I didn't even look back; my whole focus was on what was going on up top. I stopped short and carefully raised my head so I could see over the edge of the opening. He was ready for me. He had Kenna by the scruff of the neck with one hand, and his other held his weapon, and it was now aimed at my head. The expression on the guy's face told me he wouldn't hesitate to push her to her death. He forced her head and upper body over the stone wall.

She turned her head to look at me. The fucking bastard had wrapped a gag around her mouth, and her hands were zip-tied in front of her. She fought hard and desperately, her bound hands held high to protect herself. I saw her face wore a mask of determination and fury. She was not going to go easily.

He showed his gap-toothed smile. "She screamed, and you came. So, the rumors are true. You do care for her."

"You missed your mark at the square yesterday." I tried to turn the attention away from Kenna. "She's not who you want."

He tilted his head at me as Kenna pushed against him. "*Sí*, the princess is always our mark, but this time, this one," he loosened his grip, and she screamed as she went forward another few inches, "this one is a bonus, *signore*. One I was very happy to win."

"Who put out the mark on her? Tell me, and I'll pay you double." I hoped he would go for it.

"She smells so good." He got cocky and made a show of smelling her hair, and I catapulted forward and grabbed the rope that hung under the church bell and swung toward them. My legs wrapped around Kenna, and I pulled her back with me. The momentum threw the guy off balance, and he pinwheeled wildly then dropped with a scream through the opening into the church below us. His scream was cut short as he hit the pulpit.

The vibration of the bells above us rattled my brain as I prayed the old rope would hold us. I held on tight as Kenna had a death grip on my legs. We dangled there until Trigger's head appeared above the stairs.

"You fuckin' rang?" He turned his shit-eating grin on me.

"For fuck's sake, pull this damn thing over and grab Kenna before both of us end up down there!"

He pulled Kenna up to the ledge then took his sweet time settling her before he helped me.

I untied her gag as Trigger reached out with his knife and cut the zip ties that held her hands. Then he nodded at me and disappeared down the stairs. I held my anger as I pressed the gag to the deep cut on her collarbone. Her top was soaked with blood, and I knew it must be painful. I was ready to explode, but she didn't need to see that side of me at the moment.

"It's okay," I soothed her as she let go of her feelings and sobbed with relief and shock in my arms. "It's okay," I repeated and kissed her head as I squeezed her hard. "It's all right now."

"Is she okay?" Jesse stood at the top of the steps.

"Got a pretty nasty cut and a bad scare, but all things considered." I huffed a breath to release some of my own tension.

Jesse licked a cut lip and swiped a hand across his battered face and nodded. "We should talk."

Kenna barely spoke a word as I helped her out of the church. We walked past bodies and blood and got into Piero's car.

"Oh, Kenna!" Mom's face flushed when she saw

Kenna's state, but she stayed back, knowing not to fuss. "Grim?"

"Our doctor is already here." Piero pointed to the other room. "He's set up in the den." Minnie and Mom headed in that direction with their arms around Kenna.

"Living room," I directed, and everyone followed me through the other door.

Tess and Sienna sat on the couch while Trigger, Brick, Rail, and Morgan stood behind them.

"Three different phones." Jesse placed each one on the table. "All had the same info on them about the hit. Kenna was definitely the mark." I squeezed the top of the wingback chair and tried to fight the darkness that begged to take over.

Elio came in with Niccola and Vinni. "I've made some calls. Give me twenty-four hours, and my people will find out what this is about. I will leave no stone unturned, my friend. I'm sorry this has happened while you're my guests." His face was flushed with anger.

"I've doubled the security," Piero added, "and we have checkpoints set up. No one can drive by without us knowing it."

"I thought—" Tess said, "I thought this place was crawling with security."

"Most likely one of our men was paid to look the other way." Niccola stepped back and sat on the piano bench. "We pay them well, but we have learned money often outweighs loyalty."

Sienna stood. "Or in some cases they are threatened. The hit men find out where their families are and force them to look the other way."

"That's true." Niccola nodded. "Regardless, men who kill for money are ruthless, and there's a certain thrill they get if they win the mark. Bragging rights, as you Americans say. We can hire all the security in the world, but if enough money is offered, they come out of the woodwork and will do whatever it takes."

"It's true," Sienna moved to where Elio stood, "and where Kenna walked, in spite of the flowers, she was vulnerable, as there are several spots where she could be seen from the road."

I closed my eyes and wished we were back in Vegas where I was in control. "We should leave."

"If I may," Andrea pulled her sweater around her shoulders, "that young woman has been through a lot. Maybe give her a day to rest. She's hurt and upset. She will need to eat, and I'm sure our doctor will give her something for the pain. I ask you, please, don't rush her."

"Yeah, let's not thrust her from this hell into another back home before she can catch a freakin' breath," Tess added. I nodded. She was right. At this point, if Cameron even so much as breathed in my direction, I'd shove my fist down his throat and pull out his heart.

Mom and Minnie entered the room with Kenna. She looked exhausted and had a bandage across her shoulder and collarbone. The idea of the pain she suffered slashed through me. I allowed a little of the darkness to creep in. It taunted me to let it completely take over, and I fought to stay where I was while the girls fussed around Kenna.

"He gave her a shot of something," Minnie held her hand lovingly, "and some stitches, but she's got this."

Andrea immediately stood and kissed Kenna's cheek. "I'll get you something to eat, my dear. Pain medication is not good on an empty stomach." Andrea left the room with Piero behind her. The others started to talk quietly.

"Kenna," Jesse squatted on the floor in front of her, "on the phone, you said you needed to tell me something, and it sounded urgent. What was that?" *Interesting.*

Kenna looked away. "It was nothing."

"Kenna, you were very scared, and, in my experience, when someone's deathly afraid they make a confession," he went on. "Call it intuition, but is there something you're not telling us? Something you're holding back?"

"No."

"Maybe something about your father?" he pressed, and I moved closer.

"Wow," she batted her eyelashes like she was trying to hold back tears, "after all this, you think I'm holding on to secrets about my father?"

"Are you?" fell from my mouth, and I instantly regretted it. Her face twisted, first in hurt, then in anger. The whole room went silent.

"No! You mistrusting asshole," she snarled at me and stood. "I'm not holding secrets about my father!"

Mom also stood. "Grim, Jesse, stop. This is not the time for this."

Sienna stepped forward. "Kenna, maybe you should—"

"No," Kenna threw a pained look at Sienna, "please."

I knew it. "So, there is something going on?"

"What do I have to do to earn your trust?" Kenna's face was twisted in anger, but the pain was what I could see the most.

"Just tell me what's going on," I demanded.

"I'm pregnant!" The entire room gasped, and a sudden unfamiliar feeling went through me. "There. You wanted my secret. I'm pregnant," she repeated.

Many things ran through my head in that instant, but somehow Benny's fucking face was right there, and I spoke without a filter. "Is it mine?" Color drained from her face, and I could practically hear her heart break from where I stood.

Shit.

"We weren't exclusive," I tried to explain, but I needed to know, "and you had a few dates with Benny."

"Fucking asshole." Minnie glared at me, and Brick put a hand on her shoulder.

Kenna shook her head and muttered something. Then she raised her chin, and I knew I wasn't going to like what came next.

"Unlike you, Grim," her tone was now very calm, "I'm not a whore." Her words struck home. "Benny is a friend, and I told you that. I drew the line in the sand from the very start that I was not interested in being with anyone but you." She chuckled darkly. "How stupid was I?"

"That's it!" Mom waved her hands. "Everyone out!" She looked at me and shook her head. I knew she wasn't happy with me. "Go clear your head. It might do you some good." I moved quickly out the door, and Mom closed it, leaving her and Kenna alone. I moved across the hall and let my back hit the wall as her words echoed around my brain. *Pregnant.*

"She only found out last night." Sienna came up to me and joined me on the wall. "I spotted the signs and had her take a test." She smiled. "You know what she did when she read the results?"

"What?" Did I really want to know?

"For a few moments, she allowed herself to be happy. She cried and smiled and hoped it would be a boy. She wanted to look into his eyes and see you." She chuckled. "Or maybe she just wants you to meet your match."

"That sounds more like her," I admitted, then something strange went through me, and I pushed off the wall.

"What?"

I didn't answer; instead, I headed back through the doors. "Mom, I need a moment." I looked at Kenna, but she turned her face away from me.

"Okay?" she asked, and Kenna reluctantly nodded. "Think before you speak, son," she muttered as she walked by me.

I waited for the door to close before I moved toward her. She shot up from where she sat, dried her tears, then poked a finger in my chest.

"I know this wasn't planned or, hell, even wanted, but this is what you get when you have unprotected sex. A lot of unprotected sex." Her expression pierced like a dagger. "I'll sign whatever you want me to, because I'm not after your money, but we made something, you and me." Her hand moved tenderly over her stomach, and I could see the love she already had for the life inside her. "I intend to keep it," she poked me again, "and we don't need you."

"First," I carefully grabbed her wrist and pulled her close to me, "you caught me completely off guard, and I'm sorry I reacted the way I did. I want you to know I was perfectly aware of what I was doing, not wearing a condom with you. Maybe at first, I couldn't see why, but it didn't take long to see that I wanted you all to myself. I wanted to feel everything with you." I slowly let go but stepped closer to her. "We're sexual beasts, you and me, and we bring out a darkness in each other that we both need. You give me something I could never give up, not for anything." I drank in her beauty. "Second, you will sign nothing because what I have is yours, and what you have," I slid my hand down over her chest then to blanket her stomach, "is all mine." She blinked a few times as my words sank in.

"Grim, we're not ready for this." She waved between us and started to panic. She stepped back and put some distance between us. "Christ, the only thing we have in common is that…that dark sex."

"Kenna, that night in New Orleans when we were dancing, I know you felt something, because I felt it too."

"So, what if I did?" She whirled around.

"Admit it, Kenna, you have feelings for me."

"No, Grim, I'm in love with you," she blurted, and she shook her head in shock at her own words, "and I hate that I am."

"Well, I'm in love with you, too," I tossed back,

annoyed that she didn't want to be, "so get the fuck over it."

"I don't think you are." She looked at me boldly, and I glared at her assumption. "You don't hurt the ones you love," she hissed. "You don't lash out at the ones you love, and you certainly don't sleep around on them."

"I didn't sleep around," I assured her. "But, like you, I didn't want to fall in love!" I yelled at her then lowered my voice. "I tried everything to get you off my mind, but nothing worked, and the reason I took Leo's death out on you was because, it was true, I wanted you to hurt the way I did. I hoped it would drive you away, but it only entwined us together more."

"See," she whispered, "we're not good together. Maybe this is where we should end things, for the sake of our child."

I chuckled darkly. The woman was mad.

I tucked my hands in my pockets and closed the gap between us. She stepped back until she hit the wall. I hovered over her until she looked up.

"I've fallen in love for the first time in my life, and I have no plans of doing it again." I tipped her chin with both hands so she couldn't look away. "You're mine, Kenna, so nothing's going to stop me from taking you." I looked down and kissed her jaw softly. "Both of you."

"Is that so?" She swallowed hard.

I groaned and kissed my favorite spot, careful to avoid her cut. "And you're going to be my wife."

She chuckled, but it turned into a moan. "You're crazy."

"You haven't seen crazy yet." I brushed my lips over hers. She smiled, but she carried the day heavily in her expression, and I knew she was mentally beat. "Now," I took her hand and stepped back, "I want you to get some sleep. We're leaving tomorrow."

"I won't argue with that." She followed me outside where Mom paced.

"Is everything okay?"

I smiled and kissed her on the top of her head. "Everything's fine. We're having a baby, and we're going to get married."

Her face broke out into an excited smile, and she covered her cheeks. "Really?" She looked at Kenna. "Is this what you want?" I glanced down at Kenna and raised a brow, then she rolled her eyes.

"Yes, it is."

Mom jumped in the air. "I'm so happy!" As strange as it all was, I knew my family needed some happiness, and maybe this was it.

"We'll discuss everything later. First, Kenna needs to rest." I pulled Kenna to follow.

She yawned as I tucked her into bed and closed the blinds, then she leaned over and clicked on the light.

"Um," she stumbled and rubbed her arm, "you're not leaving the house, right?"

"No, I'll be right downstairs. Elio, Trigger, and I have some business to discuss. We need to know who's behind the hit on you." I set a bottle of water on the nightstand and looked at the pill bottle the doctor gave her.

"Yeah, I know." She looked at me. "I wasn't going to take those. It's just that I didn't want Minnie to know I was pregnant yet."

"You must be uncomfortable." I looked at the bandage on her collarbone.

She shrugged. "I'm more scared than anything else." I nodded and removed my suit jacket and shoes. "What are you doing?"

"You're scared," I leaned back against the headboard to lie next to her, "and you need sleep. Now you can close your eyes, and I'll be right here."

"Really?" She smiled and rolled into me.

"Really." I wrapped an arm around her as she rested her head on my stomach. "Now, go to sleep."

She half chuckled. "Always so bossy."

"That will never change, sweetheart."

Kenna slept well into the following morning, and the next day she dozed the whole way home. Mom assured me it was normal, given all she'd been through, but I felt uneasy, especially with the storm we were about to walk back into. Things had changed between us, and with a baby on the way, I suddenly saw danger everywhere. I became hyperaware of everything.

Elio, Niccola, and Vinni decided they'd travel back with us and help as much as they could. I thought they knew I needed my friends. What I really needed was to know who the hell put out a hit on Kenna.

"Hey, Grim?" Vinni joined me in the back of the plane. "I wanted to run something by you."

"Sure." I closed my laptop and sipped my drink.

Vinni looked up at his brother then back at me. "As you might know, my father wants to hand his part of the family business over to Niccola."

"I heard."

"I'm thrilled for him. Trouble is he's pushing back." He stumbled. "I mean, given what we discovered years back, I think he's reassessing." I nodded at that. I knew Niccola had taken quite a blow back then when he discovered the truth about his family. Though it was bad, it came with an unlikely surprise. "I really want this for him. He needs it. I don't look at him any differently. I never could. I wish I was sure he believed me. Anyway, for Niccola to see his true worth, I think he needs to stand on his own for a bit. I need to be taken out of the picture, just for a while."

"I understand that."

"I discussed it with Elio, and we both think since Secrets is basically ready to launch, maybe I could stay behind and help work on Elio's behalf for a bit."

"The Capri family's investment in Secrets would benefit from that," I agreed. "You never have to ask, Vinni. We're family, and you're always welcome."

Vinni's shoulders sagged with relief. Whatever he was feeling about Niccola must really be bothering him. They were incredibly close, and I knew their family had been through a lot since Sienna entered their lives years back. Some scars never completely healed.

"An extra set of trusted eyes can be invaluable."

"Thanks for that." He rubbed his face, and I saw some of the stress leave his shoulders. "How do you feel about Kenna being pregnant?"

"I think my plan worked."

"Entrapment?" He raised a surprised brow.

"No," I chuckled, "not quite like that." I bit my lip. "But it certainly ensured she'd stay mine."

"You love her?"

I let out a long breath. "Yeah, as fucked up as it is, I really do."

He grabbed his drink and finished it off. "I envy you, Grim." His smile didn't reach his eyes, and it told me he was dealing with more than just his brother. "You found your person."

"You haven't?" I didn't say it, but I knew he was seeing someone.

He shrugged. "I just don't know what I want."

"That'll come," I assured him. "Something will happen, and you'll see things more clearly."

He nodded a few times and stared at the floor then seemed to shake it off. He raised his drink to me. "To clarity." I tapped his glass, and he pushed up from the chair and left me to mull over our conversation.

When I arrived at my hotel, I saw Secrets in a new light. I wondered if I might get a house one day. Good God, what was happening to me? I shook my head.

"Jesse?" I lowered my voice as he moved to my side. "Are the men in place to watch over Kenna?"

"Yes, and as ordered, they're out of sight."

"Good." I'd warned Kenna about what I was doing and how she wasn't to leave the property without me or Jesse knowing. Shockingly, she didn't protest. I felt some progress had been made between us.

I smiled as my new dog walker greeted us in the lobby. They'd just come back from their walk.

"Mr. Gates, welcome back." He seemed uneasy. It didn't surprise me; most people were at the start of employment with me. I patted the boys, who were pleased to see me. Leal whined when he saw Kenna, and she got right down and hugged him then Zhar. "Shall I take them upstairs, sir?"

"No," I unsnapped their leashes and handed them to him, "that's all."

The man looked at Kenna, and I cleared my throat as he gawked at her. "Yes, right. Well, have a nice day."

We headed to my floor where our lunch awaited. I spotted what I was waiting for on the counter. I quickly swiped it up and tucked it away in my pocket.

"I want you to move your things up here," I ordered as I pointed and gave the command for the dogs to go to their beds, "I don't like the thought of you staying anywhere but here."

"Isn't that moving a little fast, Grim?" She disappeared into the bedroom.

I lifted the lid off the roasted chicken. "I want what I want, Kenna. You'd be wise to remember that."

"What will your girlfriend think?" She dripped with sarcasm as she stepped into the room in a new dress. It was off one shoulder, and the style conveniently covered her bandage. "Come on, Grim. That's just asking for trouble."

"I only keep Jenelle around because of her father." I pulled out her chair and pointed at it. "There was a time I thought we could be more, I have to admit. I just never seemed to want to take it to the next level." I waited for her to join me, but instead she threaded an earring on. "I think that speaks volumes for us. Now, sit."

Kenna checked the time, which pissed me off. "I can't. I have to meet Salazar at the tables in fifteen."

"No. I cleared your schedule."

She pulled out a lipstick as I glared at her. "I know you did, but I re-filled it."

"The fuck you did." My temper rose. "You went around me?"

"Yes, like you did me." She snapped her mirror closed.

I moved to stand in front of her. "Kenna, you could've been killed in Italy. Someone's after you. I'm not saying you need to live your life in hiding. I'm just saying we need to be smart with this."

She tucked her mirror away and let out a heavy sigh. "All right, I hear you. I'll spend most of my time here at Secrets, but I'm not about to give up my main clients. Hong, Salazar, and Harris are too important to me. I have a lot of time invested in them."

I didn't like it, but I respected it. "I'll agree to that, but when you're at Indulge, you'll have extra men assigned to you. They won't get in your way." I waved a hand at her expression. "I'll tell them to be discrete."

"Fine." She looked at me and tried to read my mind. "Are you jealous that I work mostly with men?" She cocked a saucy brow at me.

I laughed darkly and shook my head. She had some balls on her. I took my time and moved around the table and stroked my chin as I thought.

"Maybe I should explain it to you like this, *sweetheart*." I slowly stalked toward her and watched her gorgeous throat contract. "I've killed more men than I can keep track of, and the thrill I get when the heart stops beating is like an adrenaline shot straight to my vein. I feed off the bad stuff in this world, and I'm just looking for an excuse to indulge myself." I stopped when I was in front of her. "And when it comes to you, I wouldn't give it a second thought if I had to dispose of a body if they tried anything with you. I'm possessive and protective of anything that's mine."

"I know what to do if someone tries anything with me. Anyway, I never let them get too close."

"And they won't, because you'll be wearing this." I reached into my pocket and pulled out a box and opened it. Her face dropped when she looked at the engagement ring. The huge cushion cut diamond was set in white gold. Sienna helped me pick it out before we all left for the airport, and my jeweler had it ready by the time we arrived home.

"I can't wear that!"

"Why? You agreed to get married to me."

"Yes, and I will, but, Grim, this is huge." She reached out and touched it. "I mean, it's absolutely gorgeous. I'm supposed to appear single but not available." She looked a little panicky for some reason. "Once people see that ring, it'll spread like wildfire. I think it's fair to say I need a moment without the spotlight being on me. Just give me some time, okay?" Her eyes pleaded.

"Hey, slow down." I smiled and decided to approach the topic a little more softly. It took great effort, and I silently applauded myself. Besides, she had a point; she needed a breather. "That's fair." Her eyes widened at my understanding. "But think about what else this means." I grinned. "This goes both ways, sweetheart. You wearing this means I'm off the market too."

"Yes, it does." Her expression changed to a darker one, and she pressed her chest into mine. Slowly, her hand descended and found me. I fought not to moan. "That's right, babe, because if I see you flirting with another chick, I'll chop your balls off, sauté them up, and feed them to the boys."

"That's my girl." I slid the ring on her finger as my other hand wrapped around hers and pumped my painful erection. "Marry me?"

"Yes."

FOURTEEN

SIMON

It was strange to wake up to a gentle alarm as opposed to the obnoxious, deafening screech that tore us from sleep in prison. It had gone off for a minute straight.

I opened one eye and tapped the snooze button, but instead of falling back to sleep, I grinned because I could hit that button and take a few more minutes if I chose to. I'd taken for granted the simple pleasures and choices you made when you were free. When I found myself in the bathroom mirror, my grin turned into a big, fat smile that stretched from ear to ear. Happy tears fell when I stepped into the shower as I realized I had it all to myself. My smile remained as I sipped a coffee that actually tasted like coffee. I sat in front of the bay window and enjoyed the feeling of the warm sun on my face.

I was finally free.

Not only was I free, but all charges had been magically dropped. How? I had no idea, but I sure as hell wasn't going to question it.

I hung my terrycloth robe on the hook in my closet and got dressed for the day. Just as I grabbed my house keys and coffee tumbler, I felt my phone buzz in my hand. The screen read XX.

"Hello?" I wasn't sure how to address him.

"Have you left yet?" His voice was as strong over the phone as his presence was in person.

"I was just leaving."

"Good. You remember that you're my eyes and ears in that place. Also, you need to keep him in check. He's a loose cannon and makes impulsive decisions, not to mention his mouth is unpredictable."

"I understand." I pushed my glasses up my nose. I had to get them tightened.

"Very well," he cleared his throat, "I'll be in touch."

"All right. Have a good day." The line went dead, and I got my head on straight as I stepped out into the Nevada desert heat.

The office was only a short walk, and I made it there in a matter of ten minutes. When I came through the front doors, I caught sight of a gorgeous young woman who smiled warmly at me.

"You must be Simon." She shoved a handful of files in my arms. "I'm Calli. Dad's in his office," she jerked her

thumb over her shoulder, "and my late-as-ever sister is on her way in about ten minutes to bitch about last night's family dinner." She huffed and looked around. "That's your desk across from mine, when I'm not in school. We have a client coming in at noon that you need to be prepped on, and the coffee maker tastes like shit, so use it at your own risk." She finally took a breath with her hands on her hips. "Welcome to team Tame."

My phone alerted me of a text, and it abruptly shot me out of my memory. I knew it wouldn't be Cameron. I knew where he was; everyone did. He was terrified of being alone ever since Leo's death, and he announced his presence loudly whenever he was in public. I still couldn't understand why the Gates family hadn't taken him out. Maybe I needed to give them another reason to. I glanced at the screen.

> Construction Owner: He's here. I'll text
> you the address. Just remember what
> I told you.

Finally! I took a breath then hopped up and hurried toward the restaurant.

"Cameron." I burst into the glass room where he sat at the table he now used as if it was his personal desk. He thrust a hand in the air to indicate he was on a call.

He glared at me then looked around to see who was watching. He had given out dinner vouchers to some high-powered clients of Grim's, knowing rich people loved free stuff. In turn, it helped to keep him around people Grim valued. I had to admit there were times when the guy seemed smart. "Yes, I'll be in touch." He hung up and started to write something in his notebook.

"Cameron, you have to call that hit off Kenna. Do you know they tried to kill her in Italy?" I tugged at my tie and wondered if I should just talk to Grim myself and blow the entire thing out of the water. Trouble was, I valued my life too much and knew I couldn't do that, not if I wanted to continue to see the light of day.

"And just exactly how do you suppose I do that?" He'd been totally unemotional and detached ever since Griple had made him choose which daughter to kill. I began to wonder if it all was just an act.

"I don't know," I slammed my fist on his table, "but she's your child, dammit!"

He tossed his pen and leaned back in his seat. "No, she's a grown woman who has chosen a side, and that side just so happens to be the wrong one. For years, I tried to warn her of the repercussions of being friends with those ruthless assholes. And now," he realized he was shouting and quickly lowered his voice when a few people looked over, "she's screwing around with Gates's son."

"So is Calli!" I reminded him.

He made a face like I was an idiot. "We both know what's really going on there."

My chest heaved with the realization that he had no love for either of them. He just used his daughters as pawns in his game. "Have you no heart at all?"

"It's reserved for those who deserve it." He held my gaze then grabbed his pen and went back to work.

I couldn't believe the guy. So many things suddenly became clear to me as I walked out the door. I knew his days were numbered, and I looked forward to the Gateses making their move.

I stabbed the elevator button and stewed with all the ways I'd be happy to help remove Cameron from this world. I'd already served years for a murder I didn't commit.

"Christ, Simon," Kenna stood by the elevator and pointed at the window of the restaurant, "if looks could kill." She chuckled. I noticed a corner of a bandage peeked out from the top of her dress. I stepped back slightly. "So, you heard." She saw my eyes on it and sighed.

"I did. Are you—"

"Don't finish that question." Her smile dipped. "I'm not okay. Someone wants me dead. All I wanted was to celebrate getting rid of a stalker, only to have another crazy person try to kill me. My life's like a whack-a-mole game."

I couldn't begin to imagine how rattled she was. "Is there anything I can do?"

She touched my arm and gave it a light squeeze. "Just being my friend is enough." I wanted to pull her to me and promise I'd protect her. "I need to go, but thanks for caring."

"Always." I stepped into the elevator and pulled out my phone. I knew I was about to cross the line by doing so. I scrolled until I found the contact. My stomach fluttered as I descended toward the lobby.

"Why are you calling me?"

"I need a favor."

"You're not really in a position to ask for favors."

I pulled off my glasses and rubbed between my eyes. "I know, but…" I paused as I stepped out and nearly collided with Brick.

"Sorry, man." I stiffened at Brick's voice. He reached out and steadied me by the shoulder as he went past. I kept walking and didn't look back. It was clear something was going on. I didn't even think he even realized it was me.

The voice on the phone brought my attention back to it. "I don't have all day, Simon."

"Sorry, just one sec." I pushed my glasses back in place and rushed outside and down the street toward the office. "Can you clear the hit that's been put out on Kenna Lodge?" I blurted as I walked. Silence. After a few seconds, I had to check that the phone was still connected. "I know it's not my place, but she's a good person and—"

"There's no hit ordered on Kenna Lodge."

That stopped me dead in my tracks. "What? But I know there—"

The line went dead.

In a daze, I swung the door open to the law office and immediately snagged a bottle of water from the fridge. I was so confused.

"I know that face." Calli came out from the back office. "You need to clear your head?" She started to unbutton her blouse. "Dad's at the hotel, Knox is doing God knows what or who, but it isn't me, so it's just us in this big ol' office." She tossed her shirt aside, pulled down her panties, and hopped up on the counter. "Whatever could we do to pass the time?"

Screw it.

I dropped my pants and kicked them aside then pushed between her legs and began to kiss her throat. I was instantly ready and slid inside her.

"Wow, where did Mr. Romance go?" She chuckled.

I pulled back for a moment and pressed my forehead to hers. "It's been a day," I confessed "and I'm not wearing a condom."

"Oh." Calli shifted back and released me. "Bottom drawer. I have a few."

"Right." I quickly pulled my pants back on, tucked myself back in, and hurried to her desk.

"Will you grab me my phone too? It's on Dad's desk," she called.

"Yeah," I tossed over my shoulder. "I just found your dark secret." Candy wrappers half-filled the drawer, and I had to fish around through a sea of Twix bars before I finally found what I needed. "I think you have a sugar problem."

I headed to Cameron's office for her phone. "Damn door, it always sticks," I growled, in a hurry to get back to Calli. Three good pulls, and I made it inside. "There you are." I unplugged the phone and headed back down the hallway. "Cameron really needs a new door," I complained as I reached to unzip my pants. As I rounded the corner, the phone dropped out of my hand.

"Calli!" I cupped my mouth and ran to her. Her throat gaped from a deep cut straight across from ear to ear. In shock, I stared, numb. Then I noticed a drawing on her arm, and a cold feeling washed over me. I recognized the mark of the Potens.

"What the hell!" Oh, my God! My mind spun and fired off in so many directions at once, but the biggest one was I needed to get out of there.

I stepped back and slipped in her blood. I tossed the stuff I held, grabbed my bag, and raced blindly out the front door. Before I got far, I was grabbed from behind, and I caught a glimpse of Morgan as his fist met my face.

I blacked out cold.

Words pushed their way through my head as I lay there, but I could barely make sense of them.

"How did you guys know he was at the office?"

"We were following him," a man's voice answered. "Have been for a few days now." I gave up trying and slipped back into the comfort of the darkness.

Cold water hit me, and my mouth opened wide as I gasped desperately for air. My mind scrambled to understand what was happening. I was shot from the hell I had been in to the hell I now found myself in. It looked like a basement of a bar. Boxes of whiskey lined the walls, and as my vision cleared, my stomach dropped when I saw the Devil himself in front of me. I swallowed hard and blinked at Trigger's stare. I looked around and realized the other members of the Devil's Reach, as well as Grim and Jesse, all stood around me. Then I spotted Knox, who looked totally wrung out and pissed.

Shit.

Then it hit me. "I didn't kill her," I stammered through my fear. "One minute she was alive, and the next…" Tears came then, but I didn't care. "I really cared for her. I'd never hurt her."

"Seems real convenient that you just so happened

to be there the moment she got killed," Knox hissed from where he leaned against a pillar.

"It looks bad," I agreed. "It really does, I know. It's just that given everything that's been happening lately, I needed to get away from the hotel. Cameron and I, we're butting heads, and I..." I stopped and tried to pull myself together. "I loved her, Knox, just like you did."

"If you loved her so much, why'd you run?" He raised a brow in that way you know shit isn't going to end well. Grim did the same thing.

"It was a Potens kill." I watched their faces, but nothing showed. "Meaning a hired hit." I waited, and still nothing. "Meaning if they knew I was there, I'd be dead, too. I couldn't risk it."

Grim, who had been silent until then suddenly stepped up and grabbed a fistful of my hair and stared down at me. "Arms up," he ordered, and I obeyed. I knew what he wanted to see. The tattoo. He pulled out his switchblade and cut a slit down the sleeves of my dress shirt. Then he used the point of his knife to pull apart the fabric to check. I had one tattoo that was a quote from *Catch-22*. It read, *Anything worth dying for... is certainly worth living for*. Grim shook his head at Trigger.

"I had the chance to join them," I confessed. "My cellmate, Kurt," I glanced at Grim, "would have loved nothing more than to recruit me to the Potens. That was his job there, to bring people in. But I had zero desire to join any kind of group." I stopped myself there; I didn't need to run the risk of aggravating Trigger. "Kurt saw potential in me anyway and helped me get out of jail early. I just had to agree to work for a hotshot lawyer, and by that, I mean Cameron. I had to keep an eye on him for them."

"You went to jail for murder," Morgan grunted. "You don't get off somethin' like that."

"No?" I pushed my glasses up my nose. "I've seen miracles happen with the MC world when they're put behind bars, so let's not pretend money doesn't mean something in that system."

"Morgan?" Trigger said.

"Records are sealed on the murder," Morgan said over his shoulder, "but I'm still working on it."

Allen had done a good job to make sure he was in no way connected to the dead body in my kitchen. I had no doubt he'd managed to get the record of the whole thing wiped or at least sealed up tight. He'd been a sorry excuse as an MC President, but he'd had power, at least until, from what I heard, Trigger murdered him. His own father.

"That's where I met Calli," I went on. "It sure beat working in construction." I glanced at Brick and knew it was time. "I found him, your brother."

Brick turned to me, and something raw raced over his face. "Where?"

"Here, Vegas. It took some digging, but he's here if you want to meet him."

Brick looked across the room, and that was when I saw Minnie next to Tess. Christ, I hadn't even seen them until now.

"You get one chance," Trigger warned, and I swallowed hard as his huge body suddenly loomed over me. "Let's go."

"There's just one thing, Brick." I squeezed one eye shut, and I felt the pain of Morgan's punch. "I have to warn you about something."

Rail, with his crazy eyes, offered to drive me on the back of his bike, and I nearly tripped over my feet at the thought. Thankfully, Grim had me by the scruff of my shirt and tossed me into his car. I reevaluated my relief as I was sandwiched between his dogs again. Their shoulders were like stone, and every time we hit a bump, they'd knock against me and gave me a look as though I was the cause. One licked his lips, and I prayed they couldn't smell my fear. My earlier injuries were bad enough. I didn't need one of them to get pissed.

"I get how bad this looks," I said quietly, in a desperate need to cut the tension in the car. I felt like I couldn't breathe.

"Which part, exactly?" Grim kept his attention on my phone. He scrolled through it slowly. "The part where you were with Calli in the last moments of her life, or that you've been lying about knowing Brick's brother all this time?"

"I only just found him," I reminded him.

He pursed his lips and looked out the window but gave a small nod. "They might be blinded by what's in front of them right now," he referenced the Devil's Reach who were riding all around us, "but it's not lost on me that up until a few months ago, you never mentioned you knew anything about Brick's family. Seems pretty convenient, if you ask me. Almost like an ace in your pocket."

"Like I said, I know how bad it looks, but Grim—" I hesitated as he shot me a warning not to be so informal with him. "Mr. Gates, surely you can see why I'd keep that quiet. Dave wasn't easy to track down. I moved mountains and pulled favors just to find the guy. I couldn't bring up the fact I knew him until I had proof. I've no credibility with any of you, especially as an ex-convict and with, you know, my association with Cameron."

"Would you have ever mentioned it if Cameron hadn't outed that information at the meeting months ago?" I sighed because the truth was no, I'd had no intention of sharing I knew Brick's brother. "Okay," he went back to my phone, "so you can see why I'm finding it fucking hard to accept it now."

I seized up as one of the dogs jammed his hip bone into mine. I swore he did it on purpose.

"I brought you Kurt. He was a longtime friend, someone I considered family. I did it because he was up to no good, and it might hurt Kenna. Do you think that was easy for me?" I swallowed the lump in my throat. I didn't like showing such vulnerability to him. "I'm walking this Earth alone. Trust me or not, but I've shown nothing but respect to you and your family, and that includes Kenna."

Grim kept scrolling. I wasn't even sure if he heard me. I sat back in the seat and tucked the emotions he'd stirred up inside me deep down. I knew this moment would be challenging, but I needed the hope that things would smooth out from here on. He put the phone in his pocket, rested his arm on the armrest, and stared out the window. His finger brushed over his lips while he seemed deep in thought.

We pulled off the main street, and when we came to a stop, he locked the doors and shifted his cold gray eyes over to mine. "I want to make something perfectly clear while I have you alone." The air in my lungs froze. "The only reason you're not already tied to a cement block at the bottom of the Sultan Sea, with every bone in your body broken, is because of Kenna's fondness for you." He leaned forward. "Remember that from here on, because next time I won't be so kind." I couldn't speak. I barely gave a nod but jumped when the locks shot up and the driver opened the door for him. He gave a command, and the dogs followed. I sagged in my seat.

I'd truly stared death in the eye one too many times.

Minnie shot me a death glare as I emerged from the car, and I knew it was now or never.

"He goes by Dave." I filled Brick in as we stood next to Grim's town car. I was pleased my voice didn't give away the fact that I shook from the inside out. "There he is." I nodded toward the skinny man who walked toward us. "Just be ready." Minnie had taken Brick's hand, but as Dave got near, she stepped back slightly. I saw her run her hand down his back as if to say 'you've got this.'

Dave stopped in front of us and looked around. I waved, and he smiled but said nothing.

"Hi," Brick rubbed the back of his head, "I'm Matt." Dave just smiled again. "You might not remember, but we share the same old man." Again, Dave just stood there and listened, but the big smile never changed.

"Does anyone else remember the chicken from *Moana*?" Rail muttered, and Tess gave him a smack.

"Don't be inappropriate."

"Shit, sorry." He rubbed his head.

Brick reached into his pocket and pulled out an old photo. He held it up. "This was us as kids."

Dave studied the picture, and I felt the sweat roll as I caught Trigger's eyes on me.

Come on, Dave. Look alive.

"Family." Dave squinted at the photo, and Brick let out a relieved chuckle.

"Right," he pointed at Dave and then at himself, "we're family."

Minnie smiled at Tess, and I inhaled for what felt like forever. It wasn't much, but it was a start. Relief began to seep in slowly.

"Have you ever imagined what a belt sander can do to your face?" Morgan quietly asked as he sucked on a joint.

I shook my head. "No, not particularly."

"'Kay." He inhaled. "Just know if this goes south, you'll find out."

"Got it."

FIFTEEN

KENNA

"Your turn." Salazar grinned playfully from behind his glass. "What's your re-do?"

"I like to draw. Design, really." I rubbed my arm as I opened up. "A friend of mine is expanding her business and saw some of my drawings. She asked me to design some of the rooms. Mr. Gates also extended an invitation for me to design some rooms in Secrets."

"That's huge." He seemed impressed. "You must be good. Why haven't you pursued this before?"

"I have, actually." My smile fluttered. "Before I became a hostess, I wanted to go to a school for design, but my father needed help, and you don't say no to my father. Well, not then, anyway." I laughed awkwardly.

"Yes, Cameron Tame has an interesting way about him." He gave a sardonic smile.

"That he does."

Grim whisked across the lobby to where we were. "Excuse me, Salazar, but I need Kenna to come with me. It's important."

"I'll be right back," I assured Salazar.

"No," Grim shook his head, "she'll need the night."

Salazar stood. "Of course." He nodded at me, then Grim. "If you need anything, you know how to reach me."

"Thanks." Grim wrapped a hand around my waist and steered me away.

"Grim, what the hell?"

"I need you to come to my place. Just keep walking," he hesitated, "please." He steered me toward the elevator. An odd feeling went through me at his tone, and I didn't argue.

He didn't say a word on the ride up to his floor, but his hand kept flexing on my hip. Minnie and Tess were waiting in his living room as we entered. Jesse had the dogs by him, and I could see they looked stressed and annoyed that there were people in their space.

"Hey, babe." Minnie wrapped her arms around me then looked over at Grim. "Be careful. Stress can be dangerous at her stage."

"Out with it," I ordered. "What the hell is this? I don't like being handled, so spill it."

"Your sister was killed today," Grim carefully said.

I let his words spin around my head as I tried to get them to stick in one place.

"She was with Simon in their office, Simon went out back to grab something, and they made a move on her."

"They?"

"Potens," Minnie answered.

"But," the words fell from my lips as I went numb, "they were after me, not her."

Grim eyed me. "We don't have all the details yet, but that's what we know so far."

"Okay." I nodded a few more times than necessary. "Yeah, okay." Everything went still as a few good memories I'd had with Calli played out in front of me.

"Kenna," Minnie was in my face, "hon, did you see the doctor today?" I nodded again. "How far along?"

"Around six weeks," I whispered and looked around as the floor seemed to crumble beneath me. "I think I need to lay down." Grim was by my side immediately and steered me to the bedroom. "Why would they kill my sister?" I wondered out loud.

Grim eased me down on my side and covered me with a blanket. He sat next to me and brushed the hair off my face. "You have my word I'll get you answers."

I turned and looked up at him and saw the worry on his face. "Thank you."

"Kenna, I need you to be okay." He took my hand

and placed it on my stomach. "You both need to be okay." I nodded and sniffed. "I'm going to let you have some time alone. I'll be in my office down the hall." He kissed me. "I'm sorry about Calli."

He stood, and I felt a chill as the door quietly closed behind him. The moment he was gone, a painful, soul-shattering cry tore from somewhere deep inside. We may have been oil and water, but she was my sister, and she was a part of me.

A week went by in a blur. Grim insisted I take time off, but I couldn't imagine being left alone with my thoughts. I spent a great deal of it in a fog. Part of it was exhaustion from being pregnant, but most of it was the idea that a part of me was now gone. The worst part was not being able to tell Calli that even though we were mostly at odds, I still loved her.

My father had disappeared, and that left my mother and me to deal with everything. When I broke all my rules and asked Simon if my father was all right, he explained Dad needed time and he found it difficult to look at me because I reminded him of her. That was a slap in the face and instantly put my head back on straight. At least Simon offered to help wherever he could, and we were thankful for that.

The funeral came and went, and the whole time I

found myself wondering why they had targeted Calli. I was the one they'd been after. What had my sister done? She was just a daddy's girl. Who could she have made angry enough to kill her?

The door of the private chapel where I sat at the end of a pew opened, and without thought, I dropped low and slid into the shadow behind a pillar. It was part reaction and part just because I didn't want company.

"What do you mean he's dead?" my father hissed, and I froze. I strained to listen then risked a peek around the pillar to see if he was with someone. "You told me Ines agreed to testify even after his stupid conscience got to him." *Holy shit, Morey Ines.* That nervous, wrinkly-suit lawyer was dead? "Explain to me why every time we pay a witness to go up against the Devil's Reach, they end up with a bullet in their head." He scoffed. "I don't care it was suicide! He was a damn poor choice, and now look where it's gotten us. We've got nothing, and the police are close to solving the fucking Riverside case."

What? I shuddered as I remembered the image Brick had shown me of those poor veterans who had been murdered, their necks sliced ear to ear. It was the reason I'd gone after Matt Myers, to stop him from falsely testifying against Devil's Reach. My head spun as I pieced everything together. I had no idea they'd paid Morey to testify instead. I remembered how strangely he'd acted in my office that day with all his questions, but I would never have connected it to that.

Holy shit, my father really was the Devil in disguise.

I considered stepping out to show myself. The only thing that stopped me was I wanted to hear more of his conversation.

He plunked down on a pew, and I heard it groan under his weight. "Tell Griple I'm working on it. I'll make it happen, damn it! I said I would, and I will." I knew that tone, and I could tell his temper was flaring again. You never knew when Cameron would blow. He was his own worst enemy. "We need him out. I know that. I'll find another witness!" I heard him hang up and jumped when he cursed God's name. The candles flickered across the aisle, and I waited and hoped he'd be struck by lightning or something.

Of course, my father was up to more shady shit, only this time I was going to confront him on it. I stepped around the corner as he turned toward a sound, and I saw his face drop. I jerked back before he spotted me. I wanted to see who it was. I ducked and moved across to another pillar so I could see better.

"Sit," a familiar voice ordered. To my surprise, Jim and Laurel walked up the aisle hand in hand then sat on either side of him.

Holy shit, was I about to witness a hit?

My entire body broke out in a sweat as an uncomfortable heat flowed through me. I tightened my hold on the pillar as my palms grew damp.

They both whispered something, I wondered if it was a prayer as they looked up at the cross. Laurel looked in control and powerful again, and Jim looked strong and carried a level of darkness I'd always known was there. Yes, the Gates family was back in check, and I found my mouth stretching into a smile. *Good.*

Jim leaned back and laced his fingers together behind his head. "Cameron, do you remember when I first got sick?" My father nodded slightly. "We'd met only a few times before that happened. You were my lawyer, and you got me out of a very sticky situation I was in." Jim nodded as if to agree with himself and dropped his hands to his knees. "Then you brought me that excellent doctor, and if it wasn't for him, I'm not sure I'd be here today. He helped nurse me back to life again."

"I never believed in miracles until the day he cleared you of cancer." Laurel smiled warmly at Jim, who gave her an affectionate smile back.

"I felt I was forever in your debt. After all, you saved my life. I opened the door and let you in, I shared my wealth, connections, and family with you. I should have known by the way you behaved with your own family that something was off with you, but I was blinded with gratitude." A shadow darkened Jim's face as he flexed his jaw. "Lesson learned."

"Yes, we certainly learned our lesson." Laurel nodded in agreement.

"The worst thing a parent can do is outlive their children. That kind of pain wasn't meant for our hearts to take." Jim's voice was deeply sad, and Dad's head bobbed, but I didn't see the pain for Calli in the grooves of his face. Not the way it showed on the faces of Jim and Laurel.

"I know," Jim continued in a low but strong tone that seemed to echo through my body. "*We* know," he nodded at his wife, "and now *you* know." My father sat like stone. You would think he was already dead the way he paled, but his throat contracted as he swallowed hard.

Dad's gaze was locked on the floor. "It wasn't supposed to be Leo." His voice was emotionless, and I saw Laurel close her eyes for a moment, and Jim ran his tongue over his teeth. I covered my mouth in fear I'd cry for Leo all over again. I'd believed it was true that my father had done it, but hearing him say those words out loud sent a spear deep into my heart. I wanted to cry for Grim, too, because he'd never get over what had happened to his brother.

"Well, Cameron, now that you know what it's like to lose a child," Laurel glared at him with such hatred I blinked, "we wanted to let you marinate in that pain for a bit. We want you to feel the ache we felt, to think about the life that was stolen from them, and for what?" She looked over at Jim, and for a hair of a second, I wondered if they'd ordered the hit on my sister. They couldn't have. *Right?* They were dangerous people, but they weren't cold-hearted monsters like my father was.

"Yes, you must have wondered why we didn't end your pathetic life after you had our son murdered." My father visibly shook as Jim stood and buttoned his jacket.

Laurel squared her shoulders and made the sign of the cross. She stood and turned to look down on my father. "Never underestimate a mother who has lost a child." Her ominous words hung in the air. I held my breath and wondered what was about to happen. Jim offered his hand to Laurel, and they both walked toward the door of the church and left without even so much as a backward glance.

I took a breath and pursed my lips as I blew it out. I waited for the door to close then looked over at the man whose very DNA would forever be linked with mine. I was so terribly ashamed of that. I was his family. He was my father, and that was going to be hard to live with.

I emerged from the shadows, and the movement made him jump. He put a hand to his chest. "What the fuck, Kenna?" His fear of what was promised was written all over his face. His days were numbered, and he knew it. I could totally understand the sick thrill the Gateses got from watching him cower at every bump, but I also knew the real reason my father still had a heartbeat was because there were still some unanswered questions.

"I take it you caught the show?" he grunted and tugged at his tie.

I stepped closer until I stared down at him. It was the first time I'd seen him as small, not in size, but in character.

"I'm a dead man." He wiped his sweaty face with a handkerchief. "I want you to offer Trigger money, see if he can do something about this situation."

The nerve.

"No," I said quietly and was gifted a glare that at one time would have made me second guess my words. Instead, I remained totally calm. I kept my voice strong as I looked at him like the pathetic lump he was. "I won't grieve for you, ever. Grief is reserved for those you hold deep in your heart. You're the cancer that grows around it, that feeds on the love it holds. When the Gateses decide to make their move, I hope it isn't quick. I want you to have time to think about all that you've done to get you here." I looked around. "May your fate be as damned as the evil that lurks deep beneath our feet."

I spun around with a hollow laugh and walked out. I finally felt free.

The casino at Secrets was in full swing when I got back. The burlesque theme with all the black, red, and gold seemed to be a crowd pleaser. Of course, the half-naked girls in cages helped. It drew in the younger crowd. Men wanted to have them, and women wanted to be them.

"Table nine seems to be on a rather long lucky streak," one of the waitresses mentioned as she walked by me. "Might be worth backing up the tapes." I nodded and decided to check it out myself. Mr. Hong didn't arrive for several hours, so I had some free time.

The security room at Secrets was even more impressive than the one at Indulge, and that was saying something. I used a key and my fingerprint to gain access then stepped inside the room. I came face to face with someone I didn't recognize.

"It's okay," Grim said from behind him. "That's Kenna Tame, my fiancée." The man stepped back, and I saw Grim. He sat on the edge of a desk and smiled as he acknowledged me. "This is Agent Cooper Colins with the FBI, and these," he indicated with his hand, "are some of his associates."

My stomach bottomed out for a second, but then I

took in Grim's cool composure and steadied myself. It wasn't often the FBI was around, and I worried if something had happened.

"She's your fiancée?" Agent Colins grinned down at me with a smile that gave me the shivers. "No way." He chuckled. "She's gorgeous."

"Thanks." I moved around him and stood next to Grim, and he slid an arm around my waist.

"She sure is." He kissed the side of my head. I rather liked Grim's possessive side. "Everything okay?"

"Yes, just a possible problem at table nine." He nodded at Jesse, who slipped out of the room. "Sorry, I didn't realize you were in a meeting."

"It's fine." He didn't let me go, so I guessed I was staying. "So, what did you find out on the Potens?"

Agent Colins glanced at me then at Grim. "Not a lot, more about how they started and that they went quiet after their founder went to prison. There's been chatter they're back and after Vegas again. You, Trigger, and Elio have all been mentioned along with Melvern Trident, Jr."

Grim tossed his head back and laughed. "That little shit'll be taken out by his own gun before they'll ever get a chance at him."

"Nonetheless, your names are out there, and they're around. Give me a bit more time to dig, and in the meantime, I'll leave a few agents behind and see what they can find." Colins caught my eye as he said that and shrugged. "Let me dig some more, we'll know about it soon enough. The fact they haven't moved on it since you got back is interesting."

"Do you think it was called off? Is that a thing?" I couldn't help but ask.

"No," Grim shook his head, "once a hit's in place, it's followed through to the end."

"Grim's right. You can't take it back."

"Great," I muttered and wondered when my time would come.

Agent Colins seemed to take pity on me, and his frown deepened. "I'm sure Grim's got you well covered, and I've put a few extra men at the hotel."

"I appreciate that," Grim answered for me. "All right, so, I give you Tony Farrell, and that makes us even for you getting Agent Paul over the border?"

What did I just walk into? And who was Agent Paul?

"Agreed." Agent Colins nodded. He eyed one of his men then looked back at Grim. "There's something else." He looked at me.

"Just say it," Grim answered. "She's fine."

"I need you to pull back on your retaliation with Talya's parents." Grim's arm around me tightened, and I could almost feel the anger burn through him. "We're watching Jerry Cano, her father, and—"

Grim cut him off. "Don't speak to me like I don't

know who they are or what they did. They nearly wiped out part of the Devil's Reach and almost killed Kenna in my trailer—" His fingers flexed on my hip, and I slid my hand over his to let him know I was okay. "What I have planned for them is kinder than what they deserve."

"I'm not questioning your motives, Grim, but he's been in contact with some people we're watching, and we need him alive." Agent Colins stepped toward us. "Look I'd kill anyone who tried to hurt someone I loved, too, so consider this favor and I'll be in your debt once again."

"A debt I'll collect on," Grim hissed through clenched teeth.

"Of course."

Grim looked down at me, and I wished I could read his thoughts. "If the Canos ever step foot in Vegas," he tore his gaze off mine, "they're dead."

"Understood." Agent Colins waved to his men and left.

I relaxed and sagged into Grim's side. "Interesting men who work for the FBI." I glanced up at him.

"You have no idea."

Something hit me. "Do you think it was wise that I heard any of that?"

"It just means you can't go anywhere," he gave me a devilish grin, "because if you did, I'd have to hunt you down."

I raised a brow with a playful smirk. "I do love to be hunted." I pressed my body into his. "And whatever would you do when you caught me?"

"The question, sweetheart," he grabbed the back of my head, "is what wouldn't I do." He kissed me deeply, and my world tilted. His other hand pressed against my lower back, and I felt how turned on he was. Everything inside me came to life, and I ran my hands along his erection. I popped the button on his pants and undid his belt. I needed him.

"I want you so bad right now, but I have a meeting." He squeezed his eyes shut, and I almost cried. "Fuck it." His hands slid up my skirt, snagged my panties, ripped them down, and tossed them aside, then he sat on one of the computer chairs. He turned me to face him then lifted me onto his lap and lowered me onto him. I gasped, and our eyes met. His mouth opened as he tried to slow himself down. I leaned my head back; it felt so good. He grabbed my hips and controlled the speed as we moved together. We both knew anyone could walk in at any moment. "Say it." His neck bulged, and I knew he wanted to let loose.

"Say what?" I was confused by his question but also lost in the buildup that was budding inside.

He increased the speed, and all I could do was hold on ,to his shoulders. The only sound was our bodies as they collided and our heavy breaths. "That you'll be my wife."

I let go then, and my thighs and stomach clenched as I rode out wave after wave until I collapsed over his shoulder. He lifted me and put me against the wall with one leg over his shoulder, and his neck strained with every thrust as he took what he needed. His eyes were locked on mine.

"I'll be your wife," I promised him again, "all yours to do whatever you want with." I gasped as he sent me up the wall with all his might. I fisted his hair for balance and held on.

"All mine," he whispered as I heard him give in with a groan. His shudders continued and his teeth bared. Then he sucked in a deep breath and peeled me off. My bones felt like Jell-O as he put me down on the chair. He handed me my panties, but when I went for them, he pulled them away. "I'm a patient man, Kenna. I agreed to a few weeks, but after that," he tenderly grabbed my chin, "you're marrying me." He kissed me once. "Benny asked Minnie about you yesterday. Tell him you're taken, or I will."

I loved my possessive asshole, but I also wasn't about to start this new relationship by backing down. This was what we did.

I checked my dress in the reflection of a computer screen. "First, you're not a patient man, Grim. Nowhere close, actually. And second," I snagged my lipstick out of my purse and reapplied it, "I will tell Benny when I'm good and ready."

"Kenna," he growled and leaned down close to me, but I snagged his crotch and held him in place.

"I'm yours, Grim. I'm carrying your baby. I agreed to marry you." I pulled out the ring and slipped it on my finger to show him I was serious.

"You carry it with you?" He seemed pleased.

"I do. So don't question me when I need a moment to process things." I stepped into him, and his hand covered mine, giving himself a good pump. The man was a beast. "Now, if you'll excuse me, I have a job to do." I dragged my tongue along his neck. "Since you just did yours."

Once outside in the hall, I tucked the gorgeous ring safely back into the zippered pocket in my purse and headed down to the casino. I was almost to the end of the hall when I heard my phone go off.

"Simon, hi." I wondered why he'd call me. "What can I do for you?"

"I was hoping to steal a few moments of your time."

I bet he'd got wind about what happened at the church. "If this is about my father, I'm not interested."

"Yes, but it's important, Kenna," he pressed. "Please."

I closed my eyes; my father was the last person I wanted to talk about. "Ah." I checked my watch.

"I promise you really want to hear this."

Shit. "All right, where are you?"

I'd been to my father's office in the hotel before, but I'd never been to the office Simon used when they worked on the twentieth floor. It was tucked away around a corner from Dad's, and I usually tried to avoid that whole area whenever I could. His door was open when I arrived, and his profile looked pensive. He was hunched over in his chair, his chin rested on his palm, and his face glowed pale in the light from the computer screen. I knocked softly, and he turned his head. His warm smile had no effect on the sadness in his eyes.

"Kenna, hey," he tapped his keyboard and turned off his screen, "please come in." He got up and pointed to the couch, then he sat in a chair across from it.

"Okay." I sighed and set my purse next to me as I crossed my legs and settled in. I knew this wasn't going to be something I wanted to hear. "What do you have for me?"

"How are you?"

Ugh. "I'm sure you know people often ask that question to stall for time before telling someone crappy news." I gave him a knowing look. "Come on, Simon, we're closer than that." He leaned back with a nod. "Just spit it out." He still didn't speak, and I decided I wasn't going to waste my time, and I hooked my arm through my purse and rose to leave.

"Your father, he's done something."

"Really? That's it?" I made a face. "Like murder,

spread mayhem, destroy innocent lives, including mine?" I dripped with sarcasm.

He pushed his glasses up his nose then rubbed his lips. I almost took pity on him. I noticed the way he was sweating, and he looked like he was about to be sick. He ran his hands over his thighs and leaned forward. "Shit." I'd never heard Simon curse before, so I knew this was hard on him.

"Okay, Simon, you have my attention. What's going on?" I plunked back down on the couch.

"Screw it." He pulled his chair closer to me. "I need to tell you the truth."

"I'm listening."

"But I need to start from the beginning." I nodded and waved for him to get on with it. "Back in the early fifties, there was this group that wanted to take over the drug trade here in Vegas. They called themselves the Potens."

"Yes, it's Latin for powerful. They liked to relate themselves to the Metriorhynchidae, which is a crocodile. You can skip that part."

His brows shot up like he was impressed. "Very well, then." I had thrown him off with that. He thought for a moment and started again. "As you may know, then, the group went dormant after their head guy got life in jail. But then ten years ago or so, some of them started to re-surface. They were looking for an opening, some way to get a foothold in Vegas, and that's where your father came into play."

"Jesus."

"Your father made a show of flashing around, letting people know about all the highly powerful people he knew. Anyway, he caught the attention of the Potens. At first, they hired him to keep one of their own out of prison. Cameron made all kinds of promises, but in the end, he failed them. He had a fall guy to take the rap, but it fell through, and one of the Potens' leaders ended up getting life without parole. He was murdered shortly after. Let's just say it left a bad taste in their mouth. They weren't happy."

"Shit."

"Yeah," he agreed, "this is where it gets scary. The Potens lived by one law. They gave you one chance, then you were forever in their debt. That's why they showed up that day at your house and never left. He and your family now belonged to them."

"I remember. I answered the door, they came in, and never left."

"The downfall of being cocky," he shrugged with a grim look, "because Cameron bragged about his big client, Jim Gates, who owned many highly successful hotels all over the world, including Indulge here in Vegas. That got their attention. Cameron's debt was to get the Potens inside the Gateses' world. They were patient, and they wanted to hunker down and wait for the perfect moment to destroy them from the inside out."

"Oh, my God." I covered my mouth.

"Cameron had just gotten Jim off for embezzlement a year prior, right around the time he got sick with cancer, and your father did everything in his power to find him the best doctors. He knew how valuable the Gateses were to his survival. He couldn't risk Jim dying."

"So, you're telling me my sister and I lived with a bunch of American mafia men for years because my father got cocky?"

He nodded. "To put it simply, yes."

"That's just great." I rubbed my chin. "Well, that explains a lot." Something nagged at me. "So, who was it? Who was the head of the Potens when they approached my father all those years ago?"

"I'm not sure, exactly, and to be truthful, I'm not sure if Cameron ever really knew who their leader was. But that segues me into this next part."

"Oh, there's more?" I laughed darkly. "Super."

"I may not know who the head of the Potens is either, then or now, but I can tell you who's extremely powerful and just made a big play. His name is Elias Griple."

Hold up. "Why does that name sound familiar?"

"He's one of your father's *clients*." He finger-quoted.

I rolled my eyes. "Of course he is." I waved for him to continue.

"Griple was going down for first degree murder, so Cameron used his go-to and lined up a fall guy. This time a Martin Castillo."

"One of the big Cartel bosses." I showed him I knew who he was, too.

Simon silenced a call that came through. "Correct, but Grim got to Castillo first, and long story short, he's dead and Griple's in prison for life and pissed." He paused and reached for the water behind him. "Not to mention that Cameron got Griple's nephew Sasha killed."

"Oh, shit." A chill raced over me. I wasn't going to share that Sasha had also been one of Grim's kills.

"Kenna, this part is the worst part." Simon's face grew even paler. "Griple gave Cameron a choice after Sasha's death. To pick one of his own to be killed. You or Calli."

"What?" My entire body felt like it had been tossed across the room and slammed into a wall.

"Cameron chose you to die," he blurted. I slowly sank back into the couch cushions and pulled in my chin as I tried to take in his words. "Then, because he chose you, it showed Griple that Calli was more important to him than you were. So, he retaliated and killed Calli instead. Maybe he got the idea from Cameron's messed-up hit on Grim when he got Leo instead."

"Why?" My throat was so dry I could barely get the word out.

"I don't know." Simon dropped to his knees in front of me and took my hands. "Kenna, I know this is a lot to take in, so hear me when I say this part. I don't know if we can ever speak for this long alone again. I don't know what's going to happen now. But I do know the hit on you in Italy wasn't Griple. Someone else is making a move on you, and I need you to keep your head down and eyes open. I need you to be careful while I try to figure out who ordered that hit."

"Who ordered that hit," I parroted as his words bounced around my head and I tried to make sense of it all. "Dad put a hit on me, and they took out my baby sister instead?"

"Yes." He nodded, and tears raced down his cheeks. "I'm sorry, Kenna. I—" He closed his eyes, and more tears fell. "I loved her, too."

This was all too much, so I grabbed my purse. "I need to go."

"Kenna, wait."

"I need to think."

I flew down the hallway, and once the elevator doors closed behind me, I stared at the buttons as my body flooded with confusion, hate, and deep-rooted sadness. I covered my mouth and released a silent sob and held on to the rail to steady myself as I tried to purge the pain. My temples throbbed as a sharp pain drove through my core.

How could I not have seen what was going on? How could my father be this horrible of a human? My lungs begged for air and reminded me I was no longer alone in this world.

"Sorry, little one." I rubbed my tummy and forced myself to swallow back the sobs that wanted release. "I'm trying. I really am." Then something hit me and brought a whole new wave of devastation. Did she know? Could she have? Surely, she did.

I dried my cheeks as anger surged and strengthened me. I stood straight and ran my hands down my dress with a deep inhale. *I'm ready. Let's go.*

I rushed down the hallway, burst through the door, and found my mother. She sat and stared at the wall with a book on her lap.

"Mom!" I called, but she didn't respond. Fresh anger ripped through me, and I marched across the floor and knocked the book to the floor.

She jumped and blinked a few times. "Kenna?"

"You don't get to check out on me! Not after what's happened." I let myself open a box I'd always kept tightly closed inside me. It hurt too much. "Why did you stay married to Dad? All those years, why?"

"What's gotten into you?" She stood, swiped the book from the floor, and turned her back as she slowly placed a marker in her spot and closed it. She carefully placed it on the arm of the chair with measured movements.

"I used to travel with you everywhere, remember, but then as soon as Dad got in trouble with a client, you left me there." Tears poured down my cheeks. "Left me and Calli in a house full of strange men."

"Kenna, dear. You know I started to travel to more remote places. I didn't think it was safe for you." She looked away rather than at me. "It would have been nearly impossible to have taken you to some of those places."

I shook my head. What was she not getting? "But it was safe to leave me there, with them? You chose to leave us. You weren't there to protect us."

She sank back down into her chair and covered her forehead with the back of her hand. "You had your father there to protect you."

"Dad?" I laughed like a crazy person. "Dad was *well* aware of the type of men who were in our home. Lots of times, I was approached, and let me tell you, Mom, he never once protected me. You know what he's like. In fact, when I did break away and tried to have a better life, he sucked me back. Back to this town – back to his life."

"I didn't know."

I tossed my hand in the air. "Because you didn't want to know. Because you weren't there!" I yelled.

"Calli was completely brainwashed, and look where she ended up!"

"Oh, Kenna." She finally looked up at me, and her mournful expression told me for the first time since I was a teen, she was really listening. I softened my voice. "Mom, you need to hear this. Sasha Landry was the nephew of Dad's client. He was killed recently, and that client gave dad an ultimatum, to have me or Calli be killed."

"What?" Her eyes went wide as she looked up at me with an open mouth.

"Yes, Mom, and my father chose. He chose me." As I said it, my heart that had already been riddled with tiny cracks by my father's sins now shattered in tiny pieces at the storm inside me.

Before Mom could recover, I choked out the last painful detail. "His choice made them see who he really cared about, so they killed Calli instead." I broke into a sob.

"Kenna!" She jumped to her feet, her head shaking in denial. "Your father would never, ever do such a thing. I can't believe it. How can you make such a terrible accusation?"

I closed my eyes and let my heavy tears run freely down my cheeks. How could she say such a thing to me? "When have I ever told you anything without being able to back my truth?"

"He's your father—"

"He's a monster who got one of your children murdered."

My head jerked to the side as the sting of her slap burned my cheek. *Numb.* My mother had always heard me out before, but she usually tried to make me see that I simply misunderstood my father and his intentions. I realized now that she never really wanted to see him for who he was. She'd gone too far this time.

"Oh, Kenna," she covered her mouth in horror, "I'm so sorry, honey, but I know you must have it all wrong." She reached out, but I stepped back, as the pain of her betrayal was almost too much to bear.

"Well," I sniffed, "lucky for me Simon has a copy of the prison tape that says otherwise." He didn't have it, but I knew he could get it. I put a hand on my stomach and hoped my baby wouldn't ever feel the sting of such a hit. "You don't get to decide to be a mother one moment and the next look the other way when things go wrong. Wake up, Mother, and open your eyes. You should be a mother first before anything else! My father isn't worth your love." I turned and headed for the door.

"I know he isn't. Kenna, I'm so sorry. Please stop." I looked over my shoulder at the sudden change in the tone of her voice. "It won't count for much, but let me at least explain why I left in the beginning. Why I didn't take you with me. Will you give me a chance?" I gave a tight nod and waited for her to go on.

My mother's confession fanned the flames inside me to an all-consuming blaze. When I left her, I grabbed the elevator phone inside the steel box and furiously punched zero. "Gavin?" You couldn't miss my tone, and I knew he was looking at me through the security camera. "Where's my father?"

"Well, now, Ms. Kenna, the last time I saw him he was in his beloved showman box on display for everyone." I hit the floor button and felt my phone buzz in my hand.

> Grim: Why were you with Simon today? Is there something I should know?

I tucked my phone away. One thing at a time.

"Ms. Kenna, is there anything I can do to help?"

I waited until the doors opened for the restaurant's floor in case he tried to stop me. "Yes. Give me a head start if the police show up." I slammed the phone down and raced out.

A few employees called my name, but I ignored them as I marched toward where my father sat in his famous showcase seat. How dare he use the place of our family dinners to show what a coward he was? The place was busy, of course. That was why he stayed there. I saw his security agent's expression; he was beyond stressed. Simon just kept shaking his head as he listened to my father, who spoke to both of them. I briefly wondered if he'd found out about Simon's meeting with me. Either way, something was going to happen because I'd had enough.

I caught Laurel Gates' eye from the far side of the restaurant. She had a phone to her ear. She held up a hand, then slowly lowered it. Her expression was full of worry, but nothing could stop me now.

I slammed open the door with my palm, and it hit so hard against the glass wall it boomed throughout the whole place, and everyone looked our way.

"You Goddamn son of a bitch!" I yelled at the top of my lungs.

Someone grabbed me from behind, but I whirled and rammed the heel of my hand into his nose just like Morgan had taught me and heard it crack. He yelled and stepped back, and when I turned, Simon was in front of me. His eyes were wild with concern, and he took hold of my arm.

"For fuck's sake, Kenna, sit down or I'll make you sit down." Dad's nasty voice found me as he looked out of the corner of his eye. He knew very well that everyone now stared at us. *Fine. Now you're getting what you want.*

"Kenna." Simon looked rattled as he cupped my elbow. "Is everything all right?"

"We are far from all right, Simon."

His throat contracted, and he stepped back and got out of my way. *Smart man.* Brick popped into view, but I shook my head to keep him at bay.

"Kenna," Dad lowered his voice, but it was still sharp and nasty, "you're making a scene. Sit down."

He was right, I was, and now that I had the attention, it was time to bust this shit wide open. I wasn't in my teens anymore; I wasn't a kid desperate for his approval. I wanted nothing from him but to finish this. I lowered into a chair and slipped my mind into cool and collected.

Grim burst into the room and looked around, and relief spread through him when he spotted me.

"Gates, this is a family matter," Dad growled. "This doesn't concern you."

"I disagree." I pulled out the chair next to me. "Grim." I nodded at the chair. He was already on his way over and sat down and moved it closer to me. His hand landed on my leg. It surprised me that he didn't flip out or demand I leave. I wondered if Gavin had called him right after I hung up. His mother now watched us from a place near the bar.

As Dad looked around, I saw the corners of his mouth turn up. We were on display like a fucking National Geographic documentary. He might think he was safe from death, but he wasn't safe from the truth.

"I got a call today." I tapped my nails on the tabletop and avoided a look toward Simon. I hoped he'd know I wouldn't toss him in the line of fire. "He had a lot to share."

"I don't have time for this right now." Dad attempted to brush me off, but I grabbed a glass from the center of the table and tossed it hard at the glass wall. It burst and shattered above him, and he yelped and covered his head. The customers at the tables around us now stood and looked toward us with concern. I ignored everyone except the pathetic coward across from me.

"You will listen to me, you sorry excuse for a father." I dripped with venom. "You brag and brag about how great you are as a lawyer. Then why'd you lose a case for the Potens?" His eyes popped wide open at that. "You let them fill our home with dangerous men. You know they stepped over the line with me. And not just me, by the way," I shot him a hateful glare, "with Calli too." I noticed Simon's head tilted at me.

"I'm not listening to this drivel. Get out of here, now!" Dad glanced around like a cornered hare. "You make me sound like a mobster."

I ignored him and looked around at the now interested faces. "You went after Grim and got Leo killed, you went after me and got Calli killed. You're the worst mobster I've *ever* seen." I heard someone gasp. It might not be exactly right, but who was counting?

"That's enough!" He slammed his fist on the table, and the water glasses rattled.

"That's what I thought!" I screamed matching his volume. "But of course it keeps going because you're Cameron Tame. You're the big man who can't help but make my life much worse than you already have." Grim pulled out his gun and rested it on his thigh. I covered his hand and slipped my finger over the trigger and tried to pull it from his hand, but he wouldn't let go.

"Maybe we should all take a breather." The security agent tried to step in, but Jesse, to my absolute delight, elbowed him in the stomach, and he gasped and stepped back with a nod. I swung my gaze back to Dad. He looked stricken.

"Tell her the truth, Cameron," Simon said. "Give her that much."

Dad's face turned red as his blood pressure no doubt skyrocketed. "Did you have something to do with this? You stupid little weasel, you're trying to play me!"

"You played your entire family!"

"About that," I stepped in, "at what point were you going to admit you kept Zara around as your secretary because you were sleeping with her mother?" I pulled on Grim's gun again, but he refused to loosen his grip. Then he tried to pull it free himself, but I held on. We were in a frigging tug of war for who got to kill the asshole first. I almost smiled.

"All right!" Dad swung his arms, and I saw the sweat on his forehead. "I loathe the ground you walk on, Grim Gates. You've screwed everything up for me since you came back, and now you're sleeping with my daughter!" He pounded on his chest.

"Actually..." I interrupted and placed my left hand on the table. My huge engagement ring flashed like fire in the lights above the table, and Dad's face paled.

Grim slid his hand over my stomach and kissed my cheek. "And," he gave Dad a big smile, "she's carrying my child."

Bang!

The sound deafened me, then I registered blood as it sprayed over the glass behind his head. For a split second of fear, my eyes flew to Grim, but his head was turned away. In one long blink, I saw the gun. It was being removed from the hands of my mother by Jesse.

"He killed my baby," she sobbed. Grim's mother stepped through the stunned crowd and put an arm around her. "I'm so sorry, Kenna, I'm so sorry." Then she was whisked away by Jesse and swallowed up in the crowd of stunned dinner guests.

"Time to go," Grim pulled me to my feet, "before the police arrive." He shielded me as we made our way out of there.

SIXTEEN

SIMON

I didn't want to, but I was the only one left to clean out Cameron's office. I walked there to give myself time to think. It wasn't far, just off the Strip. I found myself dragging my feet as my mind went back to the last time I'd been there with Calli. I shuddered at the thought. If I hadn't had a few things of my own that I wanted from my desk, I would have found a reason to never step back in the place.

As I went inside, I thought of all the time I'd spent there over the years. I had disagreed with Cameron when he told me we were to split our time between the office here and the one on the twentieth floor of Indulge, but he said it was at Jim Gates' request, and I couldn't argue with that. I knew it would be a big move for Cameron and would bring him closer with them, but I struggled with the Devil's Reach always being around. It brought an element I didn't like.

I knew the place had been professionally cleaned, but the smell of her blood still lingered in the air, and a chill raced up my spine.

Calli and I had a different relationship. I was older, and she still had a lot of growing up to do, but I cared for her deeply, no matter what anyone thought. It angered me so much that she had lost her life, and the fact that it was because of her father made it worse. That son of a bitch should have been taken out years before, and Calli would still be alive.

I grabbed a box and hurried to the back to Cameron's office. The quicker I got the stuff packed up, the quicker I could get out of there.

"I'll start with his bookshelf," I said out loud.

"I didn't see you at Cameron's funeral."

"Jesus, Sonny, you scared the shit out of me." My heart pounded, as he'd come up so silently behind me.

"Sorry." He shrugged as I reached to pick up the box I'd dropped. "No one noticed you weren't there, anyway. Only people there were a few clients and no family. I think most just wanted to see that fucker in the ground. It was all a little weird, if you ask me."

"If you act like a monster?" I shrugged. "Where've you been?" I hated Sonny, but I tried not to show it. The guy was unhinged, and I couldn't wait until he was gone from Vegas. I knew Grim hated him, so it was only a matter of time.

He moved around Cameron's desk, sat, and kicked his feet up. "Layin' low."

"Why now?" I almost smiled at that. Sonny was often in shit, and usually in more ways than you could count.

He flipped open the cigar box on the desk, plucked out one of Cameron's best Cohibas, and ran his nose along the side of it. "This and that." He dodged the question. "My head's still all fucked up from Matt's death. He was a good friend."

"I see." I ran a strip of packing tape to seal the box and grabbed another as I moved toward the desk.

"Did you know about Cameron banging his secretary's mother?" He lit the tip and sucked in the smoke as he took in my expression, then he grinned and blew a ring.

I pushed his feet off the desk, and he jolted forward with a curse. I thought of Zara. She was a pretty girl and was really nice. Smart, too. "No, I didn't know, but it doesn't surprise me. It's the one thing he could do well. Cheat." I used my arm and slid all Cameron's crap into the box. I might clean up a bit, but most of it was going in the trash, and the rest I wanted to burn.

I worked quietly as Sonny smoked. He had rolled the chair back slightly to give me room.

"You know, that Benny guy told Grim that you

were around Kenna way back in her high school years. Grim wouldn't like that, Sonny, not at all." Sonny didn't answer, so I went on. "I also remember I overheard Minnie and Tess talking about it over coffee one day. A lot of people are looking to get a piece of you. Maybe you should think of leaving Vegas."

He shrugged. "Not worried."

"You should be." Something nagged at me. "Would you have any idea who put out a hit on Kenna?"

"Besides her father?" He shook his head with a laugh.

I heard doors open in front, and I froze as I wondered if Sonny had brought trouble.

"Not me." He lifted his hands.

I held a finger to my lips and peeked out the door. "Hello?"

"It's me," Zara called.

"You think her ears were ringing?" Sonny chuckled, and I rolled my eyes and hurried to the front.

I greeted her at her desk. "Hey." I noticed she glanced at where Calli's body once was.

"I'm just here to get a couple of things. I can't believe she's gone."

I pressed my lips together and wished the day would be over. "I know. Me too." I reached back and handed her a box. "Do you need any help?"

"No," she seemed to snap out of her daze, "I mostly just want my charger and my calculator. I already took most of what I wanted the other day. I guess I have no reason to be here anymore. Everything just feels like a lie now, anyway."

"I'm sorry. Truthfully, I had no idea about your mother and Cameron. I really don't think Calli did either."

She stuffed the charger and calculator in her bag. "Yeah, well, that makes three of us."

"What will you do now?"

"I got a job offer across town, but I really want to get out of this city." She checked the time. "I should go. Take care of yourself, Simon."

"You too." I locked the door after she left to ensure no one else could drop in and headed to the back. Sonny must have slipped out while Zara and I talked. *Good riddance.*

I spent the rest of the afternoon packing, then I locked up and began the walk back to Indulge to do the same at the office there. The sooner I closed this chapter of my life, the sooner I could move on. I'd been waiting for this moment; I just hadn't expected it for a few more years.

"Hey." I found Kenna on my couch. She looked deep in thought. Her tight dress hugged her waist, and her slender legs were crossed. My attention was drawn to her upper thigh, and I spotted her engagement ring.

"Wow, I guess congratulations are in order." I

nodded toward her finger. She looked down and then wiggled the ring off. "Or has it been called off?"

"No," she shook her head, "I had it on when we met some clients today. It's complicated, and I wish things in my life could just be simpler." She sounded so unhappy.

"I know a lot's happened over the last few weeks." I wanted to give her a hug.

"To top it all off," she gave a little laugh, "I'm taking one of Vegas's biggest bachelors off the market. I'm not ready for the backlash on that either." She gave another dry chuckle.

"I don't blame you for that." I smiled and dropped the box on the floor. I took two water bottles from the fridge and handed her one as I settled into a chair. "What brings you by?"

"I have a few questions."

"I figured you might." I took a sip and gave her my full attention.

"I don't understand, Simon. Why would you work with a man like my father when you knew what he was really like?"

I had known this question would eventually come, so I made sure to choose my words carefully. The life choices I'd made over the years had usually been forced on me by events I had no control over. I knew I was probably warped by a lot of those things.

"Sometimes we have to be a version of ourselves

that we don't always like in order to survive. I don't really expect you to accept that, but—"

"I understand that." She nodded emphatically. "Believe me, I understand what you're saying. It's how I got through my teens." She looked around my office. "Why did you become a PI?"

I sipped my water. "It's complicated."

"I can follow complicated." She held my gaze.

"I was framed for murder once, dead man in my kitchen and all, feds were waiting on me, and before I knew what was happening, I was behind bars."

"Do you know who framed you?"

I took another swig of water as I nodded then waited a few beats. "Yeah, I do. It was Allen, Trigger's father." Her chin pulled in and her brows pinched together. "Punishment for not joining the DR."

"You knew Trigger's father?" She swung her legs off the couch and sat up straight.

"Yes, I did. I told you it's complicated. I was smart, and I think he saw potential in me, probably thought he could control me too, unlike his son." At her astounded look, I nodded. "I know more about the Devil's Reach than you realize."

"Okay, go on." She settled back a bit.

"The club had a lot of rules, and I knew I could never live by them." I shrugged. "I wasn't interested, and Allen punished me for it. Then, once I was behind bars, things changed for me. Kurt was the guy who attacked you in the parking lot. I knew nothing about that. I was as shocked as you were, honestly." I watched as she drew her arms around herself. "He tried to recruit me, too, but I won't be forced into any club or organization. I refuse to be a member of anything."

My shirt was sweaty from all the work I'd done, but I pulled back the sleeves to show her I wasn't a Poten. "I'm not one of them, Kenna. I just wanted to prove my innocence and be free. I tried to find out what I needed, but everything had been wiped clean. It was too late. Then I heard Allen had disappeared. Word was Trigger killed him. But that's beside the point.

"I learned I was pretty good at finding out stuff, one thing led to another, and I got out with the help of my cellmate. I ended up with a new deal. Working for your father. I'm not proud that I'm working off a debt to the Potens, but they gave me my freedom, and all I had to do was keep an eye on your father."

"What did you report back and to whom?" She was all business now.

"I never met who I communicated with. I only had one phone call. After that, I just texted if Cameron couldn't or wouldn't do something, but my main job was stepping in when his temper flared and try to keep him out of trouble. They had some kind of hold over him."

"You should've gotten paid a lot for that." She

snickered. "I had no idea. I have a hard time knowing all this. You never let on."

I removed my glasses and cleaned the lenses. "My past isn't something I enjoy reliving, but it's the truth."

"It's been quite the eyeopener. You know I'll share all this with the Gateses."

"Of course."

"I appreciate your honesty. It's a lot to take in." She checked her phone. "One last thing. The Gateses know there are more Potens out there. Who else is connected to all this?"

That was a loaded question. "Who isn't? They're everywhere. This group runs so deep. It could be your driver, Shore, or the girl at the coffee cart, or one of your clients like Yen Hong, for all we know. Their tattoo is basically out of sight. Although most go shirtless here, it's still basically hidden. You wouldn't notice it unless you were looking for it."

"Very true." She seemed to slip into a thought for a moment. "I should get going." She stood. "Thanks, Simon. It's nice to have some answers and to get to know you a little better. In spite of all the surprises."

"Nice to be able to be open with you." To my shock, she leaned in and gave me a hug. I took a moment to savor it.

She headed for the door, and I looked down at the box filled with Cameron's crap that I still needed to deal with.

"Simon?"

"Mm?"

"When we last spoke in this office, you said your days were numbered here."

She didn't miss much. "I did."

"Now that Dad is dead?"

"I didn't mean your father."

"The Potens?"

"No," I turned my back, "they're the least of my problems. Have a good night, Kenna." I turned back to the box and heard the door shut behind me.

SEVENTEEN

GRIM

"Kenna was just spotted coming out of Cameron's office on the twentieth. Simon's there," Jesse whispered, and I held up a finger as a thank you. I trusted Kenna, but she was digging into her father, and I was concerned that one of these days she might get herself into more trouble.

"Everything all right?" Trigger eyed me from across the table. Smoke rose from his lips and made him squint at me.

"Kenna's digging.'" I puffed on my own joint.

He gave me a shit-eating grin. "The women we attract."

I agreed.

He looked away, but I could tell something bothered him. "So, you're gonna be a fuckin' dad."

"I am."

"And?"

"And what?" Trigger never spoke more than he had to, so it was always entertaining to make him spell shit out.

"And if you knew her parents might fuck him up, wouldn't you wanna cut their throats?" *Ah, there it is.* He didn't agree with the deal I made with Agent Colins not to retaliate against Talya's parents. I couldn't blame him. I wanted to do it. "If Talya's fuckin' parents find out who the father is, no tellin' what kind of life that kid'll get."

"Talya's a big girl. She's laying low with a friend in Mexico City. If there's a problem, she'll call me."

He stabbed out his joint. "Don't like it. Colins is gettin' way too much fuckin' power."

"I don't disagree on that, but we all know his role in the underground, and until he's not FBI anymore, we should continue to use him."

"Old mafia." Trigger shook his head. I knew it still bothered him that Colins had found out late in life that his grandfather was head of a crime family. But there was a big difference being raised in that world and entering it later in life. Then add an FBI badge on top of that, it was mind-blowing. I wasn't sure of Colins myself. It was a lot of power.

My mind shifted to someone else. "How's Brick's brother doing?"

"Fuck do I know?" He flipped his mohawk back. "I just keep lookin' for the chain to pull to start his fuckin' engine."

I glanced at Jesse, who was on a call. "How's Brick?"

"Happy." He shrugged. "Just wish this guy could give him more than a google-eyed stare. He's been waitin' long enough for it. Deserves more."

"Yeah, it's too bad. I could get a doctor to check him out, see if there's maybe some way to get through."

He tapped his lighter on the table. "Yeah." He sighed. "His fuckin' smile just—" He stopped himself.

"What?"

"I don't fuckin' like that I can't tell what he's thinkin', but it's workin' for Brick. So..." He shrugged.

"Well, that's something."

Trigger chin-pointed over my shoulder. "Deal with him. I gotta make some calls." I nodded as Knox came into view.

"I got your message." I pointed to a chair, and he unbuttoned his suit jacket and waved his hand for a drink. A woman dove in at the far end of the pool, but other than her, the place was practically empty. Most guests were at a concert at the main pool.

"Nice suit. You dress up for me?" The corners of my

mouth rose. I was impressed to see he'd made an effort and didn't look like a member of a surf club.

"I've been thinking, and I want to step up and fill in, now that Leo's not here. You two were always so close. I know you wanted him to work under you, but I guess I hoped you could teach me now. You know, do the same for me."

That was unexpected, but I remembered what he had said to me that night at Indulge. It had bothered me ever since. "Knox, I don't want you to compare yourself to Leo. I just want you to understand that you're a Gates, and you need to learn the family business. You have to get an understanding of how to protect what we've built. I'd be glad to help."

"I was hoping you'd say that." He looked pleased.

"I also know you're young and Calli did a number on you, but you need to use this." I tapped his head. "Be smarter than them."

"I know." He lowered his gaze, and I thought I'd let him in a little.

"Do you know why Dad and I went after that property we just bought?"

"Because we wanted the land?"

"No," I leaned forward, "we got it in hopes you could run your own place someday. Indulge, Secrets, and," I waited, "what would you call the hotel?"

"Sins?"

I smiled proudly, and he joined in. "We need to be united more than ever now."

He looked away, and I saw his eyes had gone glossy. "I feel like this is all my fault. I let Calli get so close."

I felt a hole open in my chest. I missed Leo so much it killed me. "Justice was served, even if it wasn't by our own hand. Calli was being used as much as you were."

He looked back at me and took a swipe at his nose. "How's Kenna?"

"She's doing okay."

"Good." He stood and pushed the chair in. I knew he was struggling to hold it together, so I stood, reached for him, and pulled him in for a hug. His arms wrapped around me, and he let out a sob. "I'm sorry, Grim, for everything."

"We're good, man, I promise."

"Yeah?" He sniffed and pulled himself together and then stepped back. "I have a dinner date I need to get to, so…"

"Oh, yeah?" I grinned, curious who the new woman might be.

"Eww, don't. It's with Mom." I laughed from deep in my belly. "I just need…" He paused, and I knew what he was saying. Mom was a force in our family, and when we needed strength, we went to her. "I'll see ya later."

I slapped his shoulder as he walked by. I was happy we'd had a chat. It was long overdue.

I lit a joint and leaned over the rail to watch the city below.

"I have Mr. Knox's drink. Is he coming back?" The waitress held up his whiskey, and I reached for it.

"No, but I'll take it."

"Sure thing." She batted her lashes at me, but I wasn't remotely interested. *Well, look at me. Growth.*

My phone alerted me I had a message.

> Kenna: Yen Hong had an emergency in Bangkok and Salazar is entertaining friends. I'm free if you are. Or I can go get into some trouble, and we can fight about it and take the long way around to what I want from you.

I broke into a grin as I responded.

> Grim: Rooftop now.

I figured the demand would fuel her fire; I went instantly hard.

"Mr. Gates?" I turned to find Hanna, Kenna's friend. She stood in front of me, totally naked. Pool water dripped from her breasts, and she casually brushed a drip from a perky nipple. I was unmoved.

"I thought that was you." She gave me a sexy look. "Like what you see?"

Anger went through me when I remembered how she bolted from the hotel room and left Kenna to deal with the aftermath of Sasha. Something about her rubbed me the wrong way, and now I saw what that thing was.

I raised a brow, totally unimpressed with whatever the hell she was trying to do. My natural urge to let my eyes roam a female body was replaced with disgust.

I raised my eyebrow at her. "When people meet me, they don't forget me."

"That's true." She pulled her wet hair to one side, and her finger dipped to her breast again as she shot me a coy look. "I'm all alone here in the pool. Are you interested in a dip?"

"No." I didn't miss a beat.

"I know my tits aren't like hers, but my mouth can work magic on your—"

"You're right. They're definitely not." I tossed the insult at her, pissed she would do this to Kenna. "Get dressed before someone sees you."

"I want *you* to see me." She stepped forward. "Touch me." She came closer until she was practically touching me. "You can do whatever you want to me."

"I don't do desperate chicks." I sipped my drink, but she boldly ran her hand up my chest. I opened my hand and dropped my drink. The glass bounced off my shoe and fell into the pool as I snagged and squeezed her wrist with a deep hiss. I hovered over her and used my size to intimidate her. She cowed, and again I thought how turned off I was. "You'd be wise to remember that I've made people disappear for a lot less than what you're doing now."

"Do you have any idea how hard it is to always be in her shadow?" She glared at me but didn't make a move. "Never being good enough. They look at me, but they're really looking at her."

"A man wants a woman with confidence." I dumbed it down for her; she wasn't getting it. "Not a woman who compares herself to those around her. People see Kenna because she's real. She doesn't try to be anything but what she is." I pushed her hands away. "You're pathetic. That's the *worst* for a man."

"I might be pathetic, but I'm not stupid. I know how to ruin a good thing when I see it." She tried to kiss me, but I was ready and grabbed her arms and twisted them, slamming her back to my front. That was a move I loved to do with Kenna, but it was anything but that with this chick. She glanced back at me, then her gaze shifted, and she moaned like she was turned on. "That's right, baby, just how I like it." She pressed hard against me.

"Wow," I muttered and dropped my hold on her. She took a couple of steps to catch her balance.

"Just let me see how you feel," she whined, and I scrunched up my face in disgust.

"Hanna?" Kenna's sharp tone made her jump backward, but something told me Hanna had seen Kenna before I did. "What the hell are you doing?" I took in her long silver dress with its sexy slit up both sides as she approached us.

She was gorgeous and all fucking mine.

"It's not what you think. Grim—"

I cut her off. "Grim did nothing."

She kept going. "He made a pass at me, and I came here to—"

Crack! The sound from Kenna's slap echoed about the pool. I waved off the bartender to give us some privacy. Hanna covered her cheek as her eyes watered.

"After all I've done for you, you hit on my fiancé?"

Hanna did a doubletake, and I was pleased that she was shocked by the news.

"Your fiancé?" She laughed like a crazy person. "Oh, that's fucking great!" She brushed her wet hair back out of her face. "Of course you nabbed the billionaire." Hanna's voice dripped sarcasm, and Kenna's face twisted. I wished I knew what she was thinking. "God, that video makes so much more sense now."

"What's that supposed to mean?" Kenna glanced at me, and I closed my eyes. I wished I'd drowned the bitch in the pool while I'd had the chance.

"I saw you," she hissed. "You're friends with the guy on the video."

"Who?"

"The fucking dude with the Harry Potter glasses who always stares at you from a distance."

"Simon?" Kenna looked more confused than ever. Then her gaze moved back to mine, and I gave her a nod. "I see."

"You played me, Kenna, and I walked right into it, because I thought we were friends."

"Friends?" Now it was Kenna's turn to laugh. "Is this the way you treat a friend? We haven't truly been friends since you started screwing around with Sasha. You hated that we had a past, but that was before I even knew you."

"I trusted that you were finished with him, but you kept stringing him along. I saw the way he watched you, too."

"Speaking of trust," Kenna pressed her lips together, "tell me how you knew Kurt." Her eyes bulged, and I knew Kenna saw the truth on her face. Hanna did feed information to Kurt about her.

"It was nothing. It was a long time ago." Hanna waved her off, but Kenna wasn't having it. "He was a friend of Sasha's. He came over one night and started asking questions about you. As you know, that's nothing new for me," she glared, "to spend my nights talking all about the amazing Kenna." She rolled her eyes. "He was obsessed with you, so I just nudged him your way, hoping Sasha would see it and focus back on me."

"You almost got Kenna killed because of that." I stepped forward to grab the bitch, but Kenna put a hand on my arm to stop me.

"That's not my fault!"

Kenna calmed herself down and placed a hand on her stomach and whispered something I couldn't make out. When her eyes opened, I saw she was channeling something darker. "Look, Hanna, I've had a very rough couple of months. I've done things I didn't even know I was capable of." Kenna took a step toward her, and I prepared myself to step in should Hanna try anything. "But one thing I'm sure of is if you ever come between me or my family again," she drew attention to her stomach, and Hanna's eyes widened, "I'll push you off this rooftop and happily watch as your soul gets slammed out of your body on impact. So, wrap up your leftover snatch and get the fuck out of here."

"Well," Hanna touched her face as if it were tender, "I hope you have a boy. At least it'll have a fighting chance not to be a whore."

"Jesse," I snapped, "see that Hanna is escorted off the property. This will be her last visit to any Gates hotel." Hanna's mouth dropped open as Jesse moved to stand next to her.

"Right this way," he commanded.

"Oh, and Hanna?" Kenna joined my side. "He feels fantastic." She flicked her tongue, and I nearly lost my nerve it was so sexy.

Hanna gave us the finger as Jesse handed her a towel then carefully shoved her naked ass in the elevator with two security guards.

"Fantastic?" I arched my brow playfully, but she rolled her eyes. "Come here." I reached to grab her, but she stepped back. Instantly, my blood heated. "Kenna."

"Not here." She headed toward the elevator, and I knew she was right to move to the privacy of the penthouse. I reached out to pull her close as I stepped inside, but she skirted around me before I could touch her. As soon as the doors closed behind us, she turned to face me.

"Why didn't you tell me Simon was on Hanna's video with Sasha Landry?"

"No one knew but me and Dad."

She didn't comment as the doors opened, and she immediately moved to the bar and poured herself a glass of sparkling water. "I should have been told."

I took a moment to admire the way her ass looked in the dress as she moved farther into the room. The dress clung to all the right places.

"Hey, babies." She patted the boys as they ran to her. Gone were the days when they came to me. Zahr licked her hand, wanting more.

"So, *they* can touch you?" I teased. I wasn't going to put up with that for much longer.

"They didn't lie to me."

"You want to know why I kept it from you?" I shrugged off my coat and draped it on the back of the chair. "Because I couldn't figure him out."

"Couldn't, as in past tense?" I nodded. "Because he helped Brick and helped catch my stalker?"

"Yeah. I needed you to act normal while I watched him."

"So, you think maybe he was looking out for me and was maybe playing Sasha?"

I shrugged. "It looks that way."

"Why don't you ask him?"

I smiled darkly. "I plan to, but I want a little more time."

She nodded and seemed to accept that answer.

"Now, did you eat dinner?"

"I'm not hungry."

"I didn't ask if you were, I asked if you ate." I snagged the tablet from the counter and ordered some food from the kitchen.

"Grim?"

I turned and found her with a puzzled expression.

"When you learned Simon was good friends with Kurt, why didn't you kill Simon too?"

"The same reason I didn't act when I found out he was on the video. I want to watch him. The guy puzzles me, and I don't like puzzles. I need to see what he's really about. What side he's on." She nodded like she was deep in thought. "You seem to know Simon pretty well. You went to his office twice in one week."

She squinted at me. "Are you jealous?"

"I'm protective," I corrected.

"Yes, I am carrying your child."

I ditched my tie and unbuttoned the collar of my shirt. "I didn't need you pregnant to become protective of you." I eyed her. "I'm protective because you're mine. Our baby is just a jumpstart to our life together." I leaned down to where she sat on the couch and caught her lips with mine. "Now, answer my question," I ordered.

"I don't see any red flags. He shared some things with me. I think he's genuinely pleased Dad is dead."

"Yeah, him and everyone else." I lifted her legs, sat, and rested them over my lap. I rubbed her thighs, enjoying how smooth her skin was. I kneaded her muscles and watched her eyes flutter closed. I slid my fingers down to her ankles and slipped her shoes off.

"That feels good," she moaned, and I studied her sexy features. Her long lashes, her pink lips, and her slender neck called to my body. When she brushed her hair back, I caught sight of her ring. I hadn't noticed it until then.

"This makes me happy." I stroked her finger.

"I figured it was time. Dad's gone, and Mom's..."

She looked away for a moment. "Your family knows, so…"

I spun the ring around her finger and thought about how a tiny piece of gold and a diamond could symbolize so much. I went back to rubbing.

"What did you discover while watching him?" She kept her eyes closed and shifted to get more comfortable.

"He watches you the way I do."

"And what way is that?"

I slid my hand up under her dress and rubbed between her legs. A smile broke across her lips. "You're the only one I can focus on in a room," I whispered. "Your body calls to me, ignites every part of my being, and my only reprieve," I slipped a finger inside her, and she granted me a helpless whimper, "is to be inside you." I shifted so I was gently lying over her with one foot on the ground to stabilize me. Two more fingers were added, and her eyes opened and locked onto mine. "And if I ever," I skimmed her jaw with my lips and watched her climb toward her bliss, "found out he acted on those thoughts," I kissed up to her ear, "I'd rip him in two," I whispered harshly.

"Keep going," she breathed as her cheeks pinkened.

"But Sonny'd be first." I fed her desire for my dark side. "I'd chain him to a chair, gag him, and let him watch me take you over and over again, then, when he's wound up to the point of pain, I'd slice his sorry excuse of a dick clean off."

She cried out and climaxed. She shook as she rode it and dug her nails into my shoulder. I dove down and sucked on her neck to increase her ride.

The bell from the elevator told me we were about to have company. I pulled my fingers out, slid a blanket over her limp body, and greeted the bellman as he pushed his cart out.

"Evening, sir," he looked at me then over my shoulder, "ma'am." He nodded in Kenna's direction.

I quickly checked everything over and tipped the man, then shot him a look to get out. He disappeared, and I found Kenna holding my tie. "What?"

"It's your turn. Strip, Mr. Gates."

I cocked an eyebrow and did what I was told.

"Excuse me, Mr. Gates?" Chef Dale caught me in the restaurant the next morning. "I wanted you to know Sonny came by last night."

That caught my attention. I scanned the place and saw we were mostly alone. "And what was Mr. Conti doing trespassing on Gates property?"

"Well, he met with Mr. Borrows," *Jenelle's father*, "at the bar. They spoke for a bit, then Sonny shook his hand, and left when security appeared."

"I see." I caught Kenna coming toward us. "Let's keep this between us for now. No need to get anyone upset," I said as Kenna joined my side.

Kenna glared at him. "Dale."

"Kenna." He smiled. "Still mad at me?"

"Yes." She rolled her eyes, but I could tell she wasn't that angry. "I'm not about to forgive you for not giving me a heads up on that feral cat Kelly. That bitch came at me when we were in the desert."

"I heard you put up a good fight, though."

"I did," her smile slipped, "but that's not the point. She's nuts, and you know it."

"She *is* a freak in bed." He looked at me like I knew what he was talking about. I kept my expression dead-pan; I liked my balls where they were. "I'm sorry. I had no clue when she told me she was going that she'd come after you because of…" He trailed off and cleared his throat.

She stuck a finger in his face. "Be a friend first. I deserve that, at least."

He frowned and nodded.

"All right," I pulled Kenna to my side, "thank you, Dale, for stopping by. I'll be in touch."

"Yeah," he turned his attention to me, "if anything comes up, I'll let you know."

"Please do." He left, and I looked down at Kenna. Her face held a death glare.

She put her hands on her hips. "What did Dale want?"

"Kitchen stuff."

"Why are you lying?" She stared at me harder, but I just got turned on.

I glanced around to see if anyone else was around. I didn't trust that someone like Sonny hadn't followed Dale. Shit, he could have set the whole thing up to get Dale to come here. I made eye contact with Jesse, and he gave me the all-clear on his end.

"Hey." She tugged on my belt, and as she stepped closer, I instantly felt a flash of heat and my body pulled toward hers like a magnet. "Don't forget that I'm carrying a Gates inside me, which means I will figure out what's going on, with or without you."

The corner of my mouth lifted, and I drank in her perfume. "Is that a threat, sweetheart?" I ran my hand around her waist.

Her brow cocked. "It's a promise."

"Fuck me, if sex had a face." Minnie grinned at the two of us. "I think I got pregnant just from looking at you two."

"Minnie," Kenna acknowledged but kept her gaze on me, daring me to look away first.

"If I didn't know you were already knocked up and in love with him, Kenna, I'd say you're about to swallow him whole."

"I already did." She grinned, and my erection begged me to give in.

"So now probably isn't a good time to tell you Sonny's been spotted talking to Yen Hong at Desires restaurant?"

"What?" Kenna broke our connection first but then looked back at me when she connected the dots to Dale. Since he worked there, it was most likely why he'd come by. I nodded, and she shook her head. "You weren't going to tell me, were you?"

"No, I wasn't." I leaned down to her ear. "The same rules apply here, Kenna. You aren't to leave Secrets unless escorted by the men I have watching you. Don't," I gritted, "make me handcuff you to *our* bed again." Her mouth opened, and I kissed her hard to make my point.

"Yup, the big bad Reaper's fuckin' gotcha." Minnie laughed as I fought to pull away.

I waved to Jesse to come over, and when he joined us, I turned to Minnie. "When did you spot Sonny at Desires?"

"Just now."

"Twice in twenty-four hours," Jesse muttered quietly. "I'd say he's trying to get your attention."

"Wait," Kenna held up a hand, "why was he talking to Yen Hong?"

Minnie held up her phone. "Brick texted and said

he was asking about you. I guess Trigger followed Sonny but lost him in the crowd on the Strip."

"Excuse me, Ms. Lodge," one of staff held up a garment bag, "I was told to hand this over to you directly and not leave it in the back."

"Oh, thank you." Kenna draped the bag over her arm. "Please send my gratitude to the seamstress."

"Of course." He slipped away.

"Is that…?" Minnie gushed over the bag.

"It is."

Her hands shot to her face and her smile widened. "That's tonight! I almost forgot."

Hold on. "What's tonight?" I couldn't catch up.

"Yen Fashions. His launch at Indulge." Minnie looked at me like I lived under a rock. "Kenna's in the show."

I laughed. "The fuck you are."

"I'm thinking those new pumps I got from Rene Caovilla." Kenna ignored me.

Minnie swooned. "The ones with the flowers that wrap up your ankle?"

"Yes!"

I thought my head was going to explode. How did we go from Sonny to a fucking fashion show? "Enough." I was going to lose it. "Jesse." I didn't have to say anything else. He knew I wanted him to go find out everything about Sonny being at Indulge.

"On it." Jesse disappeared.

"Kenna, there's no fucking way you're doing any kind of a public show—"

"Grim," she cut me off and raised her chin, "I made a commitment to Yen a long while back that I'd help him debut a few pieces from his collection."

"I don't give a—"

"But think about it." She covered my lips with her finger. "We can use this as a lure to draw Sonny out. It's perfect. I'll be on stage, so he can't touch me up there, then you guys can grab him."

My initial reaction was to cut her off and forbid it, but the idea of her being in the spotlight and untouchable interested me. I kissed her fingers, then something hit me. "What's the dress look like?" I reached for the bag, but she pulled it out of reach.

"I guess you'll just have to find out." She leaned up and kissed my cheek. "Check your calendar. I made sure the event was in there weeks ago."

I felt Minnie watching me as Kenna left. Her ass had just disappeared around the corner when Minnie snorted. "What?"

"It's so fun watching you big, scary men fall hard for a woman." She moved to stand next to me. "I call it Pussy Power." I side-eyed her, and she laughed. "Come on. Trigger wants to see you."

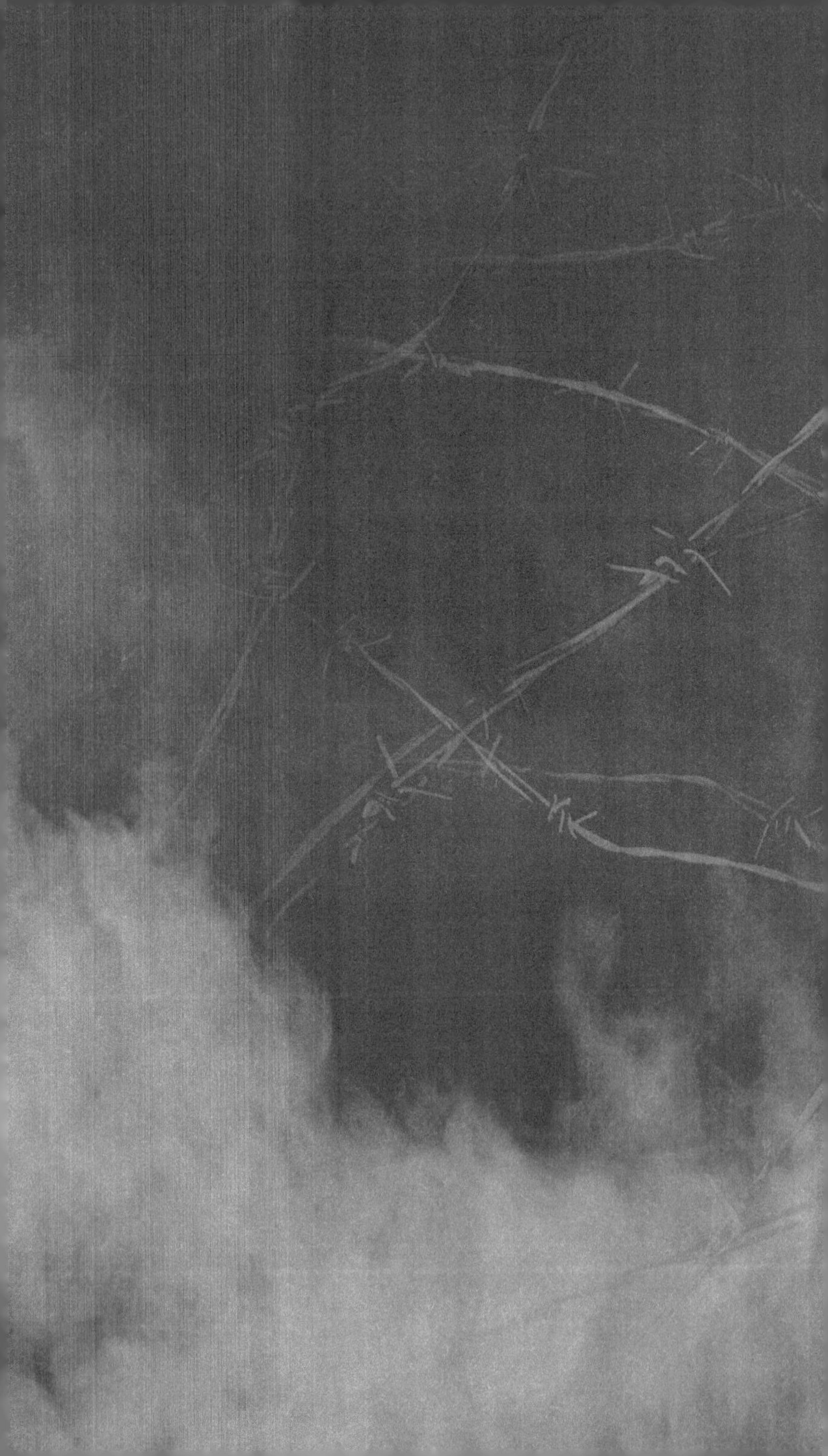

EIGHTEEN

SIMON

People tended to underestimate the quiet ones in the room. Those who didn't cause a problem, talk back, or disturb others weren't given a thought. Prison taught me the same thing. Blend in to survive and gain trust. As a PI, I saw how useful that skill really was. I was lean, nerdy, wore glasses, and only spoke when necessary. I didn't attract the focus of those around me. I was merely a plant in the room. But what people didn't know was how much I saw when they forgot I was there, and boy did I see a lot.

"Hey, new guy," Calli Tame smiled brightly at me when I looked at her, "can you pull down that file for me?" She pointed high up on the shelf.

"Yes, of course." I reached above her head and handed it to her.

She smiled and pushed it back into my hand. "Take it to Cameron for me?"

"Sure." I brushed past her; she was a pretty girl.

"If he's not there, just toss it on the rest," she called.

"Will do." I walked down the hall to Cameron's office and knocked, but there was no answer. "Cameron?" I called and heard the water running. I pushed the door open farther and set the file on top of the others, but some papers slipped out and fell to the floor. I hurried around the desk and collected them. His computer screen was on, and as I still heard the water running, I quickly glanced at it and saw he was transferring emails to a secondary hard drive. If I hadn't known already who they were, I wouldn't have thought much of it, but as the names went by on the screen, I saw they were all Potens members. Kurt had mentioned several of their names over the years. Big players in his world. I snapped a quick photo then hurried back around the desk. I snatched up the file again just as Cameron emerged from the bathroom.

"Calli wanted me to drop this off to you." I stood on the opposite side of the desk and held it out.

"Toss it there." He didn't think anything of me being there. The perk of being the quiet, trusted one paid off once again. I turned to leave. "Simon, sit down for a moment."

"Okay, sure." I sat. "What can I do for you?"

"We're opening an office at Indulge on the twentieth floor, per Jim's request." A smile tugged at his lips while I frowned. I wasn't a big fan of being at the hotel. "You'll have

an office right next to mine, but you'll work here, mostly. I know you don't like crowds."

"I don't."

He clicked a few buttons as his printer made a noise. Then I watched the reflection in his glasses as he dragged files into a folder. What was he up to? "But what I really want to know is whether you can handle being up close to the bikers who sent you to prison."

"If you're asking me if I'll say anything to Allen's son or start any type of friction, the answer's no." I looked at him, and he pushed out of his chair and paced as if in thought. Then he walked over to a shelf and picked up a photo in a thick frame. He set it down again and moved to the window. I wondered what he was thinking and decided to offer more. "You know I've seen firsthand what they're capable of. I have no reason to kick that hornets' nest."

He seemed reassured. "Happy to hear that." He looked at the picture again then nodded. "You can go."

"All right." I pushed the chair in and headed out into the hallway. I hurried outside and rounded the small building to get to Cameron's office window. As I peered in, I saw him slip some papers into the back of the photo frame then put it back on the shelf.

Later that night, I sent the photo of Cameron's computer screen to the contact marked XX in my phone. Seconds later, I got a reply.

XX: We'll take it from here.

I didn't mention I knew where he'd hidden the papers. I wondered what else Cameron was hiding. Something told me he might be a lot smarter than some people thought.

My phone rang, but when I went to answer it, no one was there.

It just kept ringing and ringing until I jolted awake. It took a moment to realize I had fallen asleep in Cameron's office at the hotel. I'd spent many nights on that leather couch, and it was often his heavy footsteps or his loud voice that would rip me from my sleep, but this time it was my phone.

"Hello?" My voice was groggy.

"I need your help getting me into the hotel." Sonny's voice made me instantly annoyed.

I rubbed my head; he was such a mess. "I can't do that."

"Why?"

"Because you tried to drug Kenna, for starters. You're reckless and unpredictable, you're—"

He sighed heavily. "For fuck's sake, get off your moral wagon and help me out."

"Sometimes I think you forget I'm not one of you. Your orders don't work on me."

"You may not be a Poten, Simon, but let's not forget they gave you your freedom."

"Only in exchange for my help because we have a mutual enemy," I reminded him.

He groaned and cursed. "Just get me alone with her

for ten minutes. It's all it'll take." He gave a nasty laugh. My face scrunched up at the thought of Sonny Conti touching Kenna in that way. Then I remembered something I heard in prison that turned men off before they attacked.

I knew I shouldn't, but Sonny needed a wakeup call that he was playing with someone good, not just one of his fuck buddies, as he called them. "Kenna's pregnant."

Sonny's unexpected laugh caught me off guard. It was so loud I had to pull the phone away from my ear. "Tell me it's Grim's."

"It is, so no. There's no way I'll help you get near her. Besides, even if I was to stoop to your level, if Grim found out, I'm as good as dead."

"You're such a pussy." He laughed harder, and I cursed under my breath. "But thanks for the heads up. Fucking with her now will be that much sweeter." The line went dead, and I closed my eyes and wished I had never answered the call.

"Shit."

"Simon?" Jim Gates stood in the doorway, and I almost felt my stomach bottom out of my ass. He never came down this way now that Cameron was gone. "May I come in?"

"Of course." I shot up and pulled out a chair, but he politely waved me off. "What can I do for you, sir?"

He looked around the office. "It's strange to think

someone you knew and trusted for nearly a decade could be so deceitful. Maybe I saw it, maybe I didn't, or maybe I didn't want to." He picked up a few items that were left on Cameron's desk. "I think that question will haunt me for all my remaining years."

"Mine too, sir," I whispered, and he nodded as he continued to look around.

"Who were you just speaking to?" My face burned with heat as he eased onto the desk and stared straight at me. I went with the truth.

"Sonny Conti."

He licked his teeth, and his face hardened. He looked a lot like Grim. They had the same stare that could make your insides twist. "And what did Mr. Conti have to say?"

"He's trying to get into the hotel."

"To Kenna?"

"Yes. I told him she's pregnant. I hoped he would leave her alone."

His brows pinched together. "And how do you know Kenna's pregnant?"

I smiled and shrugged. "People talk. I was in the elevator with you and Mrs. Gates and your security team. I didn't mean to overhear, but it was kind of hard not to."

"I see."

I smiled. "Happens all the time. I guess I'm not a noticeable person."

"And how did Sonny react when you told him this?"

"He just seemed amused. Sonny's got a beef with Grim, and since Grim and Kenna are together…" I opened my hands and shrugged again. "He's not to be trusted."

He mulled that over, and I left him to his thoughts, not wanting to break his concentration. The clock on the bookshelf ticked loudly, and I wondered what had made him come down to Cameron's office. Was he there for me, or was he there to look for something in Cameron's office?

"Speaking of trust, I don't have a reason to trust or not trust you," he finally said, "but I could use your help in getting the new lawyers settled with our accounts. Maybe in that time, you could find another job, and to that end…" He reached into his breast pocket and pulled out a business card. He scribbled something on the back of it then handed it to me. "I have a friend who needs a PI. He's in Georgia, but I think you might be happy with the pay and even the change of scenery. I've mentioned your name."

"Thank you." I took the card. "That's kind of you."

Jim stood and tucked a hand in his pocket then walked toward the open door.

"Sir," I called, and he turned around. "I understand the hesitation to trust me, given how close Cameron and I must have seemed, but if it counts for anything, I will never allow anyone to hurt Kenna. She's one of the good ones."

He pressed his lips together and let out a long breath.

"It counts." He looked at me. "And I agree, she is."

Once he left, I listened for his footsteps to become faint then lifted the picture off the shelf and peeled back the cardboard. Wedged inside was a stack of papers. I thumbed through them and saw the printed-out emails. I didn't bother to read them; I'd seen enough to know Cameron had been building a blackmail case against the Potens.

I tossed the lot in the trashcan, carried it to the bathroom, and dropped in a lit match. As it burned, I let my mind go. Secrets and sins were what drove people apart. The Tame family was no exception, and I didn't want to know what else was going on. Now no one would. Cameron had done enough damage, and it was time to end it.

NINETEEN

GRIM

Morgan found me that evening as I hurried into Indulge. "Hey, got five?"

I rolled my wrist and saw I was going to be late for a meeting on the twentieth floor. "Ride with me." I pulled out my keycard and tapped the keypad as the dogs followed us in and sat at my feet. Morgan waited until the doors closed before he started to talk.

"Everything's set for tonight. Yen Hong even added some of his own people to help us out."

"Good." I was pleased to hear that.

"It's all last minute, the whole thing. It might just throw Sonny off the scent." The doors opened.

"We'll see, won't we?" I nodded and stepped out but then caught the door as it shut. "Thanks, Morgan."

"Yeah."

I whisked down the hallway and into the conference room to find Knox, Mom, and Dad sitting around the table.

"Good evening, son," Mom greeted me, and I felt someone come up behind me.

"Sorry I'm late." Kenna slipped by me, patted the pups' heads, then took her seat with a huff. "Yen Hong wanted me to try on another dress, and, well, one thing led to another, but I'm here." I stepped back and looked out the door then back at her.

"Where's your security?"

"In the lobby." She unscrewed the cap on her water bottle and took a sip.

I shook my head. "Why aren't they up here with you?" She held up a hand and finished her drink. "Please, take all the time you need."

"Grim…" Mom scowled at me.

"I'm just trying to understand why I pay good money to have these men watch over my soon-to-be wife and mother of my child, yet she arrives alone."

"Don't get your panties in a twist," Kenna growled, and I heard Mom snicker then saw her hide a smile behind her hand. "Jesse met me at the elevator and gave them orders to check on something. He then escorted me to that door," she pointed to the door of the conference room, "then he went back down, once he knew I was with you all." She tilted her head at me, and her fingers strummed the table.

Knox clapped his hands. "See, wife-slash-baby momma is all good. So Grim can untangle his balls from his twisted panties and we can all move on with our lives. Dad, you're up."

I swatted the back of Knox's head as I took my seat and eyed Kenna, who seemed to find Knox entertaining.

"First, before we get started," Mom pulled her mini little shit of a dog onto her lap and stroked its back, "your father and I—"

"And LeeLee," Knox chimed in and threw a smug smile my way.

"Yes, and LeeLee." Mom used a baby voice toward the dog while I took the opportunity to punch Knox in the thigh. He heaved over with a laugh. "Anyway," Mom ignored us and looked at Kenna, "we *all* wanted to officially say congratulations to the two of you on your engagement and for granting us our first *human* grandbaby." She kissed the little shit's head, and I glanced at Leal and Zhar, who looked less than impressed. At least *they* got me.

"Thanks." Kenna smiled around the table. "It's all a bit fast," I glared at her, and she put her hand on mine, "but I'm very excited to start our family."

"That's wonderful." Mom covered Kenna's other

hand and squeezed it. "We'll work out the details later." She looked at Dad, and he took the floor.

"Kenna, you're family now. That's why you're here, so I won't sugar coat anything."

"Please don't." Kenna shifted right into work mode.

Dad pulled out a file and slid it over to her. "Your mother has signed everything over to you. I was hoping, with your permission, I could do some digging in Cameron's personal files. I just have to get the password."

"Whatever you need." Kenna didn't miss a beat. "How is Mom?" I knew she had a lot of mixed feelings about her mother after all that had happened, but I felt I was doing my best to help her through it all.

"I have the best lawyers on her case," Dad went on, "but she chose a very public place, and it's not the easiest situation to navigate."

I placed my hand on her leg, and she squeezed it. I hoped I could act as her anchor through all this. "I understand."

"Perhaps there won't even be a trial." Dad tried to brighten the mood. "The lawyers may be able to get her trial suspended in lieu of a mental breakdown or something. God knows Cameron's actions could snap a mother's mind."

"You know you can see her when you're ready," Mom interrupted. "We can make that happen."

"That's kind of you. I might need some time,

though." Kenna tried for a smile. Her mother had shut down. Shock had probably set in once she realized the depth of what she'd done. She had lost everything. It would take time for her to get back to normal, if she ever really did. "You'll need this." Kenna scribbled down a code. "Mom changed all the alarms at the house when Calli was killed. I have no interest in staying there, so take whatever you need."

"I appreciate that." Dad tucked the code into his pocket.

Knox leaned over the table. "Speaking of that, shouldn't we be combing through Cameron's computers now?"

"No. A week before Cameron was killed, Zara helped me copy his files," Dad explained. "I've also paid some people to watch Griple in prison. He's clearly an important member of the Potens. I'd love to know what connection he had with Cameron."

"Blackmail?" Kenna questioned. "Because Dad was notorious for compiling dirt on people."

"Maybe." I cleared my throat. "Did Simon ever mention anything?"

"No." She shrugged. "But speaking of Simon, what about him? Are you guys watching him? Or…?"

"At present, he's our only real link." Dad pulled out a file on him. "I think we keep him close." Dad glanced at me, and I wondered what the look was for. "I, ah, also spoke to him this morning. He'd been approached by Sonny, who wanted him to help gain access to Yen Hong's fashion show."

"Simon said no, right?" Kenna looked around. "Because he doesn't know our plan."

"He said no, but he did share that you were pregnant."

Kenna's face went white. "What?"

"I'll fucking kill him," I cursed, and Kenna's grabbed my arm.

"Stop, Grim." Dad stood and put out his hand to halt my murderous rampage.

"It was just his attempt at a tactic to turn Sonny off." Dad rubbed his head. "I'm sure it didn't work, but, Kenna, just be aware."

"Simon's an idiot if he thought that would work. You're not doing the show now," I fumed but settled back in my chair. Kenna was mad if she thought I would let her put herself out there after that. "Over my dead body are you allowed to do it."

"Grim…" Kenna's voice held a warning.

"I literally just heard a boxing ring bell go off between the two of you." Knox covered his face. "Grim, she's going to do it. You know she will. Kenna, you know Grim is all bark when it comes to you. As long as he doesn't drag you to the bedroom…we all remember the handcuff story."

"Knox." Mom shook her head at him.

"What, Mom? I'm just speeding up the next twenty minutes of their fight."

"He's not wrong." Kenna shrugged but conveniently avoided eye contact. Anger poured off me. Maybe I'd been wrong to encourage Knox to participate more.

Dad put a stop to our discussion. "All right, that's enough. Kenna, Simon seems to be quite fond of you. Maybe see what else you can find out."

"Of course." She smiled then raised her hand as Dad went to move on. "I should tell you that Simon was working with Cameron to pay off his debt to the Potens."

"What?" Dad and I both said at the same time.

"So, I need to fill you in." She let out a long breath. "I've had a few talks with Simon lately, and here's what I know." She began to update us.

Christ, she knew a lot more than we did, and I was impressed she was able to get Simon to fill in some blanks for us. I still didn't like the guy, but I wanted to kill him less and less, so that was a start.

I lowered my voice and leaned into her. "How did I not know this until now?"

She frowned, and in a flash, I felt like an ass because I knew the answer. "I'm sorry. I've had a lot to process lately, both the bad and the good." She glanced at her stomach. "I knew a meeting was coming, and instead of explaining it all twice, I figured a few days wouldn't make a difference." I kissed her hand; I had a need to touch her. "Besides, you get frustrated whenever you hear Simon's around."

"You mean protective," I corrected.

"Sure." Her eyes lightened.

"Well, that makes sense." Knox rubbed the back of his head and drew our attention back to the discussion. "Calli mentioned Griple a few times, and she seemed quite nervous of him. If he's as involved as Simon says he is, I'm glad we're watching him."

"Indeed." Mom seemed deep in thought.

A knock came at the door, and Jesse came into the room and handed me a small stack of printed emails. "Pardon the interruption, but you need to see this."

"What is it?" I took the stack and skimmed where he had highlighted a few things. "The fuck." I handed it to Dad. "These are emails between Cameron and Walter. Seems Walter Wallace is a Potens member and was in a position to order Cameron around."

"Why doesn't that surprise me?" Knox pulled out his phone. "I fucking hated him since I was a kid, and don't even get me started on Jayden."

Kenna stood as I did. "What? What about Jayden?"

"Nothing about him was mentioned." Jesse held his hands open. "Who knows? If you didn't know, he may not know a thing about it either."

"Where is he?" Dad handed the emails to Mom.

"In holding downstairs," Jesse answered. "Jayden too." He shrugged. "Just in case."

"You want me to handle this?" Knox asked. I pulled in my chin with surprise and noticed Mom and Dad looked taken aback at his offer as well.

"Let's do this one together," Dad suggested, and Knox nodded.

Mom lowered her head with a heavy breath. "How could so many of these people we considered close friends be secretly working against us?"

"I don't understand it either." Dad rubbed her back tenderly. "But let's flush them out and keep those we know we can trust," he looked at Kenna, "even closer." Kenna smiled at him.

When we stepped out of the conference room, Kenna's security were waiting for her. I didn't have to look over to see her I-told-you-so smile; I could feel it. I should have known better. She wasn't intentionally trying to be reckless.

I grabbed her arm and kissed her deeply then released her. "Check in with me later," I ordered.

"Yes, Mr. Gates, and up yours in the nicest way possible." She chuckled. She knew full well what that would do to my erection. Leal growled, and she turned to him and gave him a quick pat. It seemed to satisfy him, and he came back and stood next to his brother.

"Happy?" I chuckled and gave both pups an ear ruffle. Leal looked up at me. "I get it." I loved her attention as much as he did. We watched as Kenna and the others headed downstairs, then I swung around to address Jesse.

"What's your gut on all this?"

"As much as I'd like to get rid of his preppy ass, I really don't think Jayden had any clue what his father was up to. He seemed genuinely confused when I questioned him."

"Okay." I let that sink in. "And Wallace?"

"He's not saying a thing. A few blows to his fat face wiped that shit-eating grin off. He deserved it, and I was happy to deliver."

"Sorry I missed that." I chuckled softly. "You got the evidence we needed?"

"Yup, there for anyone to find, if you dared look."

"Is your gut giving you any more assholes we should deal with?"

"Not really, but there's a few I'd like to check out. Time will tell."

Jesse looked at his phone. "How are you feeling about tonight?"

"It's like I can feel something's coming." I felt myself go cold. "I just don't know what it is yet."

I had to hand it to Kenna; the outdoor lounge at Indulge had been transformed into a fun beach-themed party. The invited guests could enter as long as they dressed the part. Yen Hong's clothing line was all about sexy summer wear. Even though the summer was over, and some of us were only too happy to welcome the cooler temps of fall, it was nice for those who didn't want the heat to end.

"This is pretty nice." Rail stood next to me and sipped his massive Hawaiian looking drink. It sported a fancy bendy straw. I cringed at his board shorts, boots, and pink tank top. He caught my expression and shrugged. "Minnie told me to blend. I'm blending. Sonny would never suspect me."

I shook my head. "You look like a fucking Ken doll."

"Hey," he pointed at me, "Ken was a very important part in the *Barbie* movie." He sucked in a long drink, then used his tongue to flick the straw. I shuddered and pretended to gag as he laughed.

The crowd cheered as Kenna came out on the stage. "Oh, thank fuck," I muttered, happy for the distraction.

"You are one lucky-lucky man." Rail made a circle with his fingers and pressed it against his front teeth. I closed my eyes as he let out a high-pitched whistle. When I opened them, I tightened my fists as a few men around me barked out comments. Kenna wore a white string bikini with a sheer wrap and sparkly gold heels. Her hair was curly and pinned up on one side by a white tropical flower. Yen Hong followed hard on her heels then joined her front and center. They both introduced themselves, then the music started, and the fashion show began.

"Anything?" I mouthed to Jesse. He shook his head. I scanned the crowd in hopes Sonny would show so we could end this shit. At the same time, I wanted this show to run smoothly for Kenna. I found myself taking note of which other Indulge employees were there. I couldn't help but wonder who else might be a member of the Potens. Dad had cleared Jayden's name, but nonetheless, he was let go because of his father's involvement. He didn't like it, but I couldn't give a shit. I still found it strange that all these years he'd never suspected a thing as he'd told us. They were very close.

"I hope you all enjoyed that," Yen said clearly into the microphone, and the applause had him beaming. "We're going to take a short break, then we'll wow you even more!" He reached for Kenna's hand, and they both bowed. I tuned in to the crowd even more as a band struck up music to entertain them.

We had all our bases covered, so the commotion that started on my side of the stage surprised me. Trigger was the last person I thought I'd see steamrolling through the people toward the stage. I desperately searched for the threat but couldn't see anything.

I looked up and locked eyes with Kenna and waved her back. She nodded and took a few hesitant steps toward Yen Hong. Rail, in his ridiculous outfit, was already on the stage and had a gun out. He urged Kenna and Yen toward the edge of the stage where I was.

"Shit." I reached up, and Kenna used my shoulders to help herself jump down. Yen followed. "Go with Minnie," I ordered, but she grabbed my arm and made me look at her.

"Grim." I could see in her eyes she was scared but also determined. "Whatever it is, I can handle it." I knew she could.

"Come on." I pulled her through the sea of people and tried my best not to look worried.

Jesse met us by the door. "Get her downstairs," I yelled at him.

"I'm not going anywhere." Kenna's stance told me she wasn't going to back down.

In spite of my hope he would show up at the fashion show, Sonny had taken a big risk coming to such an event. Surely, he'd know it would be crawling with security and police. "Put this on." I shrugged out of my jacket and draped it around Kenna's nearly naked body.

"Where did Yen go?" she whispered and glanced around the elevator.

"We lost him in the crowd," Jesse answered.

"Do you have any idea what's happening? Is it Sonny?" Kenna asked.

"Not sure, but be ready for anything," I replied. "I need you to do whatever I say."

"I can handle it."

I snagged her confident chin as it lifted. "I know you can." I caught her lips with a commanding kiss.

I pulled away as the door opened and the three of us hurried out.

Jesse put his hand over his earpiece. "They're in your office." His voice was full of anger.

The unmistakable sound of a fist meeting bones sent a shiver of expectation through my body as it echoed down the hallway. I started to come alive at the sound of pain. I burst through the doors and came to a dead stop.

Trigger had his arm pulled back with a grip on someone on their knees, covered in blood. "Speak now 'cause I'm a hell of a lot more evil than my father ever was," Trigger spat.

Morgan handed me his phone at my question, and my jaw sagged open at what I read. *Son of a bitch.*

"Does *he* know?" I kept my voice low so only he could hear me.

"Not yet."

I handed it back as I looked around the room. Trigger's men stood in a tight group against the wall. Minnie moved to stand beside Brick. "Let's do this."

"Oh, my God!" Kenna gasped. "Is that Simon?"

Trigger dropped him like a rock at the sound of her

voice, like Kenna had just smacked him. He snapped out of his murderous rage and stepped back.

"Tell him or I will." Trigger's voice boomed throughout the room, and I felt Kenna step closer to me.

"Simon?" Kenna's face was shocked.

Simon's battered gaze caught Kenna's, and I stepped in front of her to shield her from his lies. His shoulders slumped, and his head dropped forward as the pain overtook him. It was clear Simon didn't live the kind of life we did. In our world, pain was a tool that fed our power, whether we were administering it or on the receiving end. I doubted he'd ever had much of it in his life, the way he gave in to it.

"Brick," Trigger snarled, "get over here."

The place went still while everyone's eyes went from the bloody man on his knees in front of Trigger to Brick.

Brick's expression went from confusion to anger, but confusion won. "What?"

"I got a DNA test run," Trigger growled, "and that sumbitch he came up with ain't your brother. He fuckin' lied."

Brick shook his head in defeat and his shoulders slumped as he shook off Minnie and brought a chair over next to Simon. "Sit." He grabbed Simon by the collar and pulled him onto it. "Is that true?"

Simon felt around his face, and Morgan cleared his

throat. "Out with it. Do it fast, or I'll get that belt sander."

"It's me. I'm your brother," Simon whispered through bloody lips.

"Liar." Brick swung and punched Simon hard in the stomach. "I've earned the right to the truth, damn it. Stop fucking with me."

"Yes, fine," he coughed and held up a shaky hand, "just stop, please. I'm telling the truth."

I muttered under my breath at Trigger. "This guy wouldn't last ten minutes in our world."

Brick stood back and studied Simon like an ant on the end of his finger. "You lie. Rowen had blue eyes. You have brown." Simon tossed his glasses on the floor and carefully stuck his finger in his eye then looked at Brick. One eye was brown, but the other was now blue. "Take out the other one. I want to see all of you." Simon removed the other contact and stared up at him.

"The last time I saw you was my birthday party. Your mother made quite the scene."

Brick's shoulders rose as he nodded at Trigger. *Holy shit.* The room went silent as the realization kicked in.

"More lies," Kenna whispered, "so many lies."

"What happened to our father?"

Simon rubbed under his nose to catch some blood. "He was killed." He looked directly at Brick. "Good riddance, too."

"The fuck does that mean?" Trig glared at Simon.

We both knew Brick had only met his father one time, and they'd never even spoken to one another. The Devil's Reach had filled in as many gaps as they could because his dad had been a life member. As far as we knew, he'd been a good man to the club.

"He was a nasty drunk with a mean right hook," Simon growled. "I was the one who took the hits, and it only increased when I refused to join your club." He groaned and stared at Trigger. "I wanted to do more with my life, and when our father was killed, I thought I was finally free of it all."

He laughed darkly. "But Allen, your fucking father," he glared at Trigger again, "stepped in and took over. It got worse. The more I refused to join the Devil's Reach, the more he made me pay, until one day a dead body was found in my kitchen, and I was suddenly serving a life sentence." He pressed his hands against his midsection. "I just wanted to be left the hell alone."

"Simon, why didn't you say something?" Kenna's face seemed sympathetic, and I wasn't having it.

"Kenna, don't fall for all this shit. This guy's making things up as sure as we're standing here." I went for Simon.

"No, Grim," Brick held up a hand, "I want to hear it."

"Suit yourself." I pulled back, disappointed, and

shook my head then caught Kenna around her middle and pulled her to me.

Simon wiped his mouth and took a breath. "Look, Brick, your club and the men who ran it have always made sure my life was miserable because I wanted no part in it. I was just a kid. So, my apologies for not wanting to out who I was when we met again as adults."

Brick bit his cheek, and his mouth twisted as he let that sink in. No one spoke for a moment.

"Brick, don't let this fuckin' nuthin' twist you up. It's all bullshit." Trigger pulled out a joint then moved to the wall. I saw Minnie move a little closer to Brick.

"Kenna, will you fill them in on the rest?" Simon's asked, his eyes desperate.

I grabbed Kenna's arm when I felt her move. All eyes shifted to her.

"I believe him." Kenna pulled her arm away. "His cellmate was a Poten. They helped him get out, and in exchange, he gave them information on my father."

"I never asked to be a part of any of it," Simon pleaded. "I'm just trying to get my life back. Now that Cameron's dead, I thought I could, but here I am right in the middle of it again."

"Did you have any intention of ever letting me know who you were?" Brick looked stricken.

"No." Simon squeezed his eyes shut. "I'm sorry, Brick. I can see how this looks, but you're connected to the one thing I want nothing to do with. The Devil's Reach stole nearly a decade of my life. We're so different. We grew up in two different worlds, and we want very different things. We're better off being strangers."

Brick looked at Trigger and chuckled. "Well, I guess we can agree on that." He reached out his hand and offered it to Simon, who looked at it cautiously. Brick helped him to his feet. "I spent years looking for you, years thinking I was missing something in my life, and now I see that was a huge mistake." He pulled his arm back and punched Simon straight in the face. He flew back and hit the floor, out cold. Brick looked at Trigger. "Let him go."

"You sure?" Morgan asked.

"It's for me, not him."

Brick reached for Minnie, wrapped his arms around her, and buried his face in her neck. I glanced at Kenna. I understood the need to hold something that would ground you. Her hand slipped back into mine and gave it a squeeze. She got me.

Trigger nodded. "Your choice."

Rail stepped up and held out his hands. "What do we do with Dave?" Rail looked worried, and Morgan looked at him in shock. "I mean, the guy's okay, even if he was used as a fake brother ploy. I've spent some time with him. He deserves more than to be dropped off in a Walmart parking lot. I know he can't stay, but…"

"I'll deal with him," Trigger said. "I got a place in mind."

Rail rubbed the back of his neck. "I want to be there when you do." Trigger nodded and caught my eye. It wasn't often Rail showed interest in anything except the female form, so Dave must have left his mark on him.

Brick whispered something to Minnie, then the two of them turned toward the door. Minnie looked excitedly at Kenna as they left.

"Morgan," Trigger chin-pointed at Simon, "wake the bastard." Morgan waved some chewing tobacco under his nose, and he jolted awake. "Simon," Trigger loomed over him, and he pulled himself into a ball like the coward he was, "Brick mighta saved your fuckin' life, but if you step out of line once, I'll crush your fuckin' bones, one-at-a-fucking-time."

"Yes. Okay." Simon's head bobbed, and Trigger looked over at me with an annoyed expression.

"Yeah, I know, Trig. It's a lot to process. Who could've ever imagined Cameron's people had a direct connection to yours? You can't make this shit up."

"Ca-can I go?" Simon felt around for his glasses then seemed to second guess himself and deliberately tossed them aside as he blinked at us.

"Morgan," Trigger looked toward the door, "get Simon back upstairs and out of our sight."

"What are you gonna do with the fake brother?" Rail asked again.

"Guy I know has a ranch. He hires people with mental shit goin' on, disabilities and the like. He'll be taken care of." Rail smiled and nodded, then suddenly looked excited.

"I'm going back up to find another of those fancy coconut drinks." He grinned. "I mean, the party's not over." He rushed out the door.

When we returned, the fashion show was in full swing. Rail greeted us with a loud slurp as he pulled hard on his bendy straw.

I shook my head and looked at Kenna, who seemed to be in a trance.

"You good?"

"I'm suddenly very tired." I could tell this news bothered her, and mix that with the pregnancy, she must be beat.

"I see Yen. I'll let him know you're not coming back." I kissed her head. "Let's go home."

Sonny never did show his face.

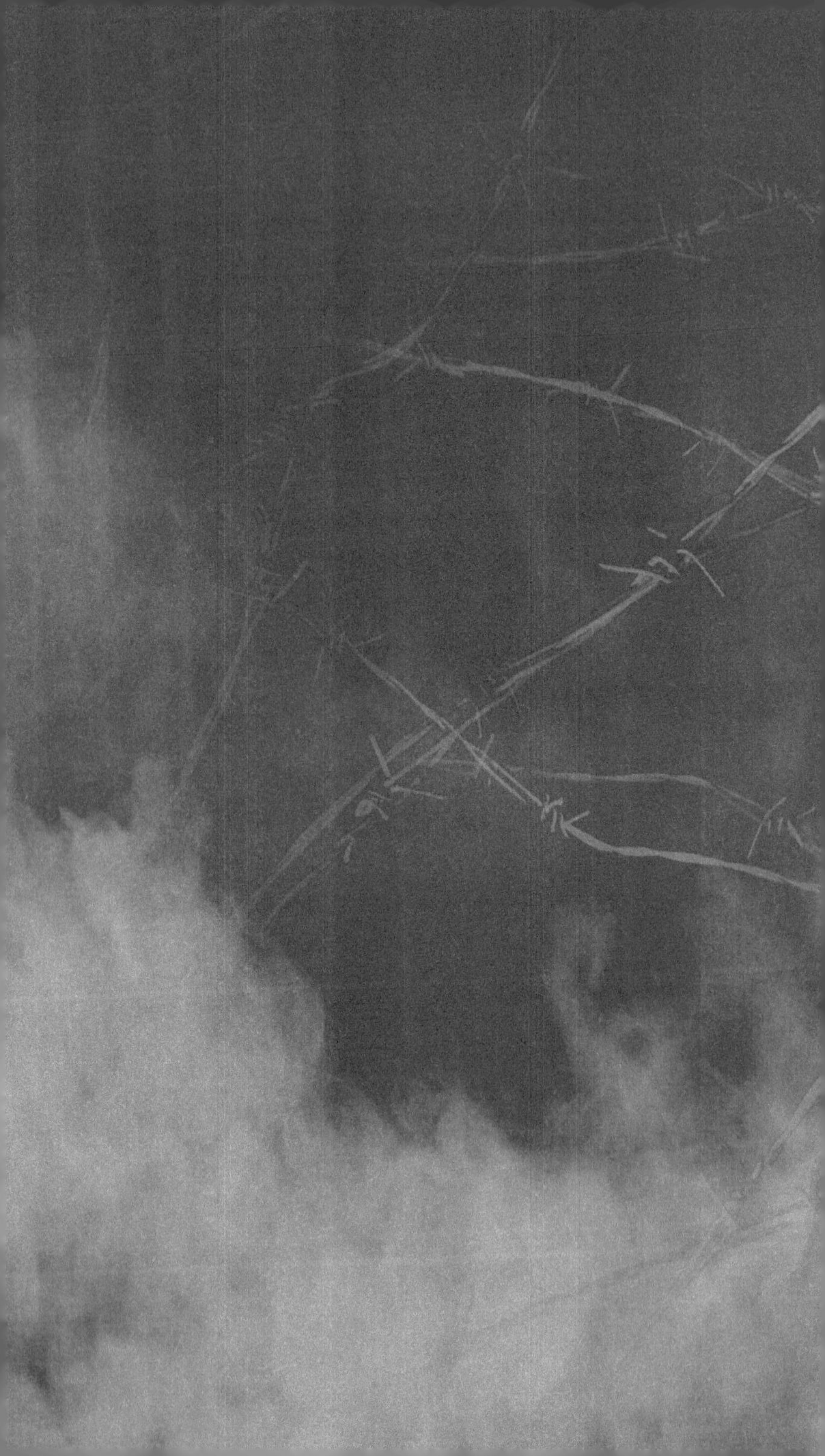

TWENTY

SIMON

"Nice place you got here. Hope you don't mind me droppin' in." Kurt moved around my living room and stopped at my bookshelf. "I see you have your beloved books." He hooked the top of the spine of a book with his finger then tilted the books forward one at a time. "I don't get why people keep books." I slid the chicken casserole into the oven with an eyeroll. "You've read 'em all, so why keep them?"

I swallowed back my surprise at his unexpected visit and decided to make an effort. "You love the movie Shawshank, right?"

"Yeah," he shrugged, "it's a classic."

"How many times have you seen it?"

"At least thirty."

"What's the difference with books?" I made my point. "I re-read them all the time. They're classics to me like your movies."

"I guess." His lips tugged upward, but I could tell he didn't get it at all. He had no understanding of the love for literature. He let the book he fingered go, and it fell back into place, then he plucked up the one and only photo I kept of my family. "Is this the notorious bastard?" I gave him a hard look to be careful on that subject, and he made a face. "I'm just shocked you have one, let alone on display."

I set the timer and tossed the oven mitt on the table. "It's the only one of my mother and me, and I can't help it if he's in it. At least he's not wearing that stupid leather vest." I pulled the photo from his hand and slammed it into a desk drawer.

"Shit, he really did a number on you, didn't he?"

I sank into the chair while he moved to the couch across from me. "My skull still has the scars from his temper," I answered rather dramatically with my hands to my head. "My father was a man who didn't take no for an answer. He beat me whenever he felt like it, and the older I got, the worse it got."

"And when it got to be too much, a Stripe Back did the deed." He smiled because he thought he knew the truth, but he didn't.

"Not entirely." I inched my glasses up my nose. "The Stripe Back was already dead, actually," I grinned and *enjoyed how delicious it felt to risk the truth for once. "He just took the blame."*

"Hold up." He threw up his hands and pulled in his chin. I could see he got a sick thrill from my confession. "You dog! How'd you kill him? Gunshot? Stabbing?"

I lifted my eyebrows at him. I ignored his question "I remember his words exactly. The ones that pushed me over the edge. 'You're such a waste.' That's when I drove an axe into his chest."

"Damn, Simon!" He looked impressed and cheered. "You are a sick son of a bitch. That's cold. Your own father, damn!" He smacked his thigh.

I looked away and took a deep breath to steady myself. His death was on my hands, it was true, but the reality was it had come down to me or him, and I'd just swung first.

"Just when I think you're too boring for me," he slapped his hands together, "bam! You hit me with another surprise. Christ, you'd make a great Potens member."

"No." I shot that shit down quick like I always did whenever he brought it up.

He raised his hands. "I know, I know, no memberships allowed." He rubbed the back of his head. "What about your mom? Did you off her too?" I glared at him, and his mouth jerked at my response. "Sorry. You just never talk about them."

I closed my eyes when I thought about my father and Allen and the unthinkable things they'd done to my precious mother. "She died." I stood when I smelled the casserole. "Which you will if you don't leave."

"Fine," he kicked his feet up on the table, "but not 'til dinner's served. It smells really good."

I rolled my eyes and headed for the kitchen. When would he learn I hated company?

My doorbell rang and jerked me from my memory. I rubbed my eyes then tapped my phone to see it was just after one in the morning. I had taken a fistful of painkillers and must have passed out on the couch. It rang again, and when I moved, I felt a sharp pain rip through my entire body.

"Answer it or I'll kick it down," Grim barked. I limped to the door and opened it to find him and Jesse looking like members of some gangster crew. "Invite us in."

"Do I have a choice?"

"No." He stepped forward as I moved out of the way.

I peeked around to see if anyone else was out there, but I couldn't spot anyone, and that almost was more nerve-wracking. "I don't have much more flesh to pound."

"There's always bones." Grim undid the button on his jacket, sat on the couch, and ran an arm along the back of the chair. "Sit."

Jesse stepped back and folded his hands in front of him. He alone was frightening, but I'd seen what the two of them were capable of, so I didn't waste any time doing what I was told.

"You lied to me." His eyes narrowed to slivers and pierced through me.

"Yeah." I didn't bother lying. "Only about that, but yes, I did."

"Why?"

I licked my dry lips. "Respectfully, Brick is a product of my father's mistakes. I owed him nothing. He was better off without me. Just like he and I were both better off without our father."

"You didn't answer my question. I don't fucking like being lied to. You could have told me the truth." His growl sent a chill through my spine. It also bothered me I was older than this man questioning me about my past, but I also liked my bones intact, so I swallowed my pride.

"Look, Grim, all I wanted was to be left alone to live a simple life, but for some reason I can't have that. I never asked to be pulled into any of this. I withheld the truth about who I was because you're, let's face it, a member of the Devil's Reach and Trigger's best friend. You're all friends of my brother's." I had to make him see how impossible it was to tell him the truth.

"I mean, jeez, think about it. I just wanted to work off the rest of my debt to the Potens and be done. I knew Cameron's days were numbered, and I thought if I could just get through that, I could leave and finally have the life I wanted." I flipped open the box on the table and tried not to groan in pain as I handed him my dream. He held the paper up to the light and studied the listing.

"What's this?"

"It's a two-bedroom cabin off the grid in Wyoming. Just me, my books, and my thoughts." I blushed a little and felt uncomfortable as I spoke about something that was so important to me.

He looked at the paper again then dropped his arm and studied me.

"Something's been bothering me." He handed the cabin listing to Jesse. "Why was Allen so interested in you joining the DR?"

"I don't know." I rethought my words at his expression. I'd had a lot of time to wonder about it, and I figured I knew why. "I'm smart, great with numbers, and made the mistake of helping my father out one time with finding a smarter way to launder their money. He was impressed, as it worked. After that, he came back again and again for my advice. The more I pushed back, the harder he came at me. But I dug my heels in and never gave up. I refused to be a part of it."

"Until you killed your father."

"What?" The word dropped right out of my mouth. I should have known Grim would figure that out. "Does Brick know?"

He picked a piece of lint off his pants and took a

moment to answer. "No, I haven't told him. You gave him something he's been searching for for years. Closure." I swallowed hard with relief. "And for that reason, I won't make my friend suffer any more grief. He's in a good place now."

"Thank you."

"Don't thank me." His gaze moved to mine. "None of this was for you." I nodded. "What you'll do now is finish what my father asked you to do, then pack your shit up and get the fuck out of town. If I ever hear you're in Vegas, California, or Italy, I will make sure you meet the same fate as your father."

"Understood." I began to see that just maybe I'd not have the shit beaten out of me again and relaxed a little.

"And how do you feel about the Devil's Reach now?" He eyed me through those slits again.

I slowly shook my head. "There was a time when I wanted to see the club go down, burn in flames for what Allen and Dad did to me, but years in jail gives you time and a different perspective. I know it was Allen and not the rest of the club who took part of me away. Life's too short to care about the past, so that ship's sailed." Grim gave a tight nod, and Jesse dropped the paper back down in front of me.

I flinched involuntarily as Grim pushed to his feet. He really was a powerful man. "Mr. Gates." I felt like I needed to say more. He turned to look at me, and his jaw ticked like he was about to snap. "If it's not too much to ask," I couldn't believe I was allowing this part of myself to open up, "could you just let Brick know I'm sorry and give him something?" I hobbled over to my desk and pulled out an envelope and thumbed through some old photos until I found the one I wanted. "I was going to toss it when I moved, but maybe Brick might want it. So..." I handed him the photo of my father standing next to Trigger's uncle Gus. It was just after he'd joined the DR. He looked happy in his leather vest. "My mother took the photo."

Grim tucked it away in his pocket and glanced at Jesse. "One more thing."

"Yes?"

"Stay the fuck away from Kenna."

TWENTY-ONE

KENNA

I leaned my hot, sweaty forehead against my arm as I emptied my stomach for the third time that morning. I heard a sympathetic whine behind me and, with what little strength I had, patted Leal on the neck.

"I'm okay," I reassured them both. "Apparently, the baby doesn't want food today." I tried to will myself to get up. "Food is overrated, anyway," I lied and closed the lid. I plunked my body heavily down on the seat. Both boys inched closer. "Can you get me some water?" I pointed to the sink and Zhar hopped up and did a spin. "Close enough." I leaned down and kissed his head as Leal moved in for some love. "For two scary dogs, you guys are very big babies."

My phone buzzed on the counter, and I knew my time to let myself feel like crap was up.

> Harris: Ready to head over when you are. Having drinks at bar in the casino, no hurry.

> Kenna: Sounds great. I'll make my way down.

This was one of those moments I wished I hadn't insisted I keep my bigger clients. I glanced in the mirror. The person who stared back at me was pale and worn out. "Christ, I look terrible." I quickly washed my face and re-applied my makeup, then brushed my teeth, pinched my cheeks, and stood straight. "You're fine," I reassured myself. "Okay, boys, let's go see the lord and master." I headed down to Grim's office to drop them off.

The elevator ride made my stomach turn, and I had to fight with my head to override it. Jesse greeted me as I stepped out, but I noticed he shot me a worried look. I gave him a little wave instead of my normal cheery good morning.

I knocked on Grim's door and stepped inside. He was on the phone. I took the boys inside as he hastily hung up from his call.

"You okay?" He studied my face.

"I'm fine." I forced a smile. I knew better than to

give Grim a reason for me to stay in the penthouse all day. "Just a late start today."

"Maybe you should've stayed in bed."

"Grim," I closed my eyes and fought back the prickle of sweat that shot across my forehead, "I have a job to do, clients who need me, and bills to pay."

"Bills?" He raised an amused brow but backed off when I didn't react with my normal feistiness. "Fine." He squinted at me. "You sure you're feeling all right?"

"Yes." Leal bumped my hand, and I swung my heavy head to smile at him. "I have to meet Harris, and then we're heading over to Indulge." He nodded but watched me carefully as he crossed the room to where I stood. He used the back of his hand to feel my forehead. I pulled away, but he steered my head back in his direction.

"What are you not telling me?"

I leaned up and kissed his lips. "That I love you." I winked and slid out of his hold.

"Kenna."

"Bye, Grim." I rushed to the door. "Bye, boys." I blew them a kiss and avoided his glare.

I hurried down the hallway, past Jesse who hit the button for me like a gentleman, and I sank into the wall when I was finally alone.

Today was going to be hard.

I spotted Mr. Harris in the bar, but the smell of a shrimp platter on its way to the private poker room had me flying into the employee's bathroom. The place still spun when I finally got cleaned up and back out onto the busy floor.

Come on, Kenna. I smacked myself back into gear and greeted Harris and his friends.

"You look pale," he whispered as we made our way outside where the fresh air felt wonderful on my sticky skin. "Fun night?"

"If your idea of fun is vomiting every thirty minutes on the dot, then, sure, *fun* night." He looked concerned. "I'm almost two months pregnant." I rubbed my stomach, and his face morphed into shock then excitement.

"Well, shit, Kenna, that's fantastic!"

I laughed lightly. "It is, but this kid is determined for me to be skin and bones. It doesn't like food."

"My sister was the same way. Sorry, that's got to be rough." He looked at the time. We were to meet some friends of his who were in town for a poker tournament. "If you don't want to go, I'm sure we can handle this on our own."

"And miss all the fun?" I tried to sound upbeat, but even I could hear my fatigue. "I'm known to be stubborn at times."

"You?" He laughed, and we hurried to join the others for the short walk to Indulge. We were almost there when I heard my name called.

"Kenna!"

I shielded my glasses and saw Jayden approach us.

Harris snickered next to me. "I've never liked that guy."

"Get in line." I excused myself and walked toward Jayden. I didn't want a client to hear anything about the Potens or that Jayden had been let go from his job at the hotel. I knew my security guys were around, and I also knew Jesse was probably getting a phone call from one of them at that moment. "Jayden."

"We need to talk."

I crossed my arms. "Why?"

"You're all that with the Gates family." He made a face. "I need you to get my job back."

"I can't do that."

"No one will touch me. No one will even hear me out. They just know I was fired from Indulge, and that's enough for them not to give me a chance."

I shook my head. "What your father did was not the Gateses' fault."

"Maybe not, but it's not mine either."

Jason stepped out of the sea of people and made sure I could see him if I needed him. He had a phone up to his ear. "Look, Jayden, I'm sorry, but I can't—"

"But you can." He grabbed my elbow, and Harris and his friends stepped forward, but Jason got there first as I ripped my arm free. "We're just talking, for fuck's sake," he snarled.

"You've always had a problem with boundaries,

Jayden." A movement behind him caught my eye, and I felt my blood pressure drop. Sonny. I looked back at Jayden and wondered if they both planned this little encounter. "It may have been your father who black-listed you, but your inability to treat a woman with respect would have brought you to the same end."

"Move it along," Jason warned him.

I went over to face Mr. Harris and his friends, embarrassed at what had happened.

"Hey, man," Harris called Jason over, "I think Ms. Lodge could use a day off. Could you please escort her back to Secrets?"

"I'm fine, really," I protested and felt mortified at the whole situation.

"I insist, Kenna." He stepped close. "I've seen enough to know you aren't yourself. You're a fabulous host, but I think you're an even better person, and therefore I'm pulling rank and saying you need some time. We'll be here once you're feeling better."

I felt unbelievably tired and was thankful for his kindness. "Thanks." I turned to Jason who looked pleased I didn't put up a fight.

By the time we got back to Secrets, I felt dizzy and disoriented. I stopped in the lobby and held on to the back of a chair.

Jason didn't know what to do, poor guy. "Miss, can I get you something?"

"I'm going to head to the kitchen to get something to eat. I think I'm just hungry."

He walked me there and seemed more than relieved when Dale took my arm.

"Oh, shit," he looked me up and down, "don't tell me that's food poisoning on your face."

"What are you doing here?" Was I that confused? "Why aren't you at Indulge?"

"Darling, this is like my sister kitchen. They can't do without my advice. I repeat, what's going on, babe?"

"I'm so very pregnant and need something I can keep down." I fell onto a stool and buried my head in my arms on the counter. I heard him tell Jason he could go, but I had no idea if he did.

"Crackers." He poured some into a bowl and set them next to me. "That's what my mom gave me whenever my stomach was hurting." I heard him whisper to someone, but I didn't care enough to listen.

I eyed the beads of salt that layered the white cracker and felt my entire body heave.

"She's over here," I heard Jason say, and a moment later, Grim was peeling me off the counter so he could look at me.

"Hey," his tone didn't match his stern but worried expression, "what's going on?" I flopped forward, too tired to care anymore. I welcomed his homey scent.

"She said she can't keep anything down." Dale's voice seemed to come from a distance.

"Chicken." Grim rubbed my back tenderly. "Protein's a natural anti-nausea. I would've already told her that, if someone hadn't been hiding things from me. Come on, sweetheart."

In the next moment, I was swept into a pair of strong arms as the room went black.

It took great effort to peel my eyelids open. I squinted and looked carefully around. I was in Grim's bedroom at Secrets. The room was almost dark with just a small glow of light from his bookshelf to give it a soft hue. Zhar made a sound then disappeared out of the room, leaving me with Leal, who had tucked himself against my side. He faintly snored, and I almost laughed.

"Hey, boy." I gently patted his head. As I lifted my arm, I was shocked to find I was hooked up to an IV. What the hell did I miss?

"You're alive." Grim was suddenly in the doorway, arms crossed, looking powerful as always. "It only took you two days to come back to me."

"I've been out for two days?"

He moved into the room and sat on the bed next to me. "You have hyperemesis gravidarum." I pinched my brows, confused as to what that meant. "Which means it's not just the baby making you sick. This is more than ordinary morning sickness. So, for now, we are to watch you closely, and get your body strong again with this." He pointed to the IV fluids. "And if you continue to lie to me," he glared, "and not eat, then I'll be forced to handcuff you to our bed until you go into labor."

"I bet you'd love that," I teased, but he didn't find it funny. "Sorry. I thought if I told you, you'd force me to stop."

"I would have."

"Grim," I pulled his hand so he'd come closer, "all of this is very new, and I'm not used to being less than a hundred percent all the time. So, I tried to muster through it. I wasn't going to wimp out."

"Kenna." He shook his head, but I held up a hand.

"No, wait. Honestly, how was I to know I had hyper-whatchacallit?"

"Hyperemesis gravidarum," he carefully pronounced.

"Yeah, that. Anyway, I see now that ignoring it isn't going to work."

"Doc says it happens sometimes during pregnancy, and it can be serious if we aren't careful. You need to eat better and take some meds he recommended."

"I'm thrilled for this little guy," I rubbed my tummy, "but there's so much going on, and sometimes

I forget that it's just—" My eyes flooded, and I fought hard to keep the tears back.

"Just?" He caught a tear as one escaped.

"Just not me anymore. I'm so used to being in survival mode, or on the defense, that I think I can handle it all."

"You're strong, Kenna. No one can say otherwise, but you need to lean on me now. We can get through this together."

"I know." I sniffed and lowered some of my walls that had shot up. Leal huffed and eyed us both, clearly unhappy to be disturbed by our conversation. "Are they always this way with you when no one's around?" I stroked Leal's head.

"We have our moments in private." He rubbed Leal's ear, and Zhar jumped up for his share of the attention. They were similar in appearance, but Zahr was slightly lighter and a lot more of a baby than Leal who tries to play the big brother role. "I've always tried to keep them at arm's length because they need to know who's the boss. They are, after all, a security tool," he shook his head, "then you came along and made them into big babies."

"Loving them isn't going to make them any less protective."

He cleared his throat. "Loving them, especially in public, shows vulnerability."

"A vulnerability in you or them?"

He thought for a moment. "Both."

"Is that why you—" I stopped myself when I suddenly felt exhaustion sweep over me.

I eyed Grim, who had stopped rubbing. "Say it," he ordered.

"Nothing." I decided not to say what was on my mind. He reached over my head and wiggled the handcuffs. "Fine. It just occurred to me that you haven't shared the news about us to Jenelle." I eyed him. "Have you?"

"Not exactly, but—"

"But you insist I wear the iceberg that hit the Titanic." I held up my ring.

"You don't like it?"

"Of course, I love it," I reassured him, "but it makes me think you want her to find out through me, instead of through you."

He didn't like that; his face turned to stone. "Are you calling me out?"

I sighed. "Maybe I am."

He cocked a brow, studied my face, then something came into his eyes.

"What?"

"You should eat." He changed topics so fast it made my head spin. He quickly left and returned a moment later with a tray. There was chicken soup, with home-made bread, and a chocolate treat. I was pleased that my stomach didn't turn at the smell. "If you can eat this, I'll allow you to leave the room. Once I get that IV removed."

"You can't hold me hostage, Grim." I draped the napkin over my lap, secretly happy he took care of me.

He gave the dogs a command, and they jumped to their feet and stood by the door. He tilted my chin up and brushed his lips over mine. "Watch me, sweetheart."

I pretty much ate everything, except the bread had proved to be a little more than I could handle. The soup was spot on. I could feel the calories bring my body back to life, my headache finally subsided, and the cobwebs were cleared away. Once a lady came and removed the IV, I cautiously showered, brushed my teeth, then pulled on a pair of yoga pants and a tank. I didn't have much energy after that to dry my hair completely, but I did a little.

I eyed the pups and wondered if they'd let me pass. "See, I ate." I showed them the tray, and they just stared. "Okay, umm…" I held up some of the bread. "Who wants a treat?" Again nothing. "Really?" I spotted my phone and thought about calling Grim, but something hit me. I remembered a command he'd used once. I straightened my shoulders and used the best Grim voice I could muster. To my absolute delight, they stepped away from the door and waited for me to lead the way. "Well, shit, look at me go." I couldn't help the grin.

The suite was quiet other than the sound of the rain pounding against the window. I squinted at the angry sky that rumbled with its warning to stay indoors. Monsoon season was in full bloom, which meant we had to be ready to hold some events inside. I shook off my constant need to be in work mode and rested my forehead against the cool glass.

Voices drew my attention, and I headed down the hall to where a light was on. Thunder clapped loudly, and I swore I felt the hotel shake.

I peeked inside the massive living room that could fit three of my suites inside and saw Grim in front of a flat screen TV. He was spread out on the couch, and to my surprise he was in sweats, a t-shirt, and a ball hat. The best part was he held a beer by its neck. Then I heard a curse and saw Jesse in similar attire with a fist raised at the screen. He sat in an armchair across from Grim and nursed his own bottle of ale.

I grinned as I came up behind them. "So, this is what you two do when you're not on duty?"

Jesse dropped his feet to the floor, nearly spilling his beer, but Grim just raised one of his sexy brows and clucked his tongue.

"And how did you get by the boys?"

I couldn't help but let him have a full-on gleeful smile. "You're not the only one who can give commands, baby."

"We'll see about that." He matched my grin, but it

turned into a scowl when Zhar trotted out and flopped on his bed on the floor. "You had one job to do," Grim threatened.

I glanced at Jesse. "I like this side of you." He smiled and raised his beer. "I promise I won't tell a soul that I saw you in something other than a suit."

"It's not often I let anyone see me without a suit on," he huffed.

"You should." I studied him until he blushed and considered who I knew that would be a good match for him.

Grim pulled a knee up and patted the couch for me to sit. We hadn't had a lot of downtime together, and I liked the idea of just hanging out. "You're looking better." I curled up in front of him, and he pulled me to his chest then drew a blanket over me.

"I'm feeling much better, thanks."

He kissed the top of my head. "Good."

"You like baseball, Kenna?" Jesse tipped his beer toward the TV.

I sighed and thought about the last time I watched a game. "I liked when Max Kepler came to town. He had dinner with me and some friends."

"Kepler," Jesse's face lit up, "from the Minnesota Twins?"

"That be him."

He whistled, clearly impressed. "When was he here?"

I did the math. "Three days before you guys came home."

"Clearly, we got back just in time." Grim slid his hand between my thighs under the blanket. "I don't need any more problems."

"He was very nice but not my type." I looked up and kissed his jaw but flinched when a crack of thunder filled the room. Zhar yelped, and Grim reached down to pat his head. Though Leal didn't show any nerves, I did notice him slink into the room and lie under the table close to his brother.

Jesse's phone lit up, and he studied the screen. "Huh." I felt Grim turn to look at him. Jesse held up a finger. "I'll be right back."

I shifted in his hold to see him better. "Let me guess. Something to do with Sonny?" I watched his throat contract as he sipped his beer. His tattoos moved like they were real.

"Sonny hasn't been seen for a few days." He traced a finger down my neck. "We're just making sure it stays that way."

"And what about Simon?" I couldn't help but feel bad for the guy. He just wanted a simple life. "How's he holding up?"

"I went to visit him the other night." That was news to me. "He knows what's expected of him now."

"I still can't believe he's Brick's brother."

Grim shook his head. "It's a bunch of mind fuckery, right there."

I tucked my hair behind my ear. "Do you think Simon's a bad guy for not saying anything about Brick or that he worked for the Potens? Like, do you think he's still a trustworthy guy?"

Grim set his beer on the table and tucked a hand behind his head, making his sexy muscles flex. "How do you feel?"

I shrugged. "I don't know. I like Simon. He's always been nothing but kind to me. I think maybe he was given a shitty deal due to his father. He didn't have much of a chance of getting what he really wanted out of life. Maybe he will now."

He nodded. "I agree with that."

"I'm a little worried about him, though, I thought maybe he'd reach out and touch base, but he hasn't."

"I'm glad to hear that," he growled, and I could see the truth written all over his face.

"You told him to stay away from me, didn't you?"

"I did." He didn't miss a beat.

I leaned back when he reached for my hand. "Why? You just agreed that he was given a shit life."

"Just because I agreed doesn't mean I want him around my soon-to-be wife." He flipped me around and was suddenly on top of me. He kissed my chest, collarbone, and neck. I closed my eyes, loving how he felt on my skin. "We need to purge our world of all things bad and start to rebuild with people we can trust." His breath was hot against my skin. "But," he leaned up and looked down at me, "if I thought Simon was truly bad, he'd already have his bones broken into little pieces. I'd have chopped him up and spread his bits around Vegas. So be happy for that." I shivered at his words, and he smirked, clearly enjoying my reaction.

"Grim," Jesse said, "We need to handle something."

"Understood." Grim kept his eyes on me. "Hey, Minnie."

"Should I leave, or can I watch the show?" Minnie swooned. Jesse must have called her to stay with me.

"My girl needs her rest." He kissed me. "Don't leave. Promise me." He glared at me.

"And risk you getting mad at me?" I wiggled my brows at him, but he wasn't having it. "I promise."

"Good." He kissed me hard then left.

Minnie swept across the room and dropped into Jesse's now vacant chair. She dug into her bag. "I come bearing comfort." She pulled out my childhood panda bear.

"Oh, my God. Did you get him from my house?"

"Yup." She grinned with shiny pink lips as she tossed him at me.

"Mr. Bamboo!" I caught my beloved stuffed animal and drank in his musty scent. "Thanks, friend."

"Anything for you." She snagged Jesse's beer.

"Now, what are we watching, because as much as I love a man in tight baseball pants, the sport itself does nothing for me."

"Hey, Min?"

"Mm?"

"You seem happy."

Her smile told me I'd hit the nail on the head. "Since Brick found out about Simon, it's like something's lifted off his shoulders. He's back to his old self again, the guy I fell in love with all those years back."

"I'm really happy for you both."

"Thanks."

I frowned as something wiggled its way through my thoughts. "Do you think love can work if you don't fully know the person?"

"You worried you and Grim won't make it?"

I rubbed Mr. Bamboo's ear while I thought. "I think I always questioned romance books when the couples fell in love so easily."

She snorted. "You guys hardly fell in love easily, Kenna. You fought your way there."

"That's true, I guess."

She muted the TV and looked at me. "Look, girlfriend. Sure, things happened fast, but look how much you two have grown since. Neither of you wanted anything more than hot sex. You fought like tigers then practically tore each other to pieces. If that ain't love at first sight, I don't know what is." She laughed and smacked her knee.

I had to join in her laughter. Then her face turned serious.

"Really, though, I don't think a wife was ever on Grim's radar. I don't know when that happened. You've both been through some horrible stuff over the last while. Heartbreak like that can be more than a person can endure. Yet here you are, on his couch, knocked up and glowing." She pointed at my belly.

"It's just so fast." I chewed my cheek again then forced myself to stop.

"Can I tell you something?" I waited for her to go on. "Jenelle made a move on Grim last night, and he didn't exactly put her off."

My blood burned instantly, and I felt it go through my body like a heatwave. I tossed the blanket off. "The fuck you say?"

"That. right there," she grinned suddenly, "that fire you have in you right now to kill someone, that's love, girlie. And I've never, ever seen that in you before."

"You fucking suck." I sat back and took a breath, then gave her a look of death.

"Why, yes, I do. Quite well, actually."

I threw a beer cap at her, and she laughed.

"If Brick and I can weather a decade-long storm, you can handle this one."

"I guess." I settled into the couch and mulled

over her words while she flicked through the channels. We settled on a comedy, and before long, I drifted off to sleep, content to be there with my best friend.

I spent the next two days mostly in bed and slept like the dead. A few times, Laurel came in and checked on me with a tasty morsel of food to tempt me. She also brought reassurance that what I was feeling now was normal. Of course, she had the doctor come in to back up her words.

Once I was back on a high protein diet in the morning, everything felt normal again. The tiredness was still there, but at least I kept my food down without the help of the IV.

Grim was in and out and seemed extra stressed. I finally got it out of Laurel that they'd been combing through Cameron's files and had flushed out another member of the Potens. He worked in the accounting department at Indulge. I knew I needed to give him the space he needed to deal and process what that must mean to them.

The day finally came when I was able to join the world of the living. "Decaf, please," I grumbled to the barista and wished I could have my normal caffeine kick.

"Nice to see you back up and kicking." I turned and hugged Morgan tightly. "I missed you."

"I missed you too." I kissed his cheek. "What have I missed?" We walked toward a table and took our seats.

"Well, now, let's see. Vinni was talking to some dude at Minnie's the other night, and Trigger came up and smoked the dude in the jaw. Guess he'd been stealing. Thought Vinni was going to shit himself."

"Sienna mentioned that even after all these years, Vinni's still terrified of Trigger." I laughed. "I mean, I get it, but Vin's mafia."

"It's 'cause Trigger's quiet. It's always the quiet ones people fear the most." Morgan rubbed his long beard. "I'm glad you're doing okay. Couple of us are going for a desert ride later, see if we can scrounge up some trouble. Maybe round up a couple of Stripe Backs." His grin made me happy. He looked past me. "I see this is my cue to leave."

Huh?

A hand slid around my neck, and I had to contain myself when his aftershave found my nose. He tilted my head back and kissed my lips.

"Who let you out?"

"Your mother." I grinned against his kiss. "I've missed you."

"Good." He kissed me again and indicated to Morgan to stay put. "I have someone who wants to see how you are." He nodded over Morgan's shoulder, and

I saw Yen Hong waving at me from where he stood with some friends. "Do you feel up to company?"

"I really do." I grinned and felt a little more life pour into me. "Thanks."

"Meet me for lunch at one up in the suite." He offered me a hand and grinned. "I want to see you eat."

"Sure thing, boss." I winked, and he gave me a look that shot straight to my core.

Minnie was right. We got this.

Later that night, we gathered outside near the pool at Tess's burlesque house. Trigger was in full swing in front of the barbecue. The house was pretty much at max capacity. I was proud of Tess; she'd taken on her mother's business and made it boom. It was the perfect fuck you to that awful woman. Not many people would be able or even want to run a place like this and make a go of it. It had been close to bankruptcy at one point, but Tess pulled it back from the dead.

"Why you gotta judge?" Rail's voice drew my attention, and I chuckled. He and Brick were always at it. "So what if I'm into foxes?"

"It's weird."

"It's not weird. The furry community are wild and let me explore a whole different side of my sexual desires." He looked at Morgan. "You get me, right? I saw you leave the other night with that mink."

"The fuck?" Trigger grunted, and Brick's face lit up.

Morgan shook his head. "She came on to me. One look at her and I was out of there. You're on your own with this kink."

"Good." Rail shrugged. "More tail for me."

"Literally," Tess jumped in, and Trigger let out an unexpected laugh. Trigger's laughter had always been rare. I'd noticed, though, that as he got older, he was loosening up a little. I was glad he allowed himself the odd moment to appreciate things around him. He took more time to enjoy family these days. It was really nice, and the joy it brought Tess couldn't be overlooked.

I made my way over to Grim where he sat with Elio by one of the fire pits. I reached over his shoulders and slid my hand down his chest. I nearly purred at how he lit up my body.

"Tess told me there's a room open upstairs," I whispered, and he drew my wrist up to his lips and kissed the inside of it softly. "You can blindfold me, and I'll be completely at your mercy." His arm slipped back, and he caught me around my waist and pulled me to his lap. I could feel how much my idea excited him.

"Oh, sweet girl," he kissed my neck, "you're already at my mercy."

"I suppose I am," I muttered without thinking, and he chuckled at my confession.

"I miss my wife," Elio grunted. I'd forgotten he was there. That was what Grim did to me; he made me forget the world was there.

Minnie cleared her throat, and I peeled myself off Grim to look up at her. "Kenna," she said loudly, trying to get everyone's attention around us. The crowd died down—well, everyone but Rail, his voice suddenly clear in the silence.

"Then she wiggled her long, fluffy tail over my lips as her front claws dug into the flesh of my ass and..." He trailed off and his eyes widened when he realized we all heard his words.

Brick gave an exaggerated shudder as Rail flipped him the bird then left. "Go on, Min," he called.

"Thank you, baby." She grinned and shot a disgusted look after Rail. "Kenna, we know you've gone through a lot lately, and we thought maybe you could use a little pick-me-up." She reached into a bag and pulled out a light green gift bag with yellow tissue paper exploding from the top. "I know it's a little premature, but..." she handed it to me, "I don't care." She beamed.

I pulled the paper out and peeked inside. Then a smile burst across my lips as I pulled out a little stuffed baby Panda made by Jelly Cat. "Oh, Min!"

"I know it's early, but you need a little excitement in your life. Well, the right kind, and that starts with celebrating the little one. Now you both have something to snuggle when you need comfort."

"This is the sweetest! Thank you." I batted tears away and hugged her hard.

I felt someone come up next to us. "My turn!" Tess cheered. "This is from me and Trigger." Trigger was hot on her heels, which made me chuckle. I ripped the paper away and opened the box and tossed my head back with a laugh. I held up a tiny Devil's Reach leather vest and showed everyone that it looked just like theirs.

"Member by blood is a special kind," Trigger grunted, and when he thought no one was looking, he swung his glance at Brick, who shared the same expression. If you watched closely enough, the guys shared a lot through looks.

"Thanks, guys. This is so thoughtful, and…" I pushed off Grim's lap as I saw a giant giraffe head floating through a sea of partiers on the deck.

Suddenly, Rail appeared, holding the rest of the seven-foot-high stuffed animal. "His name is Melman!" he shouted over the music. "Ain't he cute?" He stroked its neck. Then he fumbled awkwardly down a couple of stairs with it. He smoked several people in the head and back as he plowed through them without a care in the world. He proudly set it next to me. It was massive. "You should have heard the comments I got as I dragged him through the house. And you all thought I was the sick, twisted one?" He cocked his thumb toward the house. "Let's just say this poor guy saw a lot more than he needed to." He looked at Tess. "Who knew people were into *stuffed* animals too," he huffed with a cough. "Anyway," he grinned at us, "Melman." He pointed at it.

"Well, ah, thanks." I eyed the gigantic stuffed animal and wondered what it had seen in the last five minutes…and what it might have been exposed to even before that. I hugged Rail and gave the giraffe a pat on the chest as it stood with splayed legs listing slightly to the left.

"My turn." Morgan handed me a box, and I pulled the top off to discover an old pair of brass knuckles with a year written on the side. "My dad gave them to me when I was born, and I'm not reproducing anytime soon, so it should go to the first in the family."

Grim reached for them. "Damn straight, brother."

I realized how special his gesture was and kissed Morgan on the cheek. "That's pretty special."

"This baby is the newest generation of what's to come for the club. That's what's special."

Trigger lifted his beer. "Agreed. To fresh blood."

They all raised their drinks, as a flood of love warmed my heart. I had lost a lot over the past months, but I knew I had gained so much more.

"Kenna?" I turned to find Zara. She looked unsure of her welcome. "Can we speak?"

"Of course." I looked at Grim, and he gave me a *no idea* glance. I stepped away, as I could see she was moments away from breaking down.

"Sorry. I heard you were all up here. I've wanted,"

she closed her eyes, "to clear the air about my mother. Honestly, Kenna, I had no idea there was anything between my mom and Cameron. Truth." She bit her lip. "The very idea has me spiraling. No offense."

"None taken. I get it," I assured her. "But, Zara, I don't blame you for anything. We're friends, and I am so glad you were there when you were because I don't think I could have done what I did if it wasn't for your help."

"Yes, but—"

"No buts, Zara. Dad was never easy. You of all people know that. You were invaluable to me when I needed the inside scoop on possible clients. I won a lot of them because of you. Your ability to research at the speed you do is amazing. I hope you get to use it in your new job."

"I will." Her eyes softened, and I could tell she was relieved I wasn't upset.

Her fingers entwined in front of her stomach. "How's your mom?"

I sighed, conflicted on the topic. "Holding up."

"Good. How are you dealing with it all?"

I ran a hand through my hair. "One day at a time. I have a lot to unpack," I pointed to my head, "but I have a lot of support, so I'm lucky."

"You are." She looked at everyone chatting and laughing around us as they gave Rail shit about something. The guy was such an easy target, but I knew he loved every minute of it. "Treasure that, okay?"

"I will." I leaned in for a hug. "Thanks for stopping by."

"Thanks for understanding."

I waved goodbye and made my way back to my family.

"Everything okay?" Minnie wrapped an arm around my neck.

"Yes." I hugged my friend. "Today's been a good day. I really needed this."

"Good, because I have one last idea I think is a little wild, but…"

TWENTY-TWO

GRIM

Never did I think I'd be in one, but there I was. I glanced at Morgan a few times. I wondered if he believed this would ever happen. Then there were Elio and Trigger sitting side-by-side with a beer in their hands. Rail was winding up a fucking disposable camera like it was the damn nineties. I chuckled, and Kenna glanced up at me with hungry eyes. I grabbed her ass and pulled her closer to me.

"Do you, Minnie, take Brick to be your main man?"

"I do!" Minnie beamed with a giggle.

"Do you, Brick, take Minnie to be your main girl?"

"Fuck yeah, I do!" He grabbed her face and slammed his lips to hers as I laughed. These Vegas chapels were a riot. The Elvis impersonator went on, and then Kenna squeezed my hand.

"Do you, Kenna, take Grim to be your main man?"

"I do." She dried her tears of laughter. This entire thing was crazy, but I loved the idea of us tying our knot, and what better way than to share our date with family? Kenna elbowed me when I missed my cue. "I swear to Lucifer, Grim.

"If he don't, I will," Rail chimed in, and I grabbed Kenna by the waist and stared down into her eyes.

"I do."

"Damn right, you do." She pressed her body to mine as Mom, Dad, and Knox started to cheer. Elvis continued, but all I cared about was that Kenna was now officially mine.

"Keep your promise to me, though," I whispered for only her to hear. "I want you to have the wedding of your dreams once all this shit is over."

"I promise." She wrapped her arms around my neck. "But you know that doesn't really matter to me. All that matters is you're mine."

That pesky sound of winding made me roll my eyes as Rail came close with his plastic camera.

"Cock your hip out a little, Kenna." He snapped a photo. "Grim give me a little more of that *blue steel* in the eyes. I want to really feel this moment, not just see it."

"Christ," I muttered.

"Min, give me some sexy shots." Rail beamed as Minnie pulled Brick down and stuck her boobs in his face.

"Holy shit, are we done here?" I needed to get out of this place.

"Shall we celebrate?" Minnie squeaked as Brick pinched her ass. We all laughed.

"The rooftop, it is!" Rail shouted.

Jesse's posture suddenly changed, and I noticed he had his phone to his ear. "Trigger," he called, and Trig and I joined him and stepped away from the others. "You'll never guess who's in the lobby."

"Who?" Trigger looked at me, and I shook my head, just as curious.

"Caleb." The Stripe Back president. "Seems he's got something to tell you."

"That so?" I could almost hear the wheels turning in his head as he stroked his chin. When I made a move to head for the door, he stopped me. "You got a wife to celebrate." His green eyes lit up. "If there's any fuckin' fun comin', I'll tell ya."

I huffed. "All right." I nodded and glanced at Kenna watching us.

He called Morgan to join him, and they slipped out before the others noticed.

"We goin' or not?" Minnie called, and I joined Kenna with a grin and a wave to let her know all was okay.

"Yes, we're coming." I took Kenna's hand as Knox blocked our path. The others headed for the elevator. "Just give me one second," I said.

"Congratulations, Kenna. I know it's been said, but I'm so glad you're part of our family now."

"Thanks, Knox." She leaned in and hugged him. "That means a lot."

He smiled at me. "A year ago, I would've placed a thousand dollar bet I'd never hear you say those words to a woman. I couldn't be happier, and I know Leo would feel the same way." He held out his hand. "I love ya, brother. Thanks for all you've done for me."

"That was all you." I pushed his hand away and gave him a hug. "I love you, too." I kissed the side of his head. "Now, let's stop all this mushy shit. I need a drink." I grabbed Kenna and swept her into my arms.

Knox clapped. "Let's go have some fun!"

I woke the next morning, still inside my naked wife. Even as I thought the word, it sounded crazy. I tested it again by saying it out loud. "Hey, wife," I whispered and slid my hand down her bare skin and laced our fingers so our rings were together.

Knox was right. The idea that I would be married with a child on the way was never something I could have envisioned for myself. And now, there was nothing I wanted more. I loved the way my tattoos looked against her blank canvas. I slid my hand back and around her stomach, giving the baby a little love, too. After last night's events, I bet the little guy was dizzy. "Sorry about that." I chuckled. "But nothing can tame me when I'm with your momma." I pressed against Kenna.

"Unless you have waffles with a side of pancakes, you can keep any dirty thoughts at bay." But she still wiggled her butt against me.

"Nice to see you have your appetite back."

"Can you blame me? I burned a lot of calories keeping up with you last night."

I moaned as I let the memories flood my mind, but the sound of my alarm shut the memories down fast. "Christ." I pressed my face against her back. "I'll order some food, but I've got a business meeting with Yen Hong."

"I'll be here, playing hostess to our baby. Say hi to him for me."

I rolled her over and straddled her slim body. "Don't leave—"

"Unless I know." She finished off my line with a chuckle, and I glared at her. I reached over her head and pulled down a bar with a chain attached to each side. "Oh, hello, something new." She admired it, and I rolled my eyes, as that wasn't exactly the reaction I was looking for. "You can come out and play with me any time you want." She wiggled her brow and poked the chain.

"All right, never mind." I pushed the bar back into position, and as I rolled off her, she turned to look at the headboard.

"It's like a sex wall." She giggled and felt around. "He's leaving soon, then it's just me and you." She jumped when I swatted her ass.

"We'll explore later." I headed for the shower.

My meeting with Yen Hong went well. He wanted to invest in Secrets and open his clothing line with an exclusive store just off the lobby. I was more than thrilled to sign him on, mostly because it was something Kenna could sink her teeth into. It helped I knew he was a good friend to her. This was just one of the many avenues I hoped to bring to Kenna. She had a lot of skills we could tap into, and I knew the store idea would excite her.

"Mr. Gates, Mr. Capri." Salazar found me with Elio at the casino later that evening. "How are you gentlemen this evening?"

"Well, thanks." I pointed to an open seat. "Please join us. Would you like something to drink?"

"If you don't mind."

"Please." Elio waved for him to join us. "How has your day been?"

Salazar rubbed his chin as if something was on his mind. "I was very much enjoying a game of golf, but when I came in to get some lunch, I witnessed something that bothered me." He began to pull out his phone.

"Oh?" As I waited for him to continue, my mind suddenly flew to Kenna. I wondered if she had listened to my warning not to go out without letting me know. Perhaps she *had* ventured out and was looking for me to get her back in line. Wishful thinking on my part, perhaps.

"If you don't mind me saying, I know a lot has happened to your family lately, and you have enough on your plate, but that makes me feel even more obligated to share this with you." He handed me his phone. "Please humor me and scroll through to the right."

My mind boiled over as I studied the photos. I saw Sonny with members from one of my kitchen crews at Secrets.

"When my company decided to hire Cameron Tame as our lawyer, we did a thorough background check on him. It took a deep dive to discover he wasn't completely clean, but then who is?" He shrugged. "It's no secret I dabble in the darker side of business at times. I'm sure you will agree it's how things get done."

"Agreed," Elio purred, and Salazar gave him a slight nod. Elio's reputation and family ties were hardly a secret. His family name was respected by some but feared by many in Italy, the USA, and around the world.

"What I didn't find out until recently was that Cameron was entangled with an organization called the Potens." I felt Elio shift slightly in his seat. "From there, I dug more and discovered these men." He reached for his phone and showed me another photo of three more men. I recognized them as part of the security team that ran the poker chip supply here at Indulge. "They had interactions with Cameron on more than one occasion, including," he tilted his head to one side, "the Fourth of July, 2018." I raised a brow at him and licked the inside of my mouth. That date. It was the one and only breach we had at the hotel. Though these three had never been connected with any of it, until now…

I rubbed my hands over my thighs in a poor attempt to calm my temper. "And you discovered this how?"

"Because that was the same weekend Cameron met with my business associate, who just so happened to be staying here," he waved around the room, "and when I met Cameron for the first time."

"I see."

Elio tapped his ring on the table. "I'm sure you've met many men in your career. Why is it that these three men stand out to you?"

He turned to face Elio straight on, which I admired.

"Valid question. I think it's fair to say Sonny attracts a certain kind of person. On several occasions, I've seen these men walking into Cameron's office as I was leaving. They're not friendly and seemed to enjoy trying to intimidate me." He sighed and shook his head like they were pathetic for doing so. "Frankly, it was strange. They don't seem to be the kind of men who can afford a lawyer such as Cameron Tame. So why were they there?"

"And now Cameron's dead. So, when you spotted them here talking to Sonny, it was a red flag." Elio nodded like he followed his story.

"Exactly."

I hated that I'd lost all those years in Mexico instead of being here. Perhaps I'd have seen this cancer infesting my family's business.

Salazar ran a hand through his hair. "Forgive me if I step over a line, but I think perhaps your brother Leo saw something or felt something was off." I felt a hit to the chest at that, the pain that came whenever I realized I'd never see him again.

I squinted. "Why would you say that?"

"We had talked on occasion, and we both attended meetings with Cameron present. I thought he sensed what I did. We caught each other's eyes from time to time before I officially signed on with Cameron. I know now what a mistake that was. I have nothing concrete to tell you more than that." He shrugged. "Perhaps I'm grasping at straws."

Salazar was right. Leo had seen something, and he came to me with it. If anything, I'd hold on to the fact that Leo followed his instincts, and though it cost him his life, he saved the family.

"You're not alone in that feeling," I muttered. "And you're right. Leo did suspect something. It was the reason I came home." I wanted to make sure Leo was remembered in a good light.

"I'm truly sorry for his loss." Salazar lowered his head. "He was a good man."

"That he was," Elio agreed, and we all stayed silent for a moment.

"Mr. Gates," Salazar lowered his voice, "I bring this to you out of respect for you, your family, and for Kenna, who I have developed a kind friendship with. I've emailed you all that I've found, along with some research on the Potens. Please, take it or leave it. I just felt a need to share my findings with you."

"It's greatly appreciated." I shook his hand when he stood. "I'll look into everything you've provided me."

"All right." He turned to Elio. "Mr. Capri, thank you for letting me intrude on your evening."

Elio nodded. "*Grazie, signore.* Please, think nothing of it."

Once he left, we both took a moment to mull over what he had brought to us.

"Elio?"

He knew what I was thinking. "Niccola's done business with Salazar's company before. We have never had a reason not to trust him. At this point, I believe we should take what he said into consideration."

"Good. I agree."

I opened the email from Salazar and scanned through the photos and assorted information. Elio called Trigger to fill him in. He held the phone away from his mouth. "Shall we round them up and meet in the desert?"

"No." I nearly crushed my phone in my hand as I read the last line in the email. *From all my findings, I conclude that Sonny Conti is highly connected to the Potens, if not a direct bloodline, therefore someone to keep a close eye on.* "I have a different idea." I waved for him to follow me out back where we could speak freely.

I'd spent my fair share of time acting perfectly normal in front of someone while all my animal instincts fought to rip his body apart and break every bone one by one. When you grew up in the world I had, you learned to wait for the right moment. You lured your prey to you and let them see you lower your guard. Once they were comfortable, you attacked.

"Knock, knock." Kenna stood in the doorway of my office at Secrets in a dress that looked to be painted on her skin. Until I saw her in that, I'd been in an afternoon slump of exhaustion. No longer. "I know you have a meeting at six thirty, so I thought we could have dinner here together." She turned and waved to a waiter, and he wheeled a food cart inside. He gushed his thanks as his eyes enjoyed her sexiness. When he caught my glare, he stood straighter and looked away. "Please wait outside for the cart. We won't be long."

"Yes, Miss Kenna." He stepped quickly outside.

"Just like me," she set a plate of salmon on the table by the window, "you need to eat too."

"That's true." I admired the slight bump I could just make out under her sleek dress. "How was your day with Harris?"

She lit up. "Fun. I actually signed on two more of his friends. They spent money the moment they walked into the place. They lost six grand without blinking on the first poker hand." She looked radiant.

I gave her a hug. She molded to me and wrapped her arms over mine. "Were you wearing this at the time?" I plucked at the fabric.

"No, I decided naked was best," she teased.

I nipped at her ear, and she laughed. "Naked is only for me," I growled and spun her around, so I was pressed against her back.

"The fact that Harris told them to behave because I was pregnant was probably a major turnoff."

My erection couldn't be missed, and she chuckled, and I had to talk myself off the ledge. "Lunch can wait." I licked her ear.

"No, you need to eat first." She tried to pull away.

"I highly disagree."

She swatted at me and somehow wiggled free. She pulled out a chair to act as a barrier between us. "Eat," she commanded. "I have a client looking to meet DJ Clay, and the last thing I need is to look like I've just been thoroughly fucked by the owner of this establishment." She fanned herself dramatically.

"I disagree on that too," I muttered but took my seat. "I wanted to talk to you about something—"

A quick knock. Jesse came in with two workers who carried my new bookcase. "Just put it over there." I gave Jesse a piercing look then turned back to Kenna as he shrugged. "You should know tonight's meeting is with Jenelle and her father." She stilled but then resumed her meal.

"I was thinking of maybe green for the nursery." She switched topics. "Or we can wait until we find out the sex of the baby."

"Kenna, I'd like to discuss this with you."

"Well, I wouldn't."

I dropped my knife, and it hit the plate loudly. "You have nothing to worry about."

"Really, Grim? I came here to eat, not to discuss your girlfriend. You know what?" She tossed her napkin on the plate and pushed her chair back. "I'm suddenly not very hungry."

"Kenna," I barked, but she ignored me and whisked by the others while they tried to ignore the fact they had witnessed our argument. The waiter pressed himself against the wall as she stomped by him and slammed the door. I winced at the sound. "Jesse." I rubbed my face, and he quickly cleared the room. I needed to get my head on straight before the meeting.

A few deep breaths and an update from Jesse did the trick. We headed for the conference room. I hadn't bothered to have drinks and snacks arranged as I normally did for a meeting. The truth was I wanted nothing that could be thrown at me within arm's reach. Lord knew how this would go.

"They're here." Jesse opened the door, and I heard her heels on the marble floor.

I nearly rolled my eyes when Jenelle showed up in a dress that was clearly too small for her. Her pushup bra must have been double padded because I had never seen her boobs look that huge, ever. They nearly hit her father in the head when he skirted around her so she could close the door. I caught sight of Rail at the last second before the door shut. His eyes were as big as an owl's.

"Grim," she attempted to do a sexy walk toward

the table, but she was trying too hard, "I see you're looking well."

"I am." I flicked my pen through my fingers and caught Jesse trying to curb his grin as the chair sank and she awkwardly tried to raise it back up. "Mr. Borrows." I nodded at her father. "Thank you for joining me today. We're all busy people, so this won't take long." I slid over a file and waited for him to read it.

"What's that?" Jenelle strained to see it.

"A list of all the clients your father has brought to both Indulge and Secrets."

"Why?"

"Because as of today I wish to sever ties with our business relationship—"

Her face fell, and she looked from me to her father and back again. "What?"

"I'll honor your twenty percent, but by signing this," I handed her father another file with the contract in it, "we agree that any business between the Gateses and Borrowses is over."

"Why would it be over?" He looked confused, and rightfully so, as to him this was coming out of left field.

"My life has taken some turns lately, and I'd like to focus my energy on a different direction. I believe your clients were a good fit for Indulge, and if they want to stay, they can, but I'm moving on to a younger generation, and for that, I'll be looking elsewhere for contacts."

Jenelle hit her bulging chest with a gasp. "But what about us?"

As I expected, she wasn't hearing me. She hadn't in the past, so this was no different. "Jenelle, I've explained to you that since I've come back from Mexico, things have changed. A lot has happened, and I've changed." I kept any emotion out of my voice. Maybe this would get through to her. "We want different things."

"I want you." She tried to hold back a sob, and her father covered her hand in comfort. "And I know you want me."

"Jenelle—"

"No, Grim," she started to hyperventilate, "we're meant to be together. It's always been us. You're just scared and confused, but that's okay." She held up a hand. "I told you I'd wait."

"And I told you I didn't want you to," I reminded her. I caught Jesse's eye as he pointed to his weapon, and I hid my smirk. It was tempting.

"But I love you."

"But I'm in love with someone else." That made her expression twist into the Jenelle I'd come to know lately.

Her father put his hands up. "All right, all right, now. Let's all take a moment here and settle down."

"No, Daddy." She scowled. "I've been patient!" She stomped her foot. "I've been waiting all this time." She glared at me.

I shook my head. "Let's be honest, Jenelle. You've been dating other people, too." I wouldn't take all the blame for this. "We had fun, and maybe when I was younger, I could see more in the future with you, but it fizzled out. I've moved on, and from what I saw the other night, so have you." I saw everything, and the way she was screwing that guy in the hallway bathroom told me she was emotionally just fine about us. She just wanted to be connected to my name.

"You've moved on with that cunt?" Her words drove nails into my skull, and even Jesse stepped forward but stopped himself.

"You mean my wife?" I lifted my left hand and showed her the band of gold. "Up until now, I've tolerated your crass behavior toward her, but not any longer." I pointed to the contract. "This deal is over. I hoped we could move on from this as adults, but I see that won't be happening." I stood and gathered my things.

"I haven't signed anything." Her father started to grow angry.

I zipped the leather file folder closed. "I don't need your signature. This meeting was merely a formality. An unnecessary one, it turns out. Your lawyer told you years ago that the contract could be terminated by me at any point. As I said, I hoped we'd part ways in a civil manner. Everything comes to an end at some point, and this is that point."

"You haven't heard the end of this," Lloyd snarled.

Jenelle started to sob loudly, but I knew it was just another attempt to rope me in. "She'll never love you the way I do," she cried as her father helped her out of the chair. She sank to the floor as I walked by her. "Grim!"

"Escort them downstairs," I instructed the security guards as they left.

Moments later, as the elevator doors closed, I hit the stop button to halt our descent. Jesse and I both burst into gales of laughter. We heaved over and tried not to look at one another in fear we'd stop breathing. It wasn't often we let loose in public, but behind the steel doors and with the camera turned off, thanks to my keycard, we let it fly.

"Holy shit," Jesse held his stomach, "I knew that was going to be something, but the ending was something out of a telenovela. Grimmmm," he mimicked her high-pitched cry.

"To think young Grim considered marrying her." I cringed.

"Yes, thank God you regained your sanity." He gathered his composure. "There was a part of me that wished Kenna was there for that."

"Me too, but," I let out a long breath and straightened my tie, "that was my mess to end."

"Well," he slapped my shoulder, "I'm so fucking glad I didn't miss it." I hit the button, and we both slipped back into our normal behavior. Though I slipped once more when I caught his grin in the reflection of the door.

When the doors parted, I saw Kenna as she walked through the lobby with Rail. I spotted Jason, who made eye contact with me. Then I spotted Jenelle. She raced toward Kenna like a fucking bull.

"I can hear the bell now," Jesse whispered behind me while I fought the urge to break something. We hurried over, but Jenelle beat us there.

"Hey!" She snagged Kenna's arm and hauled her around to face her. "Look at me, bitch."

"Come again?" Kenna shook her hand away. "What did you call me?"

Jenelle towered over her. "I called you a bitch, but whore would be more appropriate."

I pushed Rail aside and shook my head as I moved between them. It was my job to shield Kenna from her wrath. "Leave, Jenelle!"

"No." Kenna fought her way around my arms and put herself in Jenelle's face. "I'm tired of you thinking I took Grim from you."

She grabbed Kenna's hand and glared at her rings.

"You did!" She used the back of her arm to wipe her snotty nose. "You married my man!"

"Your man," she used air quotes, "didn't want you. You need to move on, because desperate isn't a good look for you."

"Enough," I barked when people started to tune in to them. "Jenelle, leave, and Kenna, go upstairs," I ordered.

Kenna swung to look at me. "Let's not forget why we're even in this fight." My blood boiled. I caught Jesse's nod at someone. "You couldn't cut the cord yourself."

"That's because he loves me," Jenelle spat.

"Get upstairs, Kenna." I said each word slowly and loudly to make my point.

She pressed her lips together and stepped closer to me. "We're married, Grim, show me some fucking respect."

"I will when you've earned it."

Slap! My cheek stung, and I felt it go straight to the core of my stomach.

Kenna glared at me then stepped back and shot daggers at Jenelle. "Did he tell you that we're pregnant too?" She swiped away a tear as Jenelle's mouth dropped open like a trout. "Yup, marriage *and* a baby." She looked at me. "The perfect fairytale." She let out a laugh, and more tears fell. "If only I had the prince." She turned on her heel and headed for the door. I started after her, but she raised a hand to stop me. "Don't. I'm meeting Mr. Harris at the Wynn. Just leave me alone." Her expression was set; I knew that look.

"Jason." I pointed to Kenna. "She doesn't leave your sight."

"Understood."

As I zipped past Jenelle, I muttered. "You've done enough damage. I told you to leave."

"But, Grim—"

I turned and gave her all the anger I had built up in me. "Get the fuck out, and don't come back." She burst into tears as Jesse joined my side and we headed to the parking garage where Cartwright waited for us.

TWENTY-THREE

KENNA

"**K**enna?" Jason hurried to match my stride as he scanned the busy lobby of the Wynn. "Are you—"

"Not yet," I cut him off and waved for him to stay back as I approached Mr. Harris. He sat alone with a beer in his hand at Casa Playa. He stood when he spotted me.

"Kenna," he grinned, "thanks for meeting me here." He leaned in and kissed my cheek. "I promise I haven't spent any money."

I felt as if I was going to shake right out of my body, my adrenaline was so high. "I wouldn't blame you if you did. The Wynn is stunning," I confessed. The place truly looked beautiful. The decorator obviously had the same love for reds as I did. "Shall we move into the viewing room?"

He cleared his throat and looked at me oddly. "Are you sure?"

"Of course." I waved off his question, and we headed through the lobby, down the hall, toward the huge double doors that led into the viewing room. Harris had booked this room so he and his friends could watch a clip Paramount had produced of their last snowboarding trip. It was some sort of advertising deal they had going on. Normally, it would be held at Secrets, but it was out of my hands on this day.

The sound of his phone made me jump. He gave an apologetic smile and held up a finger. "Sorry, Kenna, this will just take a moment."

"Of course." I nodded and gave him some space to take the call. Jason hung back as if something seemed to have caught his attention. I reached for the door and stepped inside. It closed silently behind me. I walked slowly up the small ramp and tried to relax my breathing. Stress and pregnancy were not a great combo, and I fought constant fatigue. I realized I was once again far from myself and felt as though I was nearly at my limit. I figured I might need to take some more time off, then huffed a laugh at my own thought; I didn't know how to stop.

"Well, well," his voice jerked me out of my thoughts, and cold dread stopped me in my tracks, "if it isn't the gorgeous Kenna Lodge." Sonny stepped out from behind the screen and held up his arms. "I finally get you alone."

"What the hell?" I looked back toward the doors.

He made a *tisk* sound. "I wouldn't do that," he warned. Something flashed in the light and drew my eye to the gun he pointed at me. *Breathe, Kenna.* "I bet you're wondering if Harris had anything to do with this little meet-up." He laughed like a crazy man. "I'd give credit where credit is due, so no, Harris would never double cross his *beloved hostess*." He rolled his eyes. "But that's fine. I have many friends who are more than willing to keep an eye on you. Like while you ate dinner with that reaper in his office."

"I know about the Potens, Sonny, and it doesn't surprise me at all that you're one of them."

"Gorgeous and smart too." He laughed and gave a silly bow. "Kenna, how would you like to meet the star of the evening?" His arms lifted, and he waved them around like a magician.

"Todd Fairmount? Seriously." My stomach sank. I wasn't ready for two assholes at once. The waiter from earlier in the day stepped out with a shit-eating grin on his face. His blond receding hairline and matching goatee glowed under the lights.

"Lovely to see you again, *Miss* Kenna. May I say, I do love that dress." He almost licked his lips.

"I wish I could say the same." I didn't miss a beat.

"How many of you are there, for God's sake?" I knew they'd never tell, but I needed to buy a moment.

"Does it matter?" Todd checked his watch. Holy shit, were more coming?

Sonny started to walk toward me, and I did everything in my power to stay where I was. "It's funny. I've watched you for years, and I still find myself just as infatuated with you as I was back when this whole thing began. I don't even care that you're knocked up." He clapped, and I jumped. "Shit, think of the irony of it. Me raising a Gates child!"

"You're disgusting," I muttered, and he suddenly lunged at me and pointed the gun at my stomach.

"Or we can start from scratch and remove the little monster from your belly."

I reached out and ran my hand slowly down his stomach to his belt, and his eyes widened. I tried not to show my disgust as I looked deep into his eyes. "Or you can let my husband remove the monster inside your brain." His face went pale as Grim's weapon pressed into the back of his skull, and Trigger ripped the gun from his hand in one quick motion. "Checkmate, you son of a bitch." Grim smoked him in the temple, and he went down.

"Fuck, yeah!" Rail yelled as he and Harris hurried in. "Now that's how you do entrapment!"

"Jesus," Grim grabbed my arms and looked me over, "are you good? Did he hurt you?"

"I'm fine." I chuckled and realized my part was finally over. "How's the cheek?"

His expression softened then he cocked a brow. "I won't say it didn't turn me on. You're quite the little actress."

"Yeah, well, this needed to end, and I'm just glad they all bought it." Grim tilted my chin back, and something passed over his face. "What?"

"Just for the record, my wife, I do respect you." I loved that the words he'd had to say earlier bothered him. "I just needed to make a scene."

"I know." I pulled his head to mine and kissed him softly. "But thank you for clarifying."

Trigger stepped forward. "Let's get the fuck out of here."

Harris nodded at Trigger with a smile and was about to reach out and shake his hand but changed his mind as Trigger flipped back his forelock and waved the others out. They shoved Sonny and Todd ahead of them as they went out the back way. Eli, the owner's stepson, laughed. "I'm glad I agreed to host all this. It was, well, it was something!"

Harris chuckled in agreement. "At the risk of sounding crazy, it was rather fun. Intense, but fun."

"It certainly was, and thank you all for going along with it."

He smiled. "So, you suspected that Todd fellow overheard you and Grim fighting?"

"Yes." I nodded. "Grim has been narrowing in on the staff. Thanks to a friend, we've been weeding out some people who have been plotting against the hotel. Grim was able to pinpoint that Todd was a friend of Sonny's. They're all in on it. The fight between me and Grim was a farce. We planned the whole thing."

Eli grinned and shook his head. "Unbelievable. I have a whole new respect for you. I have so many questions, but perhaps I'm glad I don't know all that happens here in Vegas." He laughed. "You're fearless, Kenna."

I shrugged and smiled at that.

"Maybe you missed your calling to be FBI." Harris laughed, and I joined him.

"Maybe in my next life." I squeezed his arm gently. "Thanks for being a good friend. I'll see you back at the hotel."

Minnie came bouncing over and shut one eye as she looked me up and down. Once she was satisfied I was okay, she leaned in close. "How was *Jezelle* roped into this masterful plan?"

"Oh, Min." I slipped my arm through hers. "Well, Grim was having the meeting with her anyway, but we saw the opportunity and took it. Grim knew she'd go looking for me once he told her we got married. It's sooo something she'd do." We both laughed. "So, he stalled the elevator to give her a head start, and sure as anything, she played right into it. Todd Fairmont served us our meal. Can you believe he was in on it?"

"What the fuck, that arsehole waiter?"

"Yup, but Grim and Jesse were already on to him. Anyway, he heard everything and followed Jenelle and witnessed the whole thing. He called Sonny, and here we are."

She laughed. "You two are so meant for each other. Though I'm not gonna lie, I'm pissed I missed it all. I'd have loved to see that bitch's reaction."

"Oh, my God, Min. I guess it was a real drama! Wish I'd been there, too."

Grim motioned from the side door. "See you there, Min!" I called, and her "Fuck, you bet," made me laugh as I joined Grim.

"Ready for some desert fun?" He put an arm around my shoulders.

I stopped him. "What's going to happen to Todd?"

"Rail said he wanted to try a page out of his kill flipbook. Figured Todd would be a perfect test subject."

"I couldn't agree more." I laughed.

"Ready?"

"Yes, sir," I swatted his ass as we headed out to the car.

Wind whipped my hair around as a warning that a storm was quickly approaching. Loose sand and dirt swelled around my heels and found their way inside the fabric of my shoes.

I eyed Minnie. She was just as amped up as the rest of us as we stood in a circle surrounding the parasite.

To my discomfort, Caleb, the new President of the Stripe Backs, stood several steps away. It was still too close for my comfort.

"Who's that?" I used my chin to point as I questioned Morgan. The stone-faced man stood next to Caleb.

Morgan grunted as he looked over. "His new VP."

"What happened to the last one?"

He looked down and seemed to contemplate his answer. "Turned out he was the one who set up the hit on us that night during our party."

"What?" That was news to me.

"Yeah." Morgan stroked his long beard. "Caleb brought the news to us the day you guys got hitched. He handed him over in order to show good faith. Let's hope this guy lasts longer."

I would have thought the VP was dead by the way he stood so still, if it wasn't for the odd times he'd jerk the man on the end of the chain he held. It was wrapped around the poor guy's neck like a dog. He was shirtless and shoeless, and his expression told me he'd rather be dead than stand there like a pet.

"And the other man?" I whispered.

"Let's just say he *used* to wear their cut. Apparently,

he got caught funneling money to some other members."

"So now he's, what… their dog?"

"There's some things you just don't need to know, baby girl." He grimaced.

"Yeah," I agreed. Morgan shared a lot, maybe more than he should sometimes, so if he wasn't forthcoming with who the guys were, I didn't want to know. I just wished I knew why they were here to witness this murder. "Don't worry," he seemed to read my mind, "they were invited, and Trigger and Grim know what they're doing."

"Okay." A scraping and lip-smacking noise pulled my attention to Rail, who was inhaling a pudding cup in what could only be described as an assault to the spoon.

"Good puddin'?" Morgan asked sarcastically, and Rail grinned around the spoon and the cigarette that hung from his mouth.

"You know I like my snacks at these things. The sugar high adds to the fun. Ya want some?"

"So help me God."

I tuned them out as something strange passed through me, and I turned to find Sonny's swollen eyes latched on me. His lips curled into a smile as if he thought about something. I tugged the sides of Grim's jacket tighter around me. Leal and Zhar whined from where they stood in front of me.

"Maybe we start with his eyes," I suggested. I didn't want Sonny to know he made me uneasy.

Grim punched him in the temple when he saw his attention was on me. He fell to the ground, but Brick yanked him back to his knees with one quick jerk. He wavered from the impact but laughed, which only fueled Grim's rage.

Morgan stepped forward. "I second that. The bastard's witnessed enough in his time on Earth. He should be left alone in the dark to relive it."

Grim didn't miss a beat and grabbed the spoon from Rail's mouth then jammed it into Sonny's right eyeball and scooped it out. My knees went weak, and I looked at Morgan to anchor me. I needed to hold it together. Sonny screamed and thrashed, and Tess slipped an arm around me for comfort.

"Remember this man held a gun to your unborn baby," she whispered. "His business partner, Matt Myers, was going to testify against the DR for that mass murder of veterans, for fuck's sake. One of Trigger's oldest friends fought for our country."

"I know." I drew in a deep breath.

"He watched as your father exploited you to men to get what the Potens wanted." I nodded, feeling the embers that smoldered in my stomach come alive as she built me back up. "I'd use all that and turn off that part of my brain that says this is wrong or disgusting." I closed my eyes and used her words to shift my mind.

I'd done it before; I could do it again. "After all…" She squeezed me hard, and I opened my eyes. She pointed at Trigger's cut. "We're the extension of the Devil."

When I looked back at the group, I found Grim watching me. Blood dripped from his hands and his chest heaved with adrenaline. He didn't have to say anything. I knew he was worried, so I gave a nod to let him know I was back in check.

Sonny held his head as thick globs of saliva dripped from his lips and blood oozed down his arm.

"This could be quick and easy, or I can draw this out and make you regret all your past decisions." Grim's voice cut like glass through the cold, damp air. Thunder clapped, and dark clouds hung heavily above us.

"The only regret I have," Sonny strained his neck and cried out in pain, "was not getting your wife alone and destroying her in a way you could never repair." Trigger stepped forward when I did and warned me not to intervene. I stepped back in line, but the boys growled and inched closer.

"He's here." Rail gave me a crazed look. "Yup, he's here."

I jumped when another clap came and shook the ground. "Who?"

"The Reaper." He nodded at Grim, who suddenly looked taller and bigger as raindrops hit his face. Then on cue, like a movie, the storm beat down. His dress shirt was soaked in seconds, his shirt was rolled up over his forearms, and a few buttons were undone at the collar. It was slicked to his muscles along with his pants and left nothing to the imagination. He wore a look I'd never seen before. *Reaper.* It was just as Rail described. Grim's true self was exposed, and I'd never been more attracted to him than in that moment.

"Did you order that hit on Kenna?" Grim's voice made me shiver, it was so cold, and when Sonny just laughed, he lunged at him, grabbed him by the hair, and held up the spoon.

"Fuck!" Sonny raised his bound hands. "Yes! Yes! I ordered the fucking hit!" He panted. "I couldn't get close enough." He jerked about like a vicious animal, and it stirred up the boys even more. "When you went to Italy, I knew it was the perfect time." He was a madman drunk on pain. "I *knew* Cameron tossed her in the line of fire with Griple, and I *knew* Simon was in love with her and he'd fucking lose it with him. Everything," he shook his head and seethed in pain, "everything was perfect, but somehow that *bitch* is still alive. Fucking nine lives!" He swung his gross mess of a head toward me, but Grim still had a handful of his hair and he drove his knee into Sonny's fleshly eye socket. This time Sonny went down hard without a sound. He just lay there, his face in a disgusting puddle of eye juice and blood.

"Brick," Grim called. "Knees." Brick splashed some

whiskey from a bottle over Sonny's face, and it shot him out of his stupor with a scream. "Who canceled the hit?" I demanded.

Sonny's mouth gasped for air as the pain registered again. "I don't know! I don't know! I couldn't figure it out."

"Well, what do you know?" Grim's cold voice had zero sympathy for Sonny's pain.

"No one can stop it!" he screamed and writhed. "We all know, there's no one who can call off a hit once it's ordered. Except, maybe—" He looked up toward the sky as if to say God. "Stop at nothing, outlast your enemies, be the fear!" His screams cut through me as he chanted the Potens' motto. Leal and Zhar growled and strained their heads forward. They begged to be tapped in.

Grim rose and the Reaper finally snapped. He swung his fist into Sonny's mangled face and sent him backward. Then he reached down and took hold of his arms and snapped them both. He shook him like a rat and tossed him aside.

"Go!" Grim commanded the boys to finish off what was left of him and looked away as if something bothered him. For some reason, that action bothered me. Grim seemed to feed off this stuff, not turn away from it. It was odd.

"Morgan?" My tone said it all.

"Out of all of them, it was Sonny who got to him

the most."

"Really?"

"He tried to take away his family." He had a small smile like he understood Grim. "First time ever," he nodded toward him, "that I've seen Grim rattled." I smiled, letting his words fill me, but it was cut short by the terrible sounds the dogs made. Then suddenly they stopped as Grim called a command. Trigger whistled at a couple of his men to gather the body. I knew it would be buried somewhere in the desert. Where, I didn't want to know.

Grim's cold eyes found mine, and he hesitated for a moment. He took a breath and shook himself as if to rid his head of the Reaper. His eyes stayed on my face, and I could almost see the moment he became mine again. He swept me into his arms and buried his face into my neck and released a long breath.

"We're good?" He held me by the shoulders and pressed me away from him to study my face.

"We're good," I replied and put a hand up to his cheek. He took it and kissed my fingers.

"All right." He nodded then turned to the others. "We're done here." Trigger swung a leg over his bike, and the others began to disperse back toward the city. Grim took out his phone then waited until the roar of their bikes was gone. I didn't hear his words. I stood in silence until he finished his call.

"Sonny is finally gone." I smiled happily, and he nodded and put an arm around me. "It's such a relief."

"Yes, and Knox and Dad rounded up a lot of them while we were here. I think we got all the rats, but it'll take time to make sure. We set traps everywhere and lured them out."

I blinked the rain from my eyes and processed that part. "Why didn't you tell me?"

"That right there," he nodded at the men who had tossed Sonny's body into the back of a truck and were driving away, "was what I needed you to focus on." He kissed me quickly. "And now we can focus on us." He grabbed the back of my head and kissed me with a hungry moan. When he released me, I caught Jesse's happy face as he opened the car door, and we slipped inside. "Let's go home."

Grim got a call when we got back to the hotel, and he told me he needed a little time to meet with Trigger and Elio. I showered and changed and waited for him.

My phone buzzed on the table.

> Rail: I got a riddle for you. What's naked and has its nipples and balls attached to an electric circuit? And every time he blinks it zaps his nervous system?

A second later, a very disturbing photo of Todd showed up.

"Oh, gross!" I deleted the photo and tossed my phone aside, not wanting to think about Todd ever again in my life. I sank into a good book and lost track of the time.

Grim returned hours later, and he was in a mood I couldn't pinpoint. I gave him some space and curled up with my book while he sipped his whiskey. Later that night, we sat together next to the fire in comfortable silence on the couch in the main living room. The storm raged outside the windows, but we were both in comfy sweats and had no desire to go anywhere. The elevator was locked, so no one but Jesse could disturb us, and the pups were happily stretched out in their beds. It was nice.

Text messages kept popping up on his phone, and one moment he'd be fine, and the next he seemed agitated.

"Is everything okay? You seem distracted." I tried to read his thoughts. He nodded at my observation but didn't reply. "You can let me in, you know."

"I know." He sipped his drink. "Twenty-seven employees were rounded up today." He shook his head in disbelief. "But forty-three in total. Some were people I knew well," he went on. "It's just so hard to believe."

"It's crazy," I agreed, "and all different ages and positions around the city? How you ever found them all, I can't imagine." Grim rubbed his head. I knew it had been a big blow to the Gates family, but it was also a huge win. "I just wish I knew who was behind it all." I rested my head on the side of the couch and twined my fingers through his. "What does your gut tell you?"

"Not sure." He huffed and flipped his phone over to cover the screen. It had been pinging with emails from the media that were after an interview. "We have eyes on Griple. I bet something turns up eventually." He studied me. "What about you? What's your gut say?"

I opened my mouth then shut it quickly. What a horrible human I was for once again considering such a thought.

"What?" His eyes pierced through me, and I set my tea on the table and pulled my knees to my chest.

"Everyone around me was involved in something, and I didn't see it." I rubbed the tiny bump for comfort. "What if my mother was involved as well?"

"It's crossed my mind." He shrugged. "She's behind bars for now, so there's that. At this point, every person we know could be suspect. Everyone needs to be carefully watched."

I lifted a brow. "Is that so?" He nodded. "Even me?"

He leaned forward, and his eyes held such power

that he stole my next breath. "The only person who gets to watch you that closely is me."

That night, when we were in bed and Grim was fast asleep, I stared at the ceiling after I heard his breaths even out. The torches on the walls cast a warm glow, and I was pleased that particular design had been copied in the new hotel. I'd waited a long time for this moment, and I would be damned if something was going to get in my way. I'd made sure he had one more whiskey than his usual. I kissed away his refusal, poured him a double, and pressed it into his hand. He'd never admit it, but he was exhausted, and he needed sleep. So, I cuddled in his arms until he finished the drink then coaxed him into bed, where I rubbed his arm until he fell asleep.

Leal growled at Zhar for touching his feet, and I mouthed a string of curse words at them both and pointed at Zhar. He huffed and settled down farther from Leal. I moved onto my knees and put my plan into motion.

"Grim?" I whispered as I kissed along his jaw. "Baby, wake up."

His eyes slowly opened, and he grinned at my nakedness, until he tried to move his arms and found they were locked in place.

"The hell?" He scowled at the specially designed handcuffs that held not only his arms but legs in place too. "Kenna!"

I laughed darkly and kept kissing down his chest to his stomach. His muscles flexed under my tongue. "You left me alone with the wall," I said between kisses, "and I thought it would be fun to be the one in charge of it this time." I reached back and activated the spreader bar between his bare legs.

"Okay," he tried to act cool with it, but the tick in his jaw told me otherwise, "let's see what you got." He groaned out the last word as I swallowed him straight down to the base. Minnie had taken some lessons at Tess's club and taught me a few new tricks. She explained that just because a couple might have been together forever didn't mean their sex life should grow stale. "Holy shit." His teeth bit down as I performed the suck and dive move. I stopped, and his eyes widened.

"Oh, I see how this is going to—" Like a twister, I took him by storm and tried move number two. He tossed his head back with a laugh, trying to breathe through the intensity. Again, I stopped when I felt he was going to lose it. I crawled up on his lap and reached between the sheets and grabbed the belt. I snapped it in place so he couldn't control the thrust from the bottom. "I knew you were wild, but you have a death wish too." His eyes sparkled with dark promises.

I swung around so I was straddling him with my back facing him. "I just figured," I said over my shoulder, "this was the one thing a woman's never done with you." I slid down over his massive erection ever so slowly, savoring every inch of him. Before I got too far, I pulled up, and he growled. "We needed a first, Grim." I grinned and moved around, adjusting to his size. Holding his legs, I rode him at an angle that could normally be done only when he was in control.

"I need to touch you," he commanded, but I ignored him as I spun around and ran my hands up his body. I moved like a wave as I climbed higher and higher, and every part of me heated and swirled around inside. Grim oozed power, and I fed off it; I craved it. My fingers went to my hair, and I leaned my head back to change angles again. I groaned and slid my fingers down my neck and gave it a squeeze then grinned deliciously as I imagined it was Grim's hands. He fed my dark side, and I fed his.

"Kenna, look at me," he whispered, and I opened my eyes to see his chin was lifted and every vein popped. He was barely able to hold it together. Suddenly, I saw his finger move, and the sound of a click filled the silence. "My turn." I didn't have a second to think as I was flipped over, my leg hiked over his shoulder, and he thrust back inside.

"I should've known. Of course, you'd have an auto release button." I rolled my eyes and laughed, but my mouth turned into a circle when he hit all the right places.

He grinned. "In case of emergencies. I still give you props for trying." His body curled around mine as he took what he wanted. It was wonderful. This was how we were meant to have sex. I loved that he took me like it was our last time together. My nails clawed at his back, knowing he liked a little pain. Then he swung me to the bedpost, dropped my feet, and took me from behind. "Hold on." He grabbed both hands and held them in place while his other directed my hips. "Your body is perfect," he huffed in his wild assault. "You're so fucking perfect."

I screamed when I came, and he lifted me back onto the bed as he came, too. He kissed me back down to Earth, and when my heartbeat slowed, he pushed my hair back and grinned at me.

"What?"

"We have a first." He kissed me gently then ran his fingers down my back and held me there. "We fell in love."

A tear slipped down my cheek. "Yeah," I blinked a few times, "I guess we did."

TWENTY-FOUR

GRIM

Nine months later

"Hey, Callan, it's okay, little guy. Daddy's here." I gently lifted my son and held his tiny, swaddled body to my chest. "What's going on?" I rubbed his back as I eased into the rocking chair. "Are you hungry?" His face turned away when I tried the bottle. "I get it. Nothing like the real thing." I chuckled and stuck my finger into his little fist, and he started to relax. "There you go." I used my heel to gently rock us.

Leal lifted his head and yawned from his bed next

to the closet, and Zhar moved to my feet and sniffed at the baby. Since Callan was born, the boys had taken to sleeping in the nursery. I agreed, but every time he would stir, they'd come and wake us up. "He's okay," I assured him. "He just needs his daddy." The little guy's lip stuck out and his chin quivered. "Don't use the lip. It gets me every time." I kissed his little head then nodded at Zhar, who eased down to rest.

"Let's see." I spoke quietly and hoped he'd fall back to sleep. "Well, someday, you'll learn all about the family you belong to. You have two grandparents who have paved a pretty impressive road for you to follow. You have two blood uncles, one you can see and play with, and the other that will be right here." I gently tapped his chest. "He'll be in your heart, and you can talk to him whenever you feel lonely. I'll teach you how." I sniffed and felt Leo next to me. "You have Uncle Jesse, who is Daddy's best friend, and then you have all your DR uncles and aunts. They're wild, but they have some of the biggest hearts I know."

I rocked him a little. "Then there's me, and I'm going to teach you everything you need to know about running a business and how to rope in our kind of woman." I smirked. "I'll even teach you the keycard trick." I paused, remembering the day when I went through Kenna's art book and was so drawn to her designs. I couldn't understand how such a beautiful woman with so much skill, so much talent, would keep it to herself. Her use of all things dark and sexy completely piqued my interest.

"I don't know why I gave her that card at the time. It was a risk. It gave her full access to the whole hotel. Deep down, I must have known she was the one. And, well, here we are." I smiled down at my son. His eyes had grown heavy. "Daddy's gut was right, hey?"

Leal's ears twitched, and he rolled onto his belly and looked up at me. I knew they enjoyed story time just as much as Callan did.

My phone vibrated in my pocket, and I shifted carefully to fish it out.

> Elio: Just touched down. Looking
> forward to tomorrow. Followed that
> one lead and dealt with him. No more
> concerns there.

I felt a sense of relief. Since Sonny's death, we all had worked tirelessly to ferret out any possible Potens members. If there was even a hint of suspicion, we let them go. Though we still had no clue who their leader might be, we had purged the city of them, and I was confident we'd be ready if they ever came back.

As I rocked my son, I thought about Knox. He had really stepped up to the plate and proven that he was ready to take on a bigger role. Leo would be proud. Cameron wormed his way into my head, but I shook it off. I channeled my rage differently now.

"You and I have a lifelong job to do, little guy," I said softly. "Mommy lost everything, her entire blood family, and though she's strong, we need to make sure she knows we're always there for her." I rubbed her name that I'd had threaded through another tattoo on my left ring finger. "She deserves the world."

"Grim." I wasn't sure how long Kenna had been standing there. I was guessing our nanny ratted me out. "You left your own party early." I admired the tiny piece of silk that Yen Hong called an evening dress as she stepped into the room. She patted Zhar, and Leal jumped to his feet.

"I just needed a moment."

She leaned down and kissed me. "May I?" I lifted our son to her, and she closed her eyes and breathed him in. "My sweet boy," she whispered. "Time for bed." I watched her as she laid him in his cradle.

She stood just outside the door with her back to me and undid the string behind her neck, and the dress fluttered to her feet as she walked toward the bedroom.

"Night, boys," I whispered to the pups and rushed into the bedroom.

My parents asked us, so for them, we honored their wishes to have a church wedding. The little chapel we had built at Secrets was the perfect place to marry

Kenna the way I felt she deserved. Neither of us practiced traditional religion, but we did have it blessed by my parents' priest the night before to even the scoreboard between good and evil.

"Fuck you, you got nothin'!" Rail tried to read my mind from across the table. His cigarette bounced between his lips as he called my hand.

"Really, boys?" Mom rolled her eyes as she took in the fact that we played poker in the dressing room before the ceremony started.

"You look like honey on a warm bagel." Rail grinned at her, and she playfully gave him a huff. Mom had such a soft spot for him. "I promise we're all ready to go. I'll personally make sure he gets up there in time." He winked at me, and I arched a brow.

"Hello, Minnie," Mom called out the door, and Brick jumped up from the table.

Rail grinned. "But not until he shows me what he's got."

"Seriously!" Minnie crossed her arms. "For fuck's sake, it smells like a bar in here." She grabbed the trash can and tossed some beer cans inside.

"Winning looks so good on me," Rail bragged.

"Grim's got a full house," Minnie whispered from behind me to Rail. I didn't say a word; I just looked at him. The shit needed to fold first.

"Oh!" He pushed his chips forward. "All the

fucking way in, son!" He dropped his cards and raised his hands with a flourish.

"Royal flush." I showed my cards, and his face fell as he flung a death look at Minnie.

Mom popped her head inside. "Thank you."

"You're welcome." Minnie was in my face as I stood. "Did you do it yet?"

I batted her hand away. I opened the door and looked around. I saw Sienna holding Callan, and Filippo and Marabella stood next to her and Elio. Then I spotted him. He leaned against a doorframe and looked totally uncomfortable as he smoked his joint. Though I insisted the Devil's Reach didn't need to dress up, Trigger didn't think it was right not to, given that he was part of the wedding party. It said a lot that he wore a tux; he'd often said he felt ridiculous in one. I glanced over at Elio, who wore his tux like he'd been born in one. I made my way over to Trigger.

"I'm going to keep this short and to the point." We both hated emotion, but sometimes things needed to be said.

"'Kay," he grunted. He tugged at his collar and tilted his head to the side as he blew out a waft of smoke.

I kept my back to the others. "You took a chance on me years ago, gave me a second family and always had my back." He nodded but kept his gaze down. "I know you don't want kids, and I respect the hell out of that, but if something ever happens to me, to us, I need to know you'll be there for him. I want you for Callan's godfather. Just know this isn't just from me and Kenna. This is also coming from Laurel, Jim, and Knox." He went still. "Think about it, okay?" I held out my hand, and he grabbed it and pulled me in for a hug. Never once in all the years of knowing Trigger had he ever given me more than a quick shake or a clap on the back.

"Don't need to think. Be a real fuckin' honor," he said as he pulled back.

"Good. That goes for Tess, too, but I wanted to ask you first."

"Yeah." The corners of his mouth rose for a split second, and I turned to head back toward the others. I caught Minnie's shocked face at what she'd just witnessed, but she reined herself in and didn't comment.

"All right, boys, move it, or I'm spreading a rumor you all participated in the furry convention last month." Minnie waved at the lot of them.

Morgan scowled. "Don't lump us in with Rail's kinks."

"I have Photoshop and the web, so don't play with me. Move it." She shooed them out.

"Son," my father caught me as the others went to take their places, "a word?"

"Of course." I followed him back into the small room where we'd played poker.

"We had our talk last night at the party about how proud your mother and I are of you, but there's something I wanted to give you." He pulled out a watch, and I swallowed hard.

"That's Leo's."

"It is. I figured it should go to Callan, and it could be your something borrowed." I squinted at him and he burst out with a laugh. "I have no idea. Your mom said I should say that." He shrugged. "She said Kenna would know what it means." He waved his hand. "Regardless, I think you should wear it, so you have Leo with you."

"Thanks, Dad." I didn't waste any time replacing mine with his.

"I don't know where we'd be through this whole thing if it wasn't for you boys." He scrunched up his nose. I could see he was trying to hold it together. "We may have slipped a little, but we're coming back stronger than before."

"Agreed." I turned at the sound of the door opening. "Hey, Mom."

"You have a gorgeous woman in a white dress waiting for you." She smiled at me and took my father's arm.

I turned to Dad. "All right. Let's go."

I headed down the hall and joined the guys just as

they started down the aisle. We took our positions as the music changed, and I scanned the crowd. Mom now held Callan and stood next to Dad. I moved my gaze to the exits and re-counted the security.

"Stop that," Jesse whispered from behind me. "Best man or not, I got this." He smiled then scanned the room as I had done.

"Okay." I took a deep breath and got myself in check. Elio bumped me and cleared his throat to grab my attention. I raised my head, and for the first time in my life, I was completely unable to move. I felt my heart stop as I saw her. Kenna wore an elegant, formfitting wedding dress, and her hair was down but curled. The smile she wore nearly knocked me off my feet. When she got close enough, I found the strength to reach for her like a drowning man for a rope. I heard a few people chuckle.

"Everything is so beautiful," she whispered as the music died down. "Did you see that gorgeous archway?"

"No." I cupped her cheek with both hands, and as she looked into my eyes, everything inside me melted. "All I see is you."

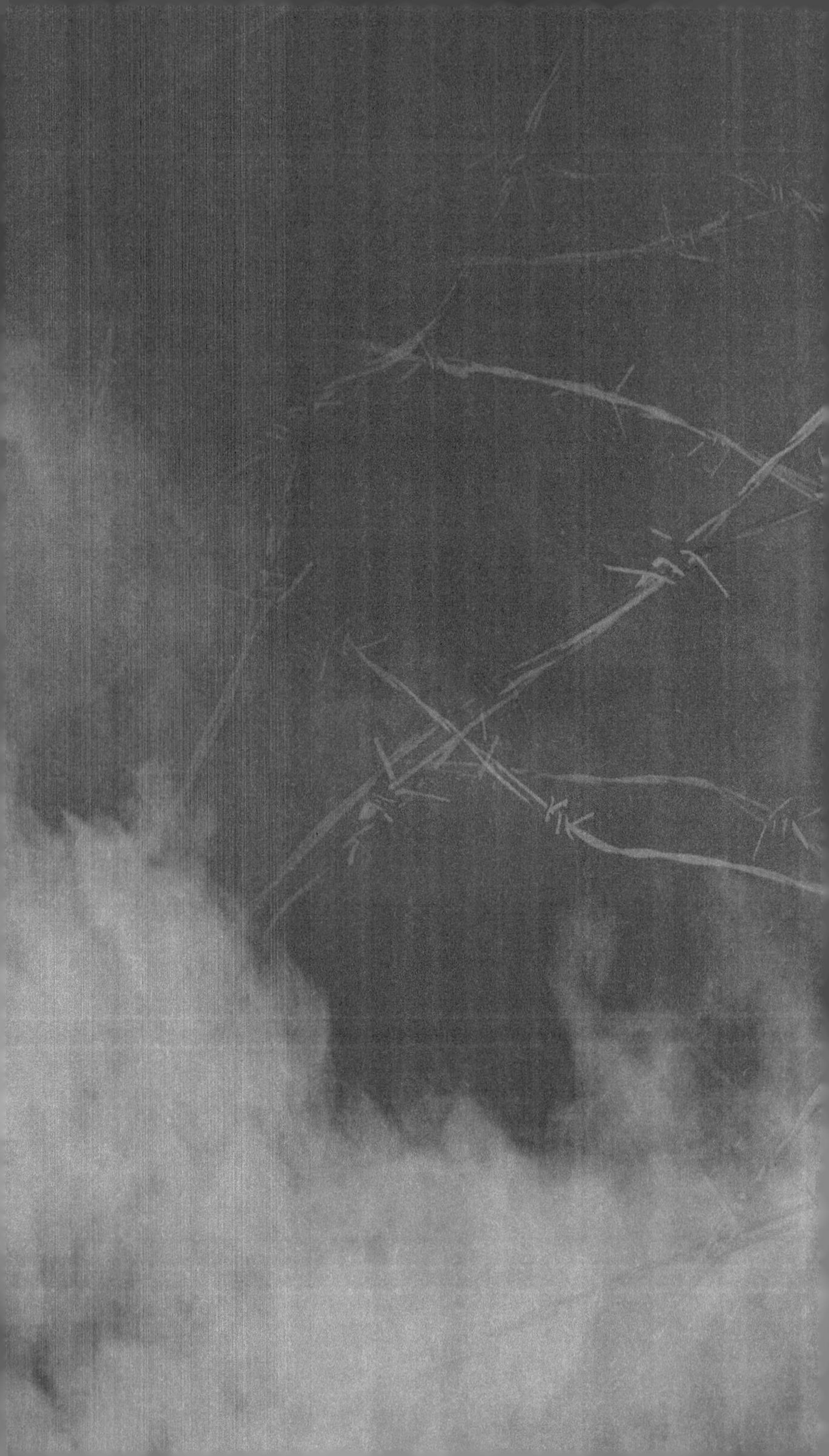

TWENTY-FIVE

SIMON

I tucked my arm under my head and relaxed the best I could. The white noise of the AC settled my thoughts as a slow smile spread across my lips. Sin City had all eyes on the Gates family as they held the wedding of the century.

"Nice to see you out and among the living." His voice was quiet as he loomed over me. I didn't open my eyes.

"Nice to be out."

He chuckled. "Hope this doesn't trigger thoughts of old times."

"Nah. As long as I get my shower to myself, I'm happy."

I felt the fabric on his suit brush against me. "That

looks good on you." I rolled my head and admired the tattoo. The bold lines stood out from the redness of my tender skin. It would always remind me that I made my own choices.

"I think so too." I smiled at him. I'd waited a long time for this. The guy nodded and finished up. He covered it with gel and plastic.

"You ready?"

"I am." I looked at the tattoo again then swung my legs over the chair and ran a hand through my shaggy hair. "I was ready years ago when you first approached me."

We headed out back from the small tattoo parlor and stepped into what looked like a room from Indulge. At least forty men moved to their seats as I took my place in front of them at the head of the table. I grinned at Salazar as they all clapped and cheered. I held up my arm and made a fist, my new tattoo visible for all to see.

"To the Potens! To our future," I boomed.

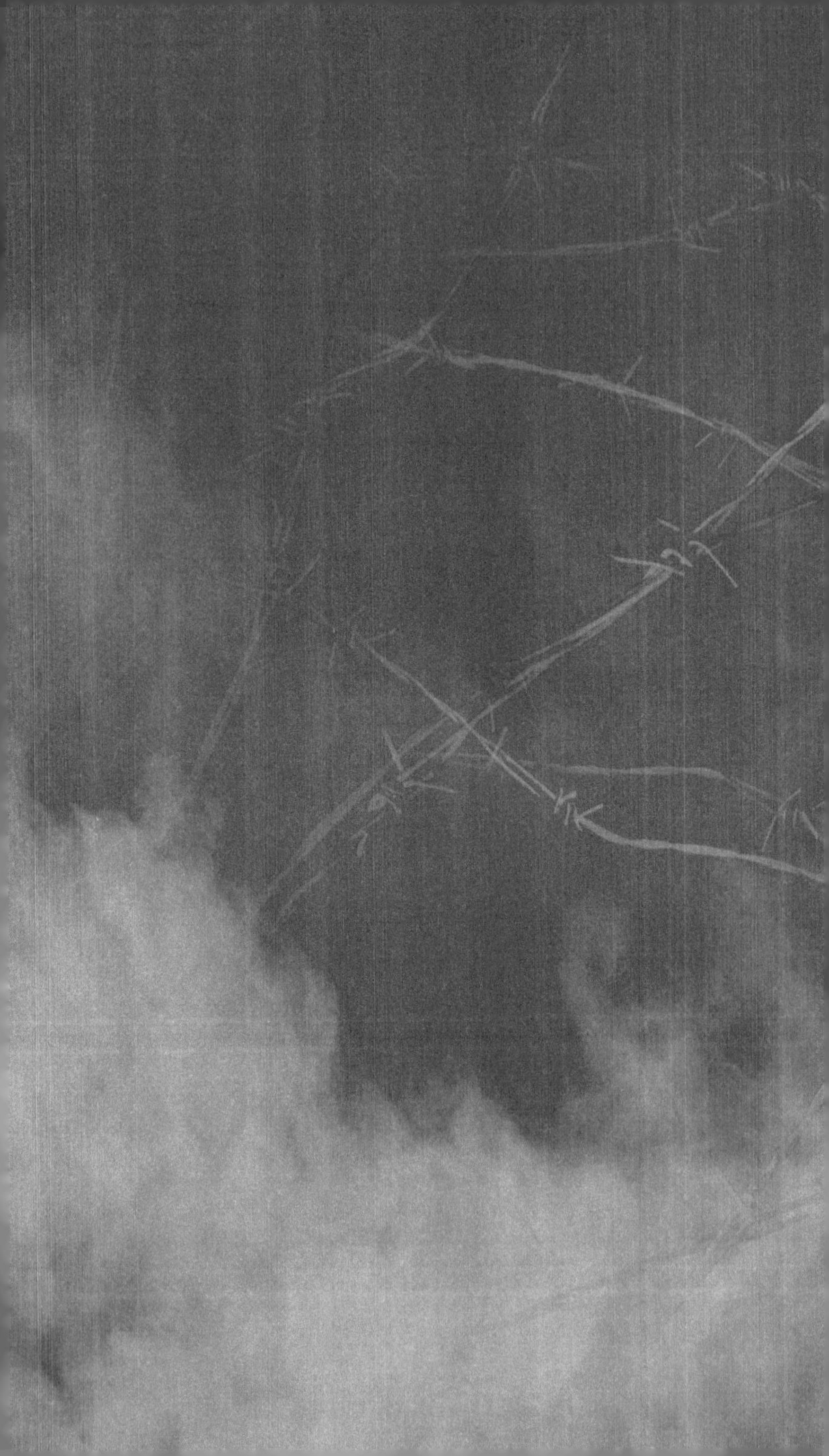

EPILOGUE

As the clapping died down and the room grew silent with anticipation, I looked around at all the smiling faces. I'd waited a long time for this day. I could hardly believe it had finally come.

"And without further ado, I'd like to introduce you to someone who has dedicated his life so the Potens can one day lead this city." The crowd cheered, and he held up his hand for silence. I give you the man who will lead us to that goal, the one and only Simon Gable!" He beamed at me and clapped wildly as I stepped up to the mic. I soaked in the moment and shook his hand as he stepped aside.

"Thank you, Salazar." I held my head high with pride. "Gentlemen, what an honor this is." I placed a hand on my chest. "When I was younger, I was faced with a choice. That choice was to join the men who wanted to control me or join the men who fought for a purpose." I slammed my fist down. "That choice came with pushback, and I had to face going to prison for murder." The crowd was silent. They knew the story, but I warmed to the tale. "We pivoted and played the long game. We made sure my cellmate, a local Potens recruiter, had my back. He wasn't told the truth about me to keep things as real as possible. That's the level of dedication our organization has." I raised my fist again, and Salazar cheered along with the crowd. "The prisons are run by the motorcycle clubs, and I had to play my part well. From there, everything fell into place, and over the years I found myself deeply embedded in the lives of the Gates family. From there, we drew other members in, wait-staff, busboys, head of the hostesses, you name it, a Potens stood tall but silent as we waited for our time to come."

"Yeah! Our time!" someone yelled. I drew off that energy.

"I know it's been a long journey, and some gave up their lives for the cause, but not all is lost." I looked around the room. "Unlike before, I come with a plan that's been in motion far longer than the last." They cheered. "We may have sacrificed some of our members by exposing them to the Gateses and their friends, but it was necessary to gain their trust. They were expendable." They nodded their agreement.

"These things sometimes have to happen for the good of the whole."

"We're all in it with you, Simon!" a woman shouted, and I smiled at her as everyone clapped. This was heady stuff, and I was going to enjoy every last drop of it. I deserved no less.

"It will require time, dedication, and strategy, but that's what it takes to be on top. And let me tell you," I slammed my fist down again, "we will not be defeated!" They raised their glasses in the air, and I swung my smile over to Salazar, who gave me a satisfied nod. "We are the Potens, and we have won this battle! We are on our way!"

As I held my fist in the air again, I was jolted backward when an explosion and gunfire tore through the crowd in a roar that morphed the cheers into cries for help. I ducked behind the podium, and Salazar threw himself on top of me.

I screamed my fury. "Who is it?"

"I couldn't see," he shouted and held up his weapon, ready to fire.

I grabbed it from him. "You shoot. They'll fire! Don't draw attention to us."

"So, do nothing?" He looked at me like I was crazy. "We're it, Simon! We're all that's left. If they die, the Potens die."

I grabbed his jacket in fear he'd out us both. "No, let them go. We can rebuild." Suddenly, the place went silent, and we stared at one another. Salazar poked his head out around the side of the podium then fell backward as a bullet hole appeared between his eyes.

A second later, a hand reached out and grabbed my ankle, and I was hauled out of my hiding place and slammed to the floor. The air was knocked from my lungs, and I fought to breathe. As my vision cleared, I blinked at the dark figures who stood around me. I scrambled backward then cringed as I felt wet flesh under my hands. The massacre was all around me; blood and death were strewn around the room. All those people who had just cheered for my victory had been slaughtered.

"You heathens!" I screamed. Everything that had led to this moment was gone; in a split second, they had taken it all away. "You monst—"

"You know what the best part of your speech was?" Grim interrupted. "When you yelled, *we won this battle!*" His eyes burned through me.

"It was all very Mel Gibson in *Braveheart*," Rail chimed in.

"Good comparison, Rail," Morgan agreed, but I wasn't listening anymore. Terror suddenly replaced my anger as the four men pointed their weapons at me.

"Shoulda killed you the first time you were on your knees." Grim's words boomed through the room. "I won't make that mistake again."

"No." Trigger added and looked at Elio. "We won't."

My brain fired off in all directions as I desperately tried to find a way out of this. "Does Kenna know you're here?" *Whack!* Grim backhanded me so hard my teeth rattled. I knew I only had moments left, so I played my last card. "If you kill me, Grim, you won't find the rest of us." He smiled down at me, and I wondered if he knew I was it. The last of the Potens.

"It's not me who gets the privilege of handing your soul over to the devil." He stepped back, and I saw Brick. He raised his gun.

"Brother," I pleaded.

Bang!

ACKNOWLEDGMENTS

To my mother, for helping me get through this book when I was at a low point.

To Jamie and Elizabeth, for all their support.

Veronica and Kasey, for digging deep into this storyline and keeping things in check.

To Rachel and Lyle Womack, for always being there when I need you. Cheers to the next series.

To my beta readers, Elizabeth Clark, Jamie Johnson, Rachel Womack, Maggie Saverese Rro, Kasey Griffin, Veronica Nelson, Deb Peach, Mandy Jones-Freeman, Tara Marie,
and I'm sure there are more!

To my editor Lori Whitwam, thanks for always being my eyes.

To my reader group, I just love that you've created a
safe place for me.

To anyone who has taken a chance on my books,
I thank you!

J.L. Drake, born and raised in Nova Scotia, Canada, later moving to Southern California. Though she loves the weather in Cali, she would sell her left kidney for a good rainstorm. Jodi's love of the seasons back home in Canada definitely appear in her books.

When she's not writing, you can often find her sitting somewhere along the coast of Huntington Beach, reading, or at home curled up on a couch with her two children and husband, binge watching a good movie.

AUTHORJLDRAKE.COM

FOLLOW ME ON SOCIAL MEDIA

facebook.com/JLDrakeauthor
x.com/jodildrake_j
instagram.com/j.l.drake
tiktok.com/@authorjldrake
bookbub.com/profile/j-l-drake

Alpha

Tango

<u>HAVOC OF SINS</u>

Grim

Havoc

Sins

<u>DARKNESS SERIES</u>

Darkness Lurks

Darkness Follows

Darkness Falls

<u>STANDALONE BOOKS</u>

Behind My Words

Christmas At The Cabin

Omerta

<u>STONEWALL TRILOGY</u>

Extraction

Embedded

Breached

For the suggested reading order, please scan the QR code: